TOO CLOSE FOR COMFORT

Eleanor Moran is an executive producer for TV Drama. She's worked on shows ranging from *Rome* to *Being Human*, as well as being behind a number of biopics such as *Enid and Shirley* during a long career at the BBC. Eleanor grew up in North London, where she still lives. This is her sixth novel.

TOO CLOSE FOR COMFORT

ELEANOR MORAN

**SIMON &
SCHUSTER**

London · New York · Sydney · Toronto · New Delhi

A CBS COMPANY

First published in Great Britain by Simon & Schuster UK Ltd, 2016
A CBS COMPANY

This paperback edition, 2018

1 3 5 7 9 10 8 6 4 2

Simon & Schuster UK Ltd
1st Floor
222 Gray's Inn Road
London WC1X 8HB

Simon & Schuster Australia, Sydney
Simon & Schuster India, New Delhi

www.simonandschuster.co.uk
www.simonandschuster.com.au
www.simonandschuster.co.in

A CIP catalogue record for this book
is available from the British Library

Paperback ISBN: 978-1-4711-7582-4
eBook ISBN: 978-1 4711-4174-4

Typeset in the UK by M Rules
Printed and bound by CPI Group (UK) Ltd, Croydon, CR0 4YY

Simon & Schuster UK Ltd are committed to sourcing paper
that is made from wood grown in sustainable forests and support the Forest
Stewardship Council, the leading international forest certification organisation.
Our books displaying the FSC logo are printed on FSC certified paper.

For Kay, with love

July 10th – Sarah

It started out quiet. It can be that way in the middle of the day – it's like I'm hidden in a big, concrete chest of drawers. The odd car pulls in and out, people staring at me, wondering why I don't climb out of this shiny piece of tat. None of their business. Sometimes I want to stick my tongue out like I'm six years old. One day I did, some old fart in a suit peering through the window like he was my headmaster, but then I remembered the last thing I needed to do was to make myself memorable. I turned my face into a smile, hoped he'd think he imagined it. It's amazing what people will imagine when the truth is too weird to believe.

Thing is, that day I barely noticed. I was too distracted, staring at my phone, sending kisses, hoping he understood. I was nearly ready to become her. I just needed a bit more time before I confirmed all the worst things he thought about me.

Suddenly it wasn't quiet any more. Not inside my head, or outside of it either. When I first got out I was walking, but then I had no choice. I was running, my trainers slipping everywhere, the ground slick and treacherous under my feet.

Then it happened. Then I was falling. My life didn't flash before my eyes; nothing like that. Everything tapered down until all I was was a single word. I don't know if I shouted it or I just became it. SORRY.

CHAPTER ONE

Georgie was pregnant. Not just pregnant, hugely pregnant – if she were to get into the delivery room and find a second baby playing hide and seek in there I wouldn't have been remotely surprised. Just to add to her discomfort, it was one of those sticky London days where the sun glowers from behind the cloud cover, giving the city a mushroom-soup kind of feel. She was flopped out on the red sofa in my office, pink and swollen feet released from her flat sandals, taking a long glug from a bottle of water. I watched her, tried to imagine how it would feel when I – if I – ever had a whole extra person strapped in for the ride. She set the bottle down heavily on the coffee table.

'I just don't know what to say to her,' she said, pushing a long, damp strand of dark hair away from her pretty face. 'Sometimes I feel like she hates me for it. But I had to do this. I had to believe that when . . .' She paused, looked at me.

'What is it this week?'

'Oscar,' she said, firmly. '. . . That when Oscar arrived she'd fall in love with him.' Georgie had been trying out names

3

week on week, talking to her ever-growing bump and seeing if they stuck. 'I decided Otto sounded like a German shot-putter,' she explained. I shrugged, smiled. 'Come on, I know you thought it too.'

Georgie was a favourite patient of mine, one of the handful I could imagine being friends with in real life. She'd decided she couldn't wait any longer for her reluctant long-term girlfriend to come round to the idea of having children, and had simply found a clinic and pushed on regardless.

'Does Maggie have any opinions on Oscar versus Otto? You were going to try asking her directly, weren't you? See how it felt if you didn't walk on eggshells?'

Georgie paused, catching the corner of her bottom lip between her teeth in the way she did when she was hurting. She turned to look out of the window, buying herself time. My offices are on the edge of Baker Street, looking out onto the steady, relentless stream of traffic that runs down the Marylebone Road. Beyond that is Regent's Park, an oasis of green that I know I should make time to escape into but somehow never do. I waited for Georgie to form a response. In the silence I heard a tiny, intrusive beep from my phone. I cursed myself for not switching it off, hoped it wouldn't take her out of the moment. She didn't seem to hear it.

'She said that he was my baby ...' Her voice had dropped low. 'That was all she said.'

I felt a hot surge of protectiveness, then yoked it in, found the professional distance I need to give my clients the best support I can. I'd been seeing Georgie for six months now, had grown to care about her. She was thirty-nine, a graphic designer with a thriving career and a happy relationship, who had known that for her it wasn't enough. Now there was an imminent Oscar. Or Otto. He'd even been Lucien on one particularly unfortunate week.

'That must've been really hard for you to hear.'

Georgie nodded, tears springing to her eyes.

'I felt like an idiot,' she said, jagged.

I felt a pang of self-doubt. Had I pushed her too hard last session? I'm not one of those therapists who barely offer an opinion, constantly bowling the problem back to the distressed client with an impassive: *'What do you think you should do?'* I get down into the dirt with them, and last week I'd encouraged her to change her own behaviour and see where it took the relationship. Another tiny, insistent beep. I pretended it didn't exist, kept my focus on her.

'I don't think you were an idiot at all,' I said. 'You were brave – you didn't want to keep existing in that passive-aggressive cold war. It's just that you didn't get the answer you were hoping for.'

Georgie's shoulders dropped, her body loosening.

'Do you have kids?'

She'd clocked my left hand long ago. The small, twinkly engagement band. The lack of a wedding band to keep it company. I was thirty-eight, and, whilst I loved the fantasy that my dewy skin would make her think I was ten years younger, she of course could guess we were roughly the same age.

'We've had this conversation before. You know I can't answer that.'

She looked at me, her face imploring. 'I know why she's angry. I did go behind her back. But if she's willing to stay, surely she's willing to give me a break?' She rubbed the taut drum of her tummy, a smile creeping across her face unbidden. 'Give us a break?'

Yet another buzz from my phone: this time we both heard it. 'I'm so sorry,' I said, 'let me just switch it off.' I retrieved my handbag from under my desk. *Lysette*, it said, not twice, but five times. I stared at the screen, unease prickling and bursting inside of me. Why would my busy best friend be calling me with the relentless determination of a stalker in the middle of a working day? I hoped it was a pocket dial, but a text told me it wasn't. Call me, it said, stark and abrupt and entirely un-Lysette. Georgie must've seen the anxiety flash across my face.

'Do you need to deal with it?' she asked.

We had ten minutes left. What difference could ten minutes make? I switched the phone off, guilt needling me as I did so, sat back down.

'Don't worry, this is your time. Let's talk about how you can approach this coming week.'

Those ten minutes felt like forever. I walked Georgie through to the waiting room, saw her out, apologised to my next client for the fact I'd need a few minutes. Lysette picked up on the first ring.

'Lys?' I said. 'What is it?'

I heard it before I heard it, if you know what I mean. It was an intake of breath, a crackle of air, no words yet, but something in the ripe gap that was more frightening than a scream.

'Can you . . .' A hiccup, a sob. 'Can you come . . .'

'What's happened?'

'It's Sarah,' she said, overcome by sobs. I had to search my brain. Sarah, Sarah. She was another mum in the pretty rural village she lived in. I'd met her once, at my god-daughter Saffron's birthday party. 'She's . . . Mia, she's dead.'

I put a hand out to steady myself. It sounded stupid, but the day I'd met her she'd seemed almost the most alive of all of us. She'd been much younger than the thirty-something mums surrounding her, but it had been about something more potent than youth.

'God. Oh God. Lysette. I'm so sorry. What happened?'

'She fell. She fell from a car park.' She gave in to the tears. 'Just come, Mia. Please. If you can, just come.'

'I'll be there as soon as I can,' I said, not insulting her by poking for details, making my voice sound stout and determined. I wanted my certainty to make her feel safe.

Nothing could make her feel safe. Soon nothing could make me feel safe either.

CHAPTER TWO

Roger Hutchins had the kind of curly nasal hair that looks like a handlebar moustache in training. Every time he angled his handsome, square-jawed face to one side — it was his listening pose, I could tell he'd perfected it over many years — all I could see was the rich jungle that was threatening to destroy his whole carefully cultivated look. It had only been a few weeks since my beloved ex-boss — no, mentor — had left, and we were still getting the measure of each other. I'd ambushed him early, before any of our patients could waylay us. The morning sky was like a crisp blue sheet, framed by the impressive window of his newly inherited office.

'Judith's shoes will be hard ones to fill, and I don't just mean the high heels.' He emitted a small, self-deprecating chuckle that sounded like a dry bark. 'I admire mavericks,' he said, in a voice which conveyed the absolute opposite. 'The therapy world needs people who don't run with the pack.'

He steepled long, almost girlish fingers under his chin, searching my face for some kind of reaction. His nails were brilliantly clean and square, like they'd been professionally manicured. When I'd heard my new boss was called Roger I'd imagined he'd be in his fifties at least – you don't meet many Rogers on a Club 18–30 holiday – but he was forty-four, only six years older than me. He was frighteningly ambitious, an ex-Army psychiatrist with a worldwide reputation thanks to his pioneering work on PTSD. Perhaps that explained his air of menace, the sense I got that he might court-martial me if I didn't obey his sugar-coated directives.

'The thing about Judith is, she's got this incredible instinct with patients.' I could hear the defensiveness in my voice and I tried to rein it in. 'She really taught me how to meet them exactly where they are, not where I think they ought to be.'

'I'm glad that you're such a fan of supervision. I'm looking forward to getting my hands dirty and getting stuck into your cases. Collaboration's the best part of our work, don't you think?' The last thing I wanted was his muddy paws all over my files, telling me how I should be dealing with patients I'd been working with for months – years, in some cases – on end.

'Absolutely!' I said, a little too brightly.

'I imagine Judith was a big support to you on the Christopher Vine case. I'd love you to fill me in on how that unfolded. It's a fascinating piece of experience you've got there – being right at the heart of a police manhunt. You can divulge it all on Friday.'

I gave a tight smile, my heart quickening at the memory, even though it was two years past. Christopher Vine was a gangster, whose angry and vulnerable teenage daughter had been my patient. Her welfare had become so paramount to me that I'd nearly torpedoed my whole career in my determination to save her from his dangerous control.

'But that's what I wanted to tell you – I'm afraid I can't make our meeting on Friday. I have to take it as leave. A close friend's had a traumatic bereavement and I've promised to spend a couple of days with her. I'm leaving right after my last session.' Roger didn't reply. 'I've rearranged my patients. A mother at her daughter's school threw herself off a car park roof.'

The words still felt like a splashy headline. I couldn't quite connect with the emotion yet – but maybe that was a choice.

'That's terrible, Mia,' said Roger, sincere, and I chided myself for my internal sniping. Real things were at play here. 'Of course you must.'

'I'll be back on Tuesday,' I told him, already rising from my seat. 'Then we can really get started.'

'Keep me posted,' he said, his eyes continuing to track me. 'Let me know if you need any support.'

I barely even heard him.

*

I dawdled. I stuffed my small, wheeled suitcase – standing upright in the corner of our bedroom like a leathery brown Dalek – with summer clothes, before panicking about the countryside being cold and starting over. I shoved the fat tube of Colgate Total in my washbag then worried about Patrick being forced to go to work with breath like Satan, and walked to the chemist halfway down the Holloway Road.

He must've sensed my nervousness, despite my insistence that I could handle it — that if anyone could handle this situation it was me. He'd barely left the police station before nine at night these last few weeks, a fact I'd been increasingly grumpy about, but now he was bounding up the internal stairs, taking them two at a time. I could hear him from the kitchen, his feet reverberating like thundering hooves through the cheap plasterboard wall of the new-build flat.

'I caught you,' he said, encircling my waist.

I put down the scalding herbal-tea bag I was dunking in a mug, and allowed myself the comfort of feeling his long arms wrapped around me. He's lanky, Patrick, ankles and wrists bony postscripts to his long limbs, constantly bursting forth from sleeves and trouser legs. It suits him, adds to the sense of him being perpetually in motion. I pulled myself closer to his lean chest, liking the way my ear landed flush against his heart. I listened to its steady rhythm, the tattoo it was beating out just for me. Then I reluctantly pulled away. I reached up and pushed the floppy cowlick of red hair out of his large brown eyes, seeing stress glimmering in them and wishing I had longer.

'I've got to go in a sec,' I told him, my feet not moving.

'I know,' he said, pulling out his car keys from the breast pocket of his crumpled suit jacket with a flourish. 'I'm driving you to the station.'

I was touched by the gesture: workaholic didn't even cover

it with Patrick. It was work that had brought us together a couple of years before – that very same Christopher Vine case I'd been dodging discussing with Roger. Gemma Vine was the last person to see her dad before he went on the run, taking down Patrick's whole case against his evil paymasters in the process. Patrick had wheedled his way into my trust, gradually convincing me that we needed to join forces to protect her and find out what it was she really knew. Christopher had ended up being shot dead in front of her eyes, a memory that still haunted me, but we had done the best we could for Gemma. And not just that – somehow along the way we'd fallen in love.

'I can take the tube,' I told him. 'The traffic'll be terrible.'

He stroked my face. 'Have you spoken to her again?'

'She still sounds awful,' I said, instantly guilty about the dawdling. 'I would've waited until the weekend, but I feel like she was sounding down even before this happened.'

'It's a lovely thing you're doing,' he said, looking down at me. 'If the cavalry were coming, you'd definitely be my top choice.'

'I have to. She's my best friend. She needs me.'

I'd known Lysette since we were thirteen-year-old convent girls, giggling in the back of maths class over a copy of *Smash Hits*. Our lives had branched out in very different directions, but she still felt more like the sister I'd always longed for than a mere friend.

'Will he be there?' he said, keeping his voice deliberately light. 'If she's in such a state.'

'I don't think so.' I didn't need to ask who he meant. He'd never met Lysette's half-brother Jim – I myself hadn't seen him for more than twenty years, apart from via a few grainy images on Facebook I'd been ashamed of calling up – but the fact that he was my first love, that he'd hurt me so badly, made him some kind of spectre for Patrick. 'And even if he was . . .' I leant upwards to kiss him. 'He's an irrelevance.' I kissed him again. 'A porky irrelevance.' I regretted the words immediately – they spoke of online stalking – but what person with functioning eyes hasn't succumbed to that modern temptation?

'I know,' he said, nonchalant. 'I just wondered.'

The truth was, I had, too. He'd moved close to Lysette a few years ago, but my visits had always been fleeting enough to avoid any danger of us bumping into each other. I'd pushed the thought away as soon as I'd had it, and now I repeated the process.

I busied myself with the kettle. 'It still hasn't come,' I said, matching Patrick's nonchalance.

'So are you going to do a test?'

'Don't want to tempt fate,' I said, not turning round. I couldn't face seeing exasperation or, even worse, pity. I poured more boiling water into my mug. 'Do you want a cup of something?'

I swung open the cupboard door, struck by how incongruous my overpriced bits of pottery still looked next to his chipped, caffeine-ringed bachelor mugs. I'd sold my South London flat nine months ago and we were saving for a house. I'd tried to restrain myself from staging a coup, but the charity shop wouldn't know what had hit it when we finally moved.

'We should get going, shouldn't we?' he said. 'I'll drop you and then I've got to go back.' I could see now that he didn't have the bulging leather man bag I got him for his birthday – a lawyer shouldn't hump round their papers in a tatty rucksack the way he had been – which was a dead giveaway that this was no more than a pit stop. He saw the irritation in my face. 'You won't be here anyway. Tonight's not Blue Bloods and a takeaway.'

'I would've cooked,' I said.

'Would've, could've. Hypothetical, darling. We'll go out for dinner when you get back. Will you be here for Sunday?'

'For Father Dracula?' I said. Unsurprisingly, Patrick O'Leary wanted a Catholic wedding. Even though I'm baptised, lapsed didn't even cover it – the thought of all the fire and brimstone made me shudder. That's probably why I'd come up with such a childish nickname for our priest, with his oiled black hair, which he insisted on slicking into a widow's peak. 'No, I'm going to stay until Tuesday morning. I really need to spend some proper time with her.'

I could see Patrick's disappointment writ large. His face was like a cinema screen, the truth projected straight onto it. He was four years younger than me, which in my more paranoid moments makes me feel like a wrinkly Mrs Robinson. But his youth is about more than calendar years. He's got a lovely innocence to him, the part of him which makes him fight tirelessly for justice, even when the odds are laughable.

'It's important, Mia.'

'I know, but so's this. Next Sunday I'll be first in the pew, I promise.'

'Fine. And I'll cook for you Tuesday night.'

'I'd love that, but Cup-a-Soup doesn't count as dinner.'

'You underestimate me. My cheezy beanz win prizes.' He fished his car key out of the pocket of his crumpled suit jacket.

'I can't wait,' I said.

All I did that day was make promises I would never keep.

CHAPTER THREE

I swayed and stumbled down the fast-moving train, suitcase trailing in my wake, feeling every twist and turn of the track. Seats were in short supply; when I eventually squeezed my way onto a square of four, my knees were virtually knocking into the skirt-suited woman opposite me. She barely registered my smiled apology, her eyes glued to her phone. I found myself mirroring her, a Pavlovian hand reaching into my bag, but I stopped myself, pushing it back underneath the bulging client files I'd brought to work on during my impromptu absence. I would do what I so often advised those clients to do: come off autopilot and be in the moment. The calmer I could be, the more calm I'd have to offer Lysette.

We passed through a thick ribbon of high-rise blocks and factories belching smoke, but then the urban sprawl gave way to something sparse and beautiful. Trees and fields, buildings as mere punctuation – I even spotted a field of munching cows. I felt myself exhale from deep in my belly, then reminded myself I'd go mad if I couldn't walk five minutes from my front door and find a decent cup of coffee.

I changed trains at Peterborough, swapping the long commuter express for a tiny local service. It was just four carriages long; a grey-haired guard walked the length of it, chatting companionably to the smattering of passengers, all of whom he seemed to know.

When I got off, Lysette's husband Ged was on the platform, his hand raised in a weary salute. Ged's handsome, but in a way that would never work for me. A carpenter by trade, he's scruffy and crumpled, with a broad chest and kind eyes. He's a stoner, a chronic under-achiever, but he loves Lysette and the three kids passionately — the fact that the eldest two aren't his has never been any kind of obstacle. He gave me a warm hug, the kind which smelt of rolling tobacco and eau de perspiration.

Eventually he released me. 'You're a complete star, coming down for her like this.'

'Of course.'

'Yeah, but we know how busy you are,' he said, and I glowed a little.

His ancient estate car was parked right outside the quaint-looking station. He threw my bags in the boot and started the engine. As we drove towards Little Copping, the landscape was bathed in the kind of ostentatious orangey-pink sunset that could have been a Hollywood special effect. The fields were village lush and green, the big houses that fringed the town built from that reassuringly old, mellow grey stone that perfectly reflects the light. We passed one that was protected by tall wrought-iron gates. Even through the bars, I could see it was in another league. It was huge and sprawling, an artful architect's take on the classical houses that surrounded it.

'Fancy,' I said, trying not to think about the shaky plasterboard and dingy communal entrance that defined my new abode.

'That's the Farthings' place.'

Lysette had told me she'd made friends with MP Nigel Farthing's wife a couple of years ago, apologising for the blatant name dropping, but unable to hide her excitement at the frisson of fame. Their kids had been hastily pulled out of private school as his star had risen, and she'd swiftly become a mover and shaker in the local community, a permanent fixture on the PTA. He was a Conservative, a rising star in the Cabinet with pretensions to future leadership. He had movie star good looks, and had become a camera-friendly fixture on the news, constantly laying out his case for compassionate capitalism with a heartfelt sincerity which gave even the haters a grudging respect. Now I could see he was the kind of MP with bulging family coffers: even the most optimistic expenses claim wouldn't give you the means for that pile.

I couldn't help but gawp. 'Is it even fancier inside?'

'You betcha,' confirmed Ged, with a certain ruefulness.

We were coming into the village proper now – there was the pretty Victorian church, its tall spire puncturing the burnt orange sky. I stared at it, feeling a jolt go through my body at the thought of Sarah's funeral. I still only knew the barest bones of what had happened, but we were so near the house that it felt unseemly to launch into a round of questions. We skirted the cobbled square, then passed the whitewashed exterior of the local pub, The Black Bull. A few drinkers were spilling out across its outside lawn, enjoying the dying embers of the sun. Ged sped up now, tearing down the country lanes with the terrifying confidence of someone who lived there.

The lights of their little cottage were blazing when we pulled up: I could see the pots of herbs that Lysette and Saffron nurtured obsessively lined up on the windowsill of the kitchen. I thought that Lysette would rip the door off its hinges, throw herself into my arms, but there was no immediate sign of her. I stepped into the messy hallway, a jumble of coats of varying sizes hanging off the pegs.

'Is she upstairs?' I asked Ged.

He put my bags down, nodded.

'Tea? Water? Something stronger?'

'Cup of something herbal. I'll just say hello to the kids quickly. Is Saffron in bed?'

'She is,' he told me, busying himself with the kettle. Now we were here, I could see how muted he was, his movements slow and careful.

It was gone eight, so it was hardly surprising my god-daughter was in bed. Still, I couldn't help missing her version of a welcome, which always made me feel like I was roughly as magnificent as Beyoncé. Lysette's two hulking teenagers, Finn and Barney, were lying on the floor of the low-ceilinged living room, hands firmly wrapped around their games consoles. Their size always shocked me anew, like we'd wandered into a fairy story and they'd downed a wizard's growth potion. The truth was that it gave me a jolt of failure, a visible reminder of my age. The idea that I too was old enough for this – that by now I could have made an almost-man – still seemed ridiculous to me. Looking at them, I couldn't deny that forty was in spitting distance – that I'd already made some of life's big choices without even noticing.

'Hello there,' I said, unexpectedly awkward, giving them a gauche little wave from the doorway.

It was sweet the way they broke away from their game, leaping up to hug me with genuine warmth. Lysette had done a great job. I hugged them back a little too fiercely, then stepped out.

It was time to go and find her.

*

She was a hump in the middle of the bed, encased in a tangle of duvet and pillows, tissues strewn around the periphery like lifeboats approaching a disaster. I made a pretence of knocking on the open door, and she slowly emerged from the mess. She sat up, grabbed the box of tissues, scrubbing at her wet, swollen face as if it was betraying her. She looked raw and unformed, as if her edges were light pencil lines, attacked by a rubber. I tried to control my expression, protect her from my shock. In twenty-five years of friendship I'd never seen her like this. She was the rock, not the wreck.

'Hi, darling,' I said, perching gingerly on the corner of

the chaotic bed, 'have you decided you're better off going fully nocturnal?'

I winced as soon as I said it, embarrassed by my flat-footed attempt at normality.

'What can I say?' she said, managing a vague semblance of a smile. 'I've always been a fox.' Then her face crumpled in on itself, and I pole-vaulted across the bed to envelop her in my arms. 'Mia ...' she said again and again as I stroked her hair, and felt the tsunami of her tears soaking through my silk shirt.

'I know,' I said, even though I didn't, not really. It's the only way we can survive, I think, telling each other these little lullaby lies, a baton pass for when life gets too hard.

Eventually her sobs grew less jagged and she pulled away, threw herself back against the pile of pillows.

'She's only twenty-seven!' she said, angry fists balled up in her lap. *Was*, I thought, the word small and devastating. 'I just can't ... she wouldn't do something like that. Max needs her too much!'

Sarah's crumpled body was found at the bottom of a car park on the edges of Peterborough, her phone in her pocket, the shattered screen covering up a text, not sent or even addressed. I'm sorry it had said, a single X on the bottom.

'The thing with depression is that it's so easy to hide. But it is a proper illness.'

'She wasn't depressed,' said Lysette firmly.

I changed tack. It was only three days since Sarah's death; of course she was too traumatised to think straight.

'When did you last see her?'

'The day ...' She gulped, voice wobbling all over the place. 'The day she ... it happened. In the morning. We were wetting ourselves laughing after drop-off about' – she waved her hand, dismissed it – 'just school stuff, the teachers – she was taking the piss that way she always did. We went for coffee and then it was suddenly lunchtime. That was what it was like with her.' She looked up at me, eyes plaintive. 'I can't imagine this place without her, Mia!'

'Of course you can't. It's just happened – it's still completely unbelievable. Have you spoken to Joshua?'

Joshua was Sarah's husband. I hadn't met him, only heard about him. 'Josh-yew-a,' Lysette would say, in a funny voice, mocking his properness. He was forty-five going on a hundred, according to her. The most improper thing he'd ever done was leaving his first family for a twenty-year-old he claimed he couldn't live without.

'Yeah, I did. He's such a fucking robot. He was talking about trying to keep everything "normal" for Max. He's sending him back to school next week!'

'Wow.'

I work with bereaved children sometimes. They might not always have the words, but they have all the feelings bottled up inside. I let them stage bloody battles and drownings in my sand tray, knowing that, unlike in real life, they can smooth out the devastation with the palm of their hand once the hour is up.

'No one's coping,' said Lysette, clutching my hand tightly.

'Kimberley and Helena and Alex are all walking round like zombies. I said maybe you could talk to them?'

'Kimberley Farthing?' I asked, and she nodded. I felt a jolt of interest about the mysterious woman behind those wrought-iron gates, then remembered what was important. 'Lys, I didn't come here to be a therapist. I'm just here to support you.'

She jerked the duvet upwards like it was a shield.

'Yeah, no. Course.'

'I'm too close. Besides, I'm only here until Tuesday morning.'

'The funeral's on Tuesday. If the, if the . . .' She can't get the words out. 'If the coroner releases the body over the weekend.' She collapsed again, body racked by sobs, the sweet, musky smell that came off her telling me she hadn't managed to leave bed all day. I held her, feeling unexpectedly useless. I hated feeling useless. 'She wouldn't kill herself, Mia. She wouldn't do that to us.'

I circled her back with my palm, determined not to reason with her.

'Whatever you need, OK? Whatever takes the tiniest piece of this off your shoulders.'

'You could take Saffron to school tomorrow,' she said, her face still pressed against my shoulder. 'You'd be a lot more fun than me.'

'Of course.'

'And you could get me a glass of red.'

I surveyed the devastation of her bedroom.

'How about we get one together?'

Lysette pulled some clothes on and we went downstairs. Finn and Barney seamlessly removed themselves from the living room, and soon we were ensconced on the tattered pink sofa, wine glasses (filled by Ged) in hand, toes touching. Mine were bare, red-nailed. Hers were sticking out of the ends of her tracksuit bottoms, clad in a pair of stripy socks. I wriggled mine against hers.

'I wish I'd had the chance to get to know her properly.'

Lysette was a little calmer now, her tears held at bay. She smiled sadly, lost in a memory.

'Yeah, you only met her that one time, didn't you? At Saffron's party.'

I felt a cold shiver at the thought that we'd been together in this very room. She'd been supervising pass the parcel, but supervising was the wrong word for what she did. The children were already jacked up on sugary birthday cake and fizzy drinks, and she turned the Black Eyed Peas up loud, shouted out instructions, made sure there was nothing pre-dictable about when the music stopped. There was a frenzy of shredded paper and squeals and hysterical tears. I sipped tea on the sidelines, impressed and judgemental all at once.

'She was really fun,' I said. Lysette was watching me closely as if she was hungry for my words. 'She was more than that though, wasn't she? She was kind of wild in a way.'

'I wouldn't call her that,' she said, quickly.

'No, I mean . . . I meant it as a compliment.'

She made a non-committal 'mmm' sound, and I tried

not to feel like I'd said something wrong. We sat there for a minute in a silence that was unfamiliar in its awkwardness.

'She was so kind,' said Lysette eventually. 'Saffron must've been two when I met her, and I felt like I was losing it a bit.'

I thought back, tried to recall her being on the edge, but all I remembered was a predictable, overwhelming mix of love and exhaustion. Perhaps I'd been too wrapped up in my own stuff to recognise the nuance of it.

'It'd been so long since I'd had a toddler, and I just . . . well, you'll find out. We came out of some mums and tots group and we were late and she was insisting on trying to unlock the car door with a twig, and I'd just had it. I mean, I properly bawled at her, and Sarah saw me. I thought she'd give me one of those looks – there are these special, patented Mummy Looks some of them give you when it's your kid throwing the Monster Munch – but she didn't. She laughed at me.'

'What, actually laughed?'

'Yeah. I was a bit taken aback, but then she just dragged us off with her. It was summer, and we ended up having gin and tonics in the garden of The Black Bull while the kids played on the swing set. I think we might've got quite pissed. She just knew exactly what I needed.' She paused. 'She knew it better than I did.'

'What happened to your car?'

It was so not the point of the story, and yet somehow it was where my brain went.

'I guess I got it the next day. She probably drove hers home.'

25

'Really?'

Why had she reacted so badly to 'wild'? Everything she was telling me was painting a picture of a cosy, rural version of that very word.

'Oh yeah. She used to run red lights on purpose when she had PMT. She was a menace in that car. I was going to have to take points for her, the way she was going.'

I reached out my hand, stroked her calf.

'You two obviously had such a laugh.'

Lysette's bottom lip crumpled again. In that moment she looked very young.

'Not only that, though. I mean she was, she was the best fun, but she really listened to me, too. However I was being, she never judged me or made me feel bad.' I tried to control my rampant, narcissistic urge to hold up our friendship against the one she was describing. 'She just loved me and I loved her back.'

'I know,' I said, hugging her again, letting her cry. 'I know how much you're hurting.'

I could barely hear her next words. 'She never meant anything bad to happen.'

'What do you mean?' I asked, but Lysette burrowed more deeply into my shoulder, didn't reply. Eventually she rubbed her eyes with her sleeve, shook herself, took a large gulp of her wine.

'Mate, thank you so much for coming down.' Her smile was still watery, but it was genuine. 'I really needed you and you just came.' I felt myself glowing from the inside. It felt primal and simple and deep all at once. 'I don't know what I'd do without you.'

'I'd always come.'

'I know you would,' she said. 'Come on, tell me what's been going on with you.'

She never meant anything bad to happen. The phrase was still flickering for me, but I didn't want to cost her this fragile calm by pushing her on it. Everything else felt so trivial, but gradually I managed to tell her about the vampiric priest, and how hard Patrick was working and, eventually, how frustrated I was by my body's refusal to play ball.

'Maybe you can ask Father Dracula to bless your woooomb,' she said, and we laughed far more than the silliness merited. 'Sorry,' she said, wiping her eyes. Her spine straightened, that bleakness settling back down over her.

'It's OK to laugh,' I said, as gently as I could. 'You probably need the release.'

'Yeah,' she said, unconvinced. She picked up the wine bottle, poured the very last dregs into her glass. I could see murky specks of sediment swirling around as she took a gulp from it.

'I bet Sarah would want you to,' I said quietly. 'I know I would want you to.' She turned to me, her eyes blazing.

'I don't know that. I don't know anything any more. The only thing I do know is that there is no way that Sarah would kill herself.'

'Is it possible that she just lost her balance?' I tentatively asked. 'Fell off?'

'No, not from the position she was found in.' She stood up abruptly. 'We should get some sleep.'

She'd sounded crazed by grief the first time she'd denied it. I'd let the words wash over me, too busy searching for a way to make her accept the reality of Sarah's suicide to even hear them properly.

This time it was different. I was more porous somehow. The words worked their way in, refused to leave me.

Sarah's Diary: February 2nd 2015

I spy, with my little eye – YOU. I watched her today, I watched her come out of her house and climb into her car, and I felt sick. She strutted to it, like she didn't just own that car, she owned the whole street. No – more than that. She owned the whole town, with me stuck right there in the middle. No escape.

When she drove off I nearly followed her, but even though she wouldn't have known, I didn't want to give her the satisfaction. I had that feeling, that feeling where I fucking wanna tear off my skin, and I nearly went into my purse, but I didn't. I went for my make-up bag instead, put on bright red lips and blew myself a kiss in the mirror, even though I was bawling. She makes me feel like shit, and I can't even admit it. Not even to Lysette, even though she knows all my deepest, darkest . . .

Does anyone ever really know our deepest, darkest, though? Because if they did, how could we know they'd still like us, let alone love us? And if they didn't love us, and WE didn't love us, how could we even carry on?

When I smooched it on Max at pick-up he rubbed his little cheek like he hated it, but I knew he loved it from the way he giggled. I snuggled him harder, and none of it mattered. NONE OF IT. It was just me and him against the world. She can't take that away from me.

Someone else loved it too. I knew he would – I see the way he looks at me. He says I'm paranoid, that I see things that aren't there, but it's not that. I've always had a bit of a sixth sense – I know things I shouldn't know. In my worst moments, I end up thinking it's a little bit dangerous.

You can get it back in an instant. Right there and then, I loved being in my skin again. I was younger, sexier. I was a MILF, a minx. The feeling didn't last all that long. That's probably why I texted him later. Something harmless, a little bit funny. He texted straight back – I knew he would, didn't need a sixth sense for that.

When I was lying in bed listening to him breathing – no, it was snoring – I wondered if what I'd done was really all that harmless. I counted each of his exhales – it sounds fucking stupid, but I was treasuring them. All the things that seem like harmless fun never end up being all that harmless, do they? I'm too stupid to remember that fact when it matters. When I'm doing it. Now I'm here in the bathroom writing it down, it's too late. It's way too late.

CHAPTER FOUR

Saffron's wellies had fat rubber bumblebees on the toes. During the ten-minute walk to school she'd managed to kick their smiley yellow faces against every conceivable obstacle: lamp-posts, walls – now her angry foot was heading for the gleaming silvery centre of a car wheel.

'Saffron!' I softened my voice, hating the shrill upturn it had. 'That's someone's car. You wouldn't like it if – I don't know, some strange man came and kicked Peppa Pig across your bedroom.'

Saffron cocked her head to look round at me like a small, mistrustful owl. She kept her foot suspended in mid-air, quietly letting me know I hadn't won.

'You don't know anything about being six. No one who is six still likes Peppa Pig unless they're a dum-dum head.'

'OK, forget Peppa Pig.' And forget my weird mental image of a Peppa Pig-hating football hooligan ambushing your bedroom. Saffron worshipped me – how could I be doing this badly, the second she decides to behave like a child instead of an acolyte? 'The fact is, you can't go

31

around kicking people's cars. Come on, we're going to be late.'

I stopped, hearing how my impatient words might ring in her ears. Hurry up and get to school, the place where your friend who's lost his mummy – any child's worst nightmare – will either be, or won't be. I dropped to my knees so I was at her height.

'Mummy calls these cars gas guzzlers.' She made a weird chomping sound, gaze still trained on the gleaming wheel arch. 'That's what we do when they won't let us go first.'

'What,' I said, making a strange *nyug, nyug, nyug* noise, muddy dampness starting to seep through the knees of my overpriced jeans, 'like that?'

'No, Mia,' she said, world-weary. 'That's not how gas guzzlers sound.' She took off like an arrow, wellies pelting down the pavement. 'Come on, slowcoach!'

*

There were only a few stragglers left by the time we squeaked through the school gates. No: stragglers was the wrong word for them. The trio of women who stood near the doors seemed energised, crackling with a nervous electricity that was almost visible. As Saffron hurtled towards the doors, they turned en masse as if they were an elegant monster.

'Slow down, sweetheart,' said a lithe blonde, her right arm shooting out to stop her with confident authority.

I expected Saffron to balk at it, but instead she ground

to a meek halt. I drew up next to her, smiling too keenly.

'Don't worry, I haven't kidnapped her. I'm Mia, her godmother.'

The blonde's cat-like blue eyes raked over me. 'That's your story and you're sticking to it!'

I laughed nervously, failing to summon up a witty riposte. I recognised the brunette standing next to her from a couple of birthday parties ago. Up close, she didn't have the blonde's thrown-together elegance; she was verging on chubby, rosy lipstick carefully painted on, fur-lined parka too obviously expensive. The third woman lacked their polish close up. She peered out through large glasses, made no great effort to smile.

'We've met, haven't we?' said the brunette warmly. 'Melissa?'

'Mia.' I paused a second too long. 'Lovely to see you again. I should get this one to class.'

'Don't panic,' said the blonde, and I tried not to prickle at the undertow of condescension. I was fairly sure by now that she was Kimberley Farthing, but I wasn't going to bestow celebrity status on her by admitting it. 'Normal service has definitely not resumed yet.'

'No, no, of course,' I said, instantly guilty for the judgements that had been spooling across my brain like a ticker tape of breaking news.

The heavy double doors swung open behind us, a stocky man in wire-framed glasses stepping through them. Teamed with a checked shirt and a pair of vaguely colonial-looking tan-coloured trousers, they made him look older than he actually was. His smooth face, topped by a mop of curly blond hair, told me he couldn't be much more than twenty-five. But it wasn't just his clothes that aged him; it was the weight of sadness that he was carrying. It was the kind of sadness that should have taken a lifetime to accumulate.

'Saffron!' he said, forced warmth in his tone. 'There you are!'

'Sorry, Mr Grieve,' she said, eyes round and guilty. 'I know it's very, very bad to be late.'

He suddenly dropped to his knees, just like I had by the car. He knew it – he knew, like I did – that she was chock full of feelings she didn't have words for.

'That's OK,' he said, extending his big paw towards her. 'You're here now.'

She slipped her small hand in his, her trust automatic, and he stood up. The mothers watched the interaction unfold, almost fascinated by it. I wanted to say something, stake a claim, I suppose, but it felt like there wasn't a role for me in this particular tableau.

'Ladies,' he said, his voice low and muted. He seemed only prepared to glance at them, his focus still on Saffron.

Kimberley stepped towards him, touched his bare arm, which was covered in a light fuzz of blond hair. 'Know that we'll all be thinking of you today.'

Mr Grieve – who must have had a real name – shook his head as if he didn't quite trust himself to speak. He moved away.

'Come on, you,' he said to Saffron, holding the door open so she could run through.

'Come for coffee if you like?' the brunette asked, and I wondered if it was an unnecessary apology for getting my name wrong. Kimberley was distracted, still looking at the swinging door, even though Saffron and her teacher had been swallowed up.

'Perhaps if you're there we'll be able to persuade Lysette she needs to face the world.' She smiled, leaned in to kiss my cheek so suddenly that I nearly flinched. 'I'm Helena, in case your memory's as bad as mine.'

Saying no felt rude. Later I would wonder if rudeness was woefully underrated.

*

The day had started overcast and murky, but by now the drizzle had turned into a full-scale downpour. We crossed the pretty square as fast as we could, fat raindrops bouncing off the flagstones. The Crumpet – its name written in thick, black, curly letters on its swinging metal sign – was over-flowing with waterlogged buggies and open umbrellas, the tables packed tightly together and crammed with damp and grumpy customers. Kimberley cut through the chaos as if she were parting the Red Sea, somehow managing to persuade the waiter to rearrange the terrain until there was a perfect corner nook that could have been designed for us. I found myself combing over what Lysette had said the night before, her plea for me to help her. A fistful of menus had appeared in Kimberley's hand, ready to distribute, a carafe of water had been automatically placed in front of her. I couldn't imagine her ever needing help, not even in a nuclear holocaust. If she was masterminding Nigel Farthing's career, I'd bet on him making prime minister by Christmas.

'No reply from Lysette,' she said once we'd settled, sitting straight-backed on her chair with the poise of a ballerina. Helena had slid into the seat next to her, the two of them like an interview panel. 'Has she messaged any of you?'

'I'm really worried about her,' said the third woman, who I was only just getting a handle on. I knew she was called Alex, and that she seemed to adore Lysette, but that was about it. 'How bad is she?' She peered at me accusingly from the seat next to mine. They'd subjected me to swift, thorough questioning as we walked here and had established I was Lysette's therapist friend. 'You must be able to tell.'

Their focus suddenly sharpened, as if a net had caught me in a wide embrace and was starting to tighten. I tried to speak, but the words dried before they reached the outside. Then the waiter arrived, a checked shirt half tucked into his jeans, a crumpled pad in his hand.

'Can I get you girls started with some drinks?'

His voice was a lazy drawl, an Aussie accent pushing up the tips of his words. He ran his hand through his collar-length brown hair, an easy smile playing across his face. We're not girls, I thought, we're pushing forty, but I knew as soon as the prim thought had landed that that was the point.

'We're all skinny lattes, Jake,' said Kimberley, turning to

me, then turning her wide green eyes back towards him as if she was my interpreter. 'What do you fancy?'

'A fat one,' I said, knowing immediately how idiotic it sounded. 'And some kind of croissant pastry thing?'

'You got it!' he said, shouldering his way back through the crush of tables towards the noisy coffee machine.

Alex stared after him, her eyes starting to fill.

'Sorry . . . sorry,' she said, wadding up a stiff paper napkin and taking off her glasses to scrub at wet eyes. Her nails were bitten and ragged, her left hand ringless, naked-looking next to their chunky diamonds. 'It just feels macabre to me. We're sitting here ordering coffees like it's OK Sarah's not here. I keep looking at the door like she's about to walk in.'

'Run in, more like,' said Helena, trying to smile. Her vowels were a bit nasal-sounding, Estuary: they lacked the cut-glass precision of Kimberley's. 'She'd be trying to pay for all the coffees to apologise, and Jake'd been giving us free stuff.'

'Jake's always charmed by her,' agreed Alex.

'We'd have a pile of muffins by now,' said Helena, laughing, her face immediately darkening as the brief respite from the truth receded. There was silence for a few seconds, before Kimberley turned back to me. I noticed how the other women's gazes seemed to follow hers.

'How is Lysette? I mean . . . sorry, that's a stupid question. Sarah was her best friend. What I mean is, what can we do?'

The feeling that rose up in me was so primal that I couldn't even scold myself for it. She's my best friend, I wanted to roar. She's been my best friend since we were thirteen; that position never became vacant.

'Bereavement, particularly traumatic bereavement, is very complex,' I said, my voice tinny and pompous. 'Lysette's in shock. It's hard to say how long that's going to last, but it will shift.'

'They were so close,' said Kimberley. I felt like she was watching me too forensically, like I was a rare Siberian tiger, trapped behind bars. 'If Sarah was going to do something like that, I can't believe she wouldn't have known something was wrong.'

Alex's eyes flicked quickly towards her, something unreadable in her gaze. She looked downwards, begun mopping up a slop of water with her soggy napkin.

'But Lysette was away last week,' said Helena, and I felt a surge of defensiveness. Lysette was already taking too much responsibility, without them providing a chorus.

'If somebody wants to' – it felt too brutal to continue – 'it's very hard to stop them.'

You stupid, coffee-swigging women, I thought, she threw herself from a building! I see the aftermath of cries for help – clients who've had their stomachs pumped or hold out wrists that are criss-crossed with shallow scars – but if you jump from a multistorey car park, you know there's no get-out clause. I shuddered, wishing suddenly that I was anywhere but here.

'I need to see her!' said Alex, intense. 'I need to talk to her properly about what she knows.'

Looking back, I think I heard something in her voice, something under the words, but I dismissed it, too busy slamming myself for being so possessive and judgemental. Jake was coming back towards us now, coffees precariously balanced on a metal tray.

'We should tell him,' hissed Helena.

'I can't,' said Alex firmly. 'I can't say it out loud again.'

'Ladies, coffee's up,' he said, unloading them from his tray, and depositing a dry-looking croissant in front of me. He looked around us, his handsome face registering the tension. Kimberley fixed him with a steady gaze, her hand already on his arm, voice low and authoritative.

'Jake, there's something we need to tell you.'

'What's happened?' he said, immediately tense.

'It's Sarah,' she said, nodding imperceptibly towards a chair that he should pull up. Customers were desperately trying to catch his attention, but his focus on her was absolute: it couldn't be otherwise. 'You know our friend, the baby? She died. She committed suicide.'

I watched her face as she said it, looked for any doubt in her mind about Sarah's fate. I couldn't detect any: it only seemed to lie with Lysette. Jake blanched. His large, strong hands started to shake.

'I can't . . . no.'

Kimberley increased the pressure on his arm, cocking her head to meet his eyes.

'I know. It's the most terrible thing. We couldn't not tell you.'

39

'The baby' – there was something so odd in that phrase. Jake suddenly stood up, his chair screeching against the stone floor, Kimberley's hand left in mid-air.

'I'm sorry. I've got to get back.'

'It's horrible,' said Kimberley, her focus still pin tight, almost as if none of us were there. To my left, Alex emitted a sob. There was something strange and unsettling about the intensity of their grief.

Jake stumbled away, shaking his head. Customers were waving at him, but he was like a stunned animal, not yet able to respond.

'You did so well,' said Helena. 'I just couldn't do it.'

Kimberley gave a small smile. She turned to me.

'Do you think I did OK?' she said, catching me completely off guard.

'It's not for me to judge.' She waited. 'Yeah, you did really well. You were very calm.'

'Thanks. It's just so hard to know how to handle . . .' She looked away. 'Any of this.'

She turned back to me, and again, they swung their gazes in unison. I ripped the nose off my croissant and chewed on its dry innards. There's a French place round the back of the Holloway Road where me and Patrick go on Saturday mornings. It's shabby and loud, presided over by a tubby Frenchman whose accent hasn't been even slightly dented by a decade in London. Right then I missed it acutely. I took a large slug of my coffee, grateful for the fact it was lukewarm. I'd be able to down it without causing offence.

'Disbelief is a natural way to feel right now,' I said. 'Death is so hard to absorb, particularly a death like this – a contemporary, right out of the blue. Try to be gentle with yourselves.'

'Thank you,' said Helena, reaching out to cover my hand with hers, gratitude in her eyes for the tiny crumb I'd given. Her skin felt almost unnaturally soft. 'I can't imagine feeling – I don't know – like the world isn't going to play some shitty trick on me.'

'Of course. It's only just happened, you've still got the funeral to get through . . .'

I felt a trickle of dread. I'd promised Lysette I'd stay; it was terrible to admit, but part of me had hoped Roger would summon me back to London, a convenient scapegoat.

'Could I talk to you?' asked Helena. 'About what counselling would be like? Lysette says you're amazing.'

Kimberley was watching me in that way she had – like she could see something that no one else could see just outside my peripheral vision. Then she gave an unexpected smile, like the sun breaking through cloud, and she looked too beautiful to pick apart.

'Sure!' I said, without allowing myself time to let the question echo inside. 'I should go, get back to Lysette, but I'll give you my number. I'll be here for a few more days.' I took another gulp of coffee, even though it tasted disgusting: the cold milk had congealed into a greasy skin that hovered on the surface. 'Thanks for . . . it was nice to meet you all.'

When I left I could feel three pairs of eyes boring into my retreating back.

CHAPTER FIVE

I normally saved this trick for teenagers — the reluctant ones, forced to see me by an irate parent. I'd take them to Hampstead Heath or the Natural History Museum, walk and talk — see if they plumped for a linear path or a chaotic zigzag across the grass, a brontosaurus or a can of Coke — little clues that oiled the hinges and opened the door.

When I'd suggested a walk to Helena she'd readily agreed, and now she had texted from outside, the hazard lights on her ostentatiously large black BMW flashing an invitation. I tried to persuade Lysette to come to the door with me, but she shook her head mulishly, reminding me acutely of Saffron, minus the bee-faced wellies. She'd been sitting at the kitchen table for the past hour, hands tightly wrapped around a mug of tea, barely communicating with me. Some pans were piled up in the sink, and the plastic carton of milk was growing warm on the kitchen counter. At least she was dressed.

I put the milk back in the fridge, wiping up a trail of it with a grey-looking sponge. Her mood had got gradually darker over the last twenty-four hours. When Helena followed up with a staccato toot of her horn I was almost grateful.

'I'll see you in a bit,' I said, leaning over her to kiss Lysette's hot cheek. She looked up at me, her eyes almost pleading.

'I know you're going to listen to her, but don't ... don't listen to everything.'

'What do you mean?' I said. I kept going back over the conversation we had that first night, chastising myself for how quickly I'd shut down what it was she was trying to say. With clients, I simply tried to listen without judgement and then work outwards from where they were starting from. Could she honestly believe that Sarah hadn't killed herself? The funeral was the next day – horrible though it was, it might at least make what had happened start feeling real. I'd wait until she'd got through it before I risked trying to reason with her again.

'Things about me.'

'Lys, I'm not going to talk about you behind your back!' I said. 'How old are we?'

'*Too* old,' she said, and we both finally smiled.

'She loves you! They all do.' Her eyes flashed: not like Sarah, they said. 'You sure you don't want to just ask her in for tea?' Lysette shook her head, took a gulp of her own tea like we might threaten her supply. 'I thought you wanted me to talk to her?' I said, trying not to let a note of exasperation creep into my voice.

'Yeah, no. It's really kind of you.'

'I think you should try and see them before the funeral,'

I said, then cursed my own bossiness. She didn't reply. 'Whatever you think. I'll be back by six.'

'See you then,' she said, voice small, her sadness making me sad.

*

The weather was less filthy today but it still didn't feel like real summer. It was warm in a muggy kind of a way, grey clouds scudding about like playground bullies. Helena was leaning against the door of her 4×4, pulling deeply on a cigarette. She threw it down as soon as she saw me, even though it was only half gone, grinding it into oblivion with the heel of a high-heeled chestnut leather boot.

'Don't worry, I brought trainers,' she said. She smiled at me, but it was brisk and efficient, lacking the overblown warmth of our last encounter. Ridiculously, I felt underdressed. My jeans were on day two, my options running short now I'd stayed on, my long-sleeved blue T-shirt a cast-off of Lysette's with tiny holes puncturing the armpits.

'Are we heading for rocky terrain?'

Everything I said to these women sounded as though I'd been practising it in my head beforehand, like it deserved a little drum roll.

'No,' she said, climbing into the driver's seat. I hopped in too. The inside smelt of Chanel No 5, and I wondered if she sprayed it around to disguise the underlying whiff of cigarette smoke. The radio came on as she flicked the key, a loud blast of Katy Perry. She didn't turn it off. 'Thanks for doing this,' she said, over the top.

'Of course. You're Lysette's friend.'

'I keep thinking of Rex,' she said, 'my little one'. Katy was reaching a crescendo by now, and I wondered if it would be rude to turn her down. 'I can't imagine it, just being gone.'

It was hard to say anything meaningful when all I was communicating with was her profile. Just like last time she was fully made up, her eyelashes so lush that they didn't convince. Her skin was taut, almost pinched, and I unconsciously traced the subtle lines that arced from my nose down to my mouth. When I waste time peering at them in the mirror, I find it hard not to experience the double punch: hating them, then hating myself for the shallowness of hating them. The mirror is not always my friend.

'Do you know how they're coping?' I asked. 'Has Joshua got people staying with them?' We'd left the village now, nothing but green fields either side of us.

'Lisa and Kyle will be helping, I'm sure.'

'Who are they?'

'His ex and her husband. They've got one of those civilised divorces,' she said, voice dripping with sarcasm. 'His older two live with them. Jack's in the top juniors at St Augustine's still.'

'Didn't he leave her for Sarah?'

'Yup. Tell you what, if Chris dumped me for someone half my age, there'd be no conscious uncoupling, not unless it was me pulling his dick off.'

I laughed, the relief making me aware that laughter had been in short supply since that first night. Patrick always made me laugh, but when I'd called him the evening before, neither of us had been in that space. He was stuck at work, his distraction palpable, whilst I was perched on my inflatable bed in Saffron's room, wanting and not wanting to tell him that my period had crept up and ambushed me.

'That's very grown-up of her,' I said.

'Lisa said in the long run she was grateful. Apparently she says she knows now the marriage was dead anyway – the affair was just the straw that broke the camel's back. Sarah was pretty bolshie about it – she said they all ended up better off.'

'Wow.' I wanted to ask more, but I checked myself. I didn't like the way I was starting to analyse Sarah, the sly mental notes I was taking.

'I guess she had to say something like that though, didn't she?' said Helena. 'Lisa, I mean.'

'Maybe. Particularly if you're all still living in the same place.' The thought of it made me shudder: it was another thing that recommended a sprawling, impersonal metropolis. I looked out at the endless-seeming fields. 'Where is it we're going?' I asked.

'There's a forest. That's a bit of an overstatement – it's a little wood. It's round to the left.'

She swung the huge car off the main road, the turn sharp and sudden. We were on a narrow lane now, trees looming on either side. She mashed the horn with the palm of her hand as the lane curved to the left, the long hoot making a couple of pheasants soar upwards in a squawking flurry. A denser patch of trees was up ahead, and she pulled the car onto a grass verge. I unbuckled my seat belt, feeling slightly sick. I opened the door and clambered out, grateful for the fresh air.

'So how old is Rex?' I asked her, following her round to the back.

She was pulling off her boots now, pristine white trainers ready to go on. She reminded me of my childhood Sindy Doll, with the perfect, interchangeable outfits – ski jackets, riding boots – that I used to hoard all my pocket money to buy. There was a reason for Sindy's outfits never wearing out; Helena's trainers also looked as if they'd never been within a hundred feet of a patch of grass.

'He's eight now. Got far too much to say for himself.' She beamed automatically as she said it, love softening her edges.

'So he's a couple of years above Max at the school?'

'Yeah. And that's like – a century – at their age.' She finished lacing her trainers, looked up at me. 'Have you got any kids?'

'No. No, I haven't,' I said, the words sounding metallic in my mouth.

I Googled statistics obsessively, cheered or terrified, depending on who it was presenting the data. Thirty-eight was either a complete fertility disaster or no biggie. We'd only been – not exactly trying, but not trying not to – for six months, and Patrick was completely relaxed about the lack of success. Lack of success and relaxed have never existed in the same sentence for me. Helena slammed the boot shut, started off towards the trees.

'So what made you want to meet up?' I asked her.

'I just feel so . . . anxious.' She stopped, thrusting her hand towards me. Her fingers were wide and stubby, a contrast to the perfect wine-red manicure her nails had been treated to. I could see the tremor running through them. 'I don't know how to stop feeling like this.'

Helena set off into the dense greenery, thick branches soon forming a canopy over our heads. I hurried my pace in an attempt to keep up with her.

'It's completely natural that you're feeling this way. But if you're asking me if talking to someone can help, then yes, I think it can, particularly once the dust settles a bit. Though obviously I'm biased.'

Helena shook her head, frustrated.

'It's *not* natural,' she snapped.

'I know . . . sorry, if that sounded crass, but . . .'

'None of this is natural.' She looked at me again, her eyes dark. 'None of this is normal.'

Her voice dropped as she said it, and I felt a shiver of unease that I couldn't pin down. Lysette reared up in my mind – was this the 'everything' she was referring to?

'What do you mean?' I asked, too quickly. 'I certainly wasn't saying that it's normal for a young woman to kill herself . . .'

'I don't know when the questions will stop going round

my head. Rex has got his hamster – he stinks, but he loves him – Mr Whiskers. He just goes round and round on his stupid wheel, claws going, can't stop.'

She'd nudged slightly ahead, more sure of the winding path than I was, but now she turned to me and pulled an ugly hamster face, her features screwed up tight, her hands clenched like tiny paws. I laughed, immediately warming to her.

'What's the one that tortures you the most?' She didn't reply. 'How she could have wanted to do something like that?'

Helena gave a little snort of a laugh that came through her nose.

'I wish.' It was an odd response. Her eyes darted towards me, then darted to the ground. The silence prickled and spat. 'She was lovely, Sarah,' she added.

'I only met her once, but Lysette can't stop saying how kind she was. How funny.'

'Yeah. no. She had a sharp tongue on her.' She saw my expression. 'She was quick,' she added, even though we both knew they were totally different things.

I drew level with her, twigs snapping underfoot. We were going deeper into the green now, the light shaded out of the sky.

'Do you think she was depressed?'

'Stupid word, isn't it?' There was a cheeky sort of challenge in the way she said it, like a convent girl swearing in church. 'We're all depressed, aren't we, every day? If Rex says I'm the meanest mummy in the world in the morning I feel like shit, but then he hugs me goodbye at the gates and I feel amazing.'

I wondered where her husband figured in her happiness ratio: there didn't seem to be much mention of him. Was Rex her first, her last, her everything? I didn't even know if she had a job.

'So she didn't seem particularly down to you?'

'She was all of it, Mia,' she said, tone devoid of warmth. 'Four seasons in one day, you know?'

'Sort of,' I said, deliberately leaving a gap in my understanding for her to fill.

Helena paused, thinking. We took a few paces, going still deeper into the closely packed trees, the path more unruly, less distinct.

'She worked in this café in Cambridge, just part-time, she was a supervisor. It's really pretentious, you know. All olde worlde, full of tourists. There was a don from Trinity who used to come in and behave like a total cock. Ordering the staff around like they were his slaves, and wanting his scones all neatly arranged with the jam on the side and his cream all whippy. Used to leave shrapnel for a tip.' Helena plunged down a path that took us still further into the density of green. 'He came in with his wife and kids on his birthday, and laid into one of the other girls about his tea being cold. Sarah iced *you're a . . .* you know, a C word – on his cake, and put it down in front of him with candles, and everything. She was singing happy birthday at the top of her voice, making all the staff join in so the whole restaurant was looking over. She got the sack on the spot.'

'Wow,' I said, trying to imagine it. 'Good for her, I suppose.'

'Thing was, she was gutted. I mean – of course she'd get fired. But she was furious about how unfair it was.'

'Why, because she'd been standing up for someone else?'

'No,' said Helena, looking at me, eyes troubled. 'I think she thought she could get away with it. I think she thought she could get away with *anything*.'

'Anything?' It could mean so many things. Helena looked down at the muddy ground, the set of her jaw telling me she wouldn't be elaborating: the push–pull of our conversation was becoming as jarring as a fairground ride. 'So your hamster wheel . . .' I paused, searching for the right words. 'Is it like – a cosmic hamster wheel – how can this happen? Or is it about what Sarah might've been hiding? What else she thought she could get away with?'

Her head turned sharply towards me.

'Is that what Lysette says? That she was hiding stuff? From her?'

'No. I think . . .' I looked at Helena, mindful of Lysette's paranoia about what we might share. 'She's struggling to believe she would've killed herself.'

Helena's eyes looked bright and wet. She stared down at the ground, quiet, and I silently chided myself. I shouldn't have been there. When I was ensconced in my treatment room diligently following the rules of patient confidentiality, there was no danger of me causing this kind of trouble. This – this was starting to feel more like the sixth form common room.

'Why would she say that? What would make her ... does she know something? Fuck.'

'No, not at all,' I said. 'No one seems to have any answers. Lysette says even Joshua's completely at a loss as to what was going through her head.'

'No change there then,' said Helena, with a slight eye roll.

'Do you think their marriage was in trouble?' I asked, the question leaving my mouth almost against my will. I couldn't help myself: I could feel a dangerous compulsion to grab hold of Sarah, understand who she was.

Helena looked into the middle distance, the weak sun dappling the path, broken up by the lattice of branches overhead. Her voice sounded faraway when it came.

'It's funny, isn't it, how things can look so different from the outside and the inside. Sort of makes you wonder whether black's white.'

'What do you mean?' I asked.

'I dunno,' she said, more clipped. 'Maybe Sarah looked more complicated than she was, and Joshua ... Maybe he's the other way round.'

She suddenly shouldered her way through a wall of brambles that were criss-crossing the path in front of us. The wood felt as if it was closing in on us, the sunlight too faint to warm me. Or was the chill more sinister than that – was it coming from the creeping realisation that she hadn't dismissed Lysette's grief-stricken accusations out of hand? The thought of Lysette brought me up short – I was doing exactly what I'd promised her I wouldn't do. Excavating a story that wasn't mine.

'Is there anything else I can tell you about the process?' I asked stiffly. 'I can email you with some suggestions for how to find someone if you do decide you want professional support.'

'Can you talk to me about this?' She stuck her hand out again, the tremor still present, and I retreated into my professional comfort zone, loading her down with tips about mindfulness and meditation and the perils of losing sleep. As my words guided us somewhere safer, the track seemed to do the same, opening out into a space that was less shadowed and enclosed.

'Thanks, Mia, that's a massive help,' she said, just as we emerged from the wood entirely, her gleaming car back in sight. 'I need to get going. There's a PTA meeting at six. I don't need to go getting myself a detention for shoddy timekeeping.'

'Is the . . .' I thought about the anxiety she'd just described, and blundered on. 'I know it's not my place, but do you any of you feel ready for it to be business as usual with school stuff?'

'Kimberley's the chairwoman. And trust me, what Kimberley says goes.' She smiled at me, her eyes lingering on my face.

'Right.' She had a look of sly amusement, a look that was designed to trap me into colluding with her. Or was I just being paranoid? 'OK then, let's hit the road.'

But as we headed towards the car, she suddenly stopped. She turned to me, her face pinched.

'You're . . .' She stopped, checked herself. 'You're a really good listener.' The way she said it didn't make it sound like a compliment. 'I shouldn't – I went on a bit, didn't I?'

'Not at all,' I said, stiff again. 'You asked to talk, and that's what we did.'

'Yeah I know, about like, candles and incense and deep breathing. All that other stuff I said – I was rambling on. We're all just freaked out right now, the funeral tomorrow.' She flicked her hands outwards, anger in the gesture. 'Just forget it.'

'OK,' I said uncertainly, not sure exactly which part I was erasing from the tapes – of course now I was spooling back through them, trying to work out what she was regretting so much. 'It's completely understandable that you're trying to make sense of it.'

A darkness crossed her face, a bright grin swiftly plastered over the top. I shivered, not sure if it was the rapidly descending sun or the change in temperature between the two of us. 'You're like a wise old owl, aren't you?' she said.

That didn't sound like a compliment either. Besides, I really wasn't. If I had been, I'd have flown out of town right there and then.

*

I could see into the kitchen when I climbed out of the car. Lysette's face was caught in half-profile, her lips moving, a sense of bustling purpose immediately apparent. I felt a tidal wave of relief, scrabbling in my bag for the spare key she'd given me. I pushed away my unease about the odd encounter I'd just had, calling out a hello as I wiped my muddy feet on the equally muddy doormat.

'How was it?' she said, turning to smile at me. Saffron was sitting on a kitchen chair, little legs swinging above the ground, the mound of rainbow-coloured vegetables in front of her telling me that supper was in progress. She had a butter knife, a half of a red pepper she was happily mauling.

'Yeah, no, fine,' I said, guilt needling me again. Had I elicited too much from Helena, overstepped the mark? 'I like her. Well – I think I like her.'

Lysette laughed. She put a wok on the hob, poured in oil.

'They can seem a bit up themselves when you first meet them – Helena and Kimberley, I mean, not Alex – but she's actually a real laugh. Not right now, obviously.' Lysette paused, leaned on the scuffed pine table. 'Thanks for doing that. Sorry if I was a bit . . .'

I shrugged, smiled at her. Was it me who should be apologising to her? 'I get it, don't worry. What's the deal with Alex? She doesn't seem like the other two at all.'

'She got friendly with Kimberley via the PTA. She's an academic at Cambridge, super clever.' Lysette crossed to the fridge. 'Do you want a cheeky glass of what I'm having?'

I sank into the chair next to Saffron, embraced by the comforting ordinariness. 'Go on then. It sounds like the PTA's a really big deal?'

'You betcha,' said Lysette, pulling out a bottle of white. There was less than a third in there, our glasses only half full once she'd tipped it all in. 'Alex comes up with all these schemes to bring in piles of cash so Kimberley loves her. She's a single mum. She didn't meet anyone so she decided to go it alone.' She glanced down at Saffron, who was cutting the pepper into ever tinier pieces with the blind focus of a serial killer. 'Cra-zy decision,' mouthed Lysette, taking a deep pull from her glass.

'Or brave,' I said, the words sounding more tart than I'd intended.

'Bravery's overrated,' replied Lysette, the momentary lightness already draining away. She was staring off into the middle distance, ignoring the sound of oil fizzing and hissing in the wok.

'How are you feeling?' I asked gently.

'Oh, you know,' she said, crossing to the stove, her face suffused with a bleakness that felt absolute. How could I have been so naive? Of course this wasn't ordinary: it was the very thing that Helena was lamenting, the outer veneer and the inner reality totally at odds. 'Dreading tomorrow.' I leapt up instinctively, enveloped her in a hug. 'Thanks, Mia,' she half whispered, her body almost surrendering but not quite. Saffron looked on, eyes round and watchful. 'Did Helena say much?'

How to answer that question? 'No, not really. She's in shock, like you all are.'

'Right.'

'Do you really think . . .' The uncomfortable meeting with Helena somehow chimed with the tenor of Lysette's grief – what kind of private hell was she in right now? 'Lys, do you really not think it was suicide? Do you think something happened?'

Her body juddered in my arms. She pulled away.

'I can't go there,' she said, face full of struggle.

'No, of course,' I said, regretting my blundering attempt at empathy. 'Is there anything – anything at all – I can do?'

'There might be actually,' she said, crossing back to the fridge. She spoke from inside there, the light illuminating her bent head. 'I need to pop out once I've cooked this. I'll be less than an hour. Could you hold the fort with madam? She's already eaten.'

'Course,' I said, grinning at Saffron who had a stray finger approaching her left nostril. I gave her a look and she put it down, giggling. 'What have you got to do?'

'It's nothing,' she said, still hidden in the fridge. As she stood up, I couldn't help noticing she hadn't taken anything out. 'Just something I need to sort out.' Her voice was too light, too breezy to convince.

I tried again. 'You're not going to that PTA meeting, are you?'

'Fuck no!' she said, vehement.

'What, to do with the . . .' My voice dropped. 'With tomorrow?'

'Yeah, kind of,' she said, her tone a full stop.

I felt a twinge of resentment. What was it she wasn't

trusting me with whilst she was busy trusting me with her only daughter?

'Right,' I said, equally clipped.

She ducked down towards Saffron's blonde head, held it between her hands and kissed the crown. 'You'll be good for Auntie Mia, won't you?' she said, face still dipped low. 'You'll take good care of her?'

The phrase didn't sound throwaway in her mouth – it rang in my ears, odd and disconcerting. In a few minutes she was gone, her car zooming off into the early evening. I stood at the window, watching it disappear, hurt and anxiety mixed up together. Where had she gone?

The question was so much bigger than I knew.

Sarah's Diary: February 21st 2015

I annoy him, I know I do. He annoys me – no, he fucking drives me crazy sometimes – but when I think about not having him, it makes me want to die. And if I think about HER stopping me having him – that would be it. Show's over, folks. The end.

I smelt it on him, her perfume. It was that sweet rose she gets out of that clunky crystal bottle she's got in her bathroom. I was sure it was that, but he said I was being loony. That I was letting the nasty voice inside of me who says I'm not good enough tell me stories. I needed to listen to him instead – listen to him telling me how beautiful I was, how special. He got me a vodka tonic, told me not to spoil things again, not when we'd finally pulled it off. I felt fuzzy then, good fuzzy and bad fuzzy all at once.

I ignored him the next day. I didn't even have to see him looking at me, I could feel it on my skin like it was lotion. I didn't turn round. I stayed talking to Kimberley like I liked her – actually liked her, rather than had to like her because it's too dangerous to listen to the voice telling me the truth about her. It's funny, the voice is either my best friend or my worst enemy and I don't know which.

She's invited us to her house. Girls only, she said, the cat's away *so the mice should play. Her eyes scorched me when she said it, and I knew exactly what she was asking me to do. I've seen it before, where it can take you — when I was a teenager I wasn't throwing up in some boarding school toilet and calling Mummy.*

Maybe the fact I know and she doesn't is my saving grace.

I might need saving. I think that more and more.

CHAPTER SIX

'Are you definitely, definitely sure you want me to come?'

Lysette was concentrating so hard on her own reflection that she didn't immediately reply. She was staring into the hallway mirror, applying a thick coat of scarlet lipstick, layer after layer, each one chased by another in a dizzying circle. She was wearing a flaring green dress, a chunky silver bangle adorning her bare arm – the only sliver of black came from her skyscraper heels. I felt Sarah then, almost as if it was her face, not Lysette's, that would be looking out of the mirror if I got too close.

I could hear Ged in the kitchen pleading with Saffron to put down the jar of Nutella and eat her nourishing bowl of porridge. He hadn't been sure he'd be able to rejig his work commitments, but now he had, I felt like a bit of a spare part. I didn't want anyone – not least Kimberley and her crowd – to think I'd muscled in on their tragedy.

'Why do you think I asked you?' she said, not turning away from her reflection. She was applying lashings of mascara now – it felt too callous to point out the obvious jeopardy in that decision. Besides, there was something intimidating about her intensity. I hadn't summoned up the courage to ask her where it was she'd gone when she'd finally returned last night from her mystery assignation, and now the moment had passed. Except it hadn't, not really. Something between us felt bruised.

'I know,' I said. 'But now Ged's here – I just don't want to intrude.'

She turned, eyes clear and bright. She looked so alive in that moment, like she'd taken on the job of two.

'I need you.'

'So I'm coming,' I said, reaching a swift hand out for my coat.

*

The day was warm and bright, sunlight playing off the stone façade of the huge church. A fleet of black cars was parked in the road, mourners streaming through the church gates. Kimberley and her friends were standing in a tight black knot near the thick wooden doors. They turned towards us as we approached, and Lysette stepped into the centre without pausing for a beat, sucked up, up and away like Dorothy, whisked off by the Kansas tornado. I could hear their sobs, all muddled up together into one sound. Was this what she'd needed, to be held in that maelstrom of shared grief, all these last difficult days? Why had she held them so fiercely at bay?

Nigel Farthing stood on the outskirts of their group, more handsome than I'd expected from his pictures. It wasn't just good looks; it was a certain charisma that was evident even without him opening his mouth. A couple came towards him, and he double kissed and shook hands, all the time exuding an appropriate sombreness. He was a straight-up professional, I could see it instantly.

I stood there awkwardly with Ged wishing I knew what to say – anything I thought of sounded too crass to utter. I liked him, but he was definitely Lysette's husband rather than my friend: we'd never quite graduated. I felt Patrick's absence like an ache – he would've been my fellow interloper, my partner in crime. Nigel stepped towards us, breaking the silence.

'You're Lysette's friend from London, aren't you?' he said, blue eyes intense and focused. He shot out a firm hand, an expensive-looking watch peeking out from beneath the sleeve of his smart navy suit. 'Nigel Farthing.'

It was hard to look away from him. It wasn't that I was attracted to him; it was that his attention was oddly transfixing.

'I am, I'm Mia. Lovely to meet you.'

'It's wonderful you're here,' he said, so sincerely that it was almost as if it was his wife that was being buried. He stepped backwards, but didn't yet look away. 'Thank you for coming. And nice to see you too, Ged.'

I looked after his retreating back, not quite sure what to make of him.

'Thank God they released the body,' said Ged, his voice low.

'Was it ever really in doubt?' I asked.

'They had to do a postmortem. They haven't even got a death certificate yet.'

I gulped in a mouthful of warm air. 'Why not?'

'They can't give a cause of death.'

'She killed herself,' I said, too sharply. Why was I so desperate for the facts to stay in straight lines? 'She died because she fell.'

'Yeah,' said Ged, 'but with suicides they don't just say it's a suicide. There's still got to be an inquest. They just give you some scrappy thing – an interim death certificate – so you can . . .' He looked over at Lysette. She was holding on to Helena, Kimberley hovering close by, her glossy blonde hair pinned into an elaborate up do. She'd obviously found the strength to get herself to the hairdresser. 'Do what you have to do.'

'It's just a formality though?'

'Yeah, sure, it's quite normal . . .' Ged winced at his choice of word. 'With suicides it's often an open verdict, if they feel like they don't know exactly what happened. It's not "beyond reasonable doubt". I've been reading up. Didn't think the Mrs was in need of regular updates.' We looked back over to her, and, almost as if she could feel our gaze, she broke away from the group. She half ran towards Ged, mascara painting her raw cheeks.

'Come on,' she said, urgent, grabbing hold of each of our hands, and pulling us towards the dark mouth of the church door.

Just for a second, my feet refused to comply. I looked behind me at the open church gates, my heart lurching. Tragedy came through the door every day in my job, but it wasn't like this.

*

The church was thronged with mourners, airless and muggy. The coffin was already there at the front like a hostess waiting for her guests. When silence eventually fell it was more like a scream. Lysette's gang were in a pew a few rows from the front and we squeezed in next to them. I perched on the end, which gave me a perfect vantage point of the front row. Joshua was in the middle, his arm firmly encircling a small boy. Max. I'd seen him outside, a doll – Woody from *Toy Story* – clutched in his hand, a big pair of glasses dominating his small, freckled face. When Joshua turned to whisper something in his son's ear, I saw his aquiline face in profile. It was lined and angular, moulded by grief into an equation all of its own. When he bowed his head down towards Max's ear, his movement was slow and measured, like he had his feelings under control, but it was taking every scrap of his energy. Max looked up at him, his face full of trust that was absolute and broken all at once. Tears rolled down my cheeks unbidden, and I searched my pockets for the wad of loo paper I'd hastily snatched from the downstairs bathroom when we left.

The vicar – a tall, spindly man with greying curls – stepped up to the pulpit. His opening words felt like thin gruel, inadequate for what it was we'd come to mourn – when he directed us to the order of service for the first hymn I was glad he'd been put out of his misery. But as the singing started – quiet at first and then swelling and rising to engulf the space – I found myself almost missing the dull monotony of his voice. This was only the beginning. It was like the first juddering shakes of a roller-coaster car, the whole tumultuous ride still to come. People were openly sobbing all around me, but the jagged, animal cries from a few rows behind were impossible to ignore. My head swivelled round before I could stop myself.

It took a few seconds to recognise him. His face was torn apart, savage and otherworldly, a million miles from the meek-looking man who had shepherded Saffron towards her classroom the other day. I quickly turned back, but the image of his ravaged expression felt like it was stamped on my retinas. I hoped there was someone there to hold his hand but I couldn't allow myself to keep looking back at him like a curtain-twitching old lady.

Joshua was crossing to the pulpit now. Kimberley slid her cat-like eyes towards Helena, quick and sly, the message one that I couldn't decode. But then . . . I saw him before he saw me, stranded as I was on the end of the pew with a perfect view of the aisle. My heart pounded in my chest, my whole body straining for an escape route. How could Lysette have failed to share this vital piece of information? I looked at her, her hand in Ged's, clenching and unclenching, her eyes trained downwards on the order of service. The last thing I wanted was to be thrown together with the man – he was technically a man now, but to me Jim would always be a boy – who had broken my heart, broken my spirit, when I was too young to protect myself from him.

He'd arrived now: I stared at him, a frozen smile hitched across my face, and he grinned back at me like it had been a week, not a couple of decades. His green eyes sparkled the way they always had, only now they had lines etched into the olivy skin that surrounded them, pads of flesh beneath. I continued with my spiky inventory: his dark hair was greying at the temples, his well-turned features hollowed out by age. He was short and wiry when we were teenagers, but now he had a cushion of flesh around his midriff. For all of that, he was still handsome: even now, I knew him well enough to know that he enjoyed that fact. His eyes darted back to me as he reached across to kiss Lysette.

'Hello, sis, sorry I'm late,' he whispered. 'Hi, Mia.'

'Hi.'

Was he evaluating me the way I was evaluating him? Of course he was. I tried not to care about the verdict.

'Thanks for coming,' gulped Lysette.

Joshua had arrived at the pulpit. He stood there for a few seconds in silence, his gaze trained on the front row where Max was wedged between two older children who I assumed were his half-siblings, his eyes glued to his dad. An auburn-haired woman – Lisa, I felt sure – was sitting directly behind them, her hands resting on the dark wood of their pew, proprietary. Joshua slowly withdrew some pages from the inside pocket of his immaculate charcoal suit.

'It's impossible to put into words what me and my family are feeling right now, so I'm not going to even attempt it. Instead I'm going to talk about the Sarah we all knew – the woman who lit up our lives and will be utterly impossible to forget.'

My eyes unconsciously moved towards the redhead. It seemed almost comical, the idea you'd be left for a younger model and then have to endure sitting through your ex's love-soaked eulogy. Another guttural sob wrenched itself out of Mr Grieve. I forced myself to focus, reaching for Lysette's hand as Joshua continued. It was as much for comfort as it was to comfort her – I was grateful for her hard squeeze back. She was meant to be giving a reading and I could sense the dread building up inside her. There wasn't really enough room on the pew now Jim had arrived, and I was uncomfortably aware of his thigh resting against mine. I wriggled away, but there was nowhere much to wriggle to.

'It's that fact that gives me a scrap of comfort. The idea that Sarah will never be forgotten. Her spark, her beauty, her . . .' He looked down at the typewritten pages that lay on the lectern. 'Life force. None of those things can be erased from our memories, and that means she'll always be part of us. She was a wonderful mother to Max . . .'

As his words continued, my eyes strayed back to the front rows. There was a man squeezed close to the auburn-haired woman, I now realised: his hand intermittently stroked her hand, which still lay on the pew where her children sat with Max. Max turned his body round as I watched, kneeling on the wooden seat to show her his Woody doll. She smiled at him kindly, nodded towards his dad. I squeezed Lysette's hand again, and she caught my eye, her fear naked and palpable.

'You can do this,' I whispered.

She gave me a tight smile, then looked back towards the still sobbing teacher. I thought she'd smile at him too, send him a crumb of comfort even if it went unseen, but instead her face stayed still. As she turned back, I saw Kimberley's mouth pucker into a barely detectable moue.

'Sarah made time for everyone, but she always fought hardest for the underdog,' said Joshua, shuffling the pages. Typewritten, neatly stacked: it was probably the only way he could make it through, but there was something about it that felt chilly. Heathcliff would've scrawled Cathy's eulogy in his own blood, thought the geeky English student inside of me. What would Patrick say, if it was him up there? Was everyone asking the same? Was Kimberley secretly watching Nigel, hoping that if she died, his politician's polish would get swept away by a torrent of grief? I snuck a glance at her. Her face was moulded into a mask of appropriate sadness.

'Even when Max was tiny, she insisted on volunteering at the homeless centre in Cambridge. She joked it was so she'd come home smelling of fags and booze and I wouldn't know what she'd been up to, but it was really because she never wanted to forget how much we had. There but for the grace of God, is what she'd say.' He tried to smile, but it was more a twist of pain. Did he believe in God, I wondered, and if he did, did he feel like God had punched him in the face? I took comfort in my own half-belief in a shadowy force that was too nebulous to make any real commitment to – I was like an ambivalent dater on Tinder, swiping right but never sending a message. Sometimes I envied Patrick his rock-solid Catholicism, however much I mocked him for it when I was feeling mean.

Joshua was finishing now, directing us to the next hymn. I sensed how much Lysette wanted it to stretch out for ever, but it didn't. She froze for a second as she made her way out of the pew, and I gave her a tiny touch, something between a stroke and a push. Once she was walking down the aisle her perilously high heels tapped out a confident tattoo. She arrived at the lectern looking more beautiful than I'd ever seen her, lit from within by purpose. She smoothed out the paper she was holding, looked down at it and then looked straight out at the packed church.

'I've got a poem here . . .' she said, 'and it's about grief and loss and all the things we're all feeling.' She looked at Joshua. 'I'm sorry, can I just junk the script? Is that OK?'

Her words had a sharpness to them, but he must've nodded because she turned straight back to face us.

'There are so many things I want to say about Sarah, but we'd be here until Christmas if I said them all. I don't know if you know this about her, but she loved Fleetwood Mac. She'd belt them out in the car, run too many red lights. I think a little bit of her wanted to be Stevie Nicks in 1977.'

When we laughed, it was like a cold compress on a fevered

brow; I could sense Lysette gaining confidence, safe in the knowledge that she was holding us in the palm of her hand. Kimberley had leaned in, eyes trained on her like a sniper, whilst Helena's overflowed with tears.

'There's a song of theirs she sings, not one of the million dollar anthems, it's called "Landslide", and it's either the most beautiful song you've ever heard or the saddest. She says she's afraid of changing, she's built her life around this "you" that she's singing it for. It's been going round and round my head since Sarah died.' Her voice dropped, thick with emotion. 'I think it's because I'd built my life around her, without even realising it. That's what she was like – she got under your skin in this incredible way without even trying. You couldn't be half-hearted about her. I can't imagine how you, her family, feel, but please know we're right there with you. We'll never forget her either. We couldn't – not even if we wanted to.' Lysette paused a moment. 'I'm scared of changing without her, leaving her behind, but like you said, Joshua, she'll always be a part of us.' She looked to the coffin, tears overwhelming her now, poise collapsing. 'We'll never leave you behind. We won't . . .'

Ged was out of his seat now, meeting her halfway down the aisle, gently leading her back as she collapsed into him, convulsing with sobs. The rest of the funeral passed in a blur, my hand covering Lysette's hot one, her tears never subsiding.

Like I said, she was doing the job of two.

CHAPTER SEVEN

It was the kind of house I'd have had to marry an oligarch to live in if I'd somehow managed to transport it back to London with me. It had Tudor beams, a huge garden, a kitchen so cavernous you could fit mine and Patrick's whole flat inside and have space left over. Even so, it was packed to the rafters, the noise and hubbub a contrast to the pregnant hush of the church. It felt oddly celebratory, a collective exhalation of breath that had been held in too tightly all day. A few uniformed waiting staff slipped between tight bodies with plates of sandwiches and bottles of wine, whilst Joshua moved between people with Max in tow, his Woody doll still clutched in his small hand.

As soon as we squeezed our way into the middle of the living room, Lysette was grabbed by a group of people I didn't know and didn't feel ready to meet. I looked around. The room was blandly chic – squishy oatmeal sofas, expensively off-white walls that whispered Farrow & Ball. Sarah jolted her way into my mind – the way she'd hugged me tightly like a long-lost friend even though it was the first time we'd met, the mingled whiff of fags and Orbit gum. I would never have imagined that she'd stepped out of this hushed good taste. I looked over at Lysette, already deep in conversation. Her beautiful words about Sarah had made her into a strange kind of star, and a petty bit of me didn't want to be the almost best friend who no one had even known existed until now. Helena waved at me from across the room, but I didn't go over there either, just waved back and went in search of a bathroom for a pee I only half needed. Jim had driven separately, but I knew he'd arrive soon: I needed a couple of minutes to practise being magnificent and imperious.

'Have we met? You're here with Lysette, right?'

It was the auburn-haired woman, Lisa, if my hunch was correct. She was standing in the doorway of the living room, signalling to a group of late arrivers where they should leave their coats. Her calm authority made me wonder if it had once been her family home – if it still held her energetic imprint, and cleaved to her will as soon as she stepped over the threshold. She wore a navy coat dress with gold buttons running down the front, elegant in a way that would not yet suit me. Her skin was porcelain, lightly criss-crossed by age in a way that didn't rob her of her attractiveness but probably would've limited her options. I found myself increasingly obsessed by age these days – I couldn't help it.

'That's right. I'm Mia. I'm her . . . her friend from London.'

'Lisa. Thanks for coming. I'm sure she really appreciates it.'

I could see Lysette from here, hands gesticulating like a puppeteer, only a shallow puddle of white wine left at the bottom of her glass. There was a controlled hysteria about her; relief like rocket fuel, grief threatening to boomerang back and fell her at any second. Ged had already gone back to work: I felt a wave of protectiveness towards her.

'I was glad to be here for her. I'm back to London in a couple of hours, I need to get back to work.' I rolled the word around in my mouth like a delicious sweet, comforted by it. 'And to my fiancé.'

'What is it you do?'

'I'm a therapist.'

'Yes! I've heard about you.'

'Have you?'

'Word travels fast in these here parts,' she said, putting on a comedy yokel accent that didn't quite land. 'I should see how my two are doing,' she added, like she knew as much. 'Good to meet you.'

*

When I came out of the bathroom, Kimberley was waiting outside, catching the door handle as it swung open. We stood there, slightly too close.

'I thought you'd left,' she said, although I couldn't see why.

'No. I was just talking to Lisa.' Kimberley's eyebrows arched up like perfect commas. 'She seemed really nice.'

'She's a close friend,' said Kimberley, wrong-footing me. I tried to keep my face neutral, but it was almost as if she could read my thoughts – how could she have been simultaneously close to the first and second wife? 'It's all very civilised with

Joshua. You'd be suitably impressed.' She paused, waiting for my reaction.

'What, you mean when I'm giving out my gold stars?'

She gave a tinkly laugh.

'It sounds like you should. Helena said you were a godsend the other day.'

'Really?'

'Oh yes! I wanted to talk to you myself by the time she'd finished, but I guess there won't be time. Shame.'

I was flattered, almost against my will. I smiled, shrugged my assent. 'I should go and find Lysette. Wasn't she amazing up there?'

A look crossed Kimberley's face that I couldn't decipher.

'I could never have done that,' she said.

'Really?'

'You get back to her. She'll be really feeling it now – Sarah not being here. She'll need you.'

Every sentence that came out of her perfect mouth left a nasty aftertaste.

*

Lysette's eyes lit up at the sight of me in a way that they hadn't all week. She still had that firework feeling about her – soaring high in the air, liable to explode. Her scarlet lipstick was bleeding outwards, a sticky red imprint left on the glass.

'Mia! Come and get a drink.'

Her glass was already held out for a top-up. I smiled at a waiter, asked him for a glass of white and took a modest sip.

I don't really like drinking in the day – growing up with an alcoholic father has given me control freak tendencies around it. That 4 p.m. muzziness that people like so much makes me feel like civilisation as we know it is crashing down around our ears.

'Everyone's saying how incredible you were,' I told her.

'Yeah well,' she said, a dismissive hand flying up. 'I had to be. That's what she deserved. She'd have done the same for me. And she wouldn't have gone to pieces at the end.'

'You didn't go to pieces,' I said, when what I really wanted to say was that I'd get up there and speak for her too, even if I was ninety years old and deaf as a post and had to shout the words down the aisle until I was hoarse. She took another slug of her wine.

'Someone had to tell the truth about her.'

'I thought Joshua spoke really well too.'

Lysette gave a tight little nod. Everything I said sounded like a press release – I couldn't quite understand why. Was it something about my vantage point, my sense of telescoping in and out, too close and then distant again? I felt relief in my body at the thought that I only had a few more hours left.

We both looked over to him, standing in the corner with Sarah's parents. Sarah's mum didn't look all that much older than him, her dark hair glowing with reddish highlights, big gold earrings framing her face. I could see that vitality of Sarah's that Lysette was holding on to like a torch. Her dad looked more grey, his shoulders slumped, eyes baggy with sadness.

'I've got to go and talk to them,' said Lysette, her voice rising dangerously like a snatched-up needle ripping across a vinyl record. I put my hand on her arm, but she pulled away, leaving it suspended uselessly in mid-air. I stood there a second, marooned again, then headed for the groaning buffet table just to give myself something to do.

'Couldn't resist the sausage rolls?'

Where had he sprung from? I kept my voice steady. 'I didn't know you were here.'

'I was going to go home, but Ged thought she might need some babysitting,' said Jim, nodding towards Lysette, her hands slicing through the air, Sarah's parents her captive audience.

'Makes sense Ged asked you. I'm going back to London in a couple of hours.'

I mapped Jim's face more closely this time, observed the passage of time etched into his skin. His confidence was so absolute back then, the world not just dancing, but waltzing to his tune. He was careless with his gifts: where had that taken him? I knew he had a gaggle of kids, a satisfyingly frazzled wife who I'd spotted at one of Saffron's parties, and a job as a TV producer. All of that was just information, though.

'So we've only got two hours to cover twenty years?' he said. 'I hope you can still talk fast.'

I kept my gaze deliberately cold, ignoring the way he was beckoning me towards our shared history. He cocked his head, smiled at me, his green eyes searching my face. He was still used to doors swinging open with the lightest of pushes.

'Edited highlights? I'm a psychotherapist, I live in

Highgate and I'm about to get married.' Why did I say Highgate? Patrick's rabbit-hutch flat was a good two miles from the leafy, celeb-riddled enclave up the hill. About to get married was an exaggeration too: we couldn't quite fix on a date, Patrick's upcoming trial a looming rain cloud that never quite broke and my work a relentless stream of clients and conferences. My voice was too high, too quick.

'Who's the lucky bastard? Although ... I bet you've got spreadsheets for the canapés and some kind of ruthless short-list for the invites.'

'And do you never get out of bed till ten unless you absolutely have to?'

Jim laughed. He'd won – he'd broken through my Teflon coating – and he was enjoying his victory. I smiled back, I couldn't help it.

'You bet.' He held up the plate of sausage rolls, offered me one, eyes twinkling. 'Although Rowena kicks my arse if I don't pull my weight.'

It was stupid, but I felt a twinge inside as he said it. It wasn't because I wanted to be with him – I'd have taken Patrick's unwavering kindness over his flighty, unreliable charm any day – it was the tangible sense of someone else having him. Someone else who'd believed in herself enough to know that kicking his arse was the way to win. Me – I let him take everything, until there was nothing left for him to stay for.

'What have you got? Three?' I said, faux casual, as if I didn't know perfectly well.

He nodded. 'That's my lot. We've got to the root of the problem now, we know what's been causing it.'

I gave a weak smile. Before I could formulate some kind of witty riposte, Joshua appeared, Max still trailing in his wake.

'Jim. Thanks so much for coming.'

'I wanted to be here.' He clapped Joshua on the shoulder, which slightly made me cringe. 'I'm so sorry, mate.' Joshua nodded, unable to summon any words. 'This is Mia. She was at school with Lysette, so we go way back.'

I felt an illogical burst of resentment – did he not want to say that I was his ex? I pushed the narcissistic thought away. It was the first time I'd properly seen Joshua up close, but even here, when we were inches apart, it was hard to really see him. I felt more absence than presence.

'It was a beautiful service,' I said.

Max's chubby hand strained upwards towards the buffet table, making a stack of three of the miniature sausage rolls. He mashed down on them and tried to stuff the triple-decker treat into his mouth.

'Max, no!' said Joshua sharply. 'That's greedy.'

Max's face, a mess of crumbs and snot, started to crumble. I fell to my knees without thinking about it.

'Hello, Max, I'm Mia. Who's your friend?' I added, pointing at his Woody doll.

Max's face brightened. He gulped down a lump of sausage, and stuck out Woody's hand, making a formal introduction. 'Woody,' he said, as I fumbled to grip his tiny plastic digits.

'He's a good friend to have,' I said.

'He's my best friend,' agreed Max earnestly. 'My mummy says I can tell him anything in the world.'

'Anything?'

'Yes. He doesn't have any other friends so if I tell him things, he never tells anyone else. Do you have a best friend?'

'I think so,' I said, looking over at Lysette. Her glass was already empty, her eyes blazing. Joshua's face was still full of reproach. I scrambled to my feet, hoping he didn't think my behaviour was presumptuous.

'Good to meet you,' he said, gliding away, Max following in his wake.

'You're going to be a natural,' said Jim, softly, and the twinge inside twisted into something tighter and harder.

We both looked back to Lysette. I could hear her, her voice cutting through the gentle hubbub of the room.

'She'd want you to know that,' she was saying, eyes trained on Sarah's father. 'She'd forgiven you for all of it.' She shrugged, grinned too widely. 'Any problems you'd had, it was all in the past.'

I watched her words land, his face like stone. This was a disaster: I looked at Jim, and he looked back at me, a half-smile playing on his face. He hadn't lost it even now – that total refusal to take anything seriously unless it was a direct threat, a herd of buffalo charging straight for him.

'Jim, we've got to persuade her it's time to go home.'

People were starting to stare. I could see Kimberley perched elegantly on the oatmeal sofa casting darting looks in Lysette's direction. Nigel sat next to her, his expression deliberately neutral. Joshua had headed out into the garden, so he wasn't there to smooth things over either. I couldn't watch any longer: I slipped my way across the room to Lysette's side, jerking my head at Jim to follow.

'She was special. I know people always say that, but . . .'

I put my arm around Lysette, which stopped her mid-flow.

'Hi,' I said, smiling awkwardly at Sarah's parents. 'I'm Mia. I'm an old friend of Lysette's. I'm so sorry to meet you in such sad circumstances.'

Jim was uncomfortably shifting from foot to foot, a bottle of beer in his hand. I felt like a prefect. Sarah's parents smiled at me, their fixed grins telling me that they needed rescuing.

'She's an old friend of my brother's too,' said Lysette, with a little roll of her eyes. This was painful.

'I need to get to the station soon. Shall we go back to yours and I'll get packed?'

'Don't go!' wailed Lysette. 'I can't have you disappearing on me too.' She turned to Jim. 'No one's going to be left.'

I looked at Sarah's parents, willing them to quietly back away. They didn't.

'I'm here, sis,' said Jim.

'You're no use to anyone though, are you?' she said, her voice a snarl.

'Bit harsh,' said Jim, comforting himself with a gulp of his beer like it was a baby's bottle.

'Let's just call a cab, or maybe Jim can drive us. Saffron'll be home from school soon.'

'Mummy time,' trilled Lysette, a poor parody of 'Hammer

81

time', fingers snapping above her head. God, I hated drunk people. 'She was such a good mum. You know that though, don't you?'

I caught a look in Sarah's mum's eye, and realised in a flash why they weren't making a speedy exit. It was hungry, her look – like she was starving and craving a morsel of food, even if it was only scraps. Anything she could learn about her daughter, however it came, was worth the risk. I felt my heart contract with the knowledge that that was how it would be for me too. I'd be wearing my heart on the outside for the rest of my life.

'She was the best daughter in the world,' said Sarah's mum, the first time I'd heard her speak. Her voice, with its sharp edges, was a contrast to Joshua's neutral tones.

'But the reason she was the best ...' said Lysette, her gaze intense, 'was because she wasn't some fucking Alpha Mummy, scoring points for her gluten-free cupcakes. She still had her wicked side.' Sarah's mum was staring at her now, willing her to continue. 'She could still be a really naughty girl.'

Sarah's dad looked down at the ground, like he wished he could tunnel his way out. Perhaps I should just back away, leave them to it, stop trying to direct operations. I looked at Jim, who shrugged and took another swig of beer.

'She always had spirit, our girl,' said her mum.

Kimberley was tracking the conversation from her vantage point on the sofa, eyes narrowed.

'Spirit's one word for it!' said Lysette, something dangerous in her voice. 'She had more than that. But you know that, don't you?'

Sarah's dad's eyes flashed. 'Good to see you again, Lysette,' he said, taking his wife's elbow. 'We should get around more of her friends.'

'Am I offending you?' said Lysette. 'I didn't mean to offend you. I just want to cut through the bullshit and talk about who she really was. The real Sarah.'

'Let's go,' I said gently, enlisting Jim with my eyes. I took her arm, tried to subtly move her.

'You don't like it when things get too real, do you, Mia?' she said, her eyes narrow. 'You like to keep everything just so.' She made a little gesture, a bow being tied up, her mouth arranged in a prissy moue. In that second I wanted to slap her.

'Mia's right, Lys,' said Jim. I shot him a grateful look. 'I need to get home. Let me drop you on the way.'

'Stop telling me what to do,' she snarled.

'Lysette . . .' I said.

We could've gone round in circles for hours. We probably would've done, but the truth is, we got stopped in our tracks. The sharp ring on the doorbell, the arrival of the two policemen, their faces painted with the kind of bad news you immediately know is set to change lives.

In the face of what we heard next, our petty argument meant absolutely nothing.

CHAPTER EIGHT

'The fact is, Mia, you're uniquely placed.'

We hadn't even left the confines of Peterborough station, and yet Roger couldn't contain himself a second longer.

'Can we grab a coffee?' I asked, playing for time. I nodded towards the chain shop opposite the ticket office, the kind of place I'd have shunned for something more artisanal and pretentious in London, but which now seemed oddly comforting. Little Copping felt hermetically sealed, and it was hard evidence that I'd made a temporary escape.

'Of course,' said Roger, pulling out his wallet as he strode across the busy concourse. How did he manage to make even the smallest action look so definitive?

Once we'd slid into a cramped booth, he began again.

'So how have the last couple of days been?' Roger took a brisk, efficient sip from his crinkly cardboard cup. 'Very challenging, inevitably.'

It had felt almost impossible to leave Lysette this morning. She'd barely left her room since the day of the funeral, her face red raw from the constant flow of tears. Mr

Grieve – Peter Grieve as I now knew him to be – had left the funeral and taken himself back to his bedsit on the outskirts of Peterborough, looped a leather belt around his neck and hung himself. He'd left a note, scrawled on the back of an exercise book that was on the top of a pile of marking. 'I'm sorry too,' it said, echoing Sarah's note, 'I never meant to make things worse.' There was a big X slashed underneath, further mirroring Sarah's text. Sarah's death was now subject to a whole new level of scrutiny. Was it the conclusion of a suicide pact or was the truth even more sinister than that? The press were starting to swarm, the connection to the Farthings bringing a whole extra level of intrigue. I'd felt unable to return to London, had rung Roger to tell him I was extending my leave of absence, and planted the seed for this plan of his in the process.

'It's been horrible,' I said. 'The whole community's in trauma. Both of them so closely connected to the school as well. Luckily term was finishing anyway.'

Roger cocked his head, considered me.

'And you yourself will be feeling that shock.'

'I mean . . . they're not my deaths to mourn.' I paused a second, moulding the rest of my answer. The truth was, I was feeling more shock than I thought I was strictly entitled to – a gnawing tension that wouldn't let me settle, and made it hard for me to soothe Lysette's savage grief. The obvious conclusion to draw was that Peter and Sarah were having an affair, and yet Lysette flatly denied it. Nor would she tell me what she thought could be a possible explanation, terse and snappy whenever Sarah's name was mentioned. 'But yes, even being close to this kind of tragedy has shaken me up.'

'It would – particularly for someone as naturally empathetic as you,' said Roger. 'You said yourself that you pride yourself on meeting your patients exactly where they are.'

Guilt needled me – had I forgotten to do that as a friend? There were times in the last couple of days when Lysette's combination of neediness and hostility had made me feel less than saintly.

I smiled at him, keen to lighten the intensity. 'Are you saying I'm a maverick?'

He laughed. 'No, but I am saying you're gifted. Which is why I think you'd be such an asset to the community if you agreed to stay on a few weeks and offer some formalised support. You're already well versed in the delicacy of a police investigation.'

Blood pounded in my ears.

'Roger ... the Christopher Vine case, it was far from my finest hour.' I ground to a halt – I didn't need to be giving my new boss a diatribe on my all-time career low. 'Gemma was a stranger when she walked through the door, and I still got too involved.' The memory of Judith suspending me – it still stung, even if now all anyone remembered was that I was the person who subsequently unlocked Gemma's dangerous secrets. 'The dead girl is my best friend's best friend.' I knew as I said it how ridiculous it sounded: I wanted him to respect me. 'I'm too close.'

Roger waved an airy hand.

'My sense of you Mia, is that you're deeply perfectionistic. I'm sure it's why you're such a high-flier, but I also doubt you ever give yourself enough credit. That was an excellent, career-defining experience. You've got a chance to build on it here.' I gave him a sceptical look, knowing all the time that the first half of his assessment was scarily accurate. Roger took a last swig, stood up. 'At least hear the Detective Chief Inspector out.'

*

The police station was on the outskirts of the town, a grim monolith on the side of a ring road: it felt a million miles away from the chocolate box prettiness of Little Copping. Roger loudly announced us to the harassed-looking woman on the front desk, and she buzzed us through the thick doors that opened into the bowels of the building. There, by a set of lifts, stood a small, trim fifty-something man in a well-cut grey suit. He pushed a clump of floppy salt-and-pepper hair out of his face, and stuck out a friendly hand, his strange kind of elegance an immediate contrast to the dingy surroundings.

'Lawrence Krall,' he said. 'A pleasure to meet you both. Come right this way.'

We made our introductions in the lift, zooming skywards to the top floor. Krall led us down a long corridor, halting suddenly at a closed door.

'Take a look,' he said, nodding towards the square of glass that let into the room. I peered inside. A huge photo of Sarah, a smile wreathed across her pretty face, was the centrepiece of a pinboard. To the right of it was a picture of Peter, his serious expression suggesting it was from his driving licence, scribbled cards and notes stuck to the available space around them. My stomach gave an unexpected lurch, my eyes meeting Sarah's. What had taken her from that moment of happiness to a crumpled heap of blood and bones on a pavement? I forced myself to look away, aware that Krall was watching me. 'Incident room,' he said, as if it wasn't obvious.

'Already a hive of activity,' said Roger. It was true: the room was full to bursting with police, all hunched over computer screens and making calls.

'It's important,' said Krall simply, leading us onwards.

He took us into a sparse office, a metal wall clock with thick black hands the only thing punctuating the bare walls. The room was light at least, and the fact we were so high in the sky meant the whole city was spread out before us. I looked out over it all; the cathedral, the jumble of office blocks, the cars on the ring road, as small as toy ones zooming around a Scalextric track from this lofty vantage point. An involuntary shudder ran through me, Sarah's smiling face still burnt into my brain. One of those random buildings was probably the one she fell to her death from: did she look over this very same skyline in her last, terrifying seconds?

As we settled ourselves either side of the ugly Formica table, Krall suddenly sprang back up and grabbed the phone in the corner of the room. There was a nervous energy about him, a sense of constant movement.

'How rude of me, let me organise some tea,' he said. 'It's fairly disgusting, I'm afraid.'

I'd imagined someone different – someone gruff and plain-speaking with a belly that strained over regulation-issue trousers. I wasn't yet sure which was preferable. My phone gave a discreet beep. I subtly slipped the screen upwards.

> Hey Mia, weird to see each other again, huh? Let alone with all this shit going on. Be good to talk more – let's meet. Worried about my sis x.

I pushed the phone back into my bag, wishing I hadn't looked. It gave me a strange feeling, irritating and gratifying all at once. It was as if I was one of those Russian dolls, my seventeen-year-old self trapped deep inside my adult exterior, rebelliously pleased to have his attention. Perhaps it was just a welcome distraction from the darkness of what was unfolding.

Krall finished relaying our requests, and then sat back down opposite us. 'So, Mia,' he said, 'I'm hoping you might be able to help us.'

Both men looked at me expectantly.

'And you two already know each other?' I said.

'Yes,' said Roger. 'Our professional paths have crossed in the past. That's why, when I saw Lawrence's name in the paper, I thought I'd give him a quick ring.'

'Such a coincidence!' said Lawrence chummily, the two of them turning back towards me, waiting for my agreement.

'A quick ring' sounded so benign. I couldn't help thinking that it was Roger who was the real high-flier, spotting a chance to raise the profile of his newly acquired practice and leaping on it.

'I don't know how much Roger's explained, but, whilst I'd love to help, I don't think it would be appropriate. Lysette's my best friend, she was very close to Sarah . . .'

'Lysette Allen,' said Krall, cutting straight across me. 'Yes, we'll be looking to interview her in the next few days.'

'Right,' I said, trying not to react; the Lysette I'd left behind this morning was in no fit state to be subjected to a police interview. I couldn't leave her, not yet. 'She is very distressed.'

'Exactly!' said Krall, leaning forward, his gaze intense. 'That's why having you on hand for this first couple of weeks would be invaluable. For people to know there's that support – it will give them the strength and clarity to share what they know. The early stages of an investigation are critical. Memories are fresh in people's minds. If they're in deep shock, we may lose key information. We'd pay to bring you on board, make sure we respected your commitments in London.'

'I certainly couldn't work professionally with a friend . . .'

'I quite see that,' said Krall, 'but I gather that you've been informally helping Sarah's wider friendship group already?'

Lisa's comedy yokel pronouncement reverberated in my head – news really did travel fast around there.

'Well – I went for one walk.'

One very odd walk – the unease it gave me had never quite dissipated. Krall was watching me, almost as if he could hear my thoughts. I could see him measuring his next words carefully.

'Mia, the investigation has taken a bleaker turn, I'm sorry to say.'

A shiver ran straight through me, as though a shadow had blotted out the sun. I looked to Roger, but he was focused on Krall. I couldn't swear to it, but his face suggested this wasn't a revelation for him.

'How?' I asked.

'We think perhaps the first team were too quick to attribute Sarah's death to suicide.' Was he confirming what Lysette had said all along? 'It's understandable, it certainly looked that way, but there are anomalies with the CCTV footage inside the car park that make us think that an unseen assailant could have been deliberately dodging the cameras. And the way she fell – well, the first postmortem was basic, the standard examination we authorise after a suicide.'

I took a gulp of my tea, looking for comfort. 'What do you mean?'

Krall paused, his face serious. 'We exhumed the body and had a senior pathologist do a much more extensive examination. There are marks on her arms which were originally attributed to the impact, but we now suspect are signs of a struggle before she died.'

'That's terrible!' I said, blood pulsing in my ears. I'd been so quick to dismiss Lysette, to try and impose a rational explanation. The irony was that her wild, non-judgemental friend – the one who was never coming back – was the only person who would have taken her seriously right from the start.

'Isn't it?' agreed Roger, suitably solemn.

My heart thumped hard in my chest, my eyes drawn back to the window, almost as if the site of her death would loom up and show itself now it seemed so real.

'Do people know that?' I asked. I didn't want to be the one to confirm Lysette's darkest fears back to her, but nor did I want to be keeping secrets.

'Joshua Bryant obviously does,' said Krall, 'and we'll be sharing the information as we interview. Seeing where it takes people's thinking.'

'So what,' I said, my words tumbling out as fast as my racing heartbeat, 'you think that Peter Grieve killed her?' There he was in front of me, every bit as real as she felt right now. The way he automatically dropped to his knees, met Saffron down there on the ground, determined not to loom over her like an ogre. 'They were having an affair?'

Krall gave an almost Gallic shrug.

'We don't know yet. That's the most probable scenario, but we need to investigate.'

'I know it's not my place, but – I met him at the school. It sounds sappy, but – he just seemed so kind.'

Krall nodded, unmoved.

'Yes. That said, there are things in his background that raise red flags for us. A history of depression, an incident at his previous school where he became involved with a mother. And even in Little Copping, we're hearing that another mother made a complaint against him that was subsequently withdrawn.'

Why had Lysette not trusted me with any of this? I might have understood then why she was so convinced there was another explanation. Had she suspected it was Peter all along? But if she had – surely she would have told the police?

'Right,' I said, playing for time again.

'But there's a great deal more we need to look into,' added Krall, 'and we'll need all the help we can get.'

Roger cut in. 'As you can see, there's a real need here. You're already familiar to Sarah's friends. The school's head-master has also specifically requested help for him and his staff. If you could get the ball rolling, handle the immediate aftermath, the local authority will look at more long-term bereavement-counselling options.'

'The fact you've already been part of a police investigation . . .' started Krall. This time it was my turn to cut in.

'But I wasn't, not formally. I was leant on.'

'By your now fiancé!' added Roger, dry.

'Yes, but it was incredibly difficult to keep the boundaries in place. I need to know that people can talk to me in confidence.'

Krall gave a reassuring smile. 'Absolutely. If someone tells you something that's critical to the police investigation then you'd be duty bound to share it if they refused to, but that seems unlikely. There's no reason for anyone you'd be seeing to be hiding anything, and you can be clear about your legal responsibilities up front.'

There was a lengthy pause. I could see his logic – I could see why, if a person chose to talk to me, it wouldn't make sense that they'd have something to hide – and yet, something deep inside was screaming at me to step back from the edge.

'But what about my clients?'

Roger had an answer for everything. 'It's holiday season now and you'll only be three weeks or so. There's Skype, phone sessions . . .'

'I suppose . . .' I said, still unsure.

'You'd be doing real good here, Mia,' said Krall.

Could I make a difference? Max whispered across my consciousness, the way he'd earnestly, painfully described his friendship with his Woody doll. Bereaved children were a bit of a speciality of mine – could the briefness of my stay make the idea of therapy palatable to his brusque father?

'Those conferences you've been speaking at – adolescent mental health.' Roger's voice was soft, cajoling. 'That last case rocketed your profile, triggered those invitations. The grey areas are what makes it interesting. You know now how to navigate them. And other people will no doubt want to learn from your experiences.'

He knew – he could sense the part of me that was like a mirror for him. The part that was hungry for it. The part that feared that, once I had a family, I'd never get to push myself like this again. I stood up abruptly, grabbed my handbag.

'I just need to nip to the bathroom.'

*

'Sweetheart, you'll be amazing. Don't forget I've seen you in action.'

I was crammed into a tiny cubicle, perched on the loo, the lid down. Just the sound of Patrick's voice, tinny and indistinct though it was, was allowing my heartbeat to slow to something approaching normal.

'Will I? Didn't go so well last time, did it? And . . .' It was so hard to wrap words around my discomfort, my sense that there was a bigger storm approaching. 'Lysette's being so odd. Why wouldn't she have told me they were having an affair?'

'Didn't want you to think badly of her friend?'

It seemed like a logical explanation, and yet something about it felt wrong. 'Yeah, maybe.'

'Thing is, you want to stay on for her anyway. So you may as well help them out.'

'I do, I really do, but . . . She was vicious to me at the funeral, Patrick.' I could hear the emotion I'd been unable to express up until now leaking out in my voice. 'She said a couple of really horrible things.'

'Did she say you had a fat arse?'

Patrick never failed to make me laugh: his pure, unadulterated silliness was one of the things I adored about him. Stress ran off me, professional confidence surging up in its place.

'I promised you I'd only be gone a few days,' I said.

'It's fine.'

I tucked my feet up on the seat, winded by an unexpected rush of insecurity. 'Aren't you bothered?'

Was he glad I was gone, relieved to be able to slide back into workaholic bachelordom without interruption? I checked myself: a childhood spent watching my mum staring at the door, willing my terminally unfaithful dad to reappear, had made me prone to paranoia. The fact my dad and I were speaking after years of estrangement was partly thanks to Patrick's gentle loyalty: I didn't need to punish him for those early crimes. He laughed softly, knowing better than to indulge me.

'Darling, three weeks is nothing. I'll come and visit you.'

'What, and snuggle up on my lilo?'

'Sounds exceedingly sexy.' Patrick paused – I could sense the cogs turning down the phone line. 'You know that thing you say sometimes? About how everyone has their Spidy skill?' Your superhero power – the thing you can do better than anyone else – it's a pet theory of mine that we all need to know what ours is. Patrick continued. 'Well, I think yours is making people feel safe when nothing else in the world does. If they want you there, you should do it.'

'Thanks,' I said, suddenly feeling way too emotional for the inside of a police station toilet. I pulled my knees up, hugged them to my chest, my cork wedges teetering on the seat. 'I should go back in there.'

'Sure. Who's the DCI trying to talk you into it, anyway?'

'Lawrence Krall, he's called. Bit odd. I feel like he's sauntered out of a moody French film.'

Patrick whistled. 'Krall?'

'You know him?' Everyone seemed to know him: I got the distinct feeling, even from the tone of his whistle, that Patrick liked him less than Roger did.

'Strange decision. He's a proper murder guy – solved a big serial killer case up North last year. If they think this is an open and shut case, I don't know why they've parachuted him in.'

I can't deny I felt it: that whisper of unease, that shivering sensation – the kind of tiny sign I always implore my patients to heed.

I didn't. I chose not to listen. So in a sense, all that came in the wake of that decision was down to me.

CHAPTER NINE

They came from nowhere, their cameras clicking and flashing, their shouted questions like white noise. It was so stupid, so naive of me, not to have prepared myself for this. I tried not to shrink, tried to keep a steady path, my eyes fixed on the two policemen who were stationed at the school gates. Then I swept my way across the bare playground, not wanting to give myself the chance to think about the last time I'd trodden this tarmac. The tight knot of mums, Saffron's small hand in mine, Peter's gentle presence. Now he was gone, and the world of the school had stopped turning, at least for now.

Patrick had somehow managed to send me a suitcase of clothes – there was no way I could exude professional authority in my two pairs of grubby jeans – and my wedges click-clacked against the floor as I passed through the echoey corridors towards the headmaster's office. I looked into the classrooms en route, splodgy artwork decorating the walls, tiny chairs empty of tiny bottoms, and wondered which one was Saffron's. His name was stencilled on the wall in the last one: *MR GRIEVE*. I stood there, rooted to the spot by the sight of those black letters, then jumped in fright as I saw movement in my peripheral vision. She stood slowly, uncoiling herself from the carpeted corner of the room – it was Kimberley. Of course it was Kimberley. She smiled widely, carefully made her way towards the door.

'You survived the mayhem at the gates?' she asked.

'It's unbelievable.' The story was igniting, a slow-news summer suddenly transformed. A blonde, photogenic wife of a cabinet minister sweeping through the school gates on Day Two could have only thrown petrol on a blazing fire. 'They must've been all over you.'

She gave a self-deprecating shrug. 'I've got used to navigating it. Ian's going to be so pleased you're here.' She touched my shoulders, lightly grazing each of my cheeks with her lips. She was wearing a pair of leg-lengthening skinny jeans topped off by a V-necked grey marl T-shirt, her skin as fresh and luminous as it always was. Now I felt overdressed, like I'd come for a job interview in a provincial bank. 'Shall I show you where his office is?'

'Don't worry. He said it was down there and to the left in his text.'

She paused, cocked her head, brooking no argument.

'No, let me. I'm just sorting through the books. I organise an auction every summer term, and the book fund's a big part of where the money goes.' She exhaled. 'I need to feel like I'm doing something useful here. Does that make sense?'

'Of course it does.'

'This was his classroom.'

She moved backwards as she said it, and I stepped in, without really wanting to. How did she do it, take total command of any space she occupied?

'Was he a good teacher?' I regretted the question as soon as I'd asked it. It felt callous, bald. Why did I feel the need to fill the space?

'He definitely made the children feel special. He always went the extra mile.' She gave a smile which didn't reach her eyes. 'Which should be a good thing, shouldn't it?'

What did that even mean? I couldn't waste energy decoding it: instead I took in the room, the project they'd obviously been doing on the environment, the clumsy crayon drawings of birds and animals, a big orange sun, a recycling bin with an ostentatious tick. Emotion surged up in me, and I looked downwards, not wanting her to see my face. She hadn't exactly ambushed me, but she'd caught me off guard. It all felt so close suddenly, Saffron's chaotic paint splatters lost somewhere in that jumble.

'Let's go and find Ian,' I said.

'Sure thing. I've got my police interview this afternoon. I need some time to psych myself up. Deep breathing, is that what you'd recommend?'

It always felt like she was mocking me, her pinches so light they left no bruises. God, I missed Lysette in that moment – she'd normally know if I was being oversensitive, and not make me feel like an idiot if I was. It's humans' fatal design flaw, the way we only appreciate the ordinary once it's no longer ordinary at all.

'I tend to find breathing helpful in most situations,' I said.

She smiled, didn't say anything for a beat longer than was comfortable.

'I really must come and see you, mustn't I?'

*

I looked at my watch as I followed Kimberley down the corridor, conscious that Lysette would be in her police interview at this very moment. By the time I got back from my meeting with Krall, the news about the cameras had leaked out, which was kind of a relief. I'd hoped it might bridge the gap I'd felt opening between us in the preceding days, the confirmation that her hunch was right, but if anything she felt more distant. Her way of psyching herself up for her interview was to get progressively angrier, convinced they'd be out to malign Sarah.

'They weren't having an affair,' she'd said, yanking the cork out of a bottle of wine like a cowboy drawing his gun. I saw a look cross Ged's face as she did it, but he didn't say anything. 'I know that's what everyone's going to say, but it's bullshit.'

'But for him to do that to himself – he must've been obsessed with her?'

She flung up a dismissive hand.

'Everyone was obsessed with Sarah, Mia. She was that kind of person.'

I tried not to feel the sting, the sense of competing with

someone impossibly perfect. An anarchic saint. Maybe dying young was the only way to square some of those impossible contradictions of being a woman.

'But it sounds like he did have problems,' I added. I was desperate to ask her about the complaint that Krall had alluded to, but I didn't want her to think I was poking around for gossip.

There was an edge to her. 'Look at you, with the inside track.'

'Lys, if you don't want me to do this . . .'

'No,' she said. 'It's not that. I'm really glad you're here.'

It doesn't always feel that way, I thought, but then I looked down at the chaos around us, her living-room floor a sea of garish plastic toys. Saffron had made me some plastic fried eggs earlier: I should've cleared them away, rather than behaving like room service would come and do it for me.

'I'm not part of the investigation. I'm just here to offer people a bit of support. Be someone to talk to.'

'I want you to be someone for *me* to talk to.'

'I'll always be that,' I promised.

Promises can be foxing – how often do we make them in a lifetime and really know they'll hold fast?

*

Ian's door was firmly shut when we got there, and Kimberley made sure that she was the one to knock. She opened it before there was a response, pushing her blonde head through the gap.

'Ian, Mia Cosgrove's here.' It felt odd to hear my whole name come out of her mouth. How had she learnt it?

'Come on in,' said a stressed-sounding voice. 'We're wrapping up.'

The office was small and poky, with a view of the roundabout in the playground and the fields that ringed the school. Ian Gardener was wedged behind his desk like it was a barricade; a man and a woman sat on the other side on boxy armchairs that looked too brown and synthetic to be comfortable – I guessed immediately that they were plain-clothes detectives. Ian probably wasn't much older than me, but he was pasty and well padded, his hair thinning at the crown, plastic glasses perched high on his sweaty nose.

Once the detectives had made their exit, Ian turned his focus onto me.

'So you managed to cross enemy lines?' he said, attempting a weak smile.

'The photographers? God, they're like swarming rats, aren't they?'

'I feel like that's unfair to rats,' he said. His voice sounded nasal to my ears, each word delivered at a similar flat pitch. 'We've got a couple of white ones in Owl class, they actually make very good pets.'

We sat there for a few seconds in silence. I like to let a first session unfold without me forcing it. Where the client instinctively wants to lead us tells me far more than I'll glean from their answer to some question I've cleverly constructed.

'Thanks for coming,' he said eventually.

'I'm glad you asked,' I said. 'I'm not arrogant enough to think I can do a great deal in three weeks, but if I can be any support to you, I'd like to try.'

He grabbed a ballpoint pen from the pen pot on his desk, started clicking the mechanism in and out. He was wearing a wedding ring that gripped the skin of his fleshy finger like it was too small for it.

'That's all we can really do, isn't it?' he said, looking up, his gaze intense. His eyes were almond-shaped, brown, too small for his wide face. 'Try?'

'In this instance?'

'More life in general,' he said, voice leaden. The next silence that came felt more loaded. I waited it out. 'These sessions are confidential, aren't they?'

'Unless you tell me something that's critical to the police investigation.' I looked at the way his shoulders hunched inwards under his bog-standard black crew neck, his fingers still fiddling obsessively with the chewed plastic pen. All I wanted – all I ever want with clients, apart from the odd one I want to drown – was to make him feel that he wasn't completely alone. 'And I know so little about it that unless you tell me you . . .' I stopped myself, then finished the sentence. 'Were directly involved, then it seems unlikely.'

'What, you mean if I'd pushed her?' he said, words laced with grim humour. 'I assume you know about the bruising on her body?'

'I do, yes.'

He shook his head. 'It still feels completely unbelievable. It's like it's a horrible practical joke, and someone's going to jump out with a camera and it'll all be over.'

'Of course it does,' I said gently. 'It's only just happened. You're in shock.'

'Shock's one word for it.'

It seemed like a strange response. Was he shooting for a fake kind of nonchalance? I see it sometimes, particularly in men – an attempt to distance themselves from their feelings to self-protect.

'If shock's one word, what would be another?'

'What do you mean?'

'You said that was one word for it, as if you were thinking about a word which might better describe your feelings.'

'Feelings.' He almost spat the word out.

'Well – how did it feel when you found out? Did the police tell you face to face?'

'Dunno,' he said, jaw rigid under the doughy flesh that covered it. 'I felt – angry, if anything.'

'Angry with who?'

'Angry about all of it,' he said, an answer to a different question. His voice dropped at the end of the sentence, like the 'all' was infinite, a stone thrown down a well, a distant splash. Was he skirting around the incident at the school that Krall had made mention of? 'I mean obviously I felt terrible for the family. For Max.'

His postscript had none of the emotion of the first half of his reply.

'Ian, can I ask what you mean by "all of it"?'

'The whole thing is obviously a huge mess. Lives have been devastated.' He was depersonalising my questions, keeping me at arm's length, but all the time he was laying down breadcrumbs, encouraging me to venture closer. 'A child's life has been destroyed,' he added for good measure.

'Of course. I appreciate all of that. I just wondered about how it felt for you, specifically. In your role.'

'What? Potentially having recruited a murderer? Fabulous, Mia, as I'm sure you can imagine.'

I laughed. I needed to take him at face value, break the tension.

'I'm sorry if that sounded trite.' He gave a smile that felt real, present in a way that he hadn't been up until now. 'You want the truth? I'm not sure I'll ever be the person I was a month ago. He seems like a fool.'

Again, it wasn't so much the words as the delivery.

'A fool?' I was going to continue but he cut straight across me.

'Can we talk practicalities?' he said, suddenly acid. 'Or is this all going to be deep and meaningful?'

'The session's for you, Ian. It's about what you find most useful.'

He drew himself up in his chair, ramrod straight. He suddenly felt like a headmaster, like he could dole out lines or a suspension without breaking a sweat.

'How do we come back from this?' he demanded. 'How do my children, my staff, ever start to feel normal again?'

'I think the truth is, that normal will have to become something different now.'

His gaze was intense. 'OK, so how do I make this place feel safe again?'

'By telling the truth,' I said, watching how his face moved downwards at the sound of the word. Did it sound more glib to his ears than I'd intended it to be? 'Or rather – by acknowledging what's happened instead of spreading a layer of fake normal over the top. Children are very resilient, but they're also very sensitive. They know when they're being lied to. I would encourage the parents to tell them that Peter's died, not feed them stories about him having gone away.'

'Really?'

'They read fairy stories, see pets die, lose grandparents. They're much better off knowing he's died, and then having lots of support to feel safe in that reality. And Max will want to talk about his mum, I imagine, if he hasn't already.'

'Right.' I could sense the anger that he was talking about, the insistent pulse of it. 'Don't they say tabloids have a reading age of nine? They should all be well and truly up to speed by the time they get back.' It was hard not to find his gallows humour repellent. 'Did you see the headlines today?'

'I did, yes. And I found it shocking to see their faces there. I can't imagine how hard it is for those of you who were close to them.'

The newsagent had been crowded with people when I'd walked past it today. Sarah and Peter's photographs had been plastered across the front pages – *Double Love Death in Farthing's Village* said one.

'I wasn't close to them,' countered Ian. 'I was an employer. A headmaster to Sarah's child. Which isn't to say that I didn't care.' His gaze was intense again. 'Or that I don't care now.'

'Absolutely. I can see how much it's affected you.'

Ian's gaze swivelled to the window.

'I tried my best.' His voice cracked. 'What does my best look like now?'

The emotion was right there on the surface. I decided to risk trying to draw him a little further.

'What do you think it would look like?'

Just for a second, he looked utterly helpless, like he himself was a child, but then something hardened and calcified.

'I asked you,' he said.

I was going too fast. Part of him wanted to spill the emotion, but the larger part couldn't risk it yet.

'I would have an assembly the day the school comes back. Talk to everyone – staff and children – and let the kids know that they can talk about it in smaller groups with their teachers. The council are going to provide ongoing access to counsellors for your teachers, aren't they?'

'Yeah, no, I get it. Talk. Talk and talk and talk.'

His face was scarlet, the pen clasped tight in his hand again.

'It's OK to be angry,' I said, making my voice gentle. 'Something terrible has happened, and you're right in the firing line. This might sound like therapy speak, and if it does, I can only apologise, but I think you need a lot of self-compassion right now. This isn't your fault. You need support so you don't feel alone with what it is you have to get through in the next few weeks.'

My eyes flicked around the room, looking for personal touches, a sense of his wider life, what might be holding him. I couldn't find anything, just dreary MDF shelves overflowing with textbooks and ring binders.

'It's useless, this, isn't it?' he spat.

'What do you mean?'

'You don't know if it's my fault. You're just coming up with phrases . . .'

I paused a second, angling my next shot. He was angry, no question: it wasn't just his face that was reddened by it, the flush spread down below the neck of his black jumper. But below the anger I sensed something else. Pain that was too raw, too dangerous, to give words to.

'Like we said at the beginning, unless you . . .' The words stuck in my throat, but I pushed them out. 'Unless you murdered those two people, it is emphatically not your fault. So no, it's not just a phrase.' His shoulders slumped, his eyes lifting to meet mine.

'OK. Point taken.' His mouth stretched into an almost-smile. 'Round one to you.'

I smiled back, paused as I formed the next thought.

'It's just so hard for us to believe in it, I think. The finality of death, even though it's the one thing that's in the job description of being human.'

He didn't speak, just stared out of the window into the empty playground. My gaze followed his, the two of us watching a single magpie swooping downwards and landing on the roundabout. It cocked its head, gimlet-eyed, its talons tightly wrapped around one of the metal bars that quartered the surface.

'I did try,' he muttered eventually, eyes still trained on the black-and-white bird. It gave a loud squawk, its beak pointing skyward.

'What did you try?' I asked.

'I tried, you know, I tried to keep the show on the road.' He gave an ironic wriggle of his hands. I stayed quiet a minute, waiting to see where he'd go. 'I'm a headmaster, not . . . some fascist dictator.'

'What show was it you were keeping on the road, do you think?" I asked him.

'Do you have kids?'

'No. No I don't,' I said, affecting a nonchalance of my own.

'Schools are very emotional places. Feelings run high.'

'The police did mention that there was some kind of incident.'

Ian gave a humourless laugh.

'If only. An incident I could've solved. Keep calm and carry on.'

He stared at me, challenge in his eyes. The room felt airless, the session infinite. This was day one, and it was already this complicated.

'So how was it if it wasn't like that?' I asked.

'Peter was someone who seemed to stir up a lot of feelings. He didn't seem like he'd be that way when I hired him.'

'And people seem to say the same thing about Sarah. How did he make you feel?' He didn't reply, his face immobile. 'Did you think he was a good teacher?'

'One of the best I've ever come across,' he said, the compliment delivered without a trace of warmth. It was every bit as ambiguous as Kimberley's answer to that same question. Then he straightened himself in his chair, the connection lost again. He'd disappeared behind his title; I could sense it. 'We haven't got long. Why don't you talk to me more about how children deal with death? Help me get into the mindset of it?'

I talked him through the accepted wisdom, illustrated it with a few examples from my own patients, but he'd left the session already. And before long it was officially over, his stiff hand shooting back over the desk to shake mine.

'Let me know if there's anything more I can do,' I said, aware how drained I felt by the hour we'd spent together.

'Is this not something we're just doing now?' he asked, terse.

'Not unless you want it to be. It can be an every day thing, or never again.'

He gave an efficient smile. 'Let me give it some thought.'

He knew how to dismiss a person from his office with just a tone of voice. It came with the territory.

*

She made me jump. She was standing there, a suspiciously polite distance from Ian's door, tapping at her iPhone with a long, manicured finger. She waited a second to look up, even though I knew she'd heard the door swing open.

'Are you all wrapped up in there?'

'For this session, yes,' I said, hoping now that Ian wouldn't tell her that it had been a complete waste of time.

'I'm so glad I ran into you today,' she said. 'What you said back there, you made me realise we can't just sit around waiting for the dust to settle. We need to move forward.'

I was sure I'd said nothing of the kind. It was a fortnight that had been punctuated by two deaths – if I, a rank outsider had said that, it would be the height of insensitivity.

'What were you thinking?' I asked.

'A dinner. You know – breaking bread together. I've already called Lysette, and she's agreed.' I tried not to look surprised by that news. 'Helena and Alex are in. Just to warn you, I'll be mortally offended if you're not too. Particularly as it was your idea.'

She grinned at me as she said it, angling her lovely face to the side as if I were a reluctant suitor.

'Well yes, if it's not an intrusion, I'd love to come.'

Would I? And also should I – all that training I'd done about confidentiality and boundaries seemed to be a complete waste of energy in Little Copping.

'Great. I'm sorry it's in such sad circumstances, but it's actually very refreshing to have a new face in the village.

It can all get a bit Desperate Housewives round here, if you know what I mean.'

I didn't, but I laughed along with her, tried to convince myself that this was evidence I should like to hear.

'Wisteria Lane here I come,' I called after her retreating back, but she was already halfway to Ian's office, our business satisfactorily completed.

Part of me dreaded it, but part of me was intrigued. How would it be to see the Farthings in their natural habitat?

CHAPTER TEN

Jim was outside the police station when I emerged, a fag trapped between the fingers of his left hand. I'd been in there signing some paperwork, the sight of the teeming incident room every bit as discombobulating second time around. What was I doing, getting mixed up in all of this? I got the distinct impression that, however much Lawrence Krall wanted me there, some of the residents of Little Copping wanted nothing less.

Because of that – but not only because of that – there was a certain pleasure in noting the way that Jim's face lit up when he spotted me. He hugged me hello without bothering to check if it was welcome. I kept my body stiff and rigid as a point of principle, even though a part of me longed to let go – I'd been holding on too tightly the last few days. The smell of him infiltrated my senses almost against my will, the same and also different. The CK One was long gone, but there was still something there, a kind of sweet, lemony musk that his skin always seemed to produce, which I now knew I'd never quite forgotten.

'You OK?' he said, still gripping me.

'I'll be fine,' I said briskly, breaking away. 'Where's good for coffee?'

A juggernaut swung past us, farting toxic fumes in all directions.

'Don't panic,' said Jim, setting off but looking back to check I was following. 'I've got a plan.'

*

It was a branch of one of those fake French bistros that I'd never ordinarily bother with – blackboard menus covered in pretentious curly writing and leathery steak frites. Still, when Jim charmed the waitress into giving us a booth, a red velvet oasis with curved walls that gave the illusion of seclusion, all my urban snobbery melted to nothing. I sank into it gratefully, then checked myself again. He didn't deserve even a drop of my gratitude. When he tried to order me a latte, I swiftly changed it to tea. I didn't want to give him the satisfaction of second-guessing me.

'So how were the rozzers?' he asked.

I hated his refusal to take all this seriously, but a part of me also welcomed it. I'd seen Lawrence Krall only briefly today, a snatched moment in a corridor, but he'd been intense and serious. He'd asked about Lysette's reaction to her interview, probing questions that were gift-wrapped in easy charm. She seemed unusually distressed, he said, far more than anyone else outside the immediate families of the dead. As a professional, did I think her reaction was in proportion? I'd told him a little waspishly that I didn't feel comfortable discussing my friend, but I felt his eyes lingering on me, analysing my reaction whilst he trotted out an apology.

'You know. Rozzer-ish.'

'Meaning?' asked Jim.

'They're nosy, aren't they? But then, it's in their job description.'

'Aah. They were asking about Lysette and you didn't want to break the Brownie code of honour and talk about her behind her back.'

He gave a little Brownie salute as he said it, grinning at me from behind his frothy coffee, which had arrived almost immediately. The place was deserted; we were in that grave-yard slot between lunch and dinner, the place populated more by staff than customers.

'Do you have to turn everything into a joke?' I snapped. It bugged me, the way he was dumb and sharp all at once.

'It's not a joke. I'm worried about her. I've been worried for months. That's why I wanted to meet up.'

'OK.'

'And I wanted to see you, obviously. It's ridiculous that we never saw each other again.' After ... after that. A sliver of the past – the ambulance swinging around the corner of our suburban street, flashing and wailing. I looked away, conscious his eyes were trained on me. I couldn't go there.

'When you say for months, what do you mean?'

'She's not been herself. If I ring her after eight, it seems like she's rambling.' I thought about that half-empty bottle she'd produced the night before the funeral: I was pretty sure it hadn't been in the fridge earlier that day. And then . . . she'd driven off, car speeding down the lane, most likely over the limit. 'I don't want to judge her for needing a sundowner, it must be pretty boring to have the school run as the highlight of your day, but it's affecting her. You've seen the temper she's got on her now. She's always been such a bloody earth mother but now she snaps at those kids for anything.'

'But . . .' I was determined he should be wrong, although it was true that I'd seen her be unnecessarily sharp with Saffron about bedtime. 'It's not like I haven't seen her, Jim! We had dinner in London a couple of months ago and . . . and me and Patrick came down for Sunday lunch as well.'

I liked saying his name out loud. Jim's eyebrows rose, almost imperceptibly.

'Bet you ordered a second bottle at dinner,' he continued. It was true: I shrugged my assent. 'And it's not like you've ever given George Best a run for his money in the drinking stakes.' Sadness settled inside me, heavy as stone. Was he right: was I was like a Brownie who'd never grown up, still insisting Lysette and I were in the toadstool set? What if she'd been putting on a good show when she saw me, humouring me, then going back to the real friends who knew her better now? Had I missed a cry for help and then come here too late to make a difference?

'But, if you are right . . . why? Why would things have changed so much? She loves the kids, Ged's a good husband. I know she gets frustrated about her career, but . . .'

It was so different, her life. I realised as I said it how hard it was to put myself in her shoes, or her in mine. Our frustrations probably looked petty and benign from the outside, but I knew that when I was dealing with a patient who was a suicide risk, or wondering if my body would ever choose to cooperate, it felt all-consuming. I got the feeling even from a few days here that the things in Little Copping that looked petty from the outside probably felt anything but, once you were trapped inside.

'You're not going to like this answer.' He grinned again. 'Scrub that, perhaps you will. I know it sounds bad to even say it, but I think it was Sarah.'

How did he know about my awful, childish, seething jealousy? I didn't give him the satisfaction of acknowledging it, just lowered my voice, switched into professional mode. It can be a good place to hide out.

'How do you mean? I thought she was this incredible support to Lysette.'

'Think she was more of a partner in crime. I could be wrong . . . it's not like my sister spends her time pouring her heart out to me, but she just had that air about her, you know?'

'I only met her the once.' Looking back on it, I realised I'd found her oddly dazzling, like I was caught in her head-lights. The light she shone was too blinding to pick out the details of her, even for a chronic over-analyser like me. 'She seemed – she seemed like a force of nature.'

'Yeah, a tornado,' said Jim, acidly. I could tell in that

instant that he really didn't like her. 'Trust me, they can rip up a whole town.'

'Stop talking in code. Just spit out whatever it is you're trying to imply.'

The anger kept creeping up on me, my words spiky and pointed. He paused, looked at me, his eyes raking my face. He didn't want me, but he wanted to know if I still wanted him. Even here, even now. I slopped some water into my glass, refusing to meet his gaze.

'I think she was a hedonist. She was a thrill-seeker, you know? I'm not sure 2.4 children and a picket fence was the life for her.'

'So they went out and got drunk? So what?'

'Thing is, I don't think it was just Chardonnay,' he said, his green eyes steady and serious now.

'Drugs? Oh come on. What, they were getting stoned? Lysette's always liked the odd spliff. You couldn't be married to Ged and not.'

'Mmm. I don't know. I might be making two and two equal seven, but Rowena said there were a hell of a lot of toilet trips at her birthday dinner in January, and the last time I heard, cystitis isn't contagious.'

'Lysette had a birthday dinner?'

Jim's look of amusement was infuriating. 'Calm down, it was on a Tuesday. It was just a local thing at the Italian in the village. You wouldn't have wanted to trek out of town for it.'

Maybe I wouldn't, but it would've been nice to have been

given the option. I sent Lysette a bunch of flowers and her thank-you text made no mention of it.

'What, so you're saying they got all Scarface on a Tuesday at Signor Luigi's? Oh come on!'

'It's called Little Sicily, and do you get all your information about what happens outside the M25 from *Country File*, is that it?'

'No, but . . .'

I knew Lysette had taken drugs in her time. She'd gone through a clubbing stage – getting all sweaty on ecstasy and leaving me loved-up messages telling me I was her best friend – but that was nearly twenty years ago. I'd never ventured out with her, never wanted the loss of self-control, so what did I really know? But still, the idea she'd reversed her way back into it two years short of forty, with three children and a husband to think about, seemed utterly inexplicable. Or maybe it wasn't. Maybe it was the absolute opposite.

'Listen, I hope I'm wrong,' said Jim, 'but there's definitely been something up with her for the last few months. I thought you might have some ideas.'

'Clearly not,' I said mulishly, still smarting from my exclusion from her party.

'What about your professional opinion?'

'I'm here as her friend, Jim,' I said, 'I can't get into that.'

We both sat there a second in silence.

'I'm worried, Mia, with what's just happened.' We looked at each other. 'She's being shifty. If she does know stuff that's relevant, you've got to persuade her to share it. I don't want her to get herself in real trouble.'

Hearing him articulate it so clearly sent a jolt of dread through my body. I shouldn't be here in the midst of all of this, and yet in another way there was nowhere else I could be.

'I can try. I just – if she felt like I was trapping her, she'd never forgive me.'

'You don't have to trap her, but you do have to help her.' Our eyes met a second too long. 'Fuck it,' said Jim, holding up his hands in surrender, the moment broken. 'I can't deny it. I want a proper drink. Don't let me be lonely.'

'We're going to Kimberley's tonight. I don't want to start early.'

'Come on, Mia, live dangerously.'

I'd been keeping everything fun to a minimum recently – coffee, sugar, wine – hoping that making my body a temple would do the trick.

'Fine. One small glass. White. The nicest one.'

'Your wish is my command,' said Jim, doffing an imaginary cap.

The waitress sailed over the second he so much as started to smile. It was no wonder he thought life was no more than the punchline to his joke.

*

'When you say Sarah was a party girl,' I said, once our drinks had arrived, 'what's your actual evidence, apart from your red hot gossip from Signor Luigi's?'

Jim was having a pretentious French lager. He raised the green bottle to his lips, his eyes narrowing as he formulated a response. I knew I should leave soon. The nosy part of me had been looking forward to observing Kimberley in her perfect show home, but now the hour was almost upon me, now this conversation had been had, I felt nothing but queasy dread. I glanced at my phone to see if Patrick had rung, but there were no missed calls. I sent him a quick X from inside my bag, then wondered if it was trite.

'Why do you want to know?' asked Jim. 'I thought you wanted to stay out of it.'

It was a good question.

'You can't drop something like that and then not qualify it.'

'Is this a roundabout way of asking if I think she was shagging the teacher?'

'Do you?' I asked.

'I don't know. It's not like I saw them together more than once or twice. And that was only thanks to that blonde ... you know, bossy but fit. She made us go to a quiz night.'

'Kimberley?' I said, irritatingly irritated by his description. Besides, she was a minor celebrity: he knew exactly who she was, which meant he'd only described her that way to try and elicit a rise.

'That's the one. She's always organising these massive fundraisers. Our kids aren't even at the school but she still ropes us in. Rowena gets on with her.'

'Does she?' I said.

'What, you don't like her?'

'I've only just got here!' I said.

'Yes, but you've always been a girl with strong opinions.' Jim cocked his head. 'You've made a career out of it. You don't like her, do you?'

'I'll know better after tonight,' I said primly.

If – if what he said was true, would they be taking drugs? That was ridiculous – I was being paranoid now. Surely Kimberley wouldn't be that stupid, with so much to lose. With Sarah barely cold in her grave, it would have to be a sombre affair.

'Your first rural dinner party! Watch yourself, Mia. You'll be chewing straw and swilling cider before you know it.'

'I've seen their house from the outside. Not much chance of that.'

Jim's eyes flicked around the space. He'd never been able to resist it – that compulsion to check he wasn't missing out on something better. I waited it out.

'I didn't trust her,' he said eventually, his voice like lead. 'Right from the first time I met her.'

'Sarah?'

'Yeah. She seemed all bubbly, but it was an act. It was a way to suck people in.'

The silence that came next felt thick. I watched Jim weighing up whether or not to go further. When I spoke I kept my tone deliberately light, my wine glass sailing towards my mouth.

'It's fine, you don't have to tell me . . .'

He fell for it.

'Violet told Rowena this thing ...' He looked at me, his expression serious. 'It frightened me, Mia. Lysette and Sarah – by the sound of things they were doing coke on a playdate. It started with testing Prosecco for some party, next thing I reckon they were doing sneaky lines off the kitchen counter.'

'What, your daughter saw them doing it?'

'No, but ... just her description of walking in on them ... that's what it sounded like to me.'

There was something so grim about the image of it. The two of them scrabbling to sweep away the drugs, concealing their high.

'So did you confront Lysette?'

Jim nodded, pain twisting his handsome face out of shape.

'I took her out. To the pub – probably the wrong call. She got really angry with me. Said Sarah was her best friend ...' He looked at me. 'She didn't mean it. It's always been you – little sis, little sis sidekick.' I wished he wouldn't keep doing that – rubbing the lamp, calling up the genie of our shared past. 'She said that Violet had got it wrong. But I know when she's lying ...' Jim's hands dropped heavily to his knees, a gesture of helplessness. 'Since Sarah died ... I'm worried she's getting worse, not better. I'm just hoping you being here will bring her back to herself.'

We stared at each other, the fear in our faces a strange kind of mirror.

'I can try.'

Jim paused. 'Did you tell her we were meeting?'

'No,' I admitted. I knew I probably should've done – the last thing this situation needed was more secrets – but the words had jammed in my throat when I tried to spit them out.

I saw him relax, grateful for a distraction from a difficult conversation. His eyes danced. 'Me neither. Let's not.'

I stiffened, wrapped my free hand around my phone, deep in the recesses of my bag, as if it were Patrick himself, not the device we communicated via. 'No. She wouldn't like the idea we'd met up to talk about her.'

We both knew that was only a partial explanation. Jim took another gulp of his lager, the bottle almost drained.

'You'll tell me if she starts saying anything important? If she needs a proper lawyer? She and Ged aren't all that sophisticated about this stuff.'

'Jim ...' I paused, waited until I knew I had his full attention. 'Are you saying that because there's more that's worrying you? I know she's being weird about telling anyone what she thinks happened, but that may just be shock. The idea that Saffron's teacher murdered her best friend is going to take time to sink in. The fact they had a few lines of charlie is kind of irrelevant in the bigger scheme of things.'

Jim paused now, his eyes trawling the restaurant. He was weighing up what to say all over again, but this time I wouldn't win the battle.

'I don't want to imply things about my sister that could be a load of bollocks. You're here now; you're the cleverest person I know. If there's anything to work out, you'll do it.'

'Stop it!' I snapped. 'Stop talking to me in riddles.'

Jim took his last sip of lager, signalled for the bill. 'That's not what I'm doing.'

'If you want me to work something out, it would help if I had more to go on.' I didn't like the wheedling quality I could hear in my voice.

'Let's just keep talking, OK?' That was the only thing I'd promised myself I wouldn't do: I'd sworn this meeting would be a one-off. He stood up, whipped my jacket off the back of my chair, held it up for me to shrug myself into. 'Even if she's not acting like it, you being here is the best thing that's happened to her in a long time.'

Jim held the restaurant door open for me, and we stepped out into the early evening. The evening was dusky now, the sun a rusty-red wound in the sky. He walked me to the cab rank, his refusal to elaborate on what we'd discussed absolute.

If I wanted to know what Lysette was hiding, I'd have to find out for myself.

CHAPTER ELEVEN

Lysette was perched on the side of her unmade bed, slipping her small, dainty foot into a red-soled Louboutin. It was black patent, skyscraper high – I couldn't take my eyes off it.

'I've never seen you in those.'

'They were in the sale.' They didn't look like they'd have made the sale. 'Don't tell Ged,' she said, shoving the box deep under the bed. She stood up, a black baby-doll dress falling into a flattering triangle, her legs elongated by the beautiful heels.

'You look lovely,' I said, hearing the relief reverberating in my voice. She didn't look like anything was wrong, and however hard we try, it's hard to remember that the outside and the inside of people are two very different things. Jim's words were ricocheting around my head too violently for me to fall for the seduction.

'Yeah, well, it's Kimberley's. I didn't want to turn up looking like trailer trash.'

I glanced at myself in the mirrored door of her wardrobe. I thought skinny jeans and a silk shirt would make me look chic without trying, but now I wondered if I'd pitched it wrong. I checked myself. What did it matter? It was a bowl of pasta in someone's kitchen. Lysette was looking at her reflection too; she grabbed her deep red lipstick. My eyes met hers in the glass as she looped it around her mouth. I sat down on the bed.

'Lys, are you alright? Sorry, stupid question. I just feel like we haven't talked enough about what's been going on –' I hesitated. 'I haven't wanted to trample in and upset you.'

She blotted her mouth with a tissue, eyes no longer meeting mine. 'You haven't.'

'But it's not like I'm not thinking about you every second. I know you thought from the beginning she hadn't killed herself, but them confirming it … You were just trying to get your head round it, and then they started questioning you.'

She turned to face me.

'I'm not alright, Mia, no. I feel like my heart's been ripped out.'

'Is there anything more I can do?' Her eyes held mine, pleading and guarded all at once. I took a risk. 'Do you still think Peter didn't do it?'

Her voice, when it came, was thin and indistinct. 'I don't know. I can't …' She paused again, like the words were expensive. 'He wasn't like that.'

I felt a shiver. She'd been right about Sarah's death, what was to say she wasn't right about this?

'But if he didn't do it – well, someone did.'

Lysette's eyes flashed. I'd gone too far.

'I can't cope with any more questions.' She looked down at her perilous heels. 'It's enough for me to put one foot in front of the other.'

'Sorry, I'm sorry,' I said, hastily apologetic. 'I just want to help. Be your friend.'

She quickly swivelled herself back towards the mirror, baring her teeth to check for lipstick.

'Thanks, Mia.' She grabbed a clutch bag from her dressing table, signalled to the door. 'And I'm sorry if I – if I was a bit – you know – *tired and emotional* at the funeral. I . . .' She smiled at me, petered out, the apology I'd so desperately wanted at the time there in her eyes.

'Don't worry,' I said. 'I'm here.'

I don't know why I thought it was down to me.

*

'You were ages at the police station.'

The cab had one of those smelly, tree-shaped air fresheners attached to the rear-view mirror. I focused on it, toying with the idea of simply telling her I'd seen Jim. The words died in my throat.

'You know what it's like,' I said. 'They kept me hanging about for hours.'

Was it a white lie? No, it was definitely grey. Back when we were teens, she'd hated the fact that me and Jim started our ultimately disastrous relationship behind her back. I didn't want to disturb that ancient burial ground.

'He's a smooth operator, that main guy, isn't he?'

'Krall?' I said. 'Yeah.'

'I think he reckons he's solved it already,' she said softly, her eyes trained out of the window, lost in the inky blackness.

The cab driver's gaze flicked towards the rear-view mirror, his eyes trained on her. I gave Lysette a warning look.

'Saffron's reading's really coming on, isn't it?' I said, hoping fervently we were almost there. The dark country lanes seemed endless to me.

*

Kimberley's house was even more impressive close up. As the cab driver got out to ring the intercom, I cast a sideways glance at Lysette, wondering how it felt to come from her modest rented cottage to something as palatial as this. With my friends in London, the gaps never felt so gaping: unless I befriended the Beckhams, everyone was getting by, mortgaged to the hilt. I wasn't sure I could handle a scenario like this.

'Well, this is a shithole!' I said, linking my arm through hers as we walked up the drive.

'I know,' she said, rolling her eyes. 'We should've eaten before we came. I hate McDonald's.'

We leaned into each other, laughing far harder than our stupidity merited, stumbling our way to the door like a four-legged animal. It was already open, but it wasn't Kimberley who stood there. The girl looked like a teenager, a cap of dark curly hair framing a pretty, timid face, a white shirt worn over a pair of black trousers, like she was approximating a waitress uniform but wanted to leave some doubt.

'Hello. The ladies are having drinks on the back lawn,' she said, her English halting.

'Thank you,' said Lysette, formally. Why had that precious warmth drained away so instantaneously?

'Hi, I'm Mia!' I said, overcompensating. I stuck out a hand. 'Lovely to meet you. What's your name?'

'Oh, I am Lori,' said the girl, quick and nervous. 'I am very pleased to meet you.'

'Where are you from?' I asked, as we followed her down a wide hallway.

'Romania,' she said.

'Lori's only been here a few weeks,' said Lysette, still uncharacteristically chilly – she was usually the last person to treat someone serving us that way.

We passed a huge sitting room, a state of the art TV blaring out something with dinosaurs. A couple of small boys were sprawled on the sofas, cans and crisps strewn across the floor. The long hallway opened up into a predictably stylish kitchen, all chrome and granite, with appliances that wouldn't have looked out of place in a Michelin-starred restaurant. The back wall was glass, sliding doors opening into a garden so large and landscaped that it could have passed for a park. The three women were standing on the patio, drinks in hand. It was odd: as I first contemplated them, they felt more like an art installation than a gang of friends, each of them sculpted and still.

'There you are!' cried Kimberley, breaking away to come towards us. She cast a look in Lori's direction. 'I was starting to think you'd lost them!'

It was a balmy evening, and she'd decided on a silky green jumpsuit, the neckline tapering into a low V, revealing the curve of her small, shapely breasts. A silver dagger hung between them, automatically drawing the eye downwards. I quickly moved my eyes back to her face, leaned in to kiss her and say my hellos.

'Thanks so much for inviting me,' I said, still taken aback by the opulence of my surroundings. She could see me gawping as she embraced Lysette.

'Let's get you some drinks,' she said, turning to Lori, who was standing nervously on the fringes of our circle. 'Off you go,' she told her, and I smiled thanks at her retreating back, moving my attention to Helena and Alex.

'Hello again,' said Alex, sticking out a stiff hand, like she was a reluctant Royal, forced to walk down a line-up of plebs. I could tell she'd also felt compelled to make an effort, but the overall effect was very different from the polish of the other women. Her dark, messy hair was pulled up into a bun, streaks of grey visible. She wore a shapeless blue dress which skimmed the ground, and had painted her mouth in an orangey-pink colour that was bleeding from her lips. 'I only just heard you were staying on.'

Helena leaned in and kissed me. 'Nice to see you again, Mia,' she said, warm and guarded all at once.

We were on the far side of the wooden decking, the view

perfect. The lawn went on for miles, a white summerhouse planted next to a pretty little pond, frogs serenading us with joyful croaks. I knew better than to think wealth equalled happiness but it was hard to imagine being unhappy in such beautiful surroundings. I remembered with a jolt why we were here.

'I'm so sorry – what's come out since we met – it's just awful.'

Helena smiled painfully, whilst Alex's face refused to register my sympathy.

'I gather you're staying on to help people to pick up the pieces,' she said briskly.

'I wouldn't go that far . . .' I started, just as Lori appeared at my elbow with a glass of champagne. It jarred somehow – champagne in the wake of what had happened?

'Just bring out the bottle,' trilled Kimberley. 'You need to remember to keep the guests topped up.'

I couldn't help sneaking a look at Lysette, observing the fact her first mouthful was more of a gulp than a sip. *Told you so*, said Jim in my head – the last thing I needed was Jim in my head.

'I'm just going to be here as someone for people to talk to for the next couple of weeks,' I continued. Alex looked deeply unimpressed. 'I'm not part of the investigation.'

'Are the police paying you?' she fired back.

'Well yes, but . . .'

'She's being modest!' said Kimberley, smiling at me as if I was a small child who'd failed to announce my triumph in a finger-painting competition. 'Ian said you were a great help to him on Monday.'

'Really?' I said.

'Oh . . .' said Kimberley, cocking her lovely head. 'Did you not think it was a success?'

'It's . . .' They were all staring at me now, even Lysette, the lush view providing an unsuitably tranquil backdrop to the awkwardness. 'It's not really a case of success or failure. It's just about providing a safe space.'

I sounded pompous even to my own ears. Helena shuddered.

'Safe isn't a word I'm using much right now.'

Alex's small, intense eyes swivelled towards her, then moved away.

'What gourmet triumph have you magicked up for us this time, Kimberley?' said Lysette. It was an odd segue, and there was a slight edge to the way she asked it. Lysette herself felt unsafe to me right now, an unexploded bomb. I slipped another question in its place.

'Is Nigel not here?'

'My better half!' laughed Kimberley. 'Were you looking forward to meeting him properly?'

'No, I just . . .'

'He's in New York, I'm afraid. Just us girls.'

Silence reigned. Why were they subjecting themselves to this? Or was it me – was my presence the reason no one was being real?

'This is so weird, isn't it?' said Helena, almost as if she'd read my thoughts. She looked around the group. 'I still just can't believe it. I keep doing normal things – going to the toilet, or making a cup of tea – and then remembering again. Sounds stupid, doesn't it?'

Lysette crossed the grass, put her arms around her in a tight hug.

'No!' she said, heartfelt. 'I know exactly what you mean.'

Alex watched them, grief etched into her pinched face. I could sense words that wanted to explode out of her, but she wouldn't let the dam burst. I felt like a complete imposter there, intruding on their raw grief. I looked towards the kitchen, spying a harried-looking Lori racing between hob and oven.

'Why don't I go and give her a hand?' I said to Kimberley, already pulling away.

'Don't be ridiculous,' she said sharply, 'you're my guest.' She looked at the huddle that Lysette and Helena were making, clapped her elegant hands high above her in the cooling air. 'We all want to honour Sarah, that's why we're here, but we can do it over dinner. It'll be ruined if we don't go inside.'

As we started across the grass, Alex turned to me. 'This was your idea, wasn't it?' she said.

Her mouth smiled, but her eyes did the absolute opposite.

*

Kitchen supper is such a terrible phrase, all faux casual and homey – at least this wasn't even making the pretence. The table was set with silver, crisp linens by each plate, small vases of fresh-cut flowers punctuating the length of it. We all ground to a halt: it didn't invite you to throw yourself into any old place and start chatting. Perhaps that was the point, a mark of respect. Kimberley stood up a little straighter. She looked out to the garden, momentarily pensive, and then back to all of us.

'Thank you for coming. I know – we all know – how hard it is right now. But the one thing we need to be able to rely on is each other.' Her gaze landed momentarily on Lysette, who looked away, suddenly fascinated by the table setting. 'You're not just my friends, you're my sisters. This is my sisterhood. In answer to your point, Helena, *this* is our safe place. We must never forget it.' She held her glass aloft. 'To Sarah.'

I hung back, watched them all step forward, their glasses colliding noisily.

'To Sarah,' they said, their voices cracking and splintering with emotion. Something was released by that toast, something I couldn't quite name. Their tears were real, but there was something else they were sharing that wasn't visible to the naked eye.

Kimberley beckoned me forward. 'Come and join the toast, you knew her too.'

I softly chinked my glass, my eyes meeting Lysette's: the depth of her pain felt like something you could drown in. I couldn't help feeling relieved when the circle broke apart. Helena moved towards a seat, and I started to subtly follow her, but Kimberley gave us an admonishing look.

'There's a seating plan, and you,' she pointed her index finger at me, 'have got the worst seat in the house, I'm afraid! Right next to me.'

It was so odd – I felt no warmth between us, and yet she was tenacious in her pursuit of me. I gave an unconvincing smile and headed for the seat she'd indicated. Alex was the other side of me, and Lysette was to Kimberley's right with Helena next to her.

'That jumpsuit looks great,' I told Kimberley, looking for an easy win, and then immediately wondering if it seemed callous. 'I'd never get away with it, but it's fab on you.'

'Really?' she said, looking pleased. She was standing up, and she patted a lollipop-stick thigh. 'I worry it makes me look like I've got saddlebags. It's old now, Isabel Marant from a few seasons ago.'

Of course – a luxurious French label that looks thrown on but has a per item cost roughly akin to the GDP of a third world country.

'Not at all,' I said. Kimberley was as bony as a skeleton, the honeyed sweep of exposed flesh taut and smooth. She knew it too – I've got plenty of clients who suffer from the female disease of refusing to appreciate their own beauty, but I could tell Kimberley revelled in her appeal. She was like a show cat, strutting around the ring on perfect paws.

'Thanks,' she said, laying a hand on my shoulder as she shouted across the kitchen to Lori. 'Lori, top-ups needed, and I just know that salmon en croute is borderline burnt!'

I subtly wriggled my shoulder, the warmth of her

hand an uncomfortable presence, and looked around for Lysette. She was talking to Helena, animated now, her glass drained. I quelled the teeming thoughts, turned towards Alex.

'So what's your specialism?' I asked. Her glass was almost full, I noticed, a smear of her odd-coloured lipstick around the rim. Her fingers, the nails bitten and ragged, worried at the plain wooden beads that hung around her neck. They could have almost been a rosary.

'Molecular biology,' she said, her voice a full stop. In one way it was a blessing – after all, my molecular biology small talk was seriously limited – but it was already feeling like a long night, and we hadn't eaten a morsel yet.

'It's so beautiful here,' I said, directing the comment to the table at large. Kimberley was still snarling about salmon somewhere in the background. 'I bet there've been some great summer parties.'

Everyone looked at me, but no one responded. The atmosphere churned and curdled.

Alex's eyes narrowed. 'Not really. I'm a single mum, most nights it's either *Bake Off* or a pile of marking. I'm right in thinking you don't have any?'

'Not yet, no,' I said. I looked across the table at Lysette, wanting some kind of reassurance. I needed her to lead the way, to teach me the rules of engagement that I blatantly didn't understand, but her face was as cold as theirs.

Helena jumped in. 'Mia works with them, though. She caters to every size. The walk we had before the funeral

138

really . . .' She looked at me, changed tack. 'She gave me some great ideas for getting the anxiety under control.'

She made a face, acknowledged the irony. The space between us felt even thicker now.

'My advice, Mia, is to enjoy the freedom while it lasts!' said Kimberley, sailing back to the table. Lori was following her, plates piled high with steaming mounds of salmon and asparagus, the distraction perfectly timed. Was it my fault, this latest awkwardness? Had I been unconsciously poking a hornets' nest that Jim had shoved me towards, then complaining when I got stung? Even if they had been partying, there was no reason to assume Sarah's death had anything to do with it. I caught Lysette's eye, managed finally to exchange a smile that felt real. Did she want to be here, or was it the very last place she'd have chosen? The fact I had no idea made me feel a rush of loneliness, even here, in the crush of women.

'Bon appétit,' said Helena, their eyes meeting in shared sadness. There were murmurs about the deliciousness of the food, heavy cutlery scraping against bone china plates.

'Are you wanting some wine?' said Lori, appearing at my elbow.

'I am, yes,' I said, giving her a grateful smile, knowing as I did that the last thing I needed was to get drunk.

'Let's put some music on,' said Lysette, that dangerous firework quality back in full force. 'Not Fleetwood Mac!'

'God, no,' said Helena, shuddering. She gave Lysette a sad smile. 'You did so well to get through it.'

Kimberley waved an imperious hand at Lori.

'If you fetch me the remote control, and then you can get the boys upstairs. It's well past their bedtime.' It wasn't quite clear from her tone whose fault that was. 'Tell them I'll be up to kiss them goodnight.'

It was gone 8.30 by now: I looked at the dark smudges under Lori's eyes, tried to imagine how she got any kind of break beyond a few snatched hours of sleep. I let the conversation eddy and drift around me, grateful that the odd number of guests created a discreet way to hang back.

When Lori reappeared, bottle in hand, Helena made sure her glass was filled to the brim. 'I shouldn't, I know, but I'm just so glad I got the police interview out of the way today.'

'Mia was there for hours today,' said Lysette, that edginess apparent again.

Alex looked to me, as if I should elaborate. Kimberley gave a tinkly laugh.

'I think old Inspector Krall is a bit of looker,' she said, then noticed Lysette's expression. 'I was being silly,' she said. 'I'm just grateful they seem confident about solving it. For Sarah's sake.'

'They don't know,' spat back Lysette.

Helena looked between them. 'Can we please – let's try and have a nice time. Be together.' Her eyes grazed me, as if she was embarrassed I was witnessing all of this, and I gave her what I intended to be a reassuring smile. It was hard to force my features into such a shape.

'Of course. That's the whole point of tonight,' said an icy Kimberley. 'To try and support each other. And you're right, we don't know. But what I do know – from personal experience – is that he was complicated.'

'OK!' said Lysette. She stood up, her chair scraping angrily across the floor. She crossed to the speaker dock, which was pumping out some kind of French jazz. 'Let's put on something stupid we could sing along to if this was ...' Tears sprang to her eyes, and I automatically crossed the room towards her. 'If this was different,' she said, her voice low. She briefly accepted my touch, then bent over her iPhone like she was engaged in important matters of national security, eventually choosing a summery playlist that you couldn't help but shake your shoulders to.

'Good choice,' I told Lysette across Kimberley, then turned my attention to her. 'This is delicious,' I told her, shovelling in a large mouthful to prove the veracity of the statement. Kimberley's fork trailed her plate, never quite making contact with the pile of food that was slowly congealing – no one was that thin without hard work. 'Did you cook it yourself? If we ever have people round, all my boyfriend wants to do is order pizza.'

Kimberley ignored the question. Of course she hadn't cooked it – she hadn't even deigned to carry a plate, so far. 'I thought you were engaged?'

'Yeah, no, I always think fiancé sounds a bit pretentious.' I fiddled with my engagement ring as I said it, aware how tiny it looked next to her ostentatious square slab of a diamond.

'*My fiancé* – you're right, I should say it.' She stayed silent. 'It must be hard for you, Nigel travelling so much.'

'We've got very good at waving him goodbye,' she said. 'That's partly why Lucas liked having Mr Grieve so much last year.'

'He had him as his teacher? I didn't know that. I'm so sorry.'

'Yes,' confirmed Kimberley. 'He got very involved.' It was unclear what he was involved in – it could have been as benign as Lucas's spelling, but somehow it didn't sound that way. 'So when are you getting married?'

'Probably in the spring. Work's been crazy for both of us . . .' I didn't want her to think I was being grand about my career. 'You know what it's like, juggling . . .'

I could see Lori out of the corner of my eye, painstakingly rinsing the plates before she loaded them into the top of the range dishwasher.

'I do,' she said, pointedly, watching where my eyes went. 'I've got a PR business. The office is in Cambridge. It's mainly for local businesses, but it's doing pretty well.'

'That's great.'

'I get some good discounts too. If you're getting married, you'll be wanting to think about those photos!'

'What do you mean?'

Kimberley leaned towards me, animated.

'There's a fantastic clinic we look after. They do peels and facials, but they also push the hard stuff.' My brain was struggling to compute, Jim's words still ringing in my ears.

'Come on, Mia, by our age we all start needing a bit of help to keep looking our best.'

'Oh, Botox and things.' Patrick always teases me for the way I say it, like 'buttocks', forgetting to emphasise the BO. I looked at Kimberley's smooth face, tried not to envy the lack of crow's feet. I knew my own eyes had started to tell a story I wanted to keep to myself.

'It's all moved on a lot. Fillers can be very subtle now. No harm in giving mother nature a helping hand.'

'Sure,' I said, non-committal.

'You don't approve? Not holistic enough for you?' she said, arching her perfect eyebrows as she hovered the wine bottle over my glass. I signalled for a tiny bit, aware how muddy my thinking was becoming.

'I just think once you start, where do you stop?'

Some of my patients seem to do it in a healthy way – a way that's not shot through with a dose of self-hatred – but some of them look like swaying, swollen poppies, faces pumped up and bodies starved down to nothing.

'It must be so hard, doing your job,' said Kimberley.

'What do you mean?' I could tell already I wasn't going to like the answer.

'It must be so hard not to analyse every choice you make to death. I'd find it exhausting.' I'd find it exhausting to try and write press releases about injecting elephant placenta into forehead creases, I thought, but I didn't say it.

'It's horses for courses, isn't it?' I said, straining forward to try and pull Lysette into the conversation. She was talking intensely to Helena, her hands flying about, her mascara now a mass of black around her wild eyes.

'I'd love to understand what it is you actually do,' said Kimberley, her tone implying that it was something so exotic and unlikely that it might turn out to be a fantasy. 'Can we book some time for a one to one before you go?' She paused, angled her face, elegant fingers stroking the stem of her crystal wine glass. 'When is it you're going?'

It felt like every single sentence she uttered spun on a contradiction.

'Don't say it!' said Lysette, jerking her body round. 'She's never going. She's going to live here for ever and ever.'

She was drunk, obviously so now, but I still felt childishly gratified by how heartfelt she was. That protectiveness surged back through me, that deep longing to make sure she was alright. I needed to be sure she was safe before I could leave.

'Not for ever and ever,' I said. 'But at least a couple more weeks.'

'Not long at all, then,' said Alex, with a hint of satisfaction. It felt as though everyone's eyes were on me again.

'I need a pee. Too much wine,' I said, standing up abruptly.

I gripped the back of my chair, suddenly acutely aware of how many times my glass had been topped up. I needed to get away. Even if it was only for a few snatched minutes, I needed time to think.

CHAPTER TWELVE

Kimberley had directed me to a little door off the main corridor, but when I tried the handle, it held fast. I waited for what felt like an age, before looking up at the sweeping wooden staircase. There must be millions of bathrooms in a house like this, and it wasn't as if I'd be prying – a woman like Kimberley would definitely do her business in a luxury en suite.

I crested the stairs, arrived on the top landing, and then stared open-mouthed at the huge wall that met me. It was covered, absolutely covered, in family photographs, all jigsawed together in beautiful frames. There were old pictures – glamorous weddings from long ago, a childhood picture of Kimberley, snub-nosed and holding a rabbit – as well as newer shots. Nigel in Washington, Nigel and Kimberley at Buckingham Palace, Nigel and Kimberley with their photogenic progeny. Naturally these ones were professional: grainy black-and-white images from their garden, posed as if the lucky photographer had chanced upon a beautiful family in their pastoral idyll and caught them unawares. Kimberley leant over her boys, her blonde tresses framing them, eyes staring outwards dreamily as her husband loomed behind them protectively. I sneered internally, then wondered if it was nothing more than jealousy. Even if we had two perfect, healthy children, I couldn't imagine Patrick ever agreeing to come home from work early to pose soulfully with a hay bale. I sensed that that was the point: there was no way you could look at that carefully curated collection of images and not feel as if you were somehow falling short.

I tore my eyes away from an ice-blonde 1940s bride in a satin gown, and inched my way down the wide corridor, my feet sinking into the soft taupe carpet. I knew I mustn't blunder into a sleeping child's bedroom: I turned the handle on the first door as lightly as I could. Success – it was a predictably chic bathroom, dominated by a rainforest shower and a large mirrored medicine cabinet that ran down the length of the wall. I sat on the loo, taking it in. It wasn't her personal bathroom, I was sure of that. In that case, I thought, once I'd washed my hands, it wouldn't be so bad to sneak a peek inside the gleaming mirrored doors. I swung them open, lights springing on inside as I did so. There were bottles and bottles of pills with Kimberley's name typed onto them, all with the kind of medically correct drug names that I didn't understand. Was she ill? It seemed like an extraordinary amount of medication. There were others too, I noticed, squat brown bottles with two or three different names, and details for an American pharmacist on the label. I moved my attention down to the lower shelves, which groaned with the kind of luxuriously packaged make-up and skin care where the wrapping's worth twice as much as the sticky stuff contained within. I pulled out a heavy gold tube of lipstick, swivelled the base, admired the deep crimson pigment that erupted out. That was when I heard the light tap on the door. I shoved the lipstick back in the cabinet, pushed the door closed as fast as I could.

'Hi,' I called, 'I'll be right out.'

I flushed the loo for a second time, smoothed down my shirt, and hurried to open the door. There was Kimberley.

'I was worried you'd got lost!'

'It's big enough!' I said, trying not to gabble. 'The down-stairs loo was locked. You've got such a beautiful home.'

She shrugged prettily, making no move to leave the door-way. 'It's only bricks and mortar.'

That was when I heard the loud creak behind me. How mortifying: the cabinet door had swung back open – in my desire to keep quiet, I hadn't shut it hard enough. Kimberley gave a slow smile. Her green eyes, perfectly painted with a flicking line of black, narrowed with satisfaction.

'Are you spying on me, Mia?'

What a schoolgirl idiot I was. 'No, not at all. I just ... I was looking for floss.'

'No, you weren't,' she said. She was more cat-like than ever: I was a mouse and her paw was extending ever closer. 'I'm just the same. I always want to know more about people than they want to tell me.'

'Do you?' I said, desperate to put an end to this. She was still barring the exit.

'Definitely. Other people are either heaven or hell in my experience.' She suddenly slipped her way past me, her body pushing so close against mine that I could feel the soft pears of her breasts. Her perfume was stronger than it had been when she'd been sitting next to me at dinner, almost as if she'd resprayed in preparation for our encounter. She crossed to the gaping cabinet, reached inside.

'You're a natural beauty, we've established that, but how about a little bit of cheating?' She pulled out that same vintage-y-looking gold tube. Was it obvious I'd moved it? She stepped towards me. I reached out my hand, but she kept coming at me, brandishing the lipstick. 'Indulge me.'

'I'm OK . . .' I said, but her hand was on my face now. My heart was thumping hard in my chest – I was desperate to shake her off me, but it felt too rude now she'd caught me snooping.

'Here,' she said, face close to mine. 'Just a little bit. It'll brighten you up.' Her long fingers wrapped around my neck, held my face steady. The lipstick pressed down on my mouth like an unwanted kiss. I froze, willing it to be over. She smiled at her handiwork, our faces far too close for comfort. 'Gorgeous,' she said, her voice low.

I jerked backwards, turned towards the mirror. My eyes were wide, my face pale. I couldn't give her the satisfaction of knowing how disturbing this was.

'It's darker than I normally wear,' I said, smoothing my hair behind my ears.

'Darker's good sometimes,' she said. 'At least for me.'

Her bright eyes met mine in the mirror. I was the first to look away.

'Thanks,' I said. 'I'm sorry I barged my way up here. We should get back, shouldn't we?'

'I'm not,' she said, pausing. 'I'm not sorry at all. But, if you like.' I took a step back towards the door, but somehow she'd anticipated me, was blocking the space again. She stepped in close, her lips suddenly meeting mine with the same firm pressure the lipstick had had. I felt her warm tongue trying to part my lips, her perfume, overpowering and sweet. 'This is what you wanted, isn't it?' she breathed. 'This is why you snuck your way upstairs and waited for me.'

Now I shoved her off me, pushing her bony shoulders back towards the cabinet. 'What are you doing?'

Her sculpted features twisted into an expression of ugly rage.

'The real question is, what are *you* doing?' she hissed, stalking her way across the tiled floor and slamming out.

I sank back down onto the closed loo, my racing heart almost exploding out of my chest, my body quivering. All I wanted to do was get out of this soft-furnished prison, but at the moment, even leaving the bathroom was too ambitious a task.

*

Ten minutes later I was carefully picking my way back down the wide staircase. I'd tell Lysette I felt ill, insist we left immediately – I just had to avoid Kimberley ambushing me before I could get to her.

I approached the kitchen door. They were trying to whisper, but emotion was making their voices peak and spike. It was Alex I heard first.

'It's unsustainable,' she said. 'I can't make that kind of promise.'

'But it's too late now,' said Helena.

'We can't . . .' said Lysette, her voice mangled by grief and alcohol. 'We can't do that to Sarah.'

Alex gave a superior-sounding snort. 'Do you honestly think this is the best thing for her?'

Something clattered, then Kimberley's voice cut across. She made no attempt to lower it.

'You don't mean it, Alex, so stop saying it. Every single one of us has too much to lose.'

Hearing her heels tip-tapping across the polished wood of the kitchen floor brought me to my senses: I couldn't be discovered like this, lurking in a dark corner, eavesdropping. I gave it a few seconds and then swung open the door, forced myself to smile. Kimberley looked at me as though I'd crawled out of a sewer, then swiftly adjusted her features. No one was looking at her anyway, they were too busy trying to approximate a normal dinner party tableau.

'There you are!' said Lysette. She stood up, a little unsteady, advanced towards me. I forced myself not to flinch, my nervous system still on high alert. 'Kimberley said you were feeling a bit shit and sleeping it off.'

Helena gave me a tight smile, then poked at the fondant pudding in front of her, thick molten chocolate oozing out of its smashed walls. It looked like a miniature crime scene all of its own, the dark liquid smearing the pristine white china.

'Yeah, no, I don't know if it's something I ate.' I looked at Kimberley. 'No offence. Can we get a cab?'

Their collective gratitude at not having to continue the façade was palpable. Cabs were called, goodbyes were said. Kimberley crossed the kitchen to hug me, as if that icy look was a figment of my imagination.

'It was so lovely you could come,' she said, her arms encircling me in a mumsy-feeling hug. I stood there, as stiff and straight as a pencil, then yanked my body away.

'I need a wee,' said an oblivious Lysette. 'You get our coats, yeah?'

Lori was standing by the cavernous coat cupboard near the door. She'd already dealt with Alex, the tail lights of her cab now sweeping down the drive.

'I get your stuff?' she asked.

'Thank you,' I said. Her bottom lip was caught between her teeth, her nerves still obvious. 'It's a trench,' I said, immediately realising how unhelpful that was – I was sure I wouldn't know the Romanian for 'trench coat' even if I lived there for a hundred years. 'I'll help you look.' As we rummaged our way through the deep closet, I kept the conversation going. It was strangely comforting in there; a simple task to perform, the two of us lost in the woolly depths, hidden from Kimberley's death stare or my mounting fears. 'How did you end up au pairing for Kimberley?'

'Susan. You know.'

'I'm not Susan. I'm Mia.'

'No, Susan,' she said, her words muffled. 'She had to go. Because of what has been.'

'She was the last au pair? She left?'

'She had to go,' she repeated, more emphatically. 'I had to come very quickly. Extra money.'

I'd found my coat now. I stepped out, and so did she. Her face was flushed and tense.

'Why did she have to go?' I asked. 'I don't live here. I'm new too.'

'She . . .' Lori shrugged, the words stopping in her throat. 'I am here now.' We stood there for a second, caught by awkward silence. 'Your coat is nice.' I wasn't the only one who'd mastered bland conversation killers.

'Thanks,' I said. She wasn't volunteering anything, but her eyes didn't leave my face. It was almost as if she wanted me to keep asking. Just then, Lysette appeared.

'Sorry. Downstairs loo was locked, so I had to use Kimberley's.'

Why would it be locked when she had a kitchen full of people? Had she deliberately set me up to venture upstairs, or was the idea pure egotism on my part?

'I have your coat,' said Lori mechanically. She'd disappeared herself behind a mask of servitude.

'Thanks,' said Lysette, barely making eye contact with her as she shrugged it on.

It was odd – this imperious creature was the exact opposite of the girl I'd known more than half my life. Nothing felt right here. I pulled my trench tight around my body, stepped out onto the gravel drive. The taxi was parked by the gates, hazards flashing. Our feet crunched as we walked back down the sweeping drive, no giggles to mask it now.

'Are you OK?' said Lysette, sounding more like her normal self. 'Do you think it was that cream sauce?'

I couldn't bear to pile lies on top of lies.

'No, I'm not. It was a really weird evening . . .'

Lysette stuck out a hand, stopping me mid-sentence. We halted a few steps from the cab, silvery moonlight from an almost full orb dappling the driveway. Kimberley's lights blazed out of the tall windows, the house dwarfing us. I almost bundled Lysette into the cab, so desperate was I to speed away from there.

'Look, we're all just completely freaked out,' she said, voice breaking up again. 'I'm sorry if it was weird for you, but I can't help that right now.'

'No, I know that,' I said, my hand inching towards the door. I didn't want to say it in the cab, but I didn't want to carry this toxic parcel away with me either. 'Kimberley – she came after me to the bathroom. She . . .' I looked into Lysette's eyes, faced again with the unsettling sense of not being able to read her. 'She tried to kiss me, Lys.'

It was relief I saw now, the sight of it like a body blow. Did she not care about my distress?

'She would've just been being silly, Mia. She was pissed.'

What was worse than that? Did she think she'd have offered me – her prissy little bluestocking friend – a line of coke?

153

'She likes to be Queen of Sheba. She gets a bit carried away.'

'It was horrible!' I said, my voice rising.

Lysette swung open the cab door. 'I'm not . . . I just know what she's like.' We rode in silence for a mile or so, before she spoke again. 'I'm sorry if she upset you.'

'Yeah, well she did,' I said. Who was this person who was impersonating my best friend? Did she really think that was normal hostess behaviour? I twisted round to look at her, dropped my voice low. 'What's going on with all of you? You can talk to me, Lys, it's me!'

'It's . . .' I could sense her wavering, and I thought about telling her what I'd overheard, but I knew that the decision could go either way – listening at doors is rarely appreciated, and our bond felt too compromised to take more strain. 'It's horrible at the moment, that's all.'

'Is there anything more I can do? I'm not here much longer, but . . .' Her gaze was intense, words teetering on the edge of articulation. 'Anything . . .' I said, willing her to break.

'There is something,' she said. 'Can I borrow a bit of cash? Not much, say a couple of hundred quid? Just till the end of the month.' I saw her register the shock on my face. She wiggled a foot in my direction, smiled in a way that was almost coquettish: I'd forgotten how drunk she was, but now it was obvious. 'Shoes like this don't grow on shoe trees.'

'Lys, of course I want to help you, but . . . if you've got money problems, borrowing a bit of cash off me isn't a solution.'

'Fine, don't worry,' she said, stung. 'I shouldn't have asked.'

The silence between us felt sticky.

'What's it for?' I said eventually.

'Just credit cards. Comfort spending, you know. You probably don't, actually. You're so well behaved.' I tried not to hear the echo of her rant at the funeral in the sly compliment. 'It's not been great with me and Ged. I can't cope with any more stress right now.'

I heard the crack in her voice when it came. I tumbled straight down it like Alice down a rabbit hole.

'If you really, really need it . . .'

The smile that spread across her face was one of pure relief.

'Thanks sooo much. I'll get it straight back to you.' She gave me a quick, unnecessary kiss on the cheek. 'Promise.'

She was too relieved, too pleased. I knew in that second I should never have said yes.

I'd gone to Kimberley's house secretly hoping for answers, but I came away with nothing but questions. The problem was, they were the kind of questions which came with answers too dangerous to learn.

Sarah's Diary – March 22nd 2015

I think he likes the idea of me and Kimberley being friends. Friends in high places. Friends in low places on Friday, more like. I bitched about it beforehand, but it was proper fun, no question.

Too much fun. I texted him. I'd promised myself I wouldn't, but I wanted the extra buzz on top – that fizzing feeling deep inside of me. A natural high. Knowing he doesn't just want me, he craves me.

When my phone beeped, I hid in her en suite, even though I knew she'd flip her lid if she found me there, and read what he said again and again. The fact he was trying not to say it was a bigger turn on than if he'd just put it out there. I keep thinking of you too. In fact it's getting hard to think about anything else X *I put some of her lipstick on, stared at my pink face in her big round mirror. My eyes looked so bright, so alive. I knew right then that I was beautiful. Then the high went really low. Cos it's not enough, is it? It's not enough for him. The fact I'm more beautiful and it's still her he wants must mean there's something wrong with me. I felt so angry I just pocketed the stupid lipstick. She won't miss it.*

Had to put the whole of the start of the night on that new credit card (thank FUCK they said yes and thank you, Mum, for letting me pretend I still live there). Dinner, drinks, the lot. You can't say anything when you're out with them. You can't say, I live in a big house but can I just have a starter? You can't say, please, miss, can we have Prosecco and not champagne? I looked over at Lysette and I knew she felt the same way, but all we could do was make a weird face at each other. If it wasn't for her, I'd feel like a right skank, like I was a teenager again, and not in a good way.

That was the other thing that happened in the bathroom — I came up with a plan. It's going to change things up a bit, level the playing field. Something good can come out of the badness, at least for me. No, for us. I reckon Lysette will go for it. She needs it as much as I do.

I woke Max up when I got in, I couldn't help it. I wasn't flying any more: all I felt was guilty. He's part of me, and he's so perfect and innocent, the purest piece of me that no one can harm. He moaned at first, pushed me away, but then he woke up a bit more and really saw me. He reached up his little arms, pulled me down so I was lying next to him. We snuggled so close it was almost like he was back in my tummy, really part of me again. Then I wondered if my plan was such a good one, if it could hurt him. Couldn't think about it. I reached into my bag, my hand creeping so slowly he didn't wake up, and took one of Kimberley's pills.

Sometimes I think I could sleep forever.

CHAPTER THIRTEEN

Too much coffee makes me twitchy. I'd foolishly ordered a second cup as I waited, the caffeine pin-balling around my system, my eyes constantly flicking towards the door of The Crumpet. It was a couple of days after the disastrous dinner party, and Krall had requested a catch-up via one of his underlings. I'd been all ready to head into Peterborough, but he'd sent word that he'd come to meet me in Little Copping. Apparently it slotted perfectly into his day, a justification I was deeply suspicious of – I know better than most that you can observe far more about an animal when you see it in the wild. I sucked up the last dregs of my now cold cappuccino. He might be good at catching serial killers, but he was clearly no great shakes at using a watch.

Jake was working today, his eyes trained on the steaming coffee machine, obsessively polishing the already gleaming pipes with a cloth and avoiding any eye contact. The café was silent and still, only a couple of tables occupied, which made the sudden clang of the bell sound like a fire engine. There was Krall, framed in the doorway, his hair dishevelled by the gusty day, a stylish Crombie coat flapping around his neat form. He pointed at me, hurried over.

'So this is the fabled Crumpet?' he said, sticking out a firm hand. 'I'm sorry I kept you waiting.'

'Don't worry,' I said, standing up. 'I've been seeing people all morning, so a bit of time to myself was no bad thing.'

'I know exactly what you mean,' he said, conspiratorial. 'It's actually a relief to escape the incident room for a couple of hours.' His dark eyes were rapidly scanning the room, adding to that sense of perpetual motion. Jake stayed resolutely still, but a twenty-something waitress I hadn't noticed stalked out from behind the counter. She had jet-black hair tied in tight bunches, heavy eye make-up, a fierce-looking nose ring that pierced the centre in a way that looked deeply painful. Krall wasn't remotely fazed. 'Hello!' he said. 'So, if this is The Crumpet, what do you have in the way of cakes?'

'Well ...' giggled the girl, her face immediately transformed by Krall's warmth. 'People say the carrot cake's nice, but I don't much like carrots.'

'Luckily I do,' said Krall, 'so I'll be having a slice. How about you, Mia?'

'I'm OK for cake,' I said, measured. What was he trying to invoke between us? This wasn't the Krall I'd encountered at the police station. 'Just an Earl Grey is fine.'

'Very restrained,' he said. 'I'll also have an espresso. The strongest your friend over there can get it to come out of his impressive machine.' He swung back to face me. 'Hello,' he said. 'Where were we?'

'Roughly at hello.'

Krall smiled at me: touché.

'How have the past few days been?' he asked.

My gaze dropped towards the table, fixed itself on the sugar bowl before I forced it back up. The aftershock of the dinner party was still reverberating through me, almost forty-eight hours later. Kimberley's mouth on mine would have been shocking enough, but I kept playing their whispered words back to myself, aware that they were muddled in my mind by alcohol. Had my heightened state meant I'd woven a significance into them that wasn't even there? One thing I know from my work is how dangerously prone we are to create a story of our own making from random facts.

'It's been tough,' I said, a little too heartfelt. I'd tried to gently broach another conversation with Lysette, but her distress meant that any spare capacity she had was rightly directed towards her children. I'd toyed with talking to Patrick, but something had stopped me, a shaming echo of Lysette's words in the cab. Had I somehow incited that situation with Kimberley? I felt like I couldn't explain it to him without seeing him face to face. The person I'd really wanted to talk to – the person I knew would understand – was Jim, and I was resolutely ignoring his suggestions of another meeting. 'I've mainly spent time with the teachers, trying to help them to understand what to expect when the kids come back. How they can hold them.'

Krall paused a beat too long. 'So not so much time spent with the mums? Or has that been more of a social thing?'

A swish of unease ran straight across me, a piano scale played too fast. What had he been told? Before I could formulate a response, the waitress sailed up to us, her chrome tray landing on the table.

'Espresso for you,' she said, putting a tiny china cup in front of Krall, 'tea for you,' she said, unloading a mug, 'and a slice of Bugs Bunny's favourite in the middle!'

'Perfect!' said Krall, effortlessly charming. As she bustled off, he changed tack. 'So how did you get into your line of work? When you were slaving away at your A levels, did you think, I just really want to know what makes people tick?'

I knew enough to be wary of him, but the sight of him sitting there, a mouthful of cake halfway to his mouth as he waited for my response, made it hard to maintain chilliness.

'I came to it later – I started out thinking I was going to be a journalist, but it didn't suit me.' An understatement – I did the first couple of months of a postgraduate course, then crashed and burned to spectacular effect, the quicksand of the years preceding it sucking me under for a few hellish months. 'I had a difficult start ... my Dad – let's say he was eccentric.' Jim flashed up in my mind as I said it, so very much a symptom of that first impossible love for a man who could never love me the way I wanted. 'Therapy saved my bacon. I wanted to pay it forward, I suppose.'

'What a stellar motivation,' said Krall, dark eyes studying me.

'How about you?' I countered.

'Nothing so spiritual,' he said, knocking back a slug of

espresso. 'Three brothers, too much time playing cops and robbers. I've always liked the good guys winning, and I seem to have a talent for making sure it happens.' He tapped the table with a flourish. 'Touch wood.'

'So I hear.' I'd Googled him now, seen his string of high-profile murder convictions. I understood why Patrick had questioned his presence. Was it the proximity to the Farthings that meant they'd rolled out the big guns, or was there more to this case than I yet realised?

'Which is what I aim to make sure happens here. How do you think your friend Lysette Allen is coping? You're staying with her, no?'

He knew full well how discombobulating it was, the zig-zags he was forcing us to take. He wanted to make me dizzy.

'She's very sad.'

'She obviously cared deeply for Sarah,' he said.

Krall paused, his slim fingers steepled in front of him. He didn't wear a wedding ring, I noticed. The thought crossed my mind that he might be gay, but his studied campness felt more like a certain type of good breeding. Or perhaps it was neither of the above: perhaps it was his version of plain clothes.

'Of course,' I said, 'she's a very loving friend.' The words felt metallic in my mouth, cold somehow.

'Which is why I'd expect her to want to do anything she could to help answer the many, many questions surrounding Sarah's death.' He paused again. I paused longer. 'But – and I may be wrong – it doesn't feel that way.'

I sounded defensive. 'She doesn't *know* what happened.'

'I'm sure she doesn't, and don't get me wrong, it's *our* job to find that out. But what I also suspect is that she's sitting on information that would make that job a good deal easier.'

'She's furious at the world for taking her friend away from her,' I said, my voice rising. 'It's possible your detectives are mistaking anger for obstructiveness. She loved Sarah. Of course she wants her killer caught.'

He was in, quick as a flash. 'Her killer? Has she talked about the death in those terms from the start?'

'I'm not saying that.'

'So what *are* you saying?' His tone was coaxing. 'I'm fascinated by how you read the situation. You understand the subtleties in a way that I'm not trained to do.' He smiled at me, his craggy face softly handsome. 'Help me out here, Mia.'

'I appreciate the compliment, but I'm not sure it's deserved.' I thought of Lysette in the cab home – cardigan wrapped tightly around her skimpy dress, her arms crossed, her gaze turned away. I found it humiliating how little I knew about what was going on inside of her. 'And I've been very clear that it's inappropriate for us to discuss her. She's my best friend, not my client.'

'Of course,' said Krall, conciliatory. 'And I'm sure it must be very hard to be so close to that overpowering grief. She seems utterly destroyed by it.'

Destroyed: the word made me flinch. 'I'm just happy to be able to comfort her,' I lied.

'She seems to have a very strong friendship group – well, Sarah's group. They're a tight knit bunch, aren't they?'

A flash of it – Kimberley advancing across the bathroom, the lipstick clenched in her hand like a Disney Princess weapon. I was so stupid, not bolting there and then.

'Aren't they just?' I said, too quickly. We smiled at each other, and he scooped up another moist forkful of cake, thick icing dripping off it. 'I thought cops were meant to go in for doughnuts?'

'Only hard-bitten New Yorkers,' he smiled. 'Are they cake bakers, do you think?'

'I'm sure Kimberley could knock out a Victoria sponge on a Bunsen burner without breaking a sweat,' I said. 'But I bet she wouldn't so much as nibble it.'

'Interesting . . .'

I felt safer now we'd strayed away from the topic of Lysette. Too safe perhaps.

'She's a classic queen bee, isn't she? She does everything with aplomb.' Did I sound bitchy? Of course I sounded bitchy. 'It's very impressive,' I added hastily.

'And you've had the chance to observe this particular gang close up, I gather. Coffee mornings. Dinner parties.'

I was determined not to let him rattle me. 'You've obviously been doing your homework.'

'I didn't really have to. Kimberley Farthing's been very forthcoming. Much more than any of the others, in fact.'

It made perfect sense – I thought of the way her voice cut across them, in total command. If she was the one deciding what information got out, she kept control. But what was the information they seemed so desperate to keep under wraps?

'If you've got Kimberley on side, I'm sure you'll have no problem getting the others to open up,' I said.

'I see what you mean. The queen bee controls the hive,' he said, cocking his head. 'But you're not under her spell as yet?'

'She's also very close to Ian,' I said, ignoring his aside. It had the very real potential to make me paranoid. I made my voice low and authoritative, one professional to another. 'He's someone I'm determined to help. He's got a huge task on his hands, trying to put the pieces back together.'

'Absolutely,' agreed Lawrence. 'And he has to shoulder his guilt about making the decision not to suspend Peter Grieve.'

'I'm sorry?'

He smiled, weighing out his words. I could see the cogs turning, behind all that sugar and icing and charm. 'There was a complaint made. Inappropriate messages, late-night calls. He hasn't told you about it?'

He knew full well it was a revelation, was milking the effect.

'What, Peter was harassing Sarah? I mean I suppose that makes sense ...' He flashed up in my mind's eye, the look on his face as he swooped down to the playground tarmac. Even through the haze of sadness he'd felt attuned, gentle.

'No. Not Sarah.' He watched me. It's a technique I use myself: stop short and see where the client goes. I wasn't falling for it.

'So who?' I asked.

'Kimberley.'

'*Kimberley?*'

'Yes. Is that shocking to you?'

'Well – yes. I mean – it was Sarah he killed himself for. Kimberley's in charge of the PTA. She's married to a Cabinet minister. Seems like a dangerous target.'

'Exactly!' said Krall, tapping the Formica surface of the table to emphasise the point. 'Don't you think it suggests a pattern of highly unstable behaviour? Stalking. Aggressive pursuit at any cost.'

I was struggling to process it, spooling back through all those subtle little hints and digs that Kimberley had uttered.

'It's hard to say that without more information. What actually happened? Why wouldn't Ian have suspended him?'

'It all blew up at a PTA fundraiser. Kimberley decided she wanted it to stay a private matter, for both their sakes. She spoke to Peter herself with Ian present. He apologised. They all agreed to move on, not put it on his record.'

I could almost see it – Kimberley all magnanimous and saintly, accepting of the dangerous power of her spellbinding beauty. And then – what, he moved on to Sarah? It was hard to make the elements of this story fit together, but perhaps it was because I was arrogantly insisting that my three-second impression of Peter in the playground held water.

'And what – he was sending – suggestive – texts?' I couldn't bring myself to use the word 'sext' in front of Krall: it was too *TOWIE* for this arch and elegant man.

'More than that. Nigel Farthing obviously travels a lot, and Grieve was spotted parked outside their house a couple of times.'

'There are big metal gates at the front,' I told him. 'He wouldn't have got much joy. Who saw him?'

'I'd have to look at the notes. The nanny, I believe.'

'Susan?' I asked.

'I don't have the name to hand. But if that's Kimberley's nanny then yes.'

'No, her nanny is called Lori. She's only just arrived. There was a Susan, but she left in a hurry. That's why I'm wondering if you tracked her down and interviewed her?'

'I'm not sure,' said Krall. 'It's possible this information just came from Kimberley, but if there was someone else living there during the period he was stalking her, we should definitely follow up on it. Are you saying you think her leaving was connected?'

I thought of Lori's small, pinched face, as pale as skimmed milk. There was something so vulnerable about her, locked up in that velvet cell. She'd wanted to snatch the name back as soon as she'd uttered it: I didn't want to get her into trouble.

'No one's said that. I might have got the dates mixed up.'

At the time I vowed that I'd ask Lysette, go back to him with more information if it seemed relevant. How simplistic I was.

Krall was already racing ahead. 'In essence, everything points to Peter having been a man with serious emotional issues. He'd taken antidepressants his whole adult life, on and off.'

'Yeah, that's been everywhere.' The headlines were getting ever more lurid, the speculations from 'close friends' and 'unnamed sources' increasingly damning and personal. I'd seen a snatched picture of Peter's parents, heads bowed as they scuttled back into a small suburban house. It was hard to imagine what they must be going through, grieving for him and defending his memory all at once. 'But do bear in mind,' I continued, 'that they get handed out very readily by doctors. It's a way cheaper solution than therapy.'

Krall arched an eyebrow. 'You don't approve, I take it?'

'I'm not saying that. All I mean is, the fact that he took them doesn't necessarily make it more likely he killed her.'

'And you're not convinced Grieve fits the profile of a killer? Is that because of what you've gleaned here?'

My hand shot up between us unbidden.

'I don't mean to be rude, Detective Inspector, but I feel like I keep needing to remind you of the boundaries. I'm not a criminal psychologist. I'm sure you've got access to plenty of them if that's what you're after.'

It was as if the words set alight as they left my mouth. He did have plenty of experts to ask, but of course it was me he wanted to question: none of them were stuck right in the eye of the storm. I looked down at my watch – we'd been here long enough for me to make an exit.

'My apologies – again,' said Krall with a rueful smile. 'The problem is, I'm genuinely fascinated by your insights. You've certainly made me think.'

My diary was lying on the table. I scooped it up, grabbed my phone, dropped them into my handbag. I paused a second.

'I don't want to patronise you, and I'm sure you know this, but our brains are hardwired to create plausible stories.' He was listening intently, his expression unreadable. 'Even highly commended detective inspectors. Your evidence all sounds very circumstantial, and he's not here to tell you different.' I paused, the photographs from the incident room looming up for me. 'Neither of them are.'

'You're right,' said Krall, serious. 'So far we can't find any phone records that definitively support it; we're still trawling through hours of CCTV, the forensics are inconclusive. So if you end up finding out anything more concrete in the course of your work, it could be critical. I respect the boundaries, but please don't forget your responsibilities to the investigation. I'm convinced that someone here knows exactly what happened.'

As I left The Crumpet, the bell ringing loudly in my wake, I had to fight the urge to think too closely about who that might be.

CHAPTER FOURTEEN

I refused Krall's offer of a lift back to Lysette's, and set off down the high street. It was a strange jumble of shops: a boutique filled with pointlessly expensive things – burnt vanilla candles you'd have to remortgage your house to afford, porridge-coloured linen scarves – next to a hardware shop, spilling out clothes pegs and plastic washing-up bowls. Every single person I passed was white.

I took a detour across a field, determined to remind myself how beautiful it was. It was baking today, the sun beating down on me, my professional sandals with their dinky little heels no match for the mulchy path. The smell of cowpat was overwhelming.

I arrived back at Lysette's hot and bothered, my meeting with Lawrence playing back in my mind on a maddening loop. Had I said too much or not enough? I put my key in the lock, even though part of me still felt I should be knocking. Lysette stuck her head out of the kitchen, her hair piled up on top of her head, a slash of lipstick brightening her face. The sight of her warmed me, as instinctive and automatic as breathing.

'Hey, stranger, you've been ages,' she said.

'It was a busy day,' I said. 'I met one of the teachers this morning – Alison? She's really sweet.'

'She's lovely, isn't she?'

'And then I met up with Lawrence Krall.' I sensed her tensing, even though it was invisible. She was right to be tense – I tried to lighten it. 'He's such a weirdo. He wanted to meet in The Crumpet. He had carrot cake!'

Lysette took the bait: she didn't want to go anywhere too dangerous either.

'Well, there's been baking going down here too!' she said, rallying, her voice pitched like a '50s children's TV presenter. 'We've been making cinnamon biscuits. They're in the oven . . .'

'Smelling magnificent, I might add!'

'Saffron and Max are playing in the garden until they're ready.'

Max was here too. The thought of him at the funeral – so earnest, clutching his Woody doll like his life depended on it – had continued to haunt me. I'd asked Lawrence's team to reach out to Joshua, to let him know that I had experience with bereaved children, but had heard nothing.

'Shall I go and see what they're up to?' I asked.

'Good call. Only an hour till wine o'clock.'

'Surely it's wine o'clock already in Bogotá?' I said, the words catching in my throat. Jim jolted his way into my mind, yet again. His presence felt more like an itch than a yearning, an insect bite that refused to be soothed.

'What time's lover boy arriving?' asked Lysette, laughing.

'Lover boy said he'd drive down as soon as he could get away from work. So probably midnight. Tomorrow. He's booked somewhere, though, so we'll be out your hair.'

'Too right he has. I don't want any hanky panky under my roof,' shouted Lysette after my retreating back.

I turned round and gave her a sneaky V sign, then stepped through the french windows into the lush garden.

'Auntie Mia!' said Saffron. She was still on a seesaw of emotion, so it was a lovely treat to see her round face light up with genuine joy. I dropped to my knees to hug her, then turned to Max. It was hard to let her wriggly, cinnamon-scented body go – I only did so that Max wouldn't feel any more alone than he probably already did. He was watching me owlishly, big, heavy-looking glasses reflecting the sun. He'd sat Woody in a chair, his legs stuck out in front of him.

'Hi, Max, do you remember me? I hear you've been making biscuits.'

'Yes, we have,' he said in a formal voice. 'I did the stirring.'

'That's great! They smell lovely. You must've done very good stirring.'

'And I . . .' said Saffron, pulling hard on my sleeve, 'I did greasing the tray and breaking the eggs.'

'Very good work. And what are you playing out here?'

'Funerals,' said Max, matter-of-fact.

'And weddings!' said Saffron, but my attention was focused on Max now.

'And how do you play funerals?' I said, keeping my voice

172

deliberately gentle. It felt very important for him to know that I wasn't shocked or angry.

'Someone has to die,' he said. 'And then you tell people they have died. I told Woody.' He turned to look at him, giving a proud smile to his plastic stoicism.

'Did Woody love the person very much?' I said, measuring out my words carefully.

Saffron was pulling on my sleeve, and I pulled her in close again, hoping it would buy me another minute or two.

'Woody's daddy died,' he said, 'but he is very brave. We've dug him a hole to live in and he is also in heaven.'

The words sounded like a tongue-twister he'd learned to recite – death is confusing enough for adults, but the way children are expected to wrap their brains around it is more for our benefit than theirs, I often think. Max gestured to a nearby flower bed. Lysette's roses grew there: I wasn't sure how thrilled she'd be at the gaping trench the children had dug, but I didn't let on.

'That's the grave!' said Saffron in a suitably dramatic tone.

Max looked at me, dark eyes searching my face for a reaction. There was so much need burning away inside of him.

'Do you want to show me?' I said softly, extending my hand. He slowly reached his hand to meet mine and we walked across the lawn, Saffron following.

'This is where he will live now,' he told me. 'Did you know that worms eat people?'

'They eat people!' shouted Saffron at the top of her voice, laughing like a hyena. She was trying to make sense of it too, in her own, very different way. She ran across the garden, returning with a bashed-up-looking doll. It was naked, curly hair askew. Other than Sindy, saved by her impeccable sense of style, I've always found dolls borderline creepy. Max solemnly took it from her and laid it in the makeshift grave.

'I am going to bury him now.'

'He' had quite a wild haircut, but it wasn't the point.

'Are you?' I asked. 'Do you want to say anything?'

'Ashes and ashes,' he said solemnly. 'Dust and dust . . .' He petered out.

'Is there anything you want to say about Woody's dad?' I said, hoping I wasn't overstepping the mark. He felt so ripe with emotion, I couldn't help but want to give him a means to let it out.

'Woody's dad,' he declared, 'you were a very kind doll. You always read Woody his bedtime story, even when he had stayed up too late because he hadn't finished his tea and needed a snack of pepperoni.' I felt my eyes prickle, but I pushed down the emotion, made my focus absolute. 'Woody will miss you very much and he will look after his daddy – no, his mummy – very much. Amen.'

'Now we sing a hymn!' shouted Saffron, immediately breaking into a rousing rendition of 'Let It Go', complete with swaying and arm waving.

Max stayed silent a second, then joined in. After a couple of lines he abandoned singing and started violently pushing the soil back into the trench with his hands, his little face intense with effort. I stayed kneeling next to him, silently telling him that he wasn't alone.

Lysette appeared at the french windows, her hands encased in big white oven mitts so she could hold the hot baking tray.

'Biscuits are served!' she trilled. 'And sauvignon blanc,' she added, sotto voce. Saffron stopped singing, rushed towards her mum like she'd been shot from a gun. Max ignored her, his hands, even his glasses, covered in soil like he was a small, bookish mole. 'Come on, Max,' she said, 'come and try your creations.'

He looked up for a split second, then went back to scrabbling in the dirt.

'We were playing funerals,' said Saffron.

The smile on Lysette's face immediately disappeared. She stared over at me, face like thunder, and I stood up, brushing grass from my knees. I walked over to her.

'I think it's really helpful for him,' I said quietly.

'Oh do you?' said Lysette, acidly. She turned on her heel, her next words spat over her shoulder. 'Well, thank God you're here then.'

I tried to keep calm, to stop the acid of her words burning into me. I crossed back to Max, aware my whole body was shaking. I knelt back down. He was patting the soil flat, filthy hands thumping hard against the ground.

'You've done such a brilliant job, Max.'

'Thank you,' he said, peering round at me.

'It's up to you, but now you've finished, we could go in and taste your biscuits?'

He looked up at me, almost dazed. 'OK,' he said automatically.

'Is there anything else left that you want to say to Woody or his dad before we go?'

'No,' he said, abruptly standing and brushing the soil off his trousers, his eyes not meeting mine. Was he ashamed of letting me see his grief, however obliquely? 'We don't always have to do talking.'

I went to reach out a hand, but there was something in his body language that told me it wouldn't be welcome.

'Then let's get Woody and go inside.'

He ran to the chair where Woody sat, and brought the doll up close to his face. I slowly approached him.

'Daddy's very proud of you,' he muttered, quite audible – his whispering skills left something to be desired. 'You can always talk to me. You don't need to talk to anybody else. Always talk to me.'

He looked up at me, his face a pale moon. It was as if summer hadn't touched him, which in a sense it hadn't.

'So Woody tells you his secrets too?' I said. Was I asking too much? It was so hard to feign indifference in the face of his obvious distress. His free hand, muddy and warm, suddenly reached for mine. 'You said to me the first time I met you that you tell him your secrets?'

'Everyone has secrets. It's what makes you like a grown-up,' he replied, like it was patently obvious.

'Right,' I said, slowly leading him across the grass. 'So do you tell Daddy your secrets like Woody does?'

I thought of Joshua at the funeral – the way he'd ignited at the felony of Max grabbing multiple sausage rolls. He wouldn't have been my first choice for a secret.

Max yanked his hand away, taking off at a run.

'Biscuits!' he yelled, careering towards the french windows. My progress was slower – I was like an amateurish puppeteer, willing my reluctant feet to do my bidding.

*

Lysette was bristling with aggressive maternity. The children were sitting at the table, white china plates in front of them, the now legendary biscuits stacked on a cake stand I would have sworn she didn't own. There seemed to be so many things I didn't know about Lysette, big and small. Blackened and misshapen, the biscuits felt almost as out of place in their surroundings as I did.

'Shall I put the kettle on?' I said, my voice ringing high and tinny in my ears. This was ridiculous. I hadn't even started the funeral game – all I'd done was help to give it parameters, made it safe – but here I was, pandering to the latest of Lysette's savage mood swings. I pulled a couple of mugs out of the cupboard, aware of the way they banged on the kitchen counter as I put them down.

'Don't worry about doing that,' said Lysette, spinning round to face me. 'You're our *guest*.'

I could see a half-empty wine glass balanced on the draining board – she was turning the '50s housewife vibe right up to the max.

'I wasn't sure if you wanted tea, or if you were just going to go with wine?' I hated myself for saying it as soon as the words had left my mouth. The last thing the children needed was to be sitting in the toxic fog of our passive-aggressive sniping. Max was oblivious, but I could see Saffron's chocolate brown eyes tracking us – even six-year-old girls know how to pinch without leaving a bruise. I put a hand on Lysette's arm, forced myself to smile without baring my teeth. 'Let me do it. Why don't you sit down and put your feet up?'

'I couldn't possibly,' she hissed, refusing to accept the rather manky olive branch I'd held out. 'I'm not the one who's been working all day.' Her eyes were narrow slits. 'Putting in *overtime*.'

I had to turn away, my teeth grinding. I turned back, all smiles.

'I'm going to go upstairs and get ready,' I said. 'Uncle Patrick's coming later,' I said, addressing myself to Saffron. I couldn't even bear to make eye contact with Lysette in that moment. 'Lovely to see you again, Max.'

But as I left the kitchen a wail erupted.

'Where are you going?' sobbed Max, inconsolable. 'Where are you *going*?' I ran back in, dropped myself down into the chair next to him.

'She's only going upstairs,' said Lysette, her eyes burning with a new level of rage. Of course – from her point of view this just confirmed my criminality. Why could no one see – why could none of these parents see – that this child needed more support than he was getting?

'That's true, Max,' I said. 'My boyfriend's coming to see me, and I want to make myself look extra pretty.' My eyes flicked to Saffron, conscious of the terrible fairy-tale-princess logic of that statement. 'We're going to talk about lots and lots of things together,' I added.

'You're old, Auntie Mia,' she piped up. 'I've got a boyfriend who is not Max. You should have a husband. Grown-ups have husbands.'

The afternoon kept going from bad to worse: I didn't need to look at Lysette to know how much she was enjoying this. Had Saffron sucked up the spiteful energy between us, recast herself as Mummy's second in command? I was about to give her a quick tutorial from Feminism For Six-Year-Olds, but unfortunately no one had written it, and my attention needed to stay focused on Max. His glasses were moist, like a car windscreen on a drizzly Tuesday.

'I promise I'll come down and say goodbye to you when your daddy comes to collect you.'

He gave a nod, tears suddenly a thing of the past, and reached a mechanical hand out for another biscuit.

'Thank you,' he said, not even bothering to make contact.

I stood up, brushing blackened biscuit crumbs off my knees. 'OK then!' I said, all fake cheer, backing out of the room. I was going to text Patrick as soon as I was out of this cinnamon-scented hell and tell him that speed limits had no place in his life right now.

*

I lay on the stupid inflatable mattress waiting for my heart rate to slow. I tried to push my fury with Lysette aside – to tell myself it was nothing more than my bruised ego taking everything too personally – but sainthood wasn't one of my strengths.

Thinking about Max was at least a useful distraction. Could I try to engage Joshua when he arrived, tell him that I thought Max would benefit from more support? What was this constant talk about secrets – was it simply a way of articulating how much he missed that deep, snuggly closeness with his mum or was it something more troubling? I rehearsed it in my head, terrified I'd come over as some chilly, childless professional, too proud of the letters after my name, pronouncing on other people's parenting styles. I felt another spurt of rage towards Lysette: I hated thinking she was using her earth mother status to keep me down, but the thought wouldn't die. The truth was, I didn't have tons of female friends – perhaps because I feared the kind of silent, deadly warfare that we'd always scorned as a cliché we'd never resort to. I'd relied too much on her to be my everything – it was humiliating to realise I might have been the only one holding on to a torn and faded photograph.

When the doorbell rang, I sprang up. I hadn't wanted to go to the bathroom in case it forced me into any more contact with Lysette, so I'd applied my make-up in the reflection of a tiny compact. My lipstick looked garishly red, my mascara smudgy. I watched Lysette open the door from my vantage point on the top landing. Of course it wasn't Patrick – it was utter insanity to expect that he'd have proved his love by defying the land-speed record – but nor was it Joshua.

'So where's the little man?' asked Lisa. Everything about her seemed so efficient. Her cleverly highlighted hair was cut in a sleek cap that fell precisely around her sharp features, her car keys were held at the ready in her left hand. She was wearing the kind of jeans that were neither fashionable nor unfashionable, simply there.

'He's been busy baking biscuits,' replied Lysette. *And playing funerals*, I silently added, forcing myself down the stairs. Why was everyone dealing in half-truths? Half-truths are so much worse than lies: they're like ruthless assassins, deadly in their invisibility.

'Hi, Lisa,' I said. For some reason I put out my hand, just as she leaned in for a brisk kiss. We laughed awkwardly. I couldn't quite bring myself to look at Lysette.

'So you're still here, working your magic?' she said. As she was speaking, Max slunk through the kitchen door and wedged himself against me.

'I'm doing my best,' I said, looking down at him. His hands looped around my leg.

'Well, it looks like you've got yourself a fan!' she said, and I braced myself for a splash of vitriol from Lysette. This was the moment to say something, but it was also the absolute opposite.

'Are you staying for a cup of tea?' I said, aware of how presumptuous it was for me to be the one to ask.

'Yeah, stay for a cup of tea,' added Lysette, although I didn't sense much enthusiasm in her tone.

Lisa pulled a disappointed face that didn't quite convince. 'I'd have loved that – I've got so many questions bubbling away about what it is you actually do – but we have to get back and get some supper into this one.' She looked down at him. 'Don't we?'

How must it feel for Max, this new normal that was being imposed with such brutal determination? I might've been imagining it, but his grip on my leg felt like a creeping vine that didn't want to let go.

'That's a pity,' I said. 'But I would love the chance to talk to you – to you and to Joshua – about what it is I'm doing here. Perhaps I could give him a call? I don't want to impose, but if I can be any support before I go . . .'

Lysette shot me a dark look which I ignored, keeping my fixed smile in place and reaching a hand down to squeeze Max's shoulder. I couldn't abandon him: if there was the slightest chance I could help him to be heard, I had to take it.

'How kind! I'll make sure to tell him that when he manages to fight his way out of the office. It's awful . . .' she added in an undertone, 'all he wants to do is spend time with this little one, but he's got a massive deal going through which he has to be there for. It's all hands to the pump for me and the kids.'

Was her husband part of the war effort? Her actual, current husband, not her ex?

'You can bring him to us any time,' said Lysette. 'You know, Sarah was here the whole time, so it's pretty much his second home.'

Was it barbed? It felt barbed. But why would it be, when their divorce was such a civilised affair?

'You're so kind,' said Lisa, 'thank you. I don't know what we'd do without you.'

Everyone was saying 'kind' a bit more than was strictly necessary. She pecked both of our cheeks, chivvying Max to follow her to the car – she felt like a kitchen appliance which had only one setting.

'Bye, Max,' I said, dropping down to my knees: as they hit the carpet a flash of Peter Grieve came floating up, unbidden. 'See you again soon. Look after Woody.'

Lisa looked down on us, her smile never wavering. Max nodded earnestly, clutching hold of Woody, then set off down the path without saying a word. Lisa looked back at me as she left.

'I don't know how you do it!' she said. 'I mean, bless them, but I enjoyed mine far more once we could have a sensible exchange about what was on the radio.'

'She's the kiddie whisperer, don't forget,' said Lysette, but I was too distracted to take the bait.

There in the car, examining her lovely face in the passenger side mirror, sat Kimberley.

CHAPTER FIFTEEN

Patrick still wasn't putting his seat belt on. I'd whipped mine across my chest, thrust in the clip, so when he tried to turn me towards him for a kiss my body twisted unnaturally like an undercooked pretzel.

'Let's just go,' I said.

Patrick leaned back in the driver's seat, looked at me, amused.

'And breathe,' he said, floating his hands upwards like a Zen master. 'Or are you just so desperate to rip my clothes off that you can't waste valuable time on pleasantries?'

He was wearing one of those flammable-looking suits that only belonged in Help the Aged. I'd sneakily push them to the back of the wardrobe, hope he'd get the hint, but they were obviously enjoying a renaissance since I'd abandoned ship. I did want to rip it off, it was true, but not for the reason he imagined. Hopefully I'd reframe my reasoning once I'd had a couple of glasses of wine. It was hard to imagine right now, my whole body fizzing with an acid frustration I couldn't expel.

'I've just had the worst day. Lysette's being a TOTAL bitch to me, and I had another meeting with Lawrence Krall, with his – his weird sugar cravings. Honestly, he sounds more like a country and western singer than a murder detective . . .'

Patrick's warm smile lost a bit of its light, but I was too wound up to register it. He turned the key in the ignition.

'It's a police investigation. Stress is gonna be part of the deal . . .'

'No, I know,' I said, trying not to sound defensive. 'Don't worry, I'll give you a proper run-down when we get there. Where *are* we going anyway?'

I'd asked him to surprise me.

'I booked the pub.'

'The pub?'

Page one error – it's something I warn couples about all the time. Of course he hadn't read my mind, but I'd imagined being whisked off to some charming hotel in Cambridge, wined and dined in style before he seduced me like we'd only just met, giving vent to all his pent-up passion. Instead we were going half a mile for a steak and ale pie and the very real danger that one of the endless list of people I didn't want to see would have the exact same idea.

'Yeah. You're always getting all wistful when we come down here. Going on about how quaint it is and sniffing the clean air with your dainty little nose. I thought we could have a night of rural bliss in a country inn.'

'Yeah. No, good idea.'

I knew I was being impossible but somehow I couldn't stop

myself. Patrick looked over at me, and I gave him a quick, unconvincing smile. The fact he let it go, pretended he was fooled, made my loneliness – the loneliness I'd banked on him sweeping aside – rear up all over again.

Max flashed up in my mind. I was going mad, aligning myself with a six-year-old boy.

*

The pub was ancient – low and white, with black beams, a thatched roof and a door so low that Patrick had to duck his long body to get inside. I took his hand and squeezed it, ashamed of my ingratitude. We were here, together.

As we walked in I couldn't help feeling curious eyes were tracking us, even though I didn't recognise anyone except the newsagent and his wife (I'd clearly spent too much time in there pretending to myself I wasn't reading the hysterical headlines). Patrick was already at the bar, giving the landlady the booking details, all Irish charm and bonhomie. She was sixty-ish, with lots of oversized gilt jewellery and the kind of coal-black hair that never quite convinces. Her small, dark eyes were bright and watchful, roving the pub as if she was anticipating trouble. After Patrick produced a credit card she disappeared off to get our room key.

'So have you been hanging round here every night having snakebites?' he whispered, lips close enough to my ear to touch my skin.

'No . . .' I faltered for a second. Jim had texted me again the night before, suggesting exactly that (well, not snakebites).

He'd asked yet again if we could meet, told me how worried he was about Lysette's distressed state. I'd put him off – claimed babysitting duties – but I hadn't shot the idea down in flames like I should've done. 'I came here with Lysette a couple of summers ago. We sat in the garden and had white wine spritzers.'

It was the kind of weird, overdetailed response you'd give if you had something to hide, and I didn't have anything to hide, not really. Patrick nodded politely, and we stood there in silence for a couple of minutes waiting for the landlady to come back.

'Here you go,' she said. She paused. 'You journalists then? We've got a houseful of them. You're lucky to get a room. We don't rent this one unless we have to.'

Great: it looked like we'd be trying to conceive a child in a pigsty. Perhaps I'd give birth to the Second Coming.

'Nope,' said Patrick. 'I'm a lawyer, and my beautiful fiancée here is a shrink.'

I always avoid answering that question before it's absolutely necessary. Either people start eyeing you with suspicion – like you're a psychic, not a therapist, and must already know they stole a Twix from the corner shop when they were twelve – or they start telling you their dreams in excruciating detail. Her expression shifted.

'You're the one helping the police? Ian was talking about you.'

'Was he?' I said, trying and failing not to care what it was that he'd said.

'He certainly was,' she said, clocking my insecurity. 'Let me show you to your room.'

We followed her up a rickety staircase round the back of the pub, Patrick bent almost double. It opened up onto an unexpectedly big landing, dried flowers splayed out in a vase on a central table, four rooms arranged in a square.

'Lovely place you've got here,' said Patrick.

'You're the next floor up,' she replied in a tone of grim satisfaction. The next staircase was even narrower than the first, a doorway right at the top.

'Don't worry,' I said, 'we can take it from here.'

'Checkout's at ten,' she said, already clattering back down the stairs on her high black wedges.

Patrick turned his head to look at me, brown eyes twinkling with the sheer ridiculousness, then turned the key in the stiff lock. It was so obviously the servant's quarters in days of yore, the tiny space cut even smaller by the fact that it was in the eaves. The bed was the smallest double I'd ever seen.

Patrick flung himself down on it, limbs erupting out of the sides. 'Well, the good news is it's bouncy.'

I sat down gingerly on the very end. There was only one small skylight, adding to the cell-like quality of the room. I reached over him and turned on the chintzy bedside lamp.

'Maybe we should just drive into Cambridge,' I said, awkwardly rubbing his knee. All our angles were wrong. 'We've got the car.' For a lawyer, Patrick's game face is pretty poor. His hurt was immediately visible to me. 'It's tiny,' I added, trying to sound like I was explaining, not whining. 'I wanted to spend proper time with you.'

'Yeah well, I'd be happy in a bus shelter as long as I was with you.'

I lay down next to him on the tiny ribbon of available space, rubbed his chest through his shirt.

'I know, me too. But ... did they not tell you they only had a coffin when you rang to book?' Just using the word jolted me out of my 'Princess and the Pea' style funk. Sarah had lost everything – even Max.

'I didn't think it through. I just ...'

'I know,' I said, crawling upwards to kiss him. 'It's fine. The food's meant to be lovely. Not that that's the point ...'

Patrick kissed me back for a minute or so, then swung his long legs round to a sitting position. 'You say that, but I think it might be. I'm starving.'

*

The landlady – who Patrick had now established was called Rita – showed us to a table near the empty fireplace and gave us a couple of menus. It was 7.30 by now, and the pub was even busier than when we'd arrived. The tables were shoved close together, and I carefully surveyed the terrain whilst Patrick went to the bar to get a round. He strode back towards me, deposited two gin and tonics on the table.

'Cheers,' he said, clinking my glass. 'Now tell me what's going on with you and Lys?'

I flapped a discreet hand in a downwards motion. 'Walls

have ears,' I muttered, and he looked at me as if I was completely delusional. 'Seriously,' I hissed, 'everyone knows everyone here, and even Madam over there admitted this place was crawling with journalists.'

'So use sign language,' he said, grinning.

What I wanted was to be stretched out on an enormous bed, in a room of our own, with a room-service glass of something delicious and all the time in the world to unravel what this last week had been like. I took a breath, tried my best to tell him. I described the afternoon as best I could, trying not to mind the fact that his eyes kept being drawn downwards to look at the menu.

'But, darling, she *is* grieving,' he said, when I paused for breath. 'She's not gonna be all there . . .'

'I know, but . . .'

Just at that moment Rita arrived, pen held aloft over her order pad.

'Hello!' said Patrick, 'I know exactly what I'll be having . . .' whilst I desperately scanned the menu, thinking how much I didn't want mutton, even in a pie.

'Um, I'll have the cod,' I said eventually, as Rita glared at me, 'and some veg. Whatever you've got.'

'It says, just there,' she said, pointing a scarlet-tipped finger at the sides section. 'Mixed salad, beans or broccoli.'

'Broccoli!' I said, unnecessarily zealous, handing back the menu. I turned back to Patrick as soon as she'd left. 'Today wasn't about her,' I said, dropping my voice. 'It was about . . .' I dropped my voice even lower. 'Max.'

'Darling, this isn't the cold war,' said Patrick. 'Let's go outside. I'll smoke a fag, give us an excuse.'

Patrick does like the odd sneaky cigarette – I try my best not to mind. Once we were in the beer garden he lit one up from an incriminatingly empty packet.

'Can I borrow your jacket?' I asked.

It was fairly deserted out there, only a couple of the wooden tables still occupied, a nip in the air. The garden sloped downwards towards a wide stream, trees overhanging. A couple of ducks quacked companionably as they swam past.

'We're not in Holloway any more, Toto,' said Patrick, smiling down at me as he took a drag, the tension in his body visibly ebbing away. I could see what he could see, but somehow I couldn't see it for myself any more.

'We're not,' I said, squeezing his hand.

'Look, I know you don't feel like it, but you being here will be doing Lysette the world of good. And you're helping all those other people too . . .'

'That's what I was *trying* to do today. Help Max. If she loves Sarah so much she should want that! He wants to talk to someone.'

'Are you sure that's not you' – Patrick waved his cigarette in the dusk, fake pompous – 'what do you call it, projecting?' He saw my face, snaked a long arm around my waist. 'I know how hard it was for you with your dad when you were little. It's gorgeous the way you try and help all those kids. But . . . he's a six-year-old who's lost his mum. Perhaps he and his dad just need to grieve.' Frustration boiled up inside me.

'It's not just Max!' I hissed. 'Even the police are saying Lysette's behaviour is bizarre. So does . . .' I stopped myself: I didn't want to say Jim. 'And the other mums are nearly as weird. That dinner I went to . . .' Again I ground to a halt. Why didn't I just tell him about Kimberley? The truth was, I still couldn't bear to tell him about *me* – my sneaking around, how gauche I'd been when she'd advanced on me. It made me irrationally ashamed.

'The police?' said Patrick, an edge to him. 'What, Lawrence Krall?'

'Yes, amongst others.'

Patrick's eyes burnt down at me. 'Don't go hitching your star to his wagon.'

'What?'

'Come on,' he said, flicking the cigarette onto the flagstones and grinding it out with his heel, 'our dinner'll get cold.'

*

The pub was even more hectic by the time we got back inside; a hubbub of voices, bodies closely packed together at the bar. As I'd suspected, our meals were yet to arrive. I offered to go up and get us a couple of glasses of red in readiness, although what I really wanted was a moment to breathe. We had so little time together: why weren't we making it count? We kept abandoning our sentences midway, the real meaning floating off into the ether like a smoke ring, its shape transformed into something else entirely when it hit the air. I was determined that we do better.

'So what's your beef with Lawrence Krall?' I asked, depositing our brimming glasses down on the table. Now it was Patrick's turn to signal me to turn the volume down. 'I thought he had this amazing clear-up rate,' I added, more quietly.

Patrick looked away, sheepish.

'He's a lady's man, that's all. Wife and kids safely tucked up at home whilst he's off gallivanting round the country, playing the hero.'

'Really?'

'Yes, really,' he said, sounding every bit as irritated as I had been when he was doubting me. His charm hadn't felt exactly flirtatious to me – the nature of his manipulation seemed like something different and more dangerous.

'Patrick.' I reached across the sticky table, took his hand. 'You can't possibly think you've got anything to worry about?'

'No, obviously.' He paused, his jaw rigid. My feelings were like a waterfall, tumbling from offended to guilty in a matter of seconds. Was he sensing that something was off, but pointing his finger in the wrong direction? Not that there was a right direction: this was why I couldn't afford any more contact with Jim, however worried I was about Lysette's secrets. 'It's just – when we met . . . you were with someone.'

'But Marcus was all wrong for me.' Now Patrick looked almost hurt on my ex's behalf. He was evidence-gathering, hearing brutality where there was none. 'I mean, he was a lovely guy, but it was my Daddy complex.' Marcus had been older than me, seductive but distant. It suited me at the time. 'It was nothing like us. And I wasn't engaged . . .'

I looked down at the tiny, sparkly diamond on my finger, using it as an anchor. I plopped my left hand on top of his, held his gaze. Rita was bearing down on us now, her tray laden with plates.

'Cod,' she said, making it sound like a swear word, 'and here's the steak for you, sir.'

'Looks delicious,' said Patrick, beaming at her. I smiled too, poking an exploratory fork into the broccoli.

'Enjoy,' she said, as Patrick withdrew his left hand to grab for his cutlery.

'I don't want you to feel like that,' I persisted. 'If you want me to come straight home, I'll come home.'

'No, darling,' said Patrick, a large rectangle of steak impaled on his fork, speeding towards his mouth. Patrick tended to eat with the pace and enthusiasm of a starving border collie. 'Forget I said anything, I'm being a dick. Besides, it sounds like you're really making a difference here.'

'I'm not sure about that,' I said, looking away.

'You say that, but . . .' Patrick paused. 'Mia, do you think, now you've been talking to people, that the teacher really did murder Sarah?'

I went to answer, then stopped myself.

'That's not what I'm here to do. I'm not Miss Marple. Don't start getting all police-y on me.'

Patrick put a hand up, his brown eyes intense.

'But do you? Because if you think someone else did it, if you have evidence for that . . .'

I looked at him, articulating something that I hadn't even voiced inside up until that point.

'I think that, even if he did, the reasons are way more messed up than anyone's even started to realise.'

*

Afterwards, we lay next to each other in the darkness.

'That was awful,' said Patrick, and I started to giggle.

'The worst ever.'

Patrick had stubbed his toe on the wooden bed frame halfway through, causing a disastrous break in proceedings.

'I lost my virginity in a bunk bed,' he said. 'I should've had some specially tailored moves.' I tilted my face upwards, kissed him.

'You've never told me about that,' I said. 'Who was the lucky minx?'

A flash of Jim and me, all those years ago. The shock of his nakedness. The sharp pain that I'd gritted my teeth through.

'Stacey Barrett. She was in my year at St Christopher's. We were on a geography field trip.'

'It's sounding sexy already,' I said, tracing my index finger down the angular contours of his chest. It's always been good with Patrick. It never feels like a performance with him, in the way it often did with the others – every inch of him is there with me. For me. 'You'll have time to work on those moves; we really ought to try and do it again in the morning.' I giggled again. 'Also sexy.' We were both quiet for a minute.

'It will happen,' said Patrick, his voice low. 'And if it doesn't – we can always get some help.'

'It's easy to say that, but even if we did do that, they don't have a magic wand. I've got so many clients it doesn't work for. All those hormones and injections . . .'

'Maybe you need to slow down a bit, give your body a chance to relax. I've been doing some Googling about it. You've been working your arse off all year . . .'

I felt my body stiffen, withdraw from his. 'Just don't, OK? Do you think I haven't done that, and every single thing I read contradicts the last thing. I love what I do – being bored out of my mind like some Stepford Wife isn't going to get me pregnant. You work all the time.'

Now it was his body that shifted and hardened. 'The case I'm doing right now, it's human trafficking. Trust me, if I didn't spare you the details, you'd know why I'm doing everything in my power to keep these people off the streets.'

I looked at the digital alarm clock, numbers glowing, on the bedside table. 'Let's not argue, OK? It's gone midnight. We should get some sleep.'

'Yeah, I need to leave by 6.30 at the latest,' said Patrick, and I felt a stab of sadness. I miss you already, I thought, but I didn't say it out loud. I lay there in the darkness, my heart pumping.

When my phone beeped, it made me jump. I crawled out of bed.

Hi Mia, this is Joshua. I heard all about today, and
wondered if we could take you up on your kind offer
to talk to Max? All best.

I quickly texted back, telling him I'd call first thing to
arrange a time. Patrick was propped up on one elbow watching me as I knelt on the scratchy carpet, my naked body
hunched over the glowing screen.

'Lysette? I knew it'd be all right.'

'No,' I said, still typing. I was sending a second text by
now, suggesting some potential times: parents are often
push – pull about the idea of someone else having a part to
play, and I wanted to lock it in as fast as I could.

'Billet-doux from Lawrence Krall?'

I put the phone back in my bag.

'No. Max's dad – he wants me to see him as soon as
possible.' I could hear the unattractive note of triumph that
had crept into my voice.

'Good job,' said Patrick, collapsing back down onto the bed.
'You know, if you do think there's more to this, it's Lysette
you should be talking to. She's not an ogre. She loves you.'

It was funny how a ninety-minute train journey had
started to carve out as big a distance between us as a flight to
Alaska might've done. There was so much I hadn't told him,
and now it was too late.

'Yeah, no. I know.' I lay down, awkwardly curling myself
around the plank of his body. 'Goodnight,' I said softly, my
thoughts fizzing and erupting.

'Night,' mumbled Patrick, already slipping into unconsciousness.

I didn't follow him there. I could have counted every one of his inhalations that night, sleep a foreign country. Perhaps I knew. Perhaps I knew what was coming.

CHAPTER SIXTEEN

Max's oversized glasses were teetering on the end of his nose, threatening to fall off, a dog-eared copy of *The Gruffalo* held up like a tent around the bottom half of his face. We were in the reading corner of the school library. The school – the catalyst for so much – was the last place I'd wanted to take the session, but it had been there or the police station, and I didn't think an interview room would be the thing at all.

I'd had a flurry of phone calls once Patrick had made his dawn flit back to London, and Joshua had eventually delivered Max to me mid-morning. Max had grinned at me as he climbed out of Joshua's black estate car, and my heart had melted a little.

'Hi, Max!' I'd said, smiling at Joshua over his head, thinking of how Max had whispered to Woody to confide in his dad. I'd been filled with a sense of shared purpose, of enthusiasm, but Joshua's face didn't reflect any of that. He was wearing a dark suit, his lined face as closed and forbidding as prison gates.

'Thanks for doing this, Mia,' he'd said, his voice flat.

'It's ... well, not a pleasure, but it's a privilege,' I said quietly, taking Max's hand. 'I'll take good care of him.'

'I'm sure,' he'd said, already turning back towards his car. The crowd of photographers had gone in search of better picture opportunities, mercifully missing out on this painful tableau. 'Well, I'll leave you to your session. It might be Lisa who comes and gets him.'

I'd taken Max to the library, asked him to give me a tour of the shelves, but he'd thrown himself down on a shabby green beanbag and hidden behind the book. Had he watched that awkward exchange and decided that trusting me would be some kind of betrayal of his dad?

'Is *The Gruffalo* your favourite book?' I asked. Silence reigned. 'Did you hear me, Max?' I asked gently.

He nodded, then nodded again, which I took to be a yes to both questions. The book stayed in place. The library had a musty kind of smell, the reading corner surrounded by high metal shelves, tucked away. I'd plonked myself down on a small wooden chair which barely contained my woman-sized bottom, and I gratefully slid down onto the carpet. I didn't want to encroach on his space, but nearer felt like it might be more promising.

'We didn't have *The Gruffalo* when I was little,' I said. 'Maybe you could read me some?'

Max swung his head back and forth so hard it could've almost swivelled right round, then proceeded to bury his nose even deeper in the book. I examined his pale profile from this new vantage point; the subtle smattering of freck-les that stretched across the bridge of his nose, his brown hair, which had been cut in a little-boy bowl cut when I first met him at the funeral but had since grown shaggier, the lengths at different levels. My heart squeezed tight in my chest, wondering what Sarah would think of it – if anyone was noticing the tiny details of his life in the brash chaos of grief.

'You didn't have *The Gruffalo*?' he exclaimed, suddenly animated. It was clearly an inconceivable state of affairs. 'My mummy can do all the voices. She does the mouse like *this*!' he said, his voice squeaky and high. 'And the Gruffalo like this,' he said, making his voice suitably gruff. He lowered the book to his knees, waiting for my explanation.

'Sounds like your mummy . . .' I paused a second, weigh-ing up the tiny bridge of a word I needed to pick, 'is very good at telling stories.'

'She can make them up too,' he said, earnestly. 'She makes up the best stories.'

I saw her then – that wild glint she'd had as the children ripped the paper off the parcel, the way she'd made us all clink our Prosecco glasses so hard they could almost have smashed when Lysette had cut Saffron's cake. 'And does your daddy tell you stories?'

'Sort of,' said Max, considering. 'Or he puts one on for me to listen to.'

'Do you like it best when he stays and reads to you?'

Maybe it was something I could pass on to Joshua, an easy way for the two of them to stay in connection.

'Yes, but I like it better when it's my mummy,' he said, his face earnest.

She wasn't just his mother, she was the heroine of his own personal fairy story: he was still holding out desperately for the happy ending that all fairy stories promise.

'It must be very hard that your mummy can't do that any more,' I said.

'Mrs Carter next door said she was sorry I'd lost my mummy,' he said, looking hard at one of the pictures of the mouse. 'But I didn't lose her. I lost my red Toyota car which has two exhaust pipes.'

People don't understand how confusing these twee analogies are for children. 'No, you definitely didn't lose her. It's just a thing that grown-ups say. What do you think happened?'

It's so important for children to tell their own story as they see it, not have adults always imposing an acceptable version of events. I wished I'd had time to have some props sent from London – my sand tray, my dolls. Staging things can be much easier for little children than finding the words. At least he knew I'd been there for his makeshift funeral.

'Mummy was very high up and then she slipped and fell,' he said, eyes turned towards me now, watching my face. 'And then she hit the ground very hard and it made her bleed and die.'

I nodded at him, acknowledging what he'd said, thinking

all the time how random and unfair it must feel, and how much more heartbreaking information was liable to force its way into his life. I'd worked with a number of children who'd had parents commit suicide – I'd witnessed their anger, helped them to believe there was nothing they could've done. The problem was, there was no definitive truth to get to grips with as yet. His small, freckled face was angled up at me, expectant. I could tell that he was proud that he'd told me what had happened with such clarity. Without crying.

'Does it feel unfair that that happened to your mummy?' I said, keeping my focus on him tight. I wanted him to know that I was really listening. 'Does it make you want to shout and scream?'

'Sometimes when you go to hospital, they can make you better,' he said.

'That's right. But they couldn't with your mummy.'

'When I went to the hospital they made me better,' he said, picking up *The Gruffalo* again. I waited to see if he'd say more. A distraction often tells me there's something very important a child's trying to smuggle out. 'The siren goes *nee-na, nee-na* and there is a blue light and everyone gets out of the way because they have to.'

'So did you go to hospital too? A different time?'

'Yes. I was very, very ill but they made me better.'

'What was wrong with you, Max?'

Max threw down *The Gruffalo* almost violently. He jumped up.

'I need a pee pee,' he said, barrelling out of the classroom.

I went after him, wanting to make sure he wasn't just making a break for freedom. He wasn't: he went to the boys', then came back down the corridor, more slowly this time. I resolved to go more gently, ensure I wasn't pushing him. He made a beeline for the beanbag, little shoulders hunching as he sank his way into it.

'What do you like best about *The Gruffalo*, Max?'

Max chose to ignore the question.

'Everyone has to go to hospital. When you're a baby, and you get born, you go to hospital.'

'That's true. Most babies do get born in a hospital. Not every single one.'

He looked up at me – just halfway, like Lady Di charming an interviewer.

'I went there when I was a baby.'

'So you were ill when you were a baby?'

'No!' he said. 'Because you didn't have *The Gruffalo* when *you* were a baby, I am going to read it to you.'

'Thank you, Max, that sounds lovely,' I said.

I stared down at his dark head, dropped low over the ragged pages. I could hear his voice rising and falling with the characters, desperately trying to do Sarah justice. I could feel tears prickling behind my eyeballs, and I forced them away. It's rare I let that kind of unbridled emotion into my work – I need to be the rock, not the sea – but it was hard that day. We both sat there a second.

'Did you like it?' he asked.

'I loved it,' I told him. 'And what I liked best was how

you read it to me. You made the mouse all mousy and the Gruffalo very gruff.'

Max climbed out of the beanbag's embrace and came over to stand close enough to me to touch me.

'Were you scared?' he asked me.

'I wanted the mouse to be OK,' I said. 'I thought he would be. He had lots of things that we call resources. Things inside him he could use to help him, like being brave.'

'Yes, he is brave,' agreed Max, sinking back into the beanbag. He kept his body close to mine.

'But brave doesn't mean having to rely on yourself. Brave can be telling people how you feel and asking them to give you cuddles and talk to you.'

Max considered that.

'Also the mouse is clever,' he said.

'When is he clever?'

'He has to tell fibs, but not because he's naughty. The fibs are clever. They stop the bad things from happening.'

I heard a firm knock on the door. We both looked up: Joshua's square-jawed face was framed in the glass square at the top of it, a perfect headshot. Max looked back at him but didn't immediately get up. I held up my finger, smiled in a way that told Joshua we were nearly finished.

'We're going to have to stop now, Max, but it was lovely spending time with you today.'

He gave a little nod, eyes trained on the worn carpet. I longed to say more, to tell him I'd be here if he wanted to come back, but I couldn't make him a promise just yet.

Instead we both got up, his hand automatically reaching for mine, and went and found his dad.

Joshua and Max said their rather formal-sounding hellos, and then we all walked down the corridor towards the entrance.

'How did it go?' asked Joshua, as Max ran ahead.

'It was good,' I said carefully. 'Do you have time to talk? I know you said Lisa might be collecting him.'

'I felt it was important I did it,' he said stiffly.

'I'm glad she told you what I said last night. I didn't want to seem interfering.'

'Oh no, Lisa didn't tell me,' he said. 'It was Max who brought it up. He was full of it at bedtime. He's been so quiet most nights, just wanting a story played, but it was Mia this and Mia that!'

'Oh,' I said, trying to compute the information. I thought of the way Lisa's car sped off, Kimberley framed in the window.

Joshua was suddenly brisk, his eyes seeking out Max. 'I can't talk now, but I'll ring you at four.'

The tone of it was oddly jarring – it felt more like an order than a request. Max was hopping his way down the hopscotch grid, calling out the numbers to himself. I got the sense that he would always look alone, even in a teeming mass of children.

'Yes, do. I might not have finished my three o'clock, but I'll pick up if I can.'

'Fine,' he said, mind elsewhere already. 'Come on, Max,

we need to get going,' he shouted, striding off towards his car with barely a backwards glance.

*

As I made slow progress back to Lysette's, the muggy day wrapped itself around me like a second skin. I was doing the journey I'd done with Saffron at the start of all of this, in reverse. Now it all looked so different, gnarly and twisted. The last thing I wanted was to lose Lysette to that darkness – Patrick was right, I should sit down and talk to her. If anything happened, if things got worse for her and I hadn't done all I could to protect her, I'd never forgive myself. Was that how she felt about Sarah's death?

I did a strange combination of knocking and key turning, apologetic and familiar all at once.

'Lys!' I called, keeping my voice deliberately warm. 'Honey, I'm home.' Silence. Perhaps she wasn't here. I heard footsteps: here she was, stepping out of the kitchen and into the hallway, her face cold and still. 'I've been thinking about you so much ...' I started, the sparkle in my voice starting to tarnish.

'So have I,' she said, cutting straight across me. 'This isn't working, is it? This isn't like – cosy girl time. This is you doing your *job*.' She spat out the word like it was something poisonous.

I put a hand back to steady myself and hit the banister, which was piled with coats. I could feel the plasticky fabric of Saffron's beloved pink raincoat sticking to my palm.

'You asked me to talk to your friends!' I said, my voice rising with the unfairness of it. 'I would never have agreed to do this if you'd said when I came back from the police station you didn't want me to.'

Lysette's mouth twisted into a rotten flower. 'This isn't me throwing you out, but I think you should stay somewhere else.'

Why do women fight so dirty? Lies and half-truths are so much more toxic than a sucker punch.

'That's fine, but just out of interest, how is that not you throwing me out?' I could feel the blood rushing to my face, a crimson tide. 'Which part of the sentence you just uttered isn't that?'

'You saw Max today, didn't you? That's why you're all perky and pleased with yourself. You cosied up to him yesterday, in my garden, and now he's part of your investigation.'

'I'm not investigating anything!' I snapped. 'I'm here to provide support. And trust me, that child needs some. Whatever else it is you're all worrying about, that's where the fire is!'

'You don't know anything.'

'Too right,' I said. 'You don't *tell* me anything, but I know enough to be really worried about you.' There was a crack in my voice, a gap we could've squeezed through and found a softer place. I saw something flicker in her eyes, took a risk. 'I heard you – I heard a bit of what you were talking about with the girls in the kitchen.'

The second I'd said it, I knew it was a disaster. Her

eyes widened in shock, her skin paling, before she quickly reframed her reaction.

'I can't believe you'd do that – spying on us! What the fuck was wrong with you that night?'

'I'm sorry? What was wrong with me? You were pissed out of your face by the time we left.'

I could hear it, our fifteen-year-old selves creeping into this argument and robbing us of any restraint.

'Kimberley told me what you did.'

My hands were balled up into fists now. 'No, *I* told you what *Kimberley* did.'

'Rifling through her stuff, sneaking around. She said you could barely stand up. She tried to steady you, and you completely freaked out and shoved her. She's upset, Mia.'

I could barely speak through my rage. 'What, and you believe her over me? Your ...' I paused, humiliated by the fact that I had to. 'Your friend you've known for more than twenty years?'

Lysette shrugged. 'Thing is, Mia, you've never been able to handle your drink. You never built up any tolerance.'

It was another crossroads, a chance to turn left. I didn't do it: I simply put my foot down and accelerated. 'The state you were in after Sarah's funeral ...'

Now it was Lysette who looked humiliated: I could tell immediately she'd already had her own dark night of the soul about that. *I hate hurting you*: the words stayed buried deep inside me, no use to anyone there.

She might have had secret words of her own, but the

209

ones that came out were missiles. 'What, your friend Sarah you're so desperate to help?' she hissed. 'Sarah never asked for diagnosis of her son.' Her eyes were like slits. 'HER son.'

'Don't you ... I *know* that. I'm just trying to give him a place where he can express what he's feeling. Surely she would want that?'

Lysette's self-righteous zeal suddenly seemed to drain away, grief flooding into the gap.

'You didn't know her!' she said, tears threatening. 'You don't know what she would've wanted. No one knew her, not really. And now it's such a mess ...'

I should've heard what it was she was saying, the clue she was giving me about how perilous the situation really was, but I was too focused on Max.

'He's hurting so much,' I said softly.

'And one plus one equals two,' she said, her mood taking another handbrake turn. 'I hate to break it to you, but motherhood isn't quite as easy as it looks on the tin.'

It wasn't just the words; it was the pleasure she took in uttering them.

'Thanks for the advice,' I spat, already halfway up the stairs. 'Let's just hope I get the chance to practise.'

I threw everything into my bag, gave the hated lilo a childish kick and slammed the door, with its peeling blue paint, as hard as I could behind me.

Sarah's Diary – April 3rd 2015

He asked me if I thought something had started, and I said I didn't know. It was hard to focus. My head was pounding, and my tongue felt like a piece of stinky old carpet. Staying up till three when the alarm – six years old and full of beans – goes off at seven, is not my idea of fun. Not when you've been lying there, heart racing almost as fast as your brain, trying to work out what's true.

Has something started? He's gone away now, three whole days. I'm trying not to think whether she's gone with him. Trying to scrub the thought out, not give in to my stalker tendencies. I've always been an excellent stalker. Should've been a spy, not a waitress. I should've been a lot of things instead of this – he tells me the same all the time. He's going to find out I lost my job when he gets back. I'll have to make something up. If I tell him the truth he'll think I'm a spoilt little bitch. He'll have that disappointed face, like he wishes I could be the person he can see in the distance, rather than the fucked up one who's right there in his eye-line spoiling the view.

He called me tonight. He said he couldn't help it, had one thing on his mind. I wish I only had one thing on my mind. It's a playground or a jungle in there depending what day it is. It's definitely a jungle today. And in fact, the playground's the biggest jungle of my life. There are predators in there that want to flat out destroy me. No sign of her today. Normally I'd have been pleased, but today – with him away – it just made the snakes worse. They writhe around inside me, invisible to anyone else, waiting to poison me.

That's why I got him off the phone as quick as I could – I couldn't stop thinking about her. Max said he didn't want to go for a drive and neither did Woody, but I told them if we did we could stop for a McDonald's on the way back. Then he put his red coat on over his pyjamas, quick as a flash.

Her lights were on, but that doesn't mean anything. If I'd been on my own, I'd have stayed there, kept scoping it out, but I'm a good mum, or at least I try to be. Even if I let him have a Big Mac after he'd brushed his teeth.

I thought I'd drop dead tonight, the sleep deprivation kicking in hard, but instead I'm sitting up writing this. If he doesn't love me, if he loves her, I don't think I can stand it. I can't lose to her, not after all of this. I need a plan. No, I need something bigger – a strategy, a new way of life.

The truth is, the only way I can survive this is if she doesn't.

CHAPTER SEVENTEEN

Rita's arms were folded across her ample chest. A thick gold necklace lay against her sun-scorched skin, her black neckline scooping low enough to expose the top of her mountainous breasts.

'I thought you said it was small . . .' she said.

It was lunchtime: I could see a few punters casting curious glances in our direction, the visiting media types standing out like sore thumbs. At least it would make it easy to dodge them.

'Well, no, you said that. I mean, it *is* small, but I do need somewhere.' She looked distinctly unimpressed. 'It's cosy. And the pub's so lovely. You really are the heart of the village . . .'

She left me hanging for a few seconds, then uncrossed her arms and gave me a semblance of a smile.

'Fine. But the rate I gave your fiancé was for mid-week. If you're staying over the weekend it'll be another matter.'

'Of course,' I said, through gritted teeth.

She looked at my wheelie case and holdall, which were languishing on the stained carpet.

'Haven't got much anyway, have you?'

I'd already worked out that I'd left my electric toothbrush at Lysette's, and I was sure it would only be the first thing on a long list.

'No. I'm going back to London next week,' I said. 'In fact, how's the Wi–Fi? I'm doing sessions with clients on Skype.'

Rita subtly rolled her kohl–lined eyes.

'I'll find you the key.'

*

I sat down heavily on the doll-sized bed, patting the surface as if it would somehow conjure Patrick up, like a genie from a lamp. I'd already tried him three times, without success. I looked yet again at my stubbornly blank phone screen. I couldn't believe that Lysette hadn't called me to apologise after delivering such a cruel parting shot.

I was hunched over the tiny sink, pushing some toothpaste around my mouth with my finger, when my phone finally rang. I snatched it up too fast to even see the name.

'What are you and Lysette playing at?'

Really? Jim?

'Has the bush telegraph delivered you a message already?'

'You'd be surprised, Mia, we've had telephones for a couple of years now. There's talk of these – computers?'

I sank back onto the bed.

'It's not actually funny,' I said.

'I do know that,' he said, his voice warm and strangely comforting. 'Where are you anyway?'

I paused a second. 'The Black Bull.'

'What, is Rita giving you the stink eye? Hold your nerve, I'll come and take you for lunch.'

'No, don't, I've got loads of stuff to do.'

I realised as I said it that it wasn't strictly true. In London I was continuously busy, continuously moaning about it, but here there were moments of elasticity in my days, time stretching out like a rope unfurling itself.

'Yeah, and you need to eat. I know what you and Lys are like,' he said. 'You're feeling like shit. I'm on my way.'

And with that, he put the phone down. I thought about ringing him back, protesting, but hunger and distress had made me weak.

That was what I told myself, anyway.

*

Jim strode into the pub, scoping out the bar as he did so. He wore expensive-looking jeans, artfully scuffed Converse, a white T-shirt with an unzipped black hoodie flung over the top. It was odd, the way this new Jim was layered over the Jim who'd been my everything – that rangy, self-confident teen with the world at his feet. Sometimes, despite the paunch and the whisper of grey at his temples, they didn't seem so different. I bet he loved all the attention he was inevitably getting from the keen young things, hair in bunches, who ran round after him on set. I was sipping an orange juice and soda in the furthest corner. I jumped up, slightly too grateful for the hug that he enveloped me in. Today had almost broken me.

'Shall we go?' I said, voice low, directly into his ear. Rita's eyes, as bright and sharp as broken glass, were trained on me. I pulled away.

'Let's stay here. The cheeseburger's great. There's no way I'm going for a stale ham sandwich at The Crumpet.'

Two places – that was it. The world of Little Copping felt like it was shrink-wrapped, and I was no more than a tiny, shrunken thing trapped inside.

'OK,' I said, trying to keep the frustration out of my voice. 'Jim, did she call you?'

'Let's just get a drink, OK? Do you want a vodka in that?'

'Of course not,' I said, trying not to imagine the delicious anaesthesia of it. I was seeing one of the teachers in a couple of hours. What was wrong with me?

'Fine. I'm ordering cheeseburgers. I saw the way you scoped out the sausage rolls so I know you've not gone vegan.'

He grinned to himself, headed for the bar. I sat back down, my body unclenching itself as I watched his retreating back. Rita looked positively animated as they chatted, Jim slapping down a £20 note on the bar. How was this life big enough for him? Or was that the point – it allowed him to be a big fish in a small pond and never have to reflect on the larger dreams that had got washed away in the process? He came back, putting a pint down on the table.

'Don't look at me like that,' he said. 'I start shooting at the end of next week. The hours are brutal – I'm not just asking people if *zey dreamed about a phallus*.'

His comedy German accent was quite funny, but unfortunately for him I'd had a sense of humour bypass.

'My job is a huge responsibility,' I snapped. 'I support people through the most devastating things.'

I knew as soon as I said it that it wasn't really him I was snapping at.

'OK, OK,' he said, putting up his palm, that smirk of his still threatening. 'Don't get your knickers in a twist.'

'Sorry,' I said, aware what bad company I was being. I hated the fact that I sort of needed him – I comforted myself with the idea that it was a small need, in perfect proportion to the shrink-wrapped claustrophobia of Little Copping itself. 'I'm just upset. What did she say to you?'

His pause was almost the worst part. For Jim to bother to reflect on how to tell me – to reflect on anything, come to that – it had to be pretty bad. 'She's upset too, Mia. She's not being herself. She'll calm down.'

'Oh what, so it's all my fault? All I was trying to do was comfort a traumatised child. His father certainly seemed to appreciate that.' Did I really know that? I paused, took a sip of my orange juice. 'Perhaps his mother would've done too.'

I'd said it. I'd invoked Saint Sarah, the hallowed friend that Lysette had turned into a deity.

'Yeah, maybe,' said Jim soberly.

'Why maybe?' I said, my voice rising. I saw a couple of heads twitch in our direction and I reined myself in. 'I'm so sick of everyone talking in riddles. What possible reason would there be for her to not want her only child to be allowed a safe place to grieve for her?'

Rita was bearing down on us now, the greasy-looking cheeseburgers wobbling menacingly on our plates.

'I'm sure you're right,' said Jim in a quick undertone, visibly relieved to have got himself off the hook. 'These look dee-licious.'

'Yeah, you're in for a treat!' said Rita. 'Mick's in the kitchen himself today. He's mixed a bit of pork he had in with Alan's beef. Makes them just right.'

Jim took a theatrical bite, and gave her a thumbs-up. 'Compliments to the chef.'

Rita beamed. 'I'm sure he'll be out to say hello.' She looked at me, her smile withering its way off her face. 'Enjoy.'

'Is she your girlfriend or something?' Jim rolled his eyes. 'And who's Alan – the cow?'

'No, he's the butcher. And Rita's just Rita. Tuck in.' His eyes briefly scoped their way down my body. 'You need feeding up.'

I felt a shiver of discomfort, a sense of the discomfort that Patrick would feel if he was a fly on the wall, but I pushed it away. These were special circumstances, and it wasn't as if I was offering him encouragement. Besides, it meant nothing: Jim was Jim, just as Rita was Rita. And I was still Mia; I would never do anything to threaten my relationship. I subtly shifted backwards in my seat.

'When we said goodbye last time, when we'd talked about the' – I made a discreet sniffing motion – 'you implied that there was more to come out.' I paused: would saying this make the situation with Lysette even less recoverable? 'When we went to Kimberley's that night – it was horrible, Jim, it definitely felt like they were hiding something. I think you were right.'

Jim didn't reply, chewing on Alan's beef for longer than was strictly necessary. I felt strangely disappointed: I wanted him to leap on my words, validate me, but he was withdrawn and quiet.

His words were flat. 'Lysette needs to look after herself.'

'Too right,' I said. 'And in answer to your question that day, I don't like Kimberley. I think she's a manipulative bitch. The first thing Lysette should do is get as far away from her as she can.'

I could feel my heart pounding, heat rising again. Jim ignored it, gave a half-smile.

'I really don't think that's going to happen.'

'I thought you were worried about her?' I hissed, increasingly frustrated. I wanted an ally, and I also wanted – no, I needed – someone else to keep watch over Lysette.

'I'd had a drink. I was overexcited, seeing you again after all this time. We had our moment back then, didn't we?'

I ignored him, tried not to let the words puncture any softer, younger part of me. A 'moment' was such an inadequate phrase for what we'd had. I couldn't go there now.

'Jim – what if it's relevant?'

'What do you mean?'

'The drugs. The police are trying to build up a picture of

Sarah's state of mind before she died.' Jim's eyes were tracking me now. 'What if it's relevant?'

His right hand was balled up into a fist.

'Jesus, Mia!' he hissed. 'Just leave it, OK? I know you're angry with Lysette, but are you planning to get her kids put into care?'

'Calm down, OK? Don't be so melodramatic.'

'How's that melodramatic? You're suggesting telling the police my sister has a drug problem.'

It wasn't just the words; it was the strength of his reaction. Jim liked to glide smoothly over the surface of life, his charm keeping him light on his feet. He was rattled.

'A problem? *Has* a problem? Do you think she's still at it, even with Sarah gone?'

I thought back to the way she'd sped off the night before the funeral, a woman on a mission. Could she even have been high at the wake?

But before Jim could reply, the huge TV on the far wall was turned up to an ear-shattering volume. There was Lawrence Krall, in a well-cut suit, standing outside the car park where Sarah had been found.

'This CCTV footage is a significant discovery,' he said, before the screen cut to a grainy scene on a busy street.

There she was: Sarah, walking down the street, laughing, turning to the man next to her. It was Peter. His arm came out, flung itself around her shoulders. They walked a few more steps, and then the picture cut out.

'This proves that Sarah Bryant was with Peter Grieve on

the day of her death,' continued Krall, 'in the immediate vicinity of this car park. Were you here that day? Can you corroborate the police timeline, or contribute any further information as to Sarah Bryant's state of mind?'

I looked at Jim, wanting him to acknowledge the way that Krall had echoed my phrase, but his eyes were trained on the screen. The whole pub was glued to it, a couple of journalists scribbling notes.

'That's it then, isn't it?' said one of them in a tone of grim satisfaction. I'd seen her here the night before, a sharp-eyed girl in her mid twenties who was more striking than pretty. She was slurping a cup of coffee as she scribbled, the sleeve of her suit jacket soaking up the spilled liquid.

Lawrence Krall continued, smoothing his slightly too-long hair back as the wind ruffled it into a peak. 'If you have any information, however small and insignificant it might seem to you, I would ask you to come forward. This investigation needs your help. Thank you.'

The picture cut back to the news studio, a photo of Sarah — a beaming smile on her face — behind the two newscasters. Within a few seconds it had evaporated, replaced by a still of military tanks, and Rita had turned the sound down. Jim took a swig of his lager.

'That proves it then, doesn't it?' he said, his mood visibly improved. 'They needed more proof, and now they've got it.'

'How is that proof?' I said. My eyes kept pulling towards the screen, as if Sarah might reappear there and reveal something different.

'You saw him up there. Your mate Lawrence Krall.'

'My mate Lawrence Krall?'

Jim play-acted pushing his hair backwards, tossed his head.

'Yeah,' he said, a note of challenge in his voice. Men clearly thought Lawrence Krall was irresistible.

'He's not my mate. And he's just doing his job. Building up a picture of Sarah's life, which no one around here seems all that keen to help him do.'

'You've always been like this, Mia,' snapped Jim, face flushed. 'Do you remember what I used to call you – Sister Mia? You're so fucking idealistic. He thinks he's got him bang to rights. They're sewing it up. And you didn't even know Sarah, so I don't know why you've appointed yourself her representative on earth.'

'Lysette doesn't think Peter did it,' I said stubbornly. 'I thought he seemed really gentle when I met him.' For approximately sixty seconds – I didn't add that crucial detail. 'And if he didn't, then someone else did.'

'Yeah, well. Sarah could make fucking Bambi lose his shit – she was a game player.'

'What do you mean?'

He ignored me. 'And Lysette's on another planet. I've got a six-month-old at home who makes more sense than she does. And for someone who's not here to investigate – who's *just here to provide support* – you seem to have a lot of opinions.'

He was being hateful, but he had a point. Why was I worrying away at this, rather than simply standing back and watching it unfold?

'Fine,' I said, feeling myself deflate. I should just get through the rest of my time here and gratefully and gracefully slip back into my own life, that standby little black dress that you forget to appreciate until the Christmas party. 'Do you want another drink?'

'When have you ever known me say no to a second drink?' he said, his twinkle restored, his words implying that the twenty-year gap in our acquaintance had been twenty minutes. I thought of his wife with that six-month-old he was holding up like a talisman; wondered how thrilled I'd be if I were her, but I still made my way to the bar.

I'd been so focused on our argument that I'd unplugged myself from the rest of the room. It was crackling, voices raised, everyone animated. I didn't want to be that sanctimonious prig that Jim had painted, but the excitement of it was repellent to me, perhaps because the image of Max – his small body hunched over his battered book – was still so fresh in my mind.

'Same again?' said Rita.

'Exactly. You can put them on my room.'

'Oh. Are you staying here too?' It was the journalist, who'd appeared as if by magic right next to me. She put out a hand, cuff still soggy with coffee. 'I'm April.'

She was smiling a little too widely, exposing the kind of gently yellowed teeth that told me that coffee and cigarettes were a mainstay of her job. Her handshake vibrated with the pulsing energy that was electrifying the room, her dark eyes fixed on me. I couldn't help thinking the question was a contrivance: she knew exactly who I was.

'Mia. Are you a journalist by any chance?'

'I am,' she said, naming her red top proudly. She carried herself with a breezy confidence that I could never have achieved at that age. 'I've been here a whole week!' she added, a sly, conspiratorial smile on her face which she was naive enough to think that Rita would miss.

'That'll be £3.10,' Rita told me, slamming the glasses down as if it was me being snide. 'But it's on your room.'

'Thanks so much,' I said. I picked them up, but April wasn't going to let me get away that easily.

'So what brings you here?' she said, subtly barring my way.

'Oh, um, my friend lives here. I came to see her.'

'And she's a psycho ... psycho thing,' interjected Rita helpfully.

'How fascinating!' said April. 'If I get the drinks in tonight, will you tell me all about it?'

'I'm happy to tell you about the job, but what people tell me is obviously confidential.'

'Of course – you must be seeing people here. I mean, that footage today's a real game changer, but I guess you're already one step ahead of the rest of us.'

She kept searching my face. Rita was cleaning glasses now, but I sensed she was listening to every word.

'It certainly looks bad for him, but it doesn't confirm anything.'

'Why do you say that?' she asked, the words tumbling fast from her lipsticked mouth.

I stepped sideways, desperate to end the conversation.

'Just – innocent until proven guilty. I thought that was the whole point of living in a civilised society.'

Jim was making a thirsty motion at me from across the bar, lifting his empty glass. God, if he could have heard my pontifications on the nature of justice he'd have had a field day.

'Right,' said April, cocking her head. 'It's just – there aren't any other suspects, are there?'

'Your guess is as good as mine,' I said.

'It's unlucky for him, isn't it?' she said, feigning concern. 'Not being here to defend himself?'

'Quite,' I said, pushing past her now: she'd lost the right to courtesy with her wheedling questions. 'Nice to meet you, April.'

'Oh, you too!' she said. 'See you later!'

Not if I see you first, I thought childishly, then remembered that the alternative was sitting in my monastic cell watching *Scandal* on my iPad. I didn't need to be burning any more bridges.

I deposited the drinks, and sat down. I played with a cold chip on my plate.

'You're just Little Miss Popular, aren't you? Who's that?'

'She's called April. She's a tabloid hack. And can you *stop* bitching at me?'

He must've heard the catch in my voice. He extended a hand across the table, but I tucked mine into my lap.

'Must run in the family,' he said. 'Sorry.' He held my gaze. 'And for all Lysette's bitching, she is really grateful you're here.'

'Maybe she was. She isn't any more.'

'Just – look, you're a very kind person. You're ridiculously clever, too, we've always known that. Just bring it down a bit. Let It Be, as John Lennon would say. No, it was Paul McCartney, wasn't it?'

'OK,' I said, my voice small.

'It is really nice to see you again, even like this.'

'Yeah, you too,' I said. The problem was, part of me meant it.

'And I'm sorry, Mia. That's what I really wanted to say. I'm really sorry for how I behaved back then. I was just a stupid boy.'

I looked at him a second too long – the white capital letters that stretched across his black hoodie, those clichéd, Converse-clad feet. He was a whole new breed of boy: a man-boy. And yet, something still tugged at me. A desire to reach back into the past and right it.

'Me too,' I said, looking away. 'What my dad did to you was horrific.'

'Fathers and daughters, man.' He didn't want to connect to it, I could tell, that was why he'd lapsed into the syntax of a Beat poet. 'I'd lock mine in a nunnery if I could. Can I have one of your chips?'

We chit-chatted a few minutes, me crowbarring in my wedding plans, the lightness of it a relief after the strange intensity of what had gone before.

'Shit, I should go,' he suddenly said, jumping up.

'So should I,' I said, childishly irritated that I hadn't said it first. 'I'm seeing a new one – Janey Sims? Do you know her?'

'Mousy,' pronounced Jim.

'If you see Lysette . . .' I couldn't bring myself to send an apology. 'She'll be feeling terrible, seeing Sarah like that. People gossiping.' I paused. 'I do care. If she needed a gun, I'd still get it for her.'

It was a stupid expression of ours, a way of measuring our friendship. I shivered: it didn't seem so funny any more.

'What are you two like?!' said Jim, grinning at me. 'She knows that. It'll be OK.'

I wondered if this Janey would have heard about the CCTV. Of course she would have done. Like Lisa had said, news travelled fast. We walked outside, me trying not to feel the eyes that were boring into my back like sniper's bullets.

'Do you want a lift to the school?' said Jim, as we approached his muddy estate car.

'Definitely not,' I said, too quickly. He smirked, enjoying the implied intrigue, which was not what I'd intended at all. 'Well, bye,' I said, giving him a quick, awkward hug.

'Bye, Mia,' he said, pulling me back into it. Too much of him was in that hug. Betrayals can be big or small, spoken or unspoken: sometimes it's the silent ones that prove to be the most devastating of all. 'I'll see you soon. You're not alone, trust me.'

Alone would turn out to be underrated.

CHAPTER EIGHTEEN

The news crews were back. A man in a nasty stripy tie was preparing to do his piece to camera. He was stabbing his finger towards the school as if it was the building's fault, his 'sad face' perfectly arranged. 'Can we do that again?' he asked, as I swerved my way past them. 'Can you comment on the latest developments?' shouted someone, but I kept my head down, hoped I was still anonymous, and pushed my way through the black metal doors that had swallowed up Peter and Saffron two short weeks ago.

Today was the first time I'd be using the staff room for a session. I always ensure I'm there in the room before my clients, but the hubbub outside the school had held me up, and I was a couple of minutes late. I needn't have worried: there was no sign of Janey Sims, just a ring of empty chairs, the fabric covers worn and tatty, arranged around a low coffee table, its surface punctuated by heat rings. There was a plastic kettle in the corner, a jar of instant coffee with a label on it and a jumble of mugs. 'Friendly reminder to put your 50p in the tin on Fridays!' the label said, in thick black marker. I felt sad for them as I read it: that petty concern would seem like a lost paradise when they got back after the so-called holidays. I filled the kettle from a half-empty bottle of water that stood nearby, hoping that it hadn't been sitting there for weeks. I didn't want tea – or their precious instant coffee – I just wanted something to distract myself from the strange eeriness of being alone here.

The door swung open behind me. I turned, a smile on my face, then stopped in my tracks. It was Kimberley. Her blonde hair was teased up in the same way it had been on the day of the funeral: it made the smooth, angular planes of her face, her swan-like neck, even more pronounced than usual. The up-do contrasted with the studied casualness of the embroidered peasant blouse she was wearing, legs like brittle twigs in her predictably skinny jeans.

'Hi!' I said, trying to control the rage that was threatening to erupt. 'I've actually got a session I'm doing in here, so . . .'

'Surprise!' said Kimberley, pointing at herself with manicured hands.

'No, it's Janey Sims,' I said, refusing to compute the full horror just yet.

'Janey couldn't . . . she's very upset about what came out today. There's footage, Peter and Sarah—'

'I know, I've seen it,' I said, interrupting her.

'She's Daniel's teacher, my older boy. All those vile journalists outside were too much for her. She was crying outside reception class, she could barely get her words out. I called her a cab and said I'd come and tell you, but then I thought ... we've been trying to do this for ages, haven't we?'

I looked directly at her, searching her perfect face for any acknowledgement of what had happened between us. She was a crime scene with nothing left to see, a seamless government cover-up – there was no trace of any of it.

'Even if it was appropriate, you'd need to formally book,' I said, icily professional. 'And it's frankly too complicated now we've got to know each other socially.' A memory like a Polaroid: her face, almost feral, as she advanced on me with the heavy gold tube. I cringed inside. 'Boundaries are a key part of the work.'

'So were you and Helena very *boundaried* when you went rambling in the woods?' she said, matching me for ice.

'Things have shifted since then. What happened at your house ...'

Her eyes flashed a barely perceptible warning, before a wide smile arrived. She waved an airy hand. 'That was all a dreadful misunderstanding. I'm sorry if I offended you – if I misread the situation. It was just a bit of a surprise to find you up there like that!'

We watched each other for a long second.

'I just don't think we can ...'

'So let's forget boundaries,' she said, voice suddenly like caramel. She sank down heavily into one of the ratty chairs, fingers gripping the wooden arms tightly, as if she were on a pirate ship, liable to be hurled overboard any second. 'Be my friend instead.' She looked up at me, wide blue eyes brimming with tears. 'I tell you what, Mia, I could really do with a friend today.'

I can see, looking back, that I was in a dangerous trance. The nagging conviction that the darkness spread even further and deeper than was apparent – that it could blot out the friend who at that moment I hated and loved all at once – wouldn't let me quit. I was like a gambler, determined each and every hand would finally deliver my winning streak.

'I've boiled the kettle,' I said, crossing to the corner where it sat.

'Nescafé and UHT milk,' said Kimberley, blotting her eyes with the thick fabric of her gathered sleeve. 'You really know how to treat a girl!'

*

We were sitting opposite each other now, Kimberley's pretty face cupped in her right hand.

'I don't know how you do what you do,' she said. 'All those secrets you must have to carry around.'

Her eyes lingered a little too long. Who was it really, holding on to too many secrets? I didn't think the irony was lost on her.

'I try not to carry them around,' I said. 'I have supervision, where I get to talk it all through with my boss.' The thought gave me a pang of guilt: Roger had been fruitlessly chasing me for a few days now. I couldn't – and shouldn't – avoid him much longer.

'Therapy for therapists? Sounds like heaven. I think I might need to get myself some of that supervision.'

She took a quick sip of her coffee, eyes darting out of the window. She was gambling too – I just hadn't yet discovered what game she was playing.

'What do you mean? Does it feel like bog-standard therapy wouldn't touch the sides?'

Kimberley gave a mirthless laugh. 'You could say that.' Her eyes met mine. 'Seeing that footage today – I mean there's a certain relief to knowing, but still, seeing her so close to death . . .' Her mouth formed a suitably shocked round, a pale hand laid across her heart. 'Although far worse for Lysette, I'm sure.'

Her gaze rested on me a second too long. News had travelled, I was sure of it. I felt myself drawing up straighter in my chair, my voice honeyed and professional.

'I don't think it's ever useful to invalidate our experience by playing the comparison game with painful emotions. What did it make *you* feel, seeing it?'

'It sounds silly, I'm sure, but it reminded me of the Peter I thought I knew.' Just Peter now – Sarah had already been expunged from her narrative. 'The way he sort of loped when he walked, his arms swinging. A bit like the orangutan in *The Jungle Book*.' The smile she gave at the memory was pure sunlight, which only served to demonstrate how many of them were like winter. She meant it.

'I did like him very much, and Lucas adored having him as his teacher. That's why . . .' She ground to a halt. I let the silence linger.

'Why?' I asked eventually.

'Why I didn't take it further.' She looked at me. 'You're no dummy, Mia, we know that. I'm sure you're aware of what happened.'

I nodded. 'I know that there was a bit of an issue between you.'

'That's putting it mildly.' She sighed. 'He was young. It was puppy love that had got out of hand. He didn't need to lose his career for it.' She gave another mirthless laugh. 'And it did get very out of hand.'

I took a sip of instant coffee – there's power in the pause. 'Out of hand, how?'

'He was obsessed with me,' she said, increasingly animated. 'I don't know *why*. I'm – I was – fifteen years older than him. I've got a mum tum.' She patted her taut stomach. 'But it didn't seem to matter to him.'

'What, so texts? Calls?'

'All of that. He even came to the house. We had to get Ian involved. We had no choice.'

'You and Nigel?'

'Yes. I mean – imagine if it had got into the press.' She gave a delicate little shudder. 'It doesn't bear thinking about.'

'Is it a lot of pressure, being a politician's wife?'

'Oh yes!' she said unconvincingly. 'I hate being on show, it's so not me, and Nigel's away such a lot. Although he was

233

there – that night. I have to go to the UN with him, and he has to go to the St Augustine's quiz night! He gets a pretty raw deal, all in all.'

The blurriness was starting to make me disorientated. Here we were, back where Jim had taken me, at the quiz night. I didn't want to be the interfering bitch that Lysette had accused me of being, and yet it was hard not to keep probing.

'Kimberley, I'm aware that none of this is my business . . .'

My words barely registered. Her hands flung themselves upwards, her cheeks as flushed as a feverish child's.

'Nigel was actually chairing it, I think that's what set Peter off.' I'd seen Nigel on *Newsnight* recently giving forth on 'economic migrants', batting away the other guests and their opinions like they were midges that he'd been brought on to swat. I was sure that the chance to chair anything – even a rural quiz night – would've made him giddy with joy. 'It was unfortunate – we both went to the loo at the same time. Coming face to face with me like that, he just – he lost it. He was shouting, crying.' She angled her face, held my gaze. 'You saw the state of him at the funeral: he was a very fragile person. Ian had to manhandle him out.'

'Was the aftermath very difficult?'

Her voice was soaked with emotion. 'You have to try to be compassionate. It's something Nigel's work – the things he sees – has really taught me.' Her eyes locked with mine: flirtation seemed as natural to her – as vital – as breathing was to us mere mortals. 'But you've pretty much got a degree in compassion, haven't you?'

'Yeah, in a way, but ...' I knew I was probing too much. The real story felt tantalisingly close, as if all I needed to do was grab hold of a loose thread and it would unravel before my eyes. 'It doesn't make me immune to emotion.' I tracked her with my eyes. 'Presumably you'd told him to back off by then? To have that happen in front of the whole village. For it to be so public ...'

Rage mangled her features, made her momentarily ugly. Her voice shook. 'He didn't have to behave like that.'

My skin felt cold suddenly, chilled by the venom in her voice. 'But you got through it?'

She'd regained control over herself by now. 'We did. Nigel's a very special man. I'm extremely fortunate.'

Her words sounded more like a public service announcement than a declaration of love.

'So do you think the same thing happened with Sarah?' Kimberley's expression invited me to carry on. 'He got obsessed, and this time it escalated even further?'

My words suddenly brought me up short. If that was the case – if that was what she thought – could she be wrestling her own survivor guilt? The suspicion that she'd left a killer in their midst? I needed to be more generous.

Kimberley sat up now, ramrod straight. 'I didn't see it with Sarah,' she said. 'They were a similar age. They were chums, you know?' She shrugged. 'But he was still in a tremendous amount of pain about what had happened, so ...'

'So you don't think that he killed her?' I said, my voice gentle.

235

'There's no other explanation.'

'Or at least, no one's found another explanation yet,' I said.

'And it did turn out there was a similar incident at his previous school. That's partly why I didn't want to make an official complaint. He'd never have been allowed to teach again.'

He kept sliding back into my memory, the automatic way he dropped to his knees to find Saffron. That Peter kept defying this Peter, refusing to slot neatly behind him in the deck.

'But you still don't think he could've been harassing Sarah? Or even – I know she was married, but – we can all be tempted.'

Kimberley arched her immaculately threaded eyebrows, smirked. 'Can we indeed?'

Did she know? Had someone spotted Jim and me having lunch in the pub?

'You know what I mean,' I said, prickling with discomfort. I'd done nothing wrong and sinned beyond measure, all at once. Nothing in Little Copping submitted itself to a simple explanation.

'If Sarah had got involved with him, I'm sure it was a momentary weakness.' There was poison in her words. 'Trust me, she wasn't exactly backward at coming forward.'

'But don't you think that everyone has secrets?' Max flitted across my consciousness, his shoulders held high at his ears, his book a protective tent. 'Could it be that nobody knew how far it had gone?'

'I think *you* think that because of the job you do,' she said.

'Whereas your job's about getting it all out there, forcing people to listen to you.'

We contemplated each other for a long second. My brief rush of compassion had all but evaporated.

'Sarah was a hedonist,' she said. 'She hated any kind of rules. Like Lysette said at the funeral, she'd run red lights on purpose.' She smiled coldly. 'But she never lost her licence.'

'So she can't have been that bad.'

'It's a metaphor. She thought rules didn't apply to her. That was why Max was late every single day. She got a formal warning.'

'So she was scatty?'

'It wasn't scattiness,' she said, her words crossing mine in her haste to get them out. 'It was a statement of intent.'

It's our own shadows, the parts of ourselves we abhor, that we hate the most in others. I thought again of her advancing on me, lipstick held in her ring-decked left hand. It didn't seem like she was such a fan of rules either.

'It sounds like it annoyed you,' I said.

'I just think that these things have consequences. It's easy to forget that when ...' She stopped herself. 'She used her phone at the quiz night. It made a nonsense of it.'

I nodded sagely: the FBI's most wanted list had clearly found its newest target. No – this was a metaphor too.

'But did it go further than Googling number one hits of the '80s?'

Was it the drugs she was edging towards?

'You'd have to ask her, only she's not here to ask.' She paused. 'Nor's Peter,' she added, more softly.

'No.'

Her sly smile was back. 'Lysette was the one who knew her best, of course'. She paused, cocked her head. 'I think she probably just needs some space.'

'I beg to differ,' I said, aware of the pomposity that was overtaking me again. I couldn't let her see how much it hurt. 'I think she needs holding and support. Otherwise all the questions about Sarah's death will drive her even more mad.'

'Do you think she's mad?' asked Kimberley, voice gossamer-light.

'No, not at all,' I said hastily. The thing was, she did seem in a state akin to madness, but Jim's description of her hoovering up drugs on a teatime playdate made me frightened that it was a madness born out of more than grief.

'The questions seem to be getting cleared up. Peter was in a dangerous state. Sarah got too close.' She rattled out the explanation like a shopping list. 'And as for Lysette . . . you seeing Max – perhaps that was a bridge too far, with Sarah being so precious to her.'

She was tracing an invisible triangle in the space between us: I tried not to let the three sharp points skewer me.

I was stiff. 'I know how close they were.'

'But you haven't been here so much, have you? I mean, I can't believe we've never met before now, considering how long you girls have known each other.' She smiled, as if it must be some kind of collective fantasy we were peddling.

'It's hard to describe it. They felt more like sisters – no – like twins, than they did friends. None of us got a look-in either.'

I felt it this time, a deep stab in the solar plexus. 'I'm glad they had that,' I said. 'And yes, considering Lysette and I grew up together – it *is* weird we didn't meet sooner.'

Kimberley bit her smile back. My pathetic defence of our friendship had done nothing but confirm for her that her attack had hit the target.

'Just, as your friend, I'd say that if you take a step back, she'll take a step forward. I've got an instinct for these things.' She giggled. 'Sometimes I think I'd make a good therapist myself.' People tell me what a great therapist they'd make with tiresome regularity, as if it's a child's game of doctors and nurses and it's just a question of taking your turn with the plastic stethoscope.

'I should get going,' I said. I paused, blood pounding in my temples. 'For the record, I think Max benefited from us having a session together. It seems to me that he's carrying a lot.'

Perhaps she'd pass that on to Lisa, encourage the idea. Kimberley gave a half-laugh.

'Oh, I'm sure! Max has always been such a creative little boy. He'll have loved the attention. Did he tell you stories?'

'Well, we talked about *The Gruffalo*.'

Kimberley nodded, almost as if she already knew, had been humouring me.

'Stories – stories and storytelling are a bit of a speciality with him.' She glanced away, voice softer. 'Sarah too.'

'He's a lovely child,' I said. The fight stirred back up in me. 'Your two seem lovely too.'

'Oh they are!' she said, puffing up with pride. 'Little terrors.'

I picked my words carefully. 'How's your au pair getting on with them? I gather she's new.'

Her jaw clenched, almost imperceptibly. 'Did *she* tell you that?'

I kept it throwaway. 'Ooh, I can't remember who said it.'

There it was: a split second flash of the molten rage she'd had when she talked about Peter at the quiz night. She damped it down, picked her words. 'It's a wonderful opportunity for the girls, but it's hard work! We do rather get through them.'

It was almost like she was talking about hoover bags or mop heads, not actual people.

'She seems great. She had it all under control the other night.'

'She is,' she said, hand shooting down to the floor to grab her bag. 'You know, I really must go and snatch an hour with the boys.' She motioned to her sculpted hair. 'We've got a do in London tonight, and time with them is so precious to me.'

'OK then.'

'You're seeing Ian later, aren't you?'

I was starting to feel like she'd embedded a camera between the pages of my diary.

'I am,' I said.

She reached a sudden hand across the coffee table, placed

it on top of my free one. I fought the urge to throw it off.

'Lucky him. I'm so glad we got to squeeze this in. It's really helped.' She gave a little shake of her upper body. 'Helped get some of the trauma of the last few months off my shoulders. Hopefully we'll all be able to start putting it behind us now.'

The pressure of her hand was spreading a sickly warmth through my body.

'I don't think I really did anything.'

'No,' she said, withdrawing her hand so slowly that it bordered on a caress, the pads of her fingers trawling the back of mine. 'You're so easy to connect to. I understand why Lysette adores you so much. And she *does* adore you. Once you're safely back in London I'm sure it'll all blow over.'

Her eyes met mine for a final time, something like a challenge or a warning contained in them. I kept my face neutral.

'Well, if I did help, I'm glad.'

'I *was* frightened of him,' she said, uncoiling her lithe body in one swift movement so she was suddenly standing over me. She pulled on her coat, made for the door, her words thrown over her shoulder. 'Unlike certain other things, there's absolutely no doubt in my mind about that.'

Sarah's Diary – April 29th 2015

Him being away for all those days in a row – it's dangerous when I have too much time to stew. I shouldn't have done it. I shouldn't have come out and asked him about her. It was like some kind of disgusting illness – I couldn't help it pouring out of me. That's what he thought, I knew it was. That I was disgusting.

He was very quiet. Cold and silent like an iceberg you might just sail right into and drown. He told me not to be so stupid. Stupid's a funny old word – it can sound like a term of endearment or a punch in the face. He knew full well it was a right hook – he's many things, but he's definitely not stupid. I burst into tears, ran out of the room. 'I can't help the fact you're so highly strung,' he shouted, like his words coming after me were enough to mean he was a nice person. I lay there and sobbed. I called Lysette before I was thinking straight, but of course I couldn't tell her about him. Made something up on the fly, an attack of my famous PMT, and stuffed myself with chocolate like it was true. It did make me feel better, in a sick kind of a way. Most things that make me feel better seem to come with that kind of kicker.

I bet he doesn't talk to her like that. He wouldn't dare. She walks around this village like she owns it, like I'm some kind of fucking peasant. Now I've got a bit more cash I've been upping my game — I clocked her looking at my arse at pick-up on Thursday when she thought I couldn't see her. If I didn't know better, I'd have thought she had a lezzie crush, but all she was doing was calculating how much my silky red maxi dress — dry clean only, naturally — had cost me. It's got that fake boho thing going on where it looks casual and costs a fucking fortune — it's the kind of shopping you learn from living in a perfect shithole like this one. Thank God for Lysette, she gets it. I burnt the tags, couldn't risk the bin, another lecture on my irresponsibility. He's clever, we know that, he finds things. I used to think it was because he cared, but now I wonder if it's the polar fucking opposite.

Later, when he tried to tell me he loved me again, I didn't pour cold water on it. I let it burn even though I knew I shouldn't. I know how he feels — it's the kind of fire that could be fatal — but it's so long since I've felt warm to my bones.

CHAPTER NINETEEN

I held the tiny screen high above my head. It seemed like the left-hand corner, near the sink, was where the signal was strongest. Although strongest was relative – Roger had frozen again, his blue eyes bulging, his mouth wide. The screen went blank, and then started to ring.

'What I was trying to say,' said Roger, without pausing for breath, 'is that you may simply be picking up on the gener-alised anxiety in the community.' God, the man was like a talking textbook. 'Your feeling of anxiety doesn't automat-ically mean that there are flaws in your work.'

I leaned back against the thin MDF wardrobe door. My wheelie case was splayed open on the other side of the room: clothes erupted out of it like entrails, a wild animal shot dead on the savannah. I really needed to unpack.

'It's just so hard for me to keep my boundaries. I'm trying to remember I'm just here for support, but because of . . .' Even the prospect of saying her name made me choke up. 'Of my friend being here, I know more than I should. And I can't help joining the dots – trying to anyway.'

I was feeling guilty about my verbal jousting with Kimberley earlier that day. I knew I'd overstepped the mark. Roger was in his office, cocooned in the soft, expensive grey armchair he'd had winched up through his office window when he joined the practice. He leaned forward.

'And now she's asked you to leave. It does sound like a very extreme reaction, when it was she who invited you there.'

'I know,' I said, swallowing down the lump in my throat. I looked away from the screen, discreetly wiped my eyes.

'And I notice that you keep alluding to what you're unearthing, in a number of different ways. Do you think you're approaching things that are relevant to the police investigation?' His eyes were bright with curiosity. 'Because if you are, it's of vital importance that you share them.'

So much easier said than done. And why was I such a Pollyanna anyway? Drugs weren't my thing, but perhaps a few lines of coke on a night out – or even on a playdate – was nothing to write home about. The words didn't ring true, even internally. I should have pushed it more with Lysette whilst I was still in her orbit.

'Of course,' I said, calculating silently that we only had eleven minutes left.

'Let's get more specific,' said Roger firmly, who'd clearly made the same calculation. 'What are these dots that you're joining?'

I chided myself. I should try and do this properly. There was a point to supervision. I needed to find that profession-alism I so smugly prided myself on.

'It's the way people talk about Sarah – it's like they don't finish their sentences. They talk in riddles, like she was up to all sorts but they can't talk about it.'

'Well, even before that CCTV footage emerged, it looked pretty likely they'd been having an affair.'

I'd noticed this already on our call: Roger was following every fact emerging in the press with the obsessive zeal of a teenage Justin Bieber fan with a Google alert.

'It's weird, though – if they were, none of her friends seemed to know about it. Not even Lysette. And Peter – he seemed so gentle to me. So broken.'

'But he did have a track record, didn't he?' pointed out Roger.

'Yes, I know,' I said, trying, and failing, not be irritated by him. It wasn't his fault – all I had was a sense of unease and a footnote that I couldn't tell him about. Or could I? I didn't have to mention Lysette. 'I think she was a bit of a party girl, if you know what I mean.'

'Meaning?'

'Maybe she took drugs?' I regretted it as soon as the words were out of my mouth. 'And when I saw her little boy today, he seemed like he was holding on to a lot of unspoken anxieties. He kept talking about fibbing. It may just be a mechanism for dealing with the grief . . .'

'Talk me through it.'

I grabbed my notes, but the bare facts didn't give me much to hang my feeling of unease on. All I seemed to be doing was recounting the plot of *The Gruffalo*, without the funny voices to pep it up.

'Hmm,' said Roger. 'Well, I'd certainly check with his father about his medical records. But the fibbing – didn't you say that Nigel Farthing's wife mentioned he was prone to making things up?'

'Yes, but ... I trust Max more than I trust her,' I said. Roger was grainy on the tiny screen, studying my flushed face. I just had to hope it wouldn't freeze on my flared nostrils. I cooled myself. 'She's very much a politician's wife. My sense is she knows how to spin.'

'And the idea that Sarah was taking drugs, did that come from her?'

'Not exactly.'

'So where did you get that from?'

'My best friend's brother who, full disclosure, I had a relationship with twenty years ago.' My skin felt prickly with humiliation. 'This is what I mean, Roger. I'm too close. It's definitely time for me to come home.'

Roger steepled his long fingers under his chin, exactly as he had when we'd met in his office. He ruminated.

'To the contrary, it sounds like you're doing excellent work. And your experience from a couple of years ago gives you a unique insight into the stress that ordinary folk are under when they find themselves in the heart of a police investigation.'

Ordinary folk?

'Thank you,' I said.

'I'm afraid I'm going to need to cut this short – I'm actually giving a lecture this evening – but it wouldn't be appropriate for us to leave it here.' He stood up. I could see him crossing to his walnut desk, opening a leather-bound diary. 'Ha, success!' he said, jerking his hypothetically handsome face upwards to look at the screen. 'With some manageable juggling, I should be able to make it down to see you on Friday morning.'

Oh no.

'That's so kind, but there's really no need. I'm very happy to work on Skype.'

'No, no,' he said, steel in his tone. 'I'm here to support you. And as you know, I've got extensive experience with PTSD. I think the combination of our skills and experience could prove to be quite unique. I said the very same thing to Lawrence Krall, who, I should add, was extremely complimentary about you.'

No wonder he'd been trying so hard to get hold of me these last few days. It would have been nice for him to mention the fact he was having a sidebar with the Chief Inspector at the top of the call, rather than in its dying minutes. All I could do was thank him, and promise to meet him off the train.

*

I don't believe in using booze to take the edge off, but in that particular moment I needed a drink. Besides, there had to be some advantage to living in a pub and it certainly wasn't my palatial quarters. I'd tried Patrick twice, without success. Gin was the only solution left to me.

It was nearly eight by now, and the bar was humming and busy, diners and drinkers mixed up together, jostling for space. April was right at the front of the crush for drinks, smiling fruitlessly at Rita. I skulked at the back of the crowd, but her keen eyes quickly met mine and it was hard to say no to her offer to include me in the round. It was still quite a wait: Rita had hordes of locals to serve before she'd so much as acknowledge her.

'Here you go!' April said eventually, putting a tall, slippery glass into my hand. She chinked hers against it. 'Cheers. I don't know about you, but this drink couldn't come too soon!'

'I know what you mean,' I admitted.

We were still standing in the midst of the crush.

'Come and join me,' she said. 'I've got a table.'

'Thanks, but I'm just going to have this and then go and get on with some work.'

'Have you eaten?' she asked, already heading for the table.

'No, but . . .'

That was how we ended up with two plates of steak and chips and a bottle of red, all squashed together on a tiny table that was worryingly close to the men's loos. April's make-up was pristine, her red mouth leaving a lipstick kiss on her brimming wine glass. I took the reapplication as a warning: these were still her working hours. To be fair, you wouldn't have known it from the stream of girlie chat that was pouring forth now we were a glass and a half down.

'He works all the time, Mia. I mean, like, all the time!' We'd established that her boyfriend was a camera man, prone to shooting in war zones. 'And it's not like I'm sitting around painting my nails. It's hard. What does your boyfriend do?'

'He's a lawyer.'

'What kind of lawyer?' she asked. April never seemed to waste time on breathing in.

'He works with the police.'

I was keeping my sentences clipped, trying to ensure that gin plus wine didn't equal a loose tongue.

'The exciting kind! Is that how you met? Are criminal cases your thing?'

'No, not at all,' I said. 'Mainly I just ask stressed-out bankers what they dreamt last night.'

If anyone else had trivialised the work I do the way I just had, I'd have slapped them. I just didn't want to start swapping confidences.

'So all of this,' her hands flapped around like frantic birds, 'is a real departure for you. You're helping officially, right?'

'Yes, I am. I've got a little bit of experience with . . . with a criminal case.' I didn't want her researching me, if she hadn't already. I prodded my steak. 'It sounds like you need to carve out some proper time to spend with Michael. If you don't, it'll be hard to know, won't it? If it's a lack of it, or that you're not right together.'

Proper time. Me and Patrick needed to book ourselves some proper time to spend together as soon as I got back. I glanced down at my phone: the screen was still blank. The distance between us felt way more gaping than a mere sixty miles.

'Yeah, you're right.'

'Mia?' said a familiar voice from above me. There was Joshua.

'Hi,' I said, getting to my feet. Part of me wanted to physically reach out, to make a gesture that would express something about what we'd all seen today, but I knew how inappropriate it would be. He was wearing a fleece, his hair more dishevelled than usual – he was a little bit cracked. 'How are you?'

'I'm doing OK,' he said. I hadn't really intended it as a question, more an expression of sympathy. April's round face was rolled upwards like an inquisitive moon. I willed him to move away, wondering if I should introduce them to make the danger clear, but too embarrassed to do so. 'Thank you for this morning. I'd say Max is your number one fan.'

There was no animation in his voice, it was like grey concrete.

'I'm his!' I said. Understandably he hadn't made his promised phone call. 'Let's catch up on it tomorrow.'

'Absolutely. Anyway ...' he said, discreetly pointing towards the door of the Gents.

As I sat down, I saw Lisa on the other side of the pub, ensconced in the same booth that Jim and I had commandeered earlier. She gave me a brisk wave.

'That's his ex-wife, isn't it?' hissed April, still staring. Kyle, Lisa's husband, was returning from the bar, three drinks mashed together between his large hands, a wide grin on his face. He was stocky and bald, a checked shirt tight across his barrel chest. I unconsciously looked between him and the door of the Gents – he seemed so utterly different from controlled, precise Joshua. Did the difference make complete sense or no sense at all? I tore my gaze away, put a stop to my drunken amateur analysis.

'It is,' I said.

'Isn't it a bit weird, to be out on the piss the night that footage is all over the TV? Your dead wife with her killer?'

She even talked in tabloid headlines. What more proof did I need that I shouldn't be here?

'He probably just needs some support,' I said, draining my glass. There was half the bottle left, but I wasn't going to let hopelessly English politeness keep me here a second longer. 'Asking for help when you need it is one of the bravest things you can do.'

'Mmm,' said April doubtfully. 'I wouldn't like it much if it was my hubby.'

Joshua emerged from the toilets at just that moment.

'You're at Lysette and Ged's, aren't you?' he said. 'I could always try and find you after work tomorrow?'

Why hadn't I used his absence to make a judicious exit?

'I'm – I'm actually not staying there now. I'm here – mad woman in the attic!'

'Oh, OK. I'll just give you a call.' He gave an awkward sort of salute, and set off across the bar.

'That's your friend, right – Lysette?' said the relentless April. 'She's one of the mums? Why aren't you staying with her? That room at the top's like a shoebox! I told Rita to piss right off when she showed it to me.'

I stood up. Why wasn't I staying with her? I missed Lysette so much in that moment – all I could see was April's red, sticky mouth moving at warp speed.

'Long story,' I said. 'I'll put half of this on my room.'

April barely heard me: she was too busy looking back across the pub.

'I shouldn't tell you this, but the news editor says there's loads more about to come out. Apparently he had loads of affairs with different women. I think they've found another phone with loads of – you know – filthy texts and stuff. He's guilty as sin.'

She was totally consumed by it, which I supposed must make her brilliant at her job.

'Maybe,' I said, knowing full well I should let her words evaporate without acknowledgement.

'Why do you keep saying that?' she demanded. 'Do you know something?' The relentless chutzpah was impressive.

'I just don't like making assumptions. One thing my work has taught me is that people are endlessly surprising.'

April cocked her head.

'What, do you think he was different from how people are making out? They just want him to take the rap now he's dead?'

'I didn't say that.'

April paused. 'Did you meet him?'

'No. I saw him – at the funeral – but I didn't meet him.'

'Was he like – hysterical? That's what I heard.'

'It was a funeral of a young woman. Everyone was upset.'

'You'd have sensed stuff, though, wouldn't you?' said April, cogs visibly turning. 'Cos it's your job to read people. Don't go! Finish the bottle. Give me more of your words of wisdom.'

'I can't,' I said, the words grittier than I intended. I stood up. 'I'll see you soon.'

*

'Darling, just call her. Or I'll call her.'

Patrick sounded tired. No, exasperated. He wasn't the only one – other than the five missed calls, I'd texted him twice to tell him how much I'd wanted to speak to him. It had taken him until 10 p.m. to deign to call me back.

'No one's calling her. She threw me out!'

'Look, I get that you're upset, but you said yourself it's been difficult. It wasn't like you were loving the lilo either. Maybe she's trying to look out for your friendship.'

This phone call had been bad from the off.

'Can't you just – for once – be on my side?'

'Of course I'm on your side,' he said, voice rising. 'And what do you mean, for once? We're getting married!'

'I know it sounds like I'm exaggerating, but she's like a replica version of Lysette. I'm really worried about this whole drug thing.'

'But that could just be gossip. Who did it even come from?'

I paused, wishing I'd told him from the outset that I'd re-encountered Jim. The fact that I was only pretending to

myself that I wished it – that I knew full well I never would –
told me how dangerous it was. When you're lying to yourself,
there's no one left to keep score.

'I just heard it.'

The fact it had come from Jim meant I also couldn't tell
him about the playdate – it was no great surprise he thought
I was being melodramatic. Jim had texted me mid-afternoon:

> Thanks for indulging me – knew you'd love a bit of
> Alan's beef. See you soon? xx

I'd sent him back an exclamation mark, no kiss, but it had
taken a worrying amount of willpower not to call him when
I'd escaped Kimberley's clutches.

'What, from one of the other mums?' asked Patrick.

I made a non-committal kind of sound.

'So you need to work out why she'd say it. Was it that
bitchy one you hate? Madame Farthing? She sounds like she
just likes to stir.'

'Doesn't she just,' I said. My skin was hot and prickly.
Strictly speaking I hadn't lied, but the deliberate omission of
truth might have been worse. More sly.

'Listen, darling, sleep on it. Call her tomorrow when
you're calm. You two are proper besties. You're both stressed.
You'll get through it.'

'There's other things as well . . .' I said quietly, but Patrick
ran on, a phone trilling in the background. He was still at
the police station, despite the late hour. He'd taken a few

audible bites from the congealing Thai takeaway on his desk as we'd been talking.

'The truth is, this investigation is going to wrap up soon,' he said. 'I did a bit of digging, and I bet they'll say they're not looking for anyone else in connection to Sarah's death within a couple of weeks. They'll have the inquest in a few months, and it'll all be done.'

'That's what everyone's saying here.'

'So you just do your last few days, come home and let it blow over with Lysette.' We both paused. 'You don't have to make everything such a battle.'

'I'm not doing that!'

'It sounds like you are to me.'

'Patrick, if there's even the slightest chance that the wrong person is about to be condemned for a murder, don't you think I've got a responsibility to try and share anything I find out?'

'But who else could've done it?'

'I don't know. I'm probably wrong. But – I said it to you in the pub – even if it was Peter, I'm convinced the reasons it happened are way more complicated than the Cluedo version everyone's hung up on.'

Patrick exhaled, his frustration audible.

'That's not what you're there for.'

'I know. But I came to help Lysette . . . to help that little boy.' The words caught in my throat. 'And if they're left living a lie . . . you never heal if the wound can't close.'

'You can't fix everyone and everything in the world,' hissed Patrick. 'You're not . . . you're not God.'

'You're the one who's big on God, not me,' I snapped back. 'And you're also the one in the police station way past his bedtime trying to make sure that good wins over evil.'

'And that *is* my job,' said Patrick, his anger fizzing and spitting down the phone line.

This was about more than this conversation, I could feel it. I knew I should step away, but I was too tired and frustrated to be the one to act like a grown-up. The truth was, my frustration was with myself as much as it was with him. That's the worst kind: the kind that turns a person into an unexploded bomb.

'What, so you only like me doing my job if it involves handing over a Kleenex and saying *there, there*?' I hissed. 'Oh – apart from when it was useful to your criminal investigation.'

'No! I just think you're letting this take you over. You're over-thinking it. You're not coming home next week at this rate, I guarantee it. You won't be able to tear yourself away.'

The sly suggestion that my engagement was for my own benefit sent me into orbit.

'If you want some little wife who's going to sit at home darning your socks and counting her rosary beads, you've picked the wrong girl.'

Patrick's voice quivered with rage.

'I'm well aware of that fact. If you had any respect whatsoever for my religion, we might have actually booked our wedding by now.'

'That's so unfair – I've agreed to get married in a Catholic church, even though I think it's a . . .' I stopped myself. 'They don't even have women priests.'

Suddenly all the ways we were different felt so much bigger than all the ways we were similar. Even worse, the differences felt catastrophic – none of that fascination you feel when you're falling in love and the other person feels like an exotic animal that you're thrilled to contemplate. Now we were nothing but a couple of unwanted rescue mutts snarling at each other.

'Yeah, and then you've hardly bothered to come. I know you think it's funny to call him names . . .'

I lay down on the bed, exhaustion settling over me like a thick blanket.

'I'm sorry, OK? I *will* be home next week and I'll come to church on Sunday.'

Patrick paused, exhaled.

'Just be careful, OK?' he said. 'Talk to your boss, talk to old snake-hips Krall. Don't be digging about yourself.' He paused. 'If there is something bigger going on, they'll be people with a vested interest in keeping it quiet. People with a lot to lose.'

I felt a little shiver run through me, as much from the tone in his voice as the words themselves. Patrick saw far more darkness than me – perhaps he saw it now.

'I will be,' I said. 'I should go. I love you, Patrick.'

I didn't know it yet, but I'd just made another promise I wouldn't be able to keep.

CHAPTER TWENTY

It was inevitable: here I was, back in the twee confines of The Crumpet. Even the way the metal sign swung in the breeze, the steaming crumpet proudly painted on, seemed unbearably smug. Joshua had finally arrived. He was shouldering his way through the morning mummy crowd, mouthing an apology. He was dressed in a well-cut suit, the shirt underneath perfectly pressed, the cracks in his veneer already plastered over.

'So sorry,' he said, dropping down into the seat opposite. 'And I'm afraid this is a bit of a flying visit. I've got a conference call at ten that I can't miss.'

'OK,' I said, forcing myself to drown out the shouty judgements that were booming inside my head. 'Have you got time for coffee, at least?'

'Coffee's a necessity in my book,' he said, signalling for the nose-ringed waitress.

Once there were two steaming mugs in front of us, I reached for the right words. 'Max seems like such a special, clever little boy,' I said.

Massaging the parental ego tends to open them up, but in this instance I believed every syllable. Joshua smiled, his brown eyes softening in a way I hadn't previously witnessed.

'We certainly think so.' He paused, looked away. 'Thought so? I never thought the past tense would be a source of such . . .' He looked back at me, rueful. 'You know.'

I gave a nod of acknowledgement, searching for the right words. 'I only met Sarah once, but I thought she was . . .' I paused, looking for something sensitive and truthful, which was surprisingly difficult. 'She was impossible to ignore.'

The phrase splintered into a thousand meanings as soon as it left my mouth. Impossible for Peter to ignore? Where was his head at? Had he thought that Peter was a crazed stalker, only to see that footage and have to perform a devastating review of his marriage?

'She certainly was,' he said, dryly.

Not least for him: he'd blown up his whole life for her. Lisa – brisk, efficient Lisa – couldn't be more different.

'It's hard to know what to say – anything is inadequate for what you're going through. A traumatic bereavement is terrible enough, without this horrific press circus.'

I'd spotted April having a fag in the car park as I'd left, talking nineteen to the dozen on her iPhone. Her eyes had widened, like she might rush after me, but I'd walked off with a cheery wave and averted disaster.

'I wouldn't recommend it,' agreed Joshua, before lapsing into silence. I let it linger a second, and then carried on.

'So, Max. He seemed very keen to talk about his mum – normal stuff. How amazing she is. It's definitely *is*, not was, for him right now. Children often fight the reality for quite a while.'

'And Sarah was never a huge fan of reality either. She liked the drama.' He paused, measuring his words. 'That was part of the fun.'

Was this a tacit acknowledgement of what was emerging about her and Peter?

'The fun of being with her?'

'Yes, I suppose,' he said, pausing for a second. 'Being around her was never boring. Max certainly agreed.'

'Yes, it's obvious how bonded they were.'

He nodded, gave a half-smile. 'Hard to infiltrate,' he said, trying and failing to make it sound like a joke.

Max's 'secrets' were starting to make more sense. Perhaps they were nothing more than a way to make sense of his parents' marriage? I could feel an echo of my own early life: that sense of responsibility for my crazy and seductive dad that had defined everything for me. Had Max felt the same blind loyalty to his charismatic mum, his dad held firmly at bay?

'And now you're having to find a whole new relationship with him, without Sarah there to broker it.' Joshua gave a pained nod. 'I'm so sorry. I don't know how you feel about therapy, for you or for him, but I do think ongoing professional support could help you both. It won't wave a magic wand, but . . .'

Joshua cut across me. 'I'm not such a fan of magic wands anyway.'

'Right. What I would say is that Max seems very keen to open up, which is a really good sign. He's not internalising his distress. You should absolutely feel safe to talk to him about what's happened as often as you both want to. If he gets upset, it may simply be emotion that he needs to be expressed and doing that with you is the safest place.'

His eyes flicked down to the large, top of the range phone which he'd left face up on the table. 'Sarah was a great believer in letting him emotionally splurge.'

It didn't sound like a compliment.

'I think she might've given him a gift there,' I said.

Joshua's eyes rolled back up to meet mine, his gaze almost confrontational.

'You saw it, I assume?' It came from left field. 'The footage?'

'I did, yes,' I admitted.

'You and all of them,' he said, making a discreet gesture out into space.

My eyes flicked around the room. The Crumpet was packed, the coffee machine hissing and spitting, Jake confidently surfing his way through the narrow gaps between tables. He was right. People hurriedly looked away as soon as they saw me look from the island of our table out towards them.

I felt a sharp burst of compassion for him. A sense of how humiliating it must have been. 'But nobody knows – no one knows what you know about her. About your relationship.'

Joshua gave a discreet snort. 'That's an understatement.'

This whole encounter felt even stranger than I'd antici-pated it would be. It was like he was slamming the door in my face and throwing me tasty breadcrumbs all at once. I cast a quick glance at the large, round clock above the counter. It was 9.45. Was he doing what clients so often do – dumping the painful bits they can't bear to explore in detail in the dwindling moments of a session?

'It looked to me last night like you've got a good network of people you love and trust around you.'

His eyes blazed suddenly – did he think I was judging him for leaving the house? 'I do. And these people – they've got no right to judge her. Marriage is harder than anyone ever warns you. I know that.' He paused. 'So did she.'

I could see in his tortured expression that he meant it, that he wasn't simply saving face.

'That's a real insight to have, particularly now.'

'She never wanted Max. I mean, of course she did once he'd arrived. She kept counting his toes, like they were the first toes to have ever been minted.'

'So she never looked back? Everyone says what a natural she was at it.'

'In one sense, yes.' I felt him change track, the charged energy starting to dissipate. 'So what else do I need to know about my son's state of mind?'

I paused a second, stirring the froth of my coffee. My

thoughts needed unscrambling. 'I'm not sure if this is meaningful or not, but did he have a difficult time at birth?'

'No, not especially. I mean – Sarah had made some choice remark about what it did to her nether regions, but, of the three births I've been at, it was probably the most straightforward.'

'OK – he talked about hospital and ambulances like he'd been treated. Anything else – tonsils, appendix?'

'No, he's always been in rude health.'

I thought about it. 'I guess it might just be another way of bonding with his mum. Taking on what he imagines she went through in her last hours.' Joshua's face was stricken. 'I'm sorry,' I said, ashamed of the paucity of what I could offer him. I wanted to explore it more, not yet satisfied with my explanation for what Max had said, but the pain it had visibly stirred in him was too great to be contained in the frantic hubbub of The Crumpet.

'Can you see him again?' he asked, simultaneously signalling Jake for the bill.

'Of course. He needs to know it's not ongoing, so he doesn't feel like I've abandoned him when I leave, but I'm very happy to fit in another session.'

'Thank you,' he said, haltingly. 'I – we – appreciate that.'

I didn't know who made up the 'we'. Was it Sarah or Max? Jake swung up to the table, the bill in his hand, a smiley face drawn on the fold – *Service not included!*. We read it at the same moment, our shared look more of a cringe, a moment of connection passing between us.

'I'll get it,' I said, dropping a tenner into the saucer. 'You get to your meeting.'

The light in Joshua's eyes snuffed out.

'No,' he said, terse. 'I'll pay.'

He picked up my crumpled note, discarding it on my side of the table. He placed his credit card in the cream saucer with a certain deliberateness, signalled authoritatively to Jake.

'Thanks, guys,' said Jake, all Aussie bonhomie, hurrying off to get the card machine.

Any bonhomie left with him: there was a painful awkwardness to us now. Once Jake returned and the transaction was complete, Joshua stood abruptly.

'I'll be in touch,' he said.

Would he? In that moment it seemed unlikely. As he weaved his way out of The Crumpet, no one made the slightest effort to look away.

*

It was only a few minutes later when the bell above the door gave a jangling peal. I'd been contemplating a second cup of coffee, replaying the nuances of my conversation with Joshua in my mind, but the sound shook me from my reverie. Kimberley was standing there looking over at me, Helena, Alex and – my heart lurched – Lysette, crowded behind her like a gaggle of ducklings. Her eyes slid towards Lysette, and then she gave me a big, empty wave.

'Hi, Mia!' she sing-songed.

Jake was already clearing a large table on the other side of the café. She pointed at it, waved a collective goodbye. I'd half stood up by now, and I sank back down into my seat, feeling about thirteen years old. My face was burning hot. I looked down at the table, making a big deal of gathering up my iPad and notebook. A well-padded midriff appeared in my eyeline.

'Why don't you come and join us?' said Helena, smiling down at me. Her brown eyes were like warm chocolate.

'Thank you,' I said, smiling back gratefully, 'but I really don't think it's a good idea.'

My eyes darted towards their table. Lysette wasn't exactly looking at me, but from the way her body was half twisting out of her chair, I could tell that she had been.

'Kimberley asked Lysette. She's fine with it.'

I tried not to bristle.

'OK,' I said. I took a deep breath, swallowed my pride. 'Thanks.'

I felt trapped in a sugary spider web. I couldn't say no – to do so would have been humiliatingly childish – but this was the last way I'd have chosen to re-encounter Lysette. My legs were shaking as I crossed the tiled floor behind Helena, my eyes trained downwards.

'Hi there, Mia!' said Kimberley, loudly yanking a chair from the adjoining table and putting it next to hers.

'Hi,' I said, scanning the table. I let my eyes settle briefly on Lysette, then looked away. Being so close made the things she'd said to me start to burn and spit.

'Let's get you a fresh coffee,' said Kimberley, her sleek mane swishing through the air as she scanned the room for Jake. 'And not staff-room instant like we had yesterday!'

Did Lysette know about our meeting, or was Kimberley stirring the pot? Jake appeared at the table before I could discreetly gauge her reaction.

'There you are!' trilled Kimberley. 'Honestly, you just can't get the staff these days.'

'Yeah, let alone riff-raff from the colonies,' shot back Jake, grinning down at her. 'Skinny lattes for you three, yeah?'

'You know us so well!' said Kimberley.

There was a pause, five pairs of eyes suddenly trained on me.

'Can I have a latte too?' I ventured. 'Just one shot?'

'Just one shot,' chimed Lysette from the other end of the table, and we finally allowed our eyes to meet properly.

As soon as they did, I felt my anger start to melt. Lysette's hair was tied back in a messy ponytail, which was something I knew she only did when it was too greasy for public consumption. Her eyes were soft, but they were ringed by blue-grey smudges, which only served to enhance the sadness I could see pooled in them. She was wearing a ratty grey sweatshirt, face devoid of make-up. Meanwhile, Kimberley looked back and forth between us as if she'd singlehandedly brokered world peace. Jake, dismissed, strutted back to the counter.

'How are you all?' I said, my eyes still fixed on Lysette.

'Well, I think the whole town's still reeling from the

aftermath of that footage,' declared Kimberley. Lysette looked down at the table: I wished I had long, extendable arms like a cartoon character and could reach down the table and make contact with her.

'I presume you've seen it?' said Alex. Every sentence she uttered was so donnish, as if she was chasing up a late essay I stubbornly refused to hand in.

'Trust me, Mia knows far more than you or I!' said Kimberley. 'She's got the inside track. We talked about it yesterday, when we finally had our heart to heart.'

'It's stupid, really,' said Helena, shaking out her shoulders. 'But there's something about watching her there, knowing she was about to die, and she's oblivious . . .'

'I suppose the only mercy is that it looks like they're close to wrapping it up,' said Kimberley.

I looked at Lysette, who was trailing her teaspoon around the inside of her cup.

'Yeah, that is something,' she said, voice flat and colourless. I tried not to stare at her, to betray my surprise.

'Do you think he definitely did it now, Lys?' I asked.

Kimberley's gaze was intense.

'There's no other explanation, is there?' said Lysette, echoing the words Kimberley had uttered in the staff room. 'And he's dead.'

What had happened? She'd been so adamant: had that tiny snippet of footage radically changed what she believed? I realised as I computed it, how much of my own anxie-ties about the direction the case was determinedly driving towards were down to her dogged conviction about Peter's innocence. For all the alienation of recent weeks, I'd always put Lysette on a pedestal, and I think she had me. It's kind of in the job description of being a best friend, even if the 'girls' involved are eighty, not eight. I looked back at her, tried to assess how much she meant what she'd just said, but I couldn't catch her eye.

'Poor Sarah,' I said, which sounded more anodyne than I meant it to. I couldn't help spooling through that footage in my head, the way she'd looked up at Peter, laughed with an abandon you could see was real even in that grainy image.

'Absolutely,' intoned Kimberley. 'Poor Sarah. I still can't believe she's not here. She'd have loved tonight.'

'Yeah – she would,' agreed Lysette.

'Don't,' said Helena, making her hand into a stop sign. 'My dress and my arse are no longer on speaking terms. I'm going to need two pairs of Spanx. And possibly a shovel for Chris to dig me back out of it when we get home.'

Kimberley gave a tinkly laugh, squeezed her wrist.

'Don't be ridiculous. You've got a perfect derrière.'

Helena shrugged, looked away. She was chubby – a classic English pear – but she also had a lovely face, kept youthful by its slight roundness. There was something so insincere about the way Kimberley – starvation-rations thin and thrilled by it – dismissed the truth of what she was saying. Jake was hovering with my coffee.

'Are you waitering tonight, Jake?' asked Kimberley. What was this event that no one seemed in any hurry to tell me about? 'Oh sorry, Mia, Nigel's hosting a ball in Cambridge for Save the Children. And Jake sometimes moonlights when we have a function.'

Kimberley's spider web seemed to wrap itself around quite a specific kind of fly.

'Wouldn't miss it,' confirmed Jake, putting my coffee in front of me without looking away from her.

'Good to know we'll be in capable hands.' Kimberley turned to me, clapping her own elegant hands. She shot a darting, complicated look at Lysette. 'You should come! She should come, shouldn't she, Lysette?'

Alex's face was like granite. 'I thought the tickets . . .'

Kimberley ignored her.

'We all need cheering up − a girls' night out. It would be so fun if you were part of it.'

It was the last thing I wanted to do. 'Um . . .'

'It's for a good cause!' she said. 'And we all know how much you care about children.'

She ignored Alex and looked around at Helena and Lysette, appealing for support.

'Yeah, you should come,' said Lysette, voice still monotone. Was it the thought of me, or the thought of the do? I looked at her wan complexion, her straggly hair. She didn't look like someone who'd relish a night on the tiles. She smiled. 'Please,' she added, suddenly, unexpectedly, vulnerable.

'You can get a pair of pliers and help me with my zip,' said Helena.

'OK then,' I said, forcibly pushing away my doubts. I

only had a few days left: this might be my only chance to mend things with Lysette. To gauge what she really thought and felt. 'Are men folk coming? I mean . . . only if there's room.'

I'd been thinking about Patrick ever since I'd woken up, trawling back through our argument looking for the hidden fault lines, the deeper dives we could take if we didn't take better care of our relationship.

'Oh, do you want to bring your mysterious fiancé?' said Kimberley.

'Mysterious isn't a word I'd use for him,' I said, thinking at the same moment of the likelihood of Jim swaggering in, his bow tie left undone over an open-necked shirt, a look he'd perfected at school balls more than twenty years previously. 'Seriously, don't worry about it. I doubt he'd be able to come anyway.'

'No, no,' said Kimberley, 'I'm sure I can muster up another ticket, we'd love to meet him. The more the merrier.' She made her blue eyes go suitably mournful. 'And it all helps the refugees.'

'Is there an auction?' I asked.

'Yes, but the tickets are also £50. Is that OK?'

It sounded like loads – a haircut, a decent item of clothing – but I could hardly say that.

'That's fine,' I said, my brain whirring. 'Actually though – unless Patrick can come, I'd be turning up in my pyjamas – I haven't got anything smart enough.'

'Not a problem!' said Kimberley, her eyes raking over my

body. 'My wardrobe's like Mary Poppins' carpet bag. We can easily find you something hidden in the depths.'

'Please don't worry. Lys, could I . . .'

A look of shame crossed her face, and I cursed my insensitivity. That was why those Louboutins were such a shock – years of scrimping and saving with three kids to feed and clothe had left her with a wardrobe that was shabby chic at best.

'*I'm* a refugee,' she said. 'Clothing bank of Kimberley Farthing for me.'

Kimberley looked between us, delighted.

'We can all get ready together! Get the champers flowing, music up loud. I was going to get my make-up artist to come round.'

I just about stopped myself telling her that her pre-party budget could probably sustain a small country's worth of refugees for a month.

'Well, you won't have to borrow any shoes!' I said to Lysette, trying to make amends for my thoughtlessness. 'Did you see her gorgeous Louboutins the other week?' I asked the others. 'They made your legs look amazing.'

Lysette looked even more uncomfortable.

'Yeah, no, I don't have them now.' I looked at her questioningly. 'I stuck them up on eBay.'

'Oh,' I said. She had the look in her eyes again, shut down and pleading all at once. How bad was her situation? She certainly hadn't mentioned that £200, despite all her promises to get it straight back to me. I rushed to fill the silence, keen that Kimberley didn't muscle her way into the strangeness of it. 'Shall we get some more drinks?' I said, taking my turn to wave at Jake.

*

'I can't believe you're stuck with Rita!' said Helena, wiping her eyes. 'Every time we go in there, she jiggles her tits at Chris and acts like I've got a pair of horns.'

It was Kimberley who'd slyly brought up the pub – I'd never have called attention to the fact that Lysette had thrown me out – but I'd gone with the comedy route of Rita's obvious distaste for me to try and take the sting away.

'It's only a few days more, it's fine,' I said. 'Besides, her husband makes a mean burger.'

'You've been scoffing burgers?' said Lysette, looking askance.

'I didn't actually order it . . .' I said, any further explanation drying in my throat.

'Oh yes, Lisa said you were having dinner with someone last night,' said Kimberley.

'Have you got a bit on the side, already?' said Helena, teasing. 'You're a fast worker. Got any tips?'

'No, that was just someone else staying in the pub,' I said.

'Who?' asked Kimberley casually.

Their focus on me was pin tight. No conversational avenue was harmless.

'Just this girl April,' I muttered. 'What time do you need us to arrive at yours?'

'April?' said Kimberley. 'I think I've seen her name on some of the coverage – it's unusual, isn't it? Is she a journalist?'

'I think so, yes. I barely know her. I sat with her for like, twenty minutes, chewing a very chewy steak.' My words felt high and tight. 'Hopefully that's the last I'll see of her.'

The bell above the door clanged loudly, and I took the opportunity to look away. It was Saffron, Ged a couple of steps behind. Her face lit up with glee: she belted across the floor, paying no attention to any obstacles in her path.

'Auntie Mia!' she said, throwing herself into my outstretched arms. 'I've been asking and asking for you to read my bedtime story. And then Max said he'd read you a story, and I said he was a liar and you were in Lon ... Lon-don, and he said ...'

I wrapped her up more tightly, as much for me as for her.

'I'm here now,' I told her.

She climbed up on my knee, an idea she'd dismissed as babyish only last week.

'Can I have a hot chocolate?' she asked.

'Ask Mum,' I said. Lysette was looking at the two of us, the way we were welded together, with a complicated expression on her face.

'There you are!' said Ged, arriving at the table. 'I thought you were meeting us at the playground?'

'Hot chocolate? Yummy hot chocolate?' asked Saffron again.

I could sense the tension between her parents: I signalled for Jake, taking an executive decision to grant her request.

Lysette and Ged continued to snipe at each other in an undertone.

'If I'd said that, I'd remember,' said Lysette.

'Well, you didn't,' hissed Ged, his mellow demeanour nowhere to be found. 'And I've got to get to work.' He was standing at the head of the table, displaced.

'Hi, Ged, do you want my chair?' I asked. 'I can't find another one.'

'No. Thanks. I need to go,' he said, forcing a smile. He paused a second. 'It's nice to see you,' he added.

'Oh, shame!' said Kimberley. 'But we'll be seeing you tonight?' Ged looked blank. 'The ball?'

He was wearing a battered pair of jeans, nails cracked and grubby, his bulging tool bag abandoned at his feet. It was hard to imagine.

'Yeah. Thanks for the invite,' he said, voice entirely devoid of enthusiasm. How could they even afford a pair of £50 tickets if Lysette was flogging treasured possessions on eBay? Nothing about this felt right.

'Great!' said Kimberley, obviously taking that as an acceptance. 'It's shaping up to be quite an evening.'

At least on that score, she would prove to be remarkably accurate.

CHAPTER TWENTY-ONE

I was sitting in the garden of the pub, the heels of my open-toed mules sinking into the grass, peering critically at the crescent of white at the base of each of my scarlet toes. My three-week-old pedicure had well and truly grown out: I'd have to invest in some polish and clippers in the chemist and DIY them back to their former glory. I shook myself. The ball didn't matter. God willing, I'd never have to see any of these people, bar Lysette, after next week.

'It's just not practical, darling.'

'No. Of course,' I said, aware of a tinge of passive aggression – blood in the water – that was creeping into my voice. I knew he wouldn't be able to – why was some childish part of me taking his inevitable pass as a rejection? 'I get it.'

Patrick was walking and talking, shouldering his way down a busy London street in search of a late lunchtime sandwich. I could hear the crackle and buzz of it, so different from the humid stillness of the pub garden.

'I would if I could.'

'I know,' I said, although I didn't really. I felt an all too familiar stab of loneliness – would work always be his mistress? 'It was always going to be a long shot. How's it going today?'

'Oh, you know,' he said. 'Had an aromatherapy massage this morning and I'll be leaving at five. How about you?'

I tore my gaze away from my disappointing toes – I'd sat around having coffee and speculating about what truths lay beneath honeyed words. An image of Lysette loomed up at me – hypnotised by her coffee cup, lost and distant. Her resignation about Sarah, her prickly awkwardness with Ged – even if it looked like frothy cappuccinos and chat, I'd been working hard. I'd be working hard tonight too. She was my mission, more than anything.

I snapped back to the conversation. 'I saw Joshua first thing.'

'Who's he?'

'You know – Sarah's husband. Max's dad.'

'Oh yeah, of course. How'd it go?' He paused, and I wondered if he was going back over what I'd told him about my strange, sad session with Max. 'What do you reckon – Pret or Eat?'

No – he was thinking about cheese.

'It was fine,' I said, my voice flat. 'You like that baguette in Pret, don't you?'

'The cheese and ham one? I do, it's true. I swear, Mia, you know me better than I know myself.'

Did I? The distance between us seemed so obvious again, as if all the 'knowing' we'd built up in the two years prior to it was a shallow puddle, not the deep lake that I'd arrogantly believed it to be.

'I should go,' I said, aware I needed to avoid blowing this up into a self-created existential crisis. 'You get to your sandwich.'

'Don't hang up. We've got the whole walk back still.'

'No, I should. I've got the session with Ian that he cancelled yesterday, and then I've got to go to Kimberley's with Lysette to get ready.' The very thought of it made my skin prickle – why had I agreed to tonight? 'He's the headmaster.'

'I know that,' said Patrick. 'Can I have a very, very strong black coffee, please?' he said, having reached the counter. 'The kind your spoon stands up in?'

Hearing him – his acute Patrick-ness – made my heart clench tight in my chest. I would wish soon after that I'd shared my rush of affection – that I'd grabbed that small, seemingly insignificant moment and made something of it.

'I'll talk to you tomorrow,' I said. 'I miss you.'

'Are you mad with me?' he asked.

'No,' I said, determined to take the harder route and be honest, not defensive. 'I'm just a bit disappointed.'

'Sounds way worse.'

'I wanted you to meet them all so you knew what I'd been droning on about. And Kimberley makes me feel like a spotty twelve-year-old at the best of times, let alone when her celebrity husband's trailing in her wake.'

'I'm sorry, Mia,' he said simply.

'I get it, I really do,' I said.

I didn't. Unhappily for me, I'd only come to realise that fact when it was too late.

*

Lysette texted from outside, and I manoeuvred my way down the creaky staircase that connected my garret to civilisation. There on the landing was April, coming out of her room. It seemed too convenient.

'Mia!' she said, her smile garishly red. 'I'd offer to show you my room, but then I'd have to kill you.' She giggled. 'Oops, inappropriate!'

'Don't worry, I've got to run anyway.'

'Anywhere nice?' she said, clocking my bulging weekend bag and thick make-up. I'd been trying to leave myself with the minimum amount of grooming left to do: I didn't need Kimberley unleashing her 'team' on me.

'Um, just this . . . this do that Kimberley Farthing's invited me to. Some charity thing her husband's organised.'

'Ooh! Where is it?'

I hesitated. 'Just in Cambridge.' I made an awkward gesture towards the stairs. 'I should go. My friend Lysette's downstairs.'

'Sounds fun. It's good that they're able to put it all behind them, isn't it? Let life move on?'

'I don't think they've put it all behind them. Anyway . . .'

'Don't you?' said April, eyes bright.

'No,' I said firmly, thinking yet again of the sadness that was etched so deeply into Lysette's face. 'Anyway – nice to see you, April.'

'Yeah, you too, darling,' tinkled April, opening her bedroom door. Was she going in or coming out – it didn't quite make sense. 'I'll miss our evening tipple.'

'Me too,' I lied, over my shoulder, taking the wooden stairs two at a time.

*

Lysette's battered car was parked outside the pub, its wheels up on the kerb at a jaunty angle. It was the kind of thing you'd have got a ticket for in five minutes flat in London, but didn't matter a jot in Little Copping. I climbed in, still a little awkward with her. Lysette leaned over the gear stick, hugged me for almost too long.

'Hello, mate,' she said, her words muffled by my hair.

'Hi,' I said, drawing away. She clearly hadn't joined me in applying her make-up obsessively early: her skin looked grey and drawn, those dark circles I'd observed earlier even more obvious close up. 'How are you doing?'

'Oh, you know,' she said, her smile unconvincing.

'I don't, no. Tell me.'

'Full of the joys of spring,' she said, turning the key in the ignition. 'How was Ian?'

How was Ian? We'd talked in more detail about how to talk to his young pupils about death – how to neither avoid the subject nor traumatise them more. He'd seemed to find it useful, had asked for it, but I'd come away somehow feeling like the session was more for me than for him. Like he was paying lip service to the process. I'd gently probed his feelings around the footage, but he'd slammed the door on it, his jaw tight and clenched. I couldn't share much of it with Lysette, but she read between the lines.

'He's not going to be feeling good about any of it,' she said, her eyes trained on the winding lane.

'What, all that business with Kimberley and Peter?' I said hesitantly. 'The quiz night?'

'Sarah was on top form that night,' she said, a note of defiance in her voice, and I wondered what she meant. The only thing I'd heard from Kimberley was about her shameless use of an iPhone.

'How so?' I asked, even though it felt risky. We had such a brief sliver of time alone: I needed to bridge the gap.

'She never took any shit,' said Lysette. 'She didn't let her friends take it either.'

'What, so she defended Kimberley?'

'No,' said Lysette, as the grand iron gates of Kimberley's palatial house loomed up in front of us. 'She defended Peter.'

Her words felt almost electric. Defended him against what, against Kimberley? Or was it Ian, shifty and uncomfortable Ian, who was the villain of the piece here? We'd arrived a minute too soon. No, it was only too soon for me – I sensed that for Lysette it was perfect timing. She hit the buzzer and the gates drew apart – glacially slowly, as if they wanted to make it clear who was boss. She parked the car on the sweeping drive, turned to me.

'Forget it. What about you? We can't keep talking about me the whole time.'

She sounded so like her old self in that moment, I could almost believe that the last few weeks were a dream, a ridiculous plot contrivance on a daytime soap.

'I'm OK. I'm – I'm better now,' I said, our eyes meeting in a silent apology.

I wanted to go further – seal the still fragile truce by having the conversation that simmered and bubbled beneath the surface – but it wasn't the time. Not here, a discarded rice cake in the footwell, Kimberley's rambling home casting its long shadow.

'Is Paddy Cakes going to make it up the motorway tonight?' she asked, opening her door. I nearly asked her to shut it: instead I reluctantly swung mine open.

'No, he's stuck in the office.'

She must've heard the insecurity in my voice. She smiled at me across the bird-poo-splattered roof of the car, incongruously parked next to Kimberley's gleaming 4×4.

'And you're not . . . you're not late any more?'

'Nope,' I said, turning towards the house.

Lysette threaded her arm through mine in solidarity. 'I know I must seem the old woman who lived in a shoe with all those kids, but I do get it. Saffron took her time to arrive. It'll happen when you're not expecting it.'

'What, like when there's been no actual sex of any kind?'

We giggled.

'The nuns really did a number on you,' hissed Lysette, as the heavy front door swung open.

It was Lori who was behind it, Kimberley bobbing up behind her, her blonde hair looped up in large rollers, a satin robe pulled around her. She was all slippery gloss and it was only teatime.

'Perfect timing!' she shrieked. 'Lori, off you go.'

Lori scuttled off, giving me a quick, tight smile of recognition, and Kimberley shooed us towards the kitchen like we were badly trained puppies. There we found Lori already twisting the cork out of a bottle of champagne, three flutes lined up on the granite counter. I shot a glancing look at Lysette: the corner of her bottom lip was trapped between her teeth, a nervous tic I remembered from exam time at school. I'd been dreading tonight, but now I suspected she'd been dreading it even more. Was that short line of glasses just serving to remind her that Sarah wasn't here to knock hers back?

'Cheers!' said Kimberley, once we were each holding one, her excitement palpable. She must have seen our faces. 'To Sarah,' she added, suitably sombre. 'I still can't believe she's not here. It's so wrong that she's not.'

Lysette's face crumpled, her glass making slow progress towards Kimberley's. Kimberley put hers down and crushed her into a hug.

'We'll have to enjoy ourselves doubly hard to make up for the fact she's not here,' she said, speaking the words directly into her ear. It felt too intimate somehow, like I was a peeping Tom.

'We will,' agreed Lysette, the small phrase thick with sadness. I stood there, observing the two of them, muddled together in a mass of complicated emotion. Kimberley's eyes briefly met mine over Lysette's shoulder, two cold rock-pools.

'Right,' said Kimberley, pulling away and clapping her hands. She took a deep glug of champagne, and shook her head like it was a hit of tequila. 'Operation Glamazon. We've got ninety minutes before Nigel pulls up in the car. The clock is ticking!'

She filled each of our glasses to the brim, signalled for us to follow her. I looked back as we left the kitchen. Lori had stopped to watch us leave, the kitchen cloth she'd been scrubbing with no longer tracing soapy circles on the counter. I wanted to stop, talk to her, but I knew it would be seen as a small, dangerous mutiny.

'Lori, bring the bottle!' shouted Kimberley, as we ascended the curved staircase.

'I could nip back down,' I said, but she waved the idea away with an airy hand.

'We need the ice bucket.'

I looked at Lysette, hoping for a tiny moment of scorn, but she seemed utterly accepting of Kimberley's caprice. We followed her down the plush hallway, me cringing as we passed the scene of the crime – the upstairs bathroom – and eventually arrived in Kimberley's bedroom. It was predictably huge, the large bay window giving a panoramic view of the beautiful landscape, an elegant rococo bed the centrepiece, a few silk pillows strewn across it.

'What a gorgeous view,' I said, as Kimberley flung open a pair of doors to reveal a dressing room.

'The pièce de résistance,' she declared. 'I made Nigel build me this. Feel free to rootle around in there.'

Lysette perched on the bed, her champagne glass already half empty. How had she managed to drink and walk with such frightening efficiency? I waited for her to say something, but she seemed to have retreated inwards again.

'Honestly, Kimberley, just chuck me any old thing. Something you don't care about too much. Have you got something in mind, Lys?'

'There's that red one I borrowed before,' said Lysette, as Lori appeared nervously in the doorway, ice bucket dripping onto the thick cream carpet.

'Just top us up and put it in the sink,' said Kimberley. Neither of us had made much of a dent in our glasses, but Lysette wiggled her half-empty one in Lori's direction. 'Let's mix it up. Try a few things on you.' She swung round to look at me, her eyes critically scanning my body. I backed towards the bed, sat down. 'I've got a *few* things that might work on you,' she said, and I tried not to think about the recent spate of calorific pub lunches and lack of yoga.

'Honestly, anything,' I protested, but she was already trawling the rails with ruthless efficiency, throwing out a mountain of dresses as she went.

'You OK?' I mouthed at Lysette.

'I'm fine,' said Lysette, perfectly audibly. 'I'm not fine. Fine, not fine,' she sing-songed. I could already feel my shoulders tightening and I tried to talk myself down: there was no need to start bracing against her two glasses of champagne. It's funny how those early survival mechanisms kick in, even thirty years later. I no longer craved Curly Wurlys, but I still hated that insidious way that booze could body snatch the people I loved, making them there and not there, all at once.

Kimberley emerged, laden down with options.

'This pile is for you,' she said, handing me a bundle of fabric, 'and these are for you,' she said, handing Lysette a larger heap. She looked at us expectantly.

'Can I just . . .' I said, gesturing to the en suite.

'We won't stare at you, will we, Lysette?' said Kimberley. I'd stripped to my underwear in too many teenage bedrooms and Topshop changing rooms to give a hoot about Lysette seeing my cellulite, but there was no way I was exposing it to Kimberley. I kept my face still. 'Of course. Go for it,' she said, waving an imperious hand.

'Unless you want it?' I asked Lysette.

'No, I'm fine,' she giggled. 'Trust me, Kimberley's seen way worse!'

It was silent as I padded my way across the carpet to the bathroom, but it was the noisy kind of silence. I could feel my skin prickling.

It was predictably tasteful in there: retro without being twee. There were two top of the range electric toothbrushes side by side above the enamel sink, with its burnished copper taps. The bath stood on chubby metal feet, expensive unguents perched on the wooden shelf above it. I studiously ignored the medicine cabinet, which looked like it had been salvaged from a wartime chemist. I shook out the first dress, a petrol-blue sheath in a satiny fabric, slashed across the shoulder from left to right. I looked at the label: it wasn't one of those designers that felt like a naughty but occasionally justifiable splurge, it was one of those names which I'd only ever seen between the pages of *Vogue*. I unzipped it, and gingerly stepped in. Well, at least I tried to step in, but it showed absolutely no desire to slither its way over my hips.

'How's it going in there?' trilled Kimberley.

'Give us a twirl,' called Lysette. Was I imagining that slight slurring?

'Um, no – this one's not right,' I protested, just as the door swung open, revealing my body bent double, my knickers proudly displayed in the wide frame of the zip, which was still in no danger of closing.

'Oh,' said Kimberley, cocking her blonde head. 'I thought that might work, it's one of my favourites, but I see what you mean.'

I let the dress drop around my ankles, then yanked it up around myself like an inadequate sheet in an attempt to cover my half-naked body. Lysette was clutching her glass, a short-sleeved red dress in a flattering jersey fabric already in place.

'First time unlucky,' she said. 'What do you think of this one?' she added, striking a pose.

'You look ...' The truth was, whilst the dress suited her, lovely didn't feel like the right word. It was more than churlishness: her face looked hollowed out, permanently in shadow, and the haunted quality in her eyes robbed her of even more. 'It's lovely.'

Hurt flitted across her face, that tiny distinction not lost on her. She knew me too well to think that it was mere semantics. Why hadn't I trotted out the well-worn line that her question demanded? It wasn't bitchiness, it came from a better place than that, but the effect was just as devastating.

'What are you going to go for next?' asked Kimberley, busying herself with the rest of the pile, which I'd left draped over the lip of the bath. I sat down on the faux antique wooden loo seat, trying to rationalise away my sense of humiliation.

'Maybe that black one?' I said.

'Oh, the black one!' said Kimberley. 'I wore that to a drinks reception Sam Cam organised at Downing Street for this wonderful addictions charity. You must try it on.' She perched on the rim of the bath expectantly, but I didn't move a muscle. 'Oh, sorry!' she said.

Lysette waved a dismissive hand in my direction as they stood up to leave.

'You're skinny as ever,' she said, 'you're still all sushi and yoga. You wait – if you do manage to get yourself pregnant you'll know about a real paunch in no time.'

A slow smile spread across Kimberley's face.

'Are you trying to get pregnant, Mia? That's wonderful.'

My heart was beating too fast now, blood thumping in my ears. I wanted to believe it was just tipsiness, but I couldn't help thinking that Lysette was sharing my most vulnerable place to punish me. I grabbed a pristine cream towel from the rail, wrapped it around me, then busied myself with the black dress.

'I mean yes, me and Patrick do want to have a family. We'll be getting married next summer, so . . .'

I pulled the dress up lengthways by its shoulders, pretended to admire it, hoping they'd take the hint. My heart was still pumping like a piston.

'Oh, so you have set a date?'

'I keep saying to her, it doesn't always happen in five minutes flat,' said Lysette. 'But when you've had straight As your whole life . . .'

I refused to look at either of them.

'It's such a mystery, isn't it?' said Kimberley in a honeyed tone. 'That's why I didn't want to leave it too long.'

I didn't bother to engage with the blatant contradiction between the two ideas, nor tell her that most women trying to get pregnant in the autumn of their baby-making years had simply failed to meet a suitable man till September, rather than fallen prey to some kind of fertility amnesia. Instead I turned my back on them, told them tersely I should get on with finding an outfit, and then cried silently for a good five minutes, scrubbing at my face with the Farthings' mercifully multi-ply toilet paper and cursing my decision to apply two thick coats of mascara before I came out in a pointless effort to assert some control.

The black dress was also doll-sized — by now I was convinced her choice of tailored fabric cages was no coincidence — but I squeezed myself into it, enjoying the sound of a stitch giving up the ghost as my hips snuggled in. I looked at myself in the small square mirror of the medicine cabinet, forced myself to take some deep breaths. I didn't like what was going on here. I didn't like what it had done to Lysette. I would watch Kimberley like a hawk, work out what her agenda was, and hit back where it hurt. I wiped the last traces of my mascara on her fluffy cream towel and stepped out of the bathroom.

Kimberley and Lysette were on the far side of the vast bedroom by the dressing table, their heads bent in towards each other. They were talking, but their voices were low. Kimberley spun round slowly to give me the full effect: she was wearing a floor-length black number with a fish tail, delicate blue flowers appliquéd across the shoulders. The deep V of the neckline revealed a complicated necklace that was either diamanté or diamonds, probably the latter. Strappy, vertiginous heels completed the look — in our knee-length cocktail dresses, we looked like her ladies in waiting.

'There you are!' she said. 'We were starting to get worried. Do you want to come and do your face? We're all done.'

I saw Lysette take in the inky smudges around my eyes, which I'd tried so hard to eradicate. She at least had the grace to look sheepish.

'No make-up artist?' I said sweetly. 'We're slumming it, are we?'

Kimberley came back, quick as a flash.

'I just thought – it's a charity event, after all.'

'The dress looks nice,' said Lysette, giving my hand a quick squeeze as I crossed to the dressing table.

I could see from the window that the metal gates were slowly parting, a black Mercedes twisting up the curve of the drive.

'Nigel's early!' said Kimberley. 'I'd better go and get a bit wifely. Chop chop, girls, we don't have long.'

As soon as she'd swept out, I turned on Lysette.

'Why did you tell her that?' I hissed.

'I'm sorry, OK? It just came out. But you know what, it will be fine.'

'You don't know that,' I said, comforting myself with the thought of the picture Georgie had sent yesterday, her face tired and jubilant all at once, staring down adoringly at the tiny bundle in her arms. She'd gone through three cycles of treatment before he'd arrived. 'And anyway, it's not the point. It's up to me who I tell. And I would never have told her.'

'She really likes you!'

Was she naive or was I paranoid? And which was worse? I sank down on the stool, reached into my make-up bag for my mascara.

'Did she get on with Sarah?' I asked casually, running the wand through my lashes.

'Yeah, on the whole,' said Lysette, pulling the champagne out of the ice bucket. 'Do you want a top-up?'

I didn't really.

'Go on then,' I said, and she divided the dregs of the bottle between our two glasses. 'So how about the quiz night? Was that just a blip?'

'The truth is, they both went a bit too far,' said Lysette. I caught her eye in the mirror, saw how stricken she looked. 'I can't . . . I can't go there right now. I want to tell you . . .' That haunted look again. 'If I think too much about Sarah – about her not being here – I won't have a chance of surviving tonight.'

'Sorry,' I said, wrapping my arms tightly around her. Her shoulders started to shake. 'I'm sorry she's gone.'

We should have stayed like that. Keeping close would have kept us safe.

CHAPTER TWENTY-TWO

It took me and Lysette an impolite amount of time to make it downstairs. First we had to inspect each other's make-up in forensic detail. Then we roared like dragons in each other's faces like our teenage alter-egos to check for bad breath, as much for the ritual as anything else, the wordless reminder of our shared history. Finally we made our way down the twisting staircase, our high heels sinking treacherously deep into the mossy pile of the taupe carpet.

We walked past the TV room on our way to the kitchen, the scene almost identical to the last time I'd come here. The two junior Farthings were sprawled out in front of the blaring television, the canned laughter and American accents a jarring contrast to the tranquil beauty surrounding the house. Their parents were, in principle, revelling in it. They were sitting on the patio outside the kitchen, cool drinks set out in front of them, neither of them feeling the need to speak. As I looked at the tableau I couldn't help thinking that it spoke of something more complicated than deep marital intimacy.

Nigel sprang to his feet as soon as he noticed us. He was

already in his dinner jacket, bow tie impeccably knotted. His black shoes shone like autumn conkers, his dress shirt was as white as a fresh dusting of snow. He gave a broad smile that seemed to welcome us not just to his home, but to something bigger, something more fundamental. His kingdom, perhaps.

'Don't you both look lovely?' he said. 'Thank you so much for joining us tonight – we're honoured to have you along for the ride. Let me organise you some drinks whilst we wait for the car.'

Nigel's voice made him sound as if he'd been catapulted directly from the 1940s. Cut glass didn't begin to cover it.

'Thank you,' I said, 'I think I'll just have a sparkling water.'

'My tipple of choice,' he said, a twinkle in his eye. 'Let's live a little and ask Lori to add a slice of lime. And you?' he asked, turning his attention to Lysette.

His gaze was like a laser beam: you could almost feel its heat as it moved.

'She'll go bubbles, won't you?' said Kimberley, waving her flute like a baby with a rattle. 'I need somebody to keep me company.'

Lori had silently appeared, her large, dark eyes tracking us.

'Oh, poor you,' said Nigel lightly. Their eyes met for a second, neither of them smiling.

'I'll get drinks,' said Lori, into the silence.

'That would be very kind,' said Nigel, his smile locking back into place.

*

294

Nigel held open the door of the large black car that had come to collect us, sweeping down into a mock bow as we lined up. Kimberley smiled haughtily, pulling her gauzy wrap around her bony shoulders as she climbed in. Watching her made me realise that I'd forgotten my trusty trench. I apologised, dashed across the crunchy gravel as agilely as heels allowed, and slipped back through the door. I'd have to ask Lori to dig it out of the coat cupboard.

'Lori?' I called.

'You're not my mum!'

The words hit me at top volume. I poked my head round the door of the TV room. The younger boy – Lucas, if memory served – was holding an enormous remote control, red in the face with rage.

'You must calm down,' said Lori, a helpless look in her eyes. 'Is time for homework.' His brother was coolly observing them, a certain relish in his cornflower-blue eyes.

'You're just my servant,' spat Lucas. 'You're my slave, like in Roman times.'

'Slave!' shouted the older boy. 'Slave, slave, slave.'

'Don't you dare speak to Lori like that,' I said, not stopping to think. 'Do you want me to go and get Kimberley?' I asked her.

'No. No, no,' she said, looking even more distressed. 'What you need?'

'I just came back for my coat. Please don't worry though ...'

'I get for you,' she said, visibly relieved to have found a face-saving exit strategy.

I stole a last look at them both – they were swaddled in logo-covered leisure wear, top of the range technology and calorific snacks strewn around them. I tried not to find them despicable. They were boys not men, after all, moulded and shaped by their environment. None of my wise inner monologue was working – they were a pair of little shits.

I followed Lori to the coat cupboard, risked putting a hand on her shaking arm.

'I should have got for you the first time,' she said, her face turned away from me.

I withdrew my hand. 'No, I should have remembered.' She pulled out my coat, turned to hand it to me. 'You sure you don't want me to get their mum? You shouldn't have to put up with that kind of behaviour.'

She paused, gave a pained attempt at a smile.

'No, no. I need this job. I was knowing it would be,' she screwed up her face as if she'd smelt something utterly disgusting, 'not so nice before I came. The money is nice though.'

'How did you know? Did Susan tell you?'

She nodded, something like fear in her eyes. She turned back, firmly closing the doors of the cupboard.

'Thank you,' she said. 'Please, though, please don't tell Mr and Mrs Farthing. I work it out.'

'No, thank *you*,' I said, slipping the coat on. 'If you ever need to talk to someone – even when I'm gone, there's my friend Lysette. She's a good egg. She'd speak to them for you.'

If she'd devoted a week to working it out, it's unlikely she'd have been able to translate 'good egg' into Romanian. Her face was shutting down again, a trace of regret that she'd revealed herself to me. Or was it the mention of Susan – elusive, mysterious Susan – that had made her back away?

I smiled a goodbye, and zigzagged my way back across the perilous gravel towards the purring black sedan. Even their car was unjustifiably pleased with itself.

*

The journey was hell. Every fibre of my being wanted to blurt out what I'd witnessed, but I'd made Lori a promise. Meanwhile, Nigel – who was sitting opposite us on a flip-down seat – was on a charm offensive. How did you train to do my job? Did I enjoy it? Did I think that criminality came down to nature or nurture? He listened to each of my answers intently, as if they were so wise that he ought to be carving them onto stone tablets for posterity. If my blood hadn't been pulsing so fiercely through my veins, it would have been hard to avoid being ground down by his silken flattery. It felt so natural, so meant. I could see why he glided down the corridors of power with the lightest of treads. The other two barely spoke for the entire length of the journey, Kimberley's face moulded into a mask of cold boredom.

'Thank you so much for indulging me,' said Nigel, as the car drew up outside a beautiful, Gothic-looking building which was part of one of the Cambridge colleges. It was floodlit, with a short red carpet, a couple of liveried officials taking tickets. 'We must talk again. I'm sure you'd have real insight into some of the problems we face with young offenders and gang culture.'

Kimberley's blue eyes rolled, almost imperceptibly. I felt my jaw clench, the memory of those two little boys – a two-man gang all of their own – fresh in my mind.

'I don't know that I would . . .' I paused a second. 'For what it's worth,' I said carefully, 'I do think it tends to be more about nurture than nature. A lot of those children need more support than they're getting.'

Kimberley stiffened, the air churning between us. Did she sense there was more to my words than a pointed comment about social inequality?

'But your job requires you to think that, doesn't it?' she said coolly. 'If it's all down to nature you might as well just pack up and go home.'

Lysette loyally jumped in.

'Mia's brilliant at her job. All her patients love her, and she unlocked a whole criminal case a couple of . . .'

She trailed off. Her words were solely for my benefit now. Nigel had climbed out, and Kimberley was following, face arranged perfectly for the flashbulbs that were erupting all around her. They stood and posed, his hand resting on the small of her back, their smiles never wavering. Kimberley turned her head towards him, rested it against his shoulder. More flashbulbs popped. Lysette and I hung back in the car, peeking round the door like a couple of urchins.

'They ain't seen nothing yet,' said Lysette, gamely placing her scuffed black heel on the ground. We clambered out, me trying to retain a modicum of elegance and not flash my knickers. I needn't have worried: the photographers briefly scoped us out, then waited for juicier prey. But then, as I walked up the red carpet, one of them grabbed my arm.

'You're the shrink, aren't you? You're working on the Sarah Bryant killing?'

It was the guy who'd been in the pub with April that first lunchtime. I looked away, refused to reply, but he was snapping photos by now, his huge camera jammed in my face.

'I can't do this!' gasped Lysette, rushing towards the doorway. He fired off a couple of rounds at her retreating back.

'Have some respect,' I hissed, hurrying after her.

Lysette was at the entrance with the Farthings, her distress written all over her face. Kimberley had an arm around her shoulders, was leaning into her, her body blocking me from getting too close.

'This is the last of our party,' said Nigel, politely downplaying Lysette's upset, and they waved us through.

We emerged into a large atrium, ancient and beautiful, the last of the evening sun glinting through the mullioned glass windows. Kimberley had pulled Lysette up ahead, Nigel and I drawing up at the rear. The room was packed with a smartly dressed crowd – they were sipping something with bubbles and sneaking looks at the Farthings. Nigel immediately began to move around the room, seeking people out, not even affording me a backward glance: he was like a bumble bee hell-bent on maximum pollination. It worked: people visibly blossomed in his presence, faces wreathed in smiles as soon as he approached. I watched him a second, his strong hand shooting out to shake hands with a curly-haired, portly man in a dinner jacket who also looked like he could have wandered in from another era. All of the people here exuded certainty and privilege, the two aspects inextricably locked. Nigel didn't allow his smile to fade, although it never quite reached his eyes. Who was it who dwelled underneath that shiny veneer?

I cast around for Lysette. She and Kimberley were doubling back, crossing the room with purpose. 'I need a minute,' she hissed, hurrying past me towards the loos. I hated the feeling it gave me, the sense I wasn't in their posse. Even if I didn't want to be, I wanted to be the one to make the choice. Why had I come here anyway? I grabbed a glass of Prosecco – no, as it hit the back of my throat I instantly knew it was champagne – and scoped out the room. Helena was arriving, her husband just behind her. The relief of seeing her was quickly offset by doom: Jim wasn't far behind, louchely handsome, his wife tightly gripping his hand. They hadn't seen me, which gave me a momentary advantage.

I wanted to avoid the comparison game, but sadly that level of spiritual self-mastery was beyond me. I'd only seen Rowena once before – at that party of Saffron's – and Lysette had deliberately avoided introducing us. She was wearing a blandly elegant long black dress – in fact most people who hadn't been offered Kimberley's cast-offs were wearing long – her auburn hair swept up in a chignon. I wanted to call it ginger, but it would have been a misrepresentation. Her brown eyes scoped the room, a certain nervous energy to her. She was perfectly attractive: nothing more, nothing less. I stopped myself analysing any further, spared both of us the indignity of trying to tally up our scores. He didn't deserve it, and my heartbroken teenage assumptions about the kind of woman who would hold his heart in a way I couldn't were irrelevant now. Being around him felt like a game of snakes and ladders, my adult self prone to slithering downwards into some kind of teenage mental hellhole. Right at that moment Jim glanced over, caught me looking at Rowena. His smile as he approached was a smug one.

'You're looking well!' he said.

'I look like an overcooked sausage,' I said. 'It's Kimberley's dress, and it's about two sizes too small.' I stuck out my hand, unnecessarily formal. 'Hello, I'm Mia,' I said to Rowena. 'Lovely to meet you.'

'Well, you look like a very classy sausage,' said Jim, his words overlapping with Rowena's.

'I'm Jim's wife,' she said, as if it wasn't blatantly obvious. 'Rowena. You're Lysette's friend from London, aren't you?'

I could see in her face, in the determined tilt of her jaw, that she knew full well that I had once been far more than that.

'I am, yes.'

Jim's smug smile was yet to evaporate: I had a feeling he was actually enjoying the awkwardness. How long could Lysette take to get back? I raised my glass to my lips, transferring it to my left hand in a pathetic attempt to ward off any hostility with a flash of my engagement ring.

'So, Mia's the investigation's secret weapon,' said Jim. 'She's right in there, finding out what everyone's been up to.'

Rowena's eyes narrowed.

'I'm not at all,' I said, trying not to sound defensive. 'I've just been offering a bit of support to people where I can. It's such a horrible thing that's happened.'

'Yes, so I've heard,' said Rowena, her tone knowing. 'That poor little boy.'

She'd obviously heard about a very specific sliver of my work. Who from? Would Lysette really be bringing me up to her? I discreetly swivelled my gaze, willing her to come back and save me, but there was no sign of her. The grand chamber was filling fast, a mass of satin and velvet. Plummy voices bounced off the stone walls, champagne flowing into eagerly tilted glasses.

'I like him very much,' I said.

'Mia to the rescue!' said Jim, dinner-jacketed arm flung forwards like a superhero mid-flight. A long-suffering look swept across Rowena's face, then swiftly disappeared.

'He's an odd one, isn't he?' she said. 'I'm sure he'll miss you once you've gone.'

Was she reassuring herself or warning me?

'I don't know about that,' I said. 'He's barely seen me.'

There was a grinding pause.

'We should say some hellos,' said Rowena eventually, her hand still tightly entwined with Jim's. 'Lovely to finally meet you, Mia,' she said, without any discernible warmth. Her eyes lingered a beat longer, making the same split-second calculations I'd already run: the grandes dames of feminism would surely have despaired of us. She led Jim away, missed him turning to mouth an unnecessary apology to me as they were swallowed up by the crowd.

There was still no sign of Lysette. Helena and her husband were deep in a conversation with another couple and I felt too unsettled by my uncomfortable encounter with Rowena to go and crash it. As I considered my options, I heard the clink of metal against glass: Nigel was stepping onto a stage that was set up at the far end of the room. He scanned the crowd as he did so, the setting sun streaming through the stained-glass windows behind him. He looked almost biblical, a prophet giving his very own sermon on the mount.

'So sorry to intrude on what's already proving to be a sparkling evening,' he said.

Kimberley and Lysette were hurrying back now, bright-eyed and conspiratorial. Nigel's eyes settled on them a second and from the set of his face I could tell that Kimberley's presence was what he'd been scanning for before he began.

'The fact that you're here, that you've taken time out of your busy lives to think about lives so much less fortunate than ours, is a source of great comfort and pride.'

The two of them had planted themselves to the left of the

stage, and now Lysette was vigorously beckoning me over. Part of me wanted to ignore her, punish her for abandoning me for a good fifteen minutes, but it was too churlish. I breathed in the crowd as I squeezed my way through the nest of their tightly packed bodies. I couldn't really imagine Patrick in this stiff environment – I knew how ludicrous and alien he'd find it. It made me only half wish he was here, a fact that made me prickle with unease.

Nigel's words washed over me as I wriggled my way through the crush of rapt guests.

'These children – facing a fate that's almost unimaginable – could be our children,' he was saying. 'And every one of us would walk through fire if they were.' I thought of those mean-spirited little boys, wondered if they really felt like their gilded, accomplished parents would walk through fire on their behalf?

I arrived next to Lysette, but she barely seemed to notice me. Her left hand was wrapped around Kimberley's, her eyes locked on Nigel. My unease sharpened. What was this? Was that kiss Kimberley gave me in the bathroom nothing but a Little Copping version of hello?

'So I ask you to dig deep. To shake out your purses and wallets until they're raining money!' He raised his hands, fire in his eyes. 'Come on, Cambridge, let's start a tsunami.' The crowd whooped and cheered. 'Let's show these families how much we care. Let's raise our glasses and drop our cash. Here's to a wonderful night.'

Lysette and Kimberley were cheering with the best of

them, stamping their feet at each other in a frenzied huddle. I primly clapped, watching Nigel zigzagging through the adoring crowd towards us. Ushers were trawling the room with buckets, people scribbling cheques and bundling in notes. Eventually he arrived at his wife's side.

'Well done, darling!' said Kimberley, reaching upwards to plant an extravagant kiss on his lips. All eyes were on them and she knew it.

'It seemed to do the job, didn't it?' he said, his face ablaze. His eyes kept scoping in the humming room, feeding off the pulsing energy.

'Abso–fucking–lutely,' said Lysette, smashing her flute against Kimberley's. There was no doubt she was well on her way to the danger zone. As I looked at her, trying to keep the worry out of my face, I caught Jim's eye. He was staring at her too, but now his face melted into a slow smile. I gave a tight one back, deliberately returning to the conversation.

'I'm definitely overdue a drink,' said Nigel, a waitress magically appearing at his side. 'You look in need of libation too, Mia. Can I oblige?'

'Thank you,' I said. 'And you totally deserve one – you did brilliantly up there.'

He plucked two glasses from the waitress's tray, threw away a dazzling smile. She visibly coloured, then shuffled off, embarrassed. I felt an unexpected stab of sympathy for Kimberley – I wasn't sure how comfortable I'd be if Patrick's offbeat charm had that effect on other women. Nigel was good-looking, sure, but not so good-looking you'd double take. It was about that mix of power and charisma, all shot through with a potent dose of self-belief.

'He always does,' said Kimberley, latticing her fingers through his and shaking out her cascading curls. 'We're really pleased you were able to come when the invitation was *so* last minute. It's just too bad Patrick couldn't make it.'

It still felt weird, hearing his name coming out of her mouth. He felt so far away right now.

'Absolutely,' agreed Nigel. 'You were very game, letting my wife clothe you. I must say, you've given that dress a whole new lease of life.'

I froze, not sure if my discomfort was an overreaction – an echo of a childhood spent calculating whether my father's latest fawning 'friend' was something more dangerous to me and my mum. No one else seemed to flinch.

'Mia's my oldest mate,' said Lysette. 'Of course she came. Helena!' she shouted, the volume turned up too high. She waved enthusiastically, arm windmilling above her head. 'Helena!'

I was deeply relieved to have our awkward little quartet broken up. Helena dispensed warm hugs, introduced me to her comfortingly normal husband Chris, congratulated Nigel.

'You look great,' she said, and I decided to take her at her word, use it as a means to take Nigel's comment as the straightforward compliment it was no doubt intended to be.

'So do you!' I said. It was true that the black lace of her dress was stretched taut, but she looked womanly and rounded, her crimson lips and chunky gold jewellery adding to her presence.

'No Ged?' Chris asked Lysette, and I saw her face crumple a little bit.

'My boyfriend couldn't make it either,' I said quickly. 'You're very game, agreeing to get suited and booted.'

He looked like a man who was used to a suit, but not in a pompous way. He had laughter lines round his eyes, a bit of a paunch under his dress shirt. I got an immediate sense of him being comfortable in his own skin.

'I just do what I'm told,' he laughed, looking fondly at Helena, but his attention came too late. She'd been sucked away by Kimberley, by the deadly vortex of her attention. Lysette was also orphaned, pain blooming in her face now she'd been denied a distraction from Sarah's absence.

'I need some water,' I said quietly. 'Come and find it with me?'

She nodded, and we slipped off. It was childish, but I felt like I'd achieved something by spiriting her away from Kimberley. I grabbed a glass, then pulled her towards a stone bench, built into the curved wall. It felt tucked away, the cacophony of voices bouncing off the domed ceiling and reverberating around us.

'Are you OK?' I said. 'That guy was hideous – grabbing at us like that. I know ...'

I didn't finish the sentence, aware I was a stuck record. Besides, I didn't know. Not really.

'He was grabbing at *you*,' she said, morose. Her eyes

scanned the room, an expression of bitterness on her face. 'I didn't matter at all.'

'What do you mean?' I asked.

'I knew Sarah better than anyone.'

Their circle of two. All of us — even Kimberley — were now the consolation prize.

'Better than Joshua?' I said lightly. I was needling her, I knew I was.

'Way better,' she said, emphatic. 'It's different, isn't it? Men just don't get it a lot of the time.'

The words felt burdened with meaning, overripe. She'd always been so relaxed with Ged, accepting of both of their imperfections; in the years before I'd met Patrick, I'd envied them that ease.

'I don't know,' I said. 'I think it's dangerous if we start thinking of them as a different species. I'm not sure they are from Mars, really.' A look of irritation scudded across her face. 'I'm not saying it's easy. I need to put some serious work in with Patrick when I get home.'

'You've always got a curriculum, haven't you?' she said, and I tried not to feel stung. The trust between us was still so shaky: it had that juddering quality that might or might not signal an earthquake.

'I try to make an effort with things,' I said, my voice high and unnatural.

'I need to make an effort with Ged,' she said, her shoulders suddenly drooping. 'It's not good between us, Mia. Hasn't been for ages.'

I felt a wash of guilt – all those months I hadn't noticed how troubled she was. Her problems with Ged – they were only a fragment of a bigger whole. And I was fast running out of time to see the big picture.

'Is it about money? I know you're really strapped . . .'

'I know I owe you that money,' she said, snappy in a way that smacked of shame. 'I will get it back to you.'

'It's not important . . .' As I said it, I knew it wasn't true. It was the official version of my feelings, presented to cause minimum upset.

'The way it's been between us – that's why I've needed my friends so much. Not having Sarah . . .' Her eyes filled. 'Thanks for putting up with me.'

'I'm not putting up with you,' I said. 'You're – you're my friend.' Now it was my words which were too pregnant with meaning. 'And you and Ged – he really loves you, Lys. Friends are a different thing. We'd wind each other up too if we permanently had to share a bathroom.' A painful, wrenching memory of her asking me to leave – the twist of her face as she did it. I couldn't risk venturing back there. 'Though it's true I wouldn't leave the loo seat up and pee around the side,' I added, my smile forced.

She shrugged her shoulders, a discomfort about her.

'Kimberley thinks you don't like her,' she said quickly.

Of course. A passive-aggressive masterstroke.

'Really?'

'She's worried she's upset you.'

'Right,' I said, trying to quell the heat building up inside

309

me. I looked out into the hubbub, buying myself a few precious seconds. My eyes alighted on Jake, expertly choreographing a fleet of waiting staff. They were filing out of the kitchens, canapés piled high on silver trays, fanning out into the crowd like synchronised swimmers. Increasingly tipsy guests grabbed at the tasty morsels, barely looking at the human beings delivering them. 'So why does she think that?'

'She thought you were a bit weird with her in the car. And you didn't really say thank you for the dress. Don't worry – I smoothed it over. I told her it was my fault – you were upset I'd shot my mouth off about the baby stuff. It's fine.' It was absolutely not fine. I bit my lip, my mouth forming itself into a grim line. 'Maybe just say thank you later. If you get the chance.'

Frustration finally got the better of me, erupted out.

'If I *was* weird in the car, it was because I'd just seen her vile, entitled brats telling that poor au pair she was their slave. She must be so desperate to put up with it – whoever Susan was, she obviously couldn't stand it.' Lysette's face froze as she heard the name, blanched itself of colour. I should've stopped, asked her where the shock was stemming from, but I was on too much of a roll. I'd trotted out the party line instead of the truth for too long, and now it became a toxic tide. 'She's always undermining me – did you not hear that dig she made about how useless my job was in the car? And I had every right to be upset about you telling her about . . . about that. It's none of her fucking business.'

Lysette's pale face had closed in on itself like an origami fold. We'd lost each other all over again.

'So you *were* upset with her. She was right.'

The edit she'd made of what I'd just said felt like a kick in the guts. How long was the list of friends who meant more to her than I did?

'You don't think she's even a tiny bit manipulative?' I hissed. 'From what you said about the famous quiz night, it certainly sounds like Sarah did.' I wanted to call the words back as soon as they'd escaped my stupid mouth, but it was too late. Lysette stood up, her hands visibly shaking.

'Lys, I'm sorry. Sit down, I shouldn't have brought Sarah into it . . .'

'I need to get some air.' She threw the words over her shoulder, already stalking off.

CHAPTER TWENTY-THREE

I should have slipped away, trusted the cold light of day to make things better, but something inside me wouldn't let me accept defeat. Instead I sat there on the bench – my bum aching from resting on cold and unyielding ancient stone, my heart pounding so hard I could hear the pulse in my ears – waiting to decide what I should do. The crowd acted as a human curtain, but I was too close to the loos to rely on staying hidden from all the people I wanted to avoid. Eventually Alex appeared out of the crush, looking left and right like a suspicious dormouse coming out of hibernation. She gave me a brisk smile and made her way over.

'You made it, then,' she said. 'Kimberley got you all kitted out?'

Her own outfit was wilfully dowdy, a shapeless and faded cotton dress, black its only concession to formality. Her shoes were flat and buckled, reminiscent of the kind I endlessly battled with my mum about when I was at primary school. I looked at them now with a certain envy, my feet aching and throbbing in the deluxe torture chamber of my borrowed high heels.

'She certainly did,' I said. Was there something knowing in that smile? It emboldened me. 'Did you not fancy the chance to run wild in her wardrobe?'

'I know my limitations, Mia. Glamour isn't something I prize.'

The way she said it sounded liberated, not bitter. What had brought her into their inner sanctum, brought her here?

'Fair enough.' I felt foolish suddenly, sitting there alone on my bench. I stood up. 'Are you having a nice evening?'

'Useful might be a better word. There's a lot of faculty here.' I followed her gaze, the players more visible now I was standing up. Kimberley was laughing at something Jake was saying, her head thrown back, Lysette kept close, like a toddler's favourite toy. 'There's a certain irony in raising money for desperate children with a champagne knees-up rather than a tax rise, but if it works ...'

This time the look we exchanged said it all.

'Isn't there just?' I said.

'You're going home in a few days, aren't you?' she said, intelligent eyes searching my face. 'Maybe we'll see each other again in happier circumstances.'

I sensed it was a tacit apology.

'I need a pee,' I said, not trusting myself to come up with the right reply. 'I'll see you in a bit.'

*

313

I headed for the immaculate gardens first in a vain attempt to clear my head. I stood there in the half-light, surrounded by women in mountains of taffeta, who looked like they'd stepped straight out of the pages of a mildewed copy of *Country Life*. Most people were smoking, blissfully unaware of how flammable their dresses likely were. I did need a pee it turned out – three glasses of champagne and a bucketload of stress will do that to a person – so I slipped back inside. I couldn't face crossing the main room again; instead I headed deep into the warren-like building in search of alternative facilities.

Even the loos were ancient: the cubicles had wooden doors and the china cisterns had elaborate pull flushes that wouldn't have looked out of place in *Downton*. The bathroom was deserted, so I sat there longer than necessary, reluctantly admitting to myself that what I should probably do was quit while I was ... not exactly ahead, but in a place where things were still salvageable. I felt a stab of sadness. Salvageable wasn't good enough, not for any of my relationships. I scrabbled in my bag for my phone: nothing from Patrick. I didn't text him – anything I came up with sounded either maudlin or shallow or both. I could've called him, but I couldn't face him humouring me, listening with half an ear to my schoolgirl complaints whilst he dealt with the kind of gruesome horrors that he routinely shielded me from. The clockwork mechanism inside a relationship is so fine, so delicate. If one tiny piece ceases to work, the whole can simply shudder to a stop.

I yanked the flush, water cascading into the bowl, Niagara style. I heard it immediately: a scrabbling sound, a muted giggle which seemed to be coming from another cubicle. 'Ssh,' said a low voice, which sounded suspiciously like Kimberley's. More giggling. A cubicle suddenly burst open, two pairs of heels clacking loudly across the stone floor like energetically played maracas. I could've rushed out, copped a look, but I didn't. Instead I sat there, my brain whirring. Was it what I thought it was? *Who* I thought it was? Would Kimberley really be that stupid? To threaten Nigel's career like that – to take drugs at a charity ball, press more present than ever in the aftermath of Sarah's death – surely not? I thought of their stamping, wild-eyed frenzy after his speech, the jagged unpredictability of Lysette's mood: I needed to get out of here. I crossed to the sinks, my actions calm and deliberate. I washed my hands, the old-fashioned bar of soap heavy and slippery between my palms. I applied more lipstick, baring my teeth to check for smearing. I'd go and say some polite goodbyes, thank Kimberley for her uncomfortable dress through gritted teeth. I'd be dignified. Dignified and distant. Anything more would only cause more harm.

When I stepped back into the main room, I could sense immediately that something had shifted. The music was no longer elegant and tinkly; it had a beat to it. People were more raucous, empty glasses stacking up on the tables that ringed the room. I stood on the sidelines a second.

'Mia? There you are!' It was Helena. 'I thought you'd snuck off. Decided it was all a bit Home Counties for you.'

'Of course not,' I said, half wishing I had. Why was I still trying to win the PR battle?

I spotted them then, Kimberley and Lysette, dancing together near the makeshift stage. Kimberley was elegantly gyrating, lithe body corkscrewing to the music, but Lysette was doing something else entirely. She'd given herself entirely to it, her eyes somewhere else, somewhere unreachable. A cold, trickling sensation gripped my insides, the impossibility of detachment obvious the minute I laid eyes on her. Helena followed my gaze, then looked away, her discomfort like static electricity.

'They certainly know how to have a good time,' I said.

'Yeah, yeah, they do,' said Helena, sounding almost guilty. Lysette's pale, bare arms were flung above her head, whirling through the air: it was hard not to feel hurt at her total lack of concern for what had happened between us. A few more people had started dancing now, but no one else was behaving like they'd been transplanted directly from Studio 64. I discreetly scanned the room for Jim, but there was no sign of him. If he wasn't with Rowena, I knew instinctively that he'd be outside, chain smoking Marlboro Lights and smirking at the taffeta. The certainty irritated me – the reminder that you can't ever un-know someone who has at one time been your everything. That there will always be a place deep inside of you that they'll have somehow annexed, made uninhabitable for anyone who sets up camp in your future.

'It's a shame your boyfriend couldn't come,' said Helena,

turning towards me. I could tell she was trying to distract me from the heightened tableau ten yards away. 'I reckon Chris would've appreciated someone new to hang out with. He hates this kind of thing.'

Despite her pretence at conversation, her eyes were still trained on Lysette and Kimberley, an air of distraction about her. Was she breakable right now?

'Lysette seems . . .' But before I'd had time to broach what it was I wanted to say, Nigel had glided between us. I felt a light touch on the small of my back, his other hand landing briefly on Helena.

'How are you glamorous creatures enjoying your evening?' he asked, his fingers increasing their pressure. 'Would you deem it a success?'

Helena's smile was bashful: I found it almost repellent how starstruck everyone seemed to be, even their inner circle. I discreetly shifted my body away.

'It's impressive,' I said, cool. 'You certainly know how to create an occasion.'

Nigel gave a modest shrug.

'I'm just the figurehead. Glad you approve.'

His eyes had moved to Kimberley. They watched each other a second, before she beckoned him over with a feline curl of her hand.

'Don't let us keep you from the dancing,' I said. Lysette had spotted me now.

'Not really my thing,' he said, the words as dry and stiff as cardboard. He gave a rueful shrug, headed towards her, as much for the benefit of the bug-eyed guests as anything else, I suspected. There was an odd dislocation about them. Lysette meanwhile was crossing the floor in the opposite direction.

'Mia,' she said. I'd expected slurring, a lack of focus, but the opposite was true. Her eyes were sharp and bright, her expression determined. 'Let's go outside, talk.' The words came fast, each one tumbling on top of the next. 'Sorry, Hels, you don't mind, do you?'

Helena murmured her assent, and she pulled me away, brooking no argument. She took a deep swig from her glass, her jaw subtly moving up and down.

'The garden's full of smokers,' I said, mulish.

'We're not going there,' she said, fingers digging into my bare arm. 'We're going round the back. It's an adventure!'

She led me through some more labyrinthine corridors, then out into a small stone courtyard. The darkness had fully taken hold now, with only a faint glow from the main atrium offering a trace of light. The silence was absolute too – we'd strayed too far from the party to hear an echo of the hubbub. Ivy hung low from the ancient brickwork, and I pushed it away from my face. It was all a bit too Gothic for my liking. There were a couple of wrought-iron chairs next to a little table, and Lysette threw herself down in one, scrabbling in her clutch bag for a cigarette. As she flamed her lighter, her face – familiar and alien all at once – loomed out of the darkness. That manic glint in her eye was more than adrenalin and alcohol, I knew it for sure now. I felt a chill run through me that was about more than my bare arms. I'd never been around her on drugs – until a few weeks ago I'd never even considered the idea they were still a part of her life. Did I really want to start now?

'So why did you want to come out here?' I said, a coldness in my voice.

'Don't, OK? Don't let's be like this with each other any more. I can't stand it. Let's just ...' She reached across the metal table, her chair legs squealing against the flagstones, and grabbed both my hands. 'Truce?'

Any words I could summon up seemed to be lodged in my throat. I couldn't bring myself to trust the rambling sentimentality that comes from a bottle or a line – I'd been burned too many times, seen my dad turn on a sixpence and ultimately become so dangerous to my emotional health that I'd had to spend twenty years estranged from him.

'Of course I don't want to fall out with you,' I said, my formality like a straitjacket. I shivered, wrapped my arms around myself in a poor approximation of a hug.

'Don't be like that!' she begged. 'Don't be all ... Mia 2.0. I just haven't been able to talk to you properly. I haven't been able to talk to you for ages.'

'Why not?' I said, the hurt blooming in my voice. Here it was: the confirmation that it was more than Sarah's death that had alienated us. That I'd somehow failed her.

She spoke with a quiet intensity. 'Because you wouldn't have liked me.'

My hurt and anger intensified.

'You set me up every time. You make out that I'm this

judgemental bitch, who thinks I'm better than you, and it's not true.'

'I see the way you watch my wine glass, Mia . . .'

She took a defiant gulp as she said it.

'That's . . . you know what I'm like. My dad . . . you were there!' I paused, our shared history rearing up towards me. 'Is it so bad, anyway, that I worry about you? When you're going through all of this? You asked me to come here!'

Even in the faint light, I could pick out the bleakness in her face that felt like more than grief. She pulled the last drag from her fag, lit the next one off it, her hands shaking.

'Our lives are like . . .'

She held her hands apart.

'But it doesn't matter!' I said. 'It shouldn't matter – we all get so hung up on what's different. Do you not think I feel like I've failed when everyone's going on about their perfect families? Women get set these impossible ideals and then we end up turning on each other . . .'

Now I'd climbed onto my soapbox she'd stopped listening. She gave a dry laugh.

'Perfect? Is that what it looks like?'

'No, of course not. I'm not that naive. I can see you've been having a hard time for ages. You're in debt – you're . . . Lys, I know you're taking coke. You've taken it now, haven't you? I'm not judging you for any of it. I just want to be a friend to you. That's all I've ever wanted,' I added, my voice cracking a bit.

'Me too,' she said, her voice wobbling. 'I've been a shit friend. I've just had nothing left.'

She swooped down, grabbed her clutch. She shook some powder onto a make-up mirror, straightened it with a card, pulled out a rolled-up note.

'Lys, don't. You don't need to do that.'

Her eyes blazed.

'What about if I like it? What about if it's the only thing getting me through? Why don't you try some and then tell me what I should do?'

She leant down low over the wrought-iron table and snorted it up, defiant, made a little noise of satisfaction once it disappeared. It took everything I had to not simply stand up and walk away, but I couldn't leave her there, wallowing in the confirmation of everything she'd just said. I felt so far away from her right then, so lonely, even though we were sitting inches apart. I knew it was the same for her, alone on her dark high.

'I don't want to,' I said, even though part of me, in that moment, actually did. Or at least I wanted to want to. I wanted to be brave enough, abandoned enough, far enough away from my painful childhood. 'But I'm not judging you.'

It was a lie, and we both knew it. Why had truth become so ruinously expensive for us? She drained her glass, that manic quality back in full effect as the drugs took hold.

'Why did you say that thing about Susan?' she demanded.

I paused – I didn't want to make Lori's life any harder than it already was.

'I don't know – I just keep hearing her name.'

Lysette took a pull on her cigarette, an accusing look on her face. 'What, from the police?'

I started calculating, aware I could use the advantage of my relative sobriety. 'I'm not sure.'

Lysette stared at me, her face an appeal for clemency. 'We did look after her, Mia, we did.'

'Right,' I said.

'I didn't even think we should let her take the blame for it, but it was Kimberley's house.' Her eyes blazed. 'It would've been all over the papers. He'd have had to resign. And for Sarah – she could've . . .' Tears began to run down her cheeks, laying her mascara to waste: she looked almost ghoulish in the faint-light.

'She could've gone to prison, Mia!' I could hear the desperation in her voice. 'Imagine how that would've been for Max. And my kids – Ged could've left. But now . . .'

I couldn't keep treating her like a difficult patient – I pulled my chair closer, flung out my arms to gather her close. 'Tell me what happened, Lys. I won't judge you, I promise you that.'

'Everyone's acting like it's over,' she said, her voice low and intense. 'But it's not over for me! It's such a fucking mess, and Sarah's not here to clean it up.' Her voice rose, desperate. 'It's getting worse!'

'What do you mean?' Lysette shook her head, refused to answer. 'You don't need to go through this on your own.'

'I'm not on my own – but I am on my own!' Her fists balled with frustration. 'It's not just down to me.'

'What – Kimberley and Alex and Helena? You know I heard

you in the kitchen . . .' I stared at her, willing her to focus. This was our chance. 'I know you're all hiding something.'

'I know you don't like her, but she is my friend.'

She was too drunk, too high, to follow a straight line. I had to dodge and weave to keep us on the same track.

'I know she is,' I said, my voice deliberately soothing. 'And you know her much better than I do.'

It was like we'd summoned her up with the power of our words – a spiteful blonde sprite. She sailed into the isolated quad, the heavy door slamming behind her.

'There you are! I was worried.'

'Hi, Kimberley,' I said, through gritted teeth.

She pulled up another chair, perched on it. I considered her, Lysette's words blaring in my head. *It was Kimberley's house. He'd have had to resign.*

'Have you kissed and made up?' she asked, looking between us expectantly.

'I love Mia,' said Lysette, squeezing in closer. I couldn't help thinking it was the kind of sentimental line which came from a line.

'It's freezing out here!' said Kimberley. She rubbed hard at Lysette's bare arm, taking in her ravaged face but choosing not to pass comment. 'Don't you want to come back inside? Quick trip to the loos and hit the dance floor?'

'Don't worry about the loos,' I said, emboldened. 'Lysette's been quite open about the coke out here.'

Her eyes betrayed her, but she immediately got herself under control.

'Your make-up's a little bit ...' she said, gesturing to Lysette. She turned to me, gaze intense. 'I'm so sorry if I upset you earlier.'

I shot straight back. 'You didn't.'

'No ... I should've known it would be a sensitive area.'

Sucker punch: so many ways to read that sentence.

'It's fine.'

'I always tell my childless friends, enjoy it while it lasts!' It was obviously her stock phrase: I'd already heard it at dinner. 'You were telling Lysette my two terrors were on pretty feisty form, weren't you? Giving you a taste of the nightmare!'

Her mouth was smiling, but her eyes were doing nothing of the kind. I couldn't do this. I stood up.

'Let's go in,' I said, but neither of them moved.

'We'll catch you up,' said Lysette, words too fast, too staccato. I couldn't leave her.

'Lys ...'

'Honestly, you're so thoughtful,' said Kimberley, syrupy sweet, 'but you're off duty. You really don't need to babysit.'

*

I stumbled back inside on shaky legs. It wasn't just my legs: all of me was shaking, inside and out. Lysette had brought out a bottle of white – I hadn't realised how much I'd been tipping back as we talked. Now all I wanted was to get away, but the back corridors Lysette had led me down all looked the same. I skittered my way down a seemingly endless one, portraits of long dead dons looking down at me from the walls, stern and disapproving.

After a couple of wrong turns, I finally arrived on the periphery of the main room. I leaned against a stone pillar, took a moment to collect myself. Nigel's smile still hadn't faltered: he was in the centre of a group of smartly dressed acolytes, all of them laughing in unison. Sarah whispered across my consciousness. I couldn't imagine her there in that group, all velvety and smug. How did she fit in – or was the fact that she didn't the reason she wasn't here any more? I had an illogical stab of fear for Lysette, then came back down to earth. Kimberley was a bitch, not a killer.

'You waiting for them to play "Careless Whisper"?'

Jim was the other side of the pillar, eyes dancing even if his body wasn't.

'I was going to go, actually.'

'Don't do that. The night is young,' he added in a silly voice.

I looked at my watch, my goose-bumped arm shaking as I raised my wrist. It was shortly before ten but it felt more like midnight to me.

'I don't want to turn into a pumpkin,' I said.

'No danger of that,' he said, voice low.

'Where's Rowena?' I asked, deliberately steely.

'She's gone. She's got an early start.' With your kids, I thought. 'I was actually coming to ask you where Lysette was.' I looked at him, searching for the right words. I didn't need to: he read them anyway. 'Come and tell me about it,' he said, jerking his head back towards the door I'd come through. I didn't move immediately. 'Mia, this is about my sister.'

I felt foolish – vain and young all at once. My aching feet obediently followed his – it wasn't like I didn't need someone to talk to, and he was the only person I could confide in without it constituting a betrayal. I briefly looked back as I did: there was Lisa, her flouncy dress made out of a fabric more suited to a country house sofa, her hair lacquered into a solid cone. It might've been paranoia, but it felt like her eyes were directly trained on me.

Luckily Jim didn't head for the quadrangle I'd left Kimberley and Lysette behind in. After a few dead dons he took a sharp right and led me through swing doors to an area behind the kitchens. I'd have worried about rats if we'd been in London, but here in Cambridge all I could smell was honeysuckle. There was a wooden bench. Jim threw himself down, extracted a packet of fags from the inside pocket of his artfully creased dinner jacket. Lights blazed from the kitchen, chatter and shouts coming from the chefs and waiting staff.

'Want one?' he said, cocking his head. 'No, of course you don't.'

'Yes,' I said, defiant. I'd had enough of their family's narrative about me. Jim lit a cigarette for me, waited for my first puff with a look of amused fascination. I took a tiny, pathetic drag, tried not to choke. He took a puff on his.

'I envy you,' he said. 'Row's constantly on my tail to give up.'

Was he protecting himself by mentioning her, or subtly implying unhappiness? Sometimes I preferred my treatment room to real life: at least it was there in my job description to force clarity from people.

'Yeah, Patrick likes a sneaky fag when he thinks I'm not looking.'

'Your boyfriend?'

'Fiancé.'

'Right.' He sounded faintly amused by the idea – like I'd said back then to Kimberley, it was a ridiculous word, the kind of thing Hyacinth Bucket would say. 'Where's my sister? I looked all over for her.'

'She's . . .' The words jammed, that feeling of shock reverberating back through me. All of this, all of this meaningless, ephemeral flirtation was bullshit. Sarah was dead, and Lysette was on the edge of something very dangerous. 'Jim, I'm really worried about her.' My voice shook. 'You were right about the coke. I went outside with her and she was just snorting it off a table. Anyone could've come out.' Kimberley did: I'd get to that. 'Even without what's happened to Sarah, she's obviously in a huge amount of debt, it's bad with Ged . . . I just don't know how to help her any more.'

Jim looked down at the ground, his face still and grim. A part of me hoped that he'd spring into action, that their sibling bond would afford him a metaphorical magic wand to wave. He stood up. I looked up at him, expectant.

'We need a drink,' he said. 'I'm going to ask Jake for some wine.'

He loped off to the kitchen. I shivered, dropped the cigarette I'd pretended to want, ground its glowing tip into the
flagstones with my heel, then guiltily hid it under the bench.
Jim emerged with another bottle of white. Jake stuck his head
out of the kitchen door a couple of seconds later.

'There you go, mate,' he said, pressing a couple of glasses
into his hand. He didn't register me, there in the shadows.
Jim sat back down, and I subtly edged down the seat away
from him.

'Don't you find it weird,' I said, 'the way everyone knows
everyone here? I'd feel like I was under surveillance.'

'You're clearly a lot more interesting than me,' he said,
balancing the glasses on the slats of the bench and slopping
wine into them. He handed me one, his fingers brushing
mine. 'And the surveillance hasn't worked so well the last
few weeks, has it?'

'Everyone seems to think they know what happened.
Who needs cameras?'

Jim rolled his eyes, took a gulp of his wine.

'So where is she?'

'We were out the back. We had this stupid little fight
earlier, like we keep doing, and she dragged me off. She was
coming out with all this stuff . . .' I stopped, took a sip from
my drink. It tasted sweet and bitter all at once. I was drunk
now, properly drunk. I took another gulp, trying to untan-
gle the chaos inside my head. I couldn't betray Lysette – her
rambling half-confidences – but equally I needed his help. *She*
needed his help. 'She's torturing herself. She started saying

something about it not being over, about it getting worse. But then your fit blonde trotted through the door and shut her up.'

Jim was smirking, childishly grateful for a reason to focus on the least important part of the story. Then his face became serious again, the silence lingering.

'I have tried to talk to her . . .' he said eventually. 'After her birthday party, and when I heard about the playdate. Then there was the quiz night – Sarah was out of control. I didn't even try that time. I knew by then it wouldn't do any good.'

'Joshua's so straight . . . why were they even together?'

'Opposites attract, don't they?' He was trying to hold my gaze but I didn't let it snag me. 'At least for the first few years. Once you've got kids, you're in it to win it.'

'He wasn't the first time around.'

'All the more reason to stick it out,' said Jim. 'Trust me, men don't like looking like fools.'

He looked away, distracted by a thought, a silent calculation taking place. I was sure it was the same piece that he'd backed away from in the French bistro, the thing that had made him so angry in The Black Bull. I was gentle, light. I sensed he wanted to unburden himself.

'What is it, Jim?'

'Violet told Rowena this thing . . .' He looked at me, face stricken. 'It frightened me, Mia. Lysette took her and Saffron into Cambridge one day, and they met up with Sarah. They were buying all this stuff, shoes and make-up. They were paying for everything in cash – they had loads of it. Violet had never seen so much.'

'Maybe – maybe Ged got paid in cash for a job, and—'

I could hear myself scrabbling around for a comforting explanation. Jim cut across me.

'They bribed her not to tell us. Bought her some perfume. Row was furious – she's only nine. She doesn't like her having stuff like that.'

'You must've confronted her that time?'

'Had to. Row won't let even let the kids go over there without us now. She was . . .' He had that faraway look again, like he'd like to be anywhere but here, squaring up to uncomfortable truths. 'You know what she's like. She's emotional but she's not a bitch.' His gaze met mine now. 'She was fucking vile about it – she was screaming at me. She looked crazy.'

I was shaking, as much from fear as from the rapidly dropping temperature. I shifted closer to Jim, wanting the comfort of his proximity. The slippery fabric of Kimberley's black dress rubbed against the grain of the bench, catching me as I moved.

'The way she's spoken to me the last few weeks . . .' I said. I traced a sharp peak with my hand. 'Her moods are like that.'

'It's a nightmare,' said Jim, his body subtly meeting mine. 'She said if I talked to Ged she'd never speak to me again, and the way she said it, was like she meant it.' His hands dropped heavily to his knees, a gesture of helplessness. 'Since Sarah died . . . I know she's getting worse, Mia. I hoped you being here would sort her out. To be honest, I was just grateful it wasn't her who died.' It was his voice which broke now. 'I'm no good at this stuff. You know that better than anyone.'

'No, I don't,' I said. 'I haven't seen you for twenty years.'

'Exactly. I'm a fucking hopeless case.'

Now we looked at each other properly, eyes locking in the sodium glow of the kitchen window. His child – the baby I'd known I couldn't have, and yet mourned so deeply when it had made its own decision to leave my body. My father – violent and terrifying – attacking him so viciously the morning of my planned abortion that all of our lives had been indelibly changed. It wasn't just Jim I hadn't spoken to for twenty years. We'd made a tentative recovery, my dad and me, now he was sober and contrite. And here was Jim, in front of me. There was only one piece I didn't know could ever be made better – no wonder Kimberley's sly aside had reduced me to a sobbing mess. It was about so much more than today. I felt those tears threaten again, took a couple of minutes before I trusted myself to speak.

'My dad should never have done that. It was right that he went to prison.'

'I know,' said Jim, putting his arm around me now and pulling me close. I let him. I couldn't not – in that moment it felt as if we were outside of time and space. 'But it wasn't your fault. And I was an immature little prick. I should have called you. You lost the baby. Our baby.' His face was near to mine, his eyes burning with feeling. 'It wasn't like I didn't think about it. Think about you. When I had kids too.'

The shame I'd felt in the aftermath had come from so

many different places. It had locked parts of me up, thrown away the key.

'Thank you for saying that,' I said. A sense of relief — unexpected and overwhelming — seeped through my whole being. I let my head rest against his chest, his heartbeat softly pumping against my cheek. Exhaustion followed the relief — I closed my eyes, unable to move. After a few seconds his body shifted, his lips suddenly on mine, smoky and alcoholic. I remembered that taste too well. It was intoxicating, and I was already intoxicated. I lost myself in it, our bodies pressed tight together, his fingers tangled up in my hair. Then I came to my senses, twisting my face away.

'Jim, no. We've got to stop. We shouldn't have done that.'

'What?' said Jim. 'I thought that's what you wanted?'

Our bodies were still dangerously close. His arm was tight around my waist, scooping my flesh towards him.

'You're married!'

'Yeah, and you're engaged,' countered Jim, scowling down at me.

'Exactly.' The thought of Patrick — steadfast, loyal Patrick — was fast sobering me up. 'That's why.'

'Really? You don't feel like it's been building up between us ever since you turned up here?'

We stared at each other, our faces only inches apart. In one sense it was true, and in another it was an absolute falsehood. That younger, more vulnerable part of me had splintered off without me knowing, it provided what she craved. Not the kiss, but the validation of it.

'Not so we should've done anything about it. You just introduced me to your wife!'

'Chill out, Mia, seriously. Fine. I misread your fucking confusing signals. Forget it.'

He ripped his fags out of his breast pocket with his left hand, scrabbling around for a light, then caught the cigarette between his full lips, his scowling profile lit up by the savage flame of his lighter. We still hadn't pulled apart – I knew it was imperative, and yet it seemed hypocritical to treat him like a predator when I'd co-authored this sorry mess.

A familiar voice called out. 'Mia?'

'She'll definitely be lurking around here somewhere!'

And then they were there, right in front of us. Patrick, his face crumpling in on itself with hurt, and Kimberley, lit from within by her ugly sense of triumph.

Sarah's Diary – June 15th 2015

Oh my God. Oh my God. First off, we took it too far, no question. When you're leaning over a kiddie toilet, hoovering up lines, you've gone over the edge. Lys looked at me like, is this bad? and then we took a bit more for the road. We were like gangsta rappers – Fuck The PTA. We kept chanting it and pissing ourselves laughing.

Something happens here – the way it all looks so pretty, and it's so ugly underneath. It makes everything twist out of shape. Last night Max begged me to read him The Gruffalo *for like, the millionth time, and I told him he didn't need to beg, it's my favourite story. All those scary animals coming out of the dark, dark wood. It's always dark here, even when the sun's shining its heart out and it's getting darker all the time. Thank God for Lysette.*

I nearly told her tonight, when we were giggling and scraping the little white flecks off the top. I can see the pain in his eyes, the wanting – I saw it tonight. That was when it hit me: it's not that I'm not hurting anyone, it's just that I'm choosing who to hurt. It was starting to eat away at me, wanting to be said, but then we skipped back out there, all of them with their stupid answer sheets and their special trivia faces, and I got distracted. I saw them, the two of them, their heads pushed together like no one else could know the answer. Like they were a double act. I felt this stabbing, deep inside, that sense of how much I love him. I'm addicted to him, I always have been. And then all I wanted was to win. I wanted her to know I wasn't just a stupid little waitress who got lucky.

There was too much flying around, silent agendas filling the space while it looked like all anyone cared about was how many African countries began with S. Kimberley saw, she saw the way he looked at me, and then she couldn't keep her eyes off me. I shouldn't have been so stupid as to use my phone, but I had the devil in me by then.

She punished both of us that night. You could say I deserved it, but there's no way he did. I'm not having it. I've got the devil in me all over again, but it's for different reasons now. She thinks she's in control, that she's pulling the strings. She's got a shock coming. With everything that's happened, everything I've seen, I can cut them any time I like and she'll be the one taking the fall. Her and all her fancy mates. They've got more to lose than any of us.

CHAPTER TWENTY-FOUR

'I don't want to play your game.'

Max wasn't the only one. Every time I thought about last night – and it was hard not to with a snare drum pounding out a relentless beat inside my aching temples – I felt disgusted with myself. How had I got into that situation with Jim? It was so hard to switch my phone off and come into this session, try not to think about whether Patrick would have finally responded to me.

'Do you want to play a different game?' I asked him, my voice bright and tinny.

I forced myself to focus: I needed to show up for him like I'd promised. A client of any size silently senses when you're only half there. It was Max who'd pulled out Hungry Hippos, laid it between us on the scratchy brown carpet of the reading corner, but now his face was mangled by a scowl.

'I hate Hungry Hippos.'

'Do you? So why do you think you got it out of the cupboard if actually you hate it?'

Max thought about it. His voice was a snarl when it came. 'I thought *you* liked *Hungry Hippos*.'

'Did you? I just asked if you wanted to play a game, and you went and got it.'

Was he trying to please me, then resenting me for making him do something he didn't want to do? If he was, he wasn't the only one. Every tiny event somehow managed to echo Patrick, sending another shockwave of guilt and regret through my battered system. 'What are you doing here?' I'd stuttered, which was absolutely the wrong thing to say: what was *I* doing drunk and entwined with the ex-boyfriend I'd totally whitewashed out of my account of the last few weeks? I could see from his expression as his eyes burnt into Jim that I wasn't the only one who'd done some furtive Facebook stalking. Our lips may not have been locked, but the tension between us was as subtle as a blaring car alarm on a suburban street. The hurt in Patrick's face made any explanation turn to dry ash in my mouth.

'You said you weren't mad, you were disappointed. Well, I didn't want to be a disappointment.'

The way he said it left no doubt as to who was the disappointment now. I sprang up, but I was left clutching a handful of his suit jacket. He was already pushing his way out: I chased him to the car, but all I got was a few angry words, the suggestion I stay with a friend if I ever bothered to come home, and finally a mouthful of exhaust fumes. I'd sent him a Bible's worth of texts, left countless messages, but he was point blank refusing to respond. Could something so stupid, so meaningless, really have ruined things between us? I had to believe this state of affairs was temporary.

'Games are stupid,' said Max, repetitively flicking the blue hippo's plastic jaw. The crashing sound sent a bolt of pain through my head on every flick. 'They're for babies.'

'Not always. Even grown-ups play games sometimes.'

'Only stupid grown-ups.'

His anger was simmering and spitting. I was actually quite heartened to see it: he had every right to be angry, and sending its flames out into the universe was infinitely better than letting them burn away inside himself. The children who fatally struggle are the ones who make sense of the senseless by blaming themselves. They get scarred deep within where no one can see, whilst the adults around them marvel at how well they're 'coping'.

'Do you think that grown-ups are stupid sometimes?' I asked.

I could answer that question for him very easily, I thought, as I subtly reached for the bottle of water I'd been forced to bring into session with me.

'My mummy isn't stupid,' he said, defensive.

'I know she isn't. What words would you choose for your mummy if you could have any ones you liked?'

He plunged small hands into the plastic balls that had pooled between the hippos, letting them trickle through his fingers, then scrunched them up into tight fists. The energy felt taut, as if he was summoning up all his inner strength to do her justice. I tried to silently send him support, my focus pin tight.

'She is very, very pretty. Not now, now she's buried in the ground – in the ground the maggots and worms eat you, that's what William said – but she is also in heaven, and there she is as pretty as when she's going out and she says goodnight and she gives me a Marilyn kiss.'

'What's a Marilyn kiss?' I asked.

He touched his cheek reverentially, grimy nails making black crescent moons against his pale skin.

'When you kiss with red lipstick on and it leaves your lips behind. If I woke up and she wasn't there, it meant she was still giving me a kiss.'

I saw her then, conjured up by his words, as clearly as if he'd caught her in a camera flash. She leant down deep over his small bed, perfume rising from her pores, white wine on her breath, chestnut hair a heavy curtain that fell against exposed flesh. Her kiss was extravagant, rendered more so by the smacking sound she gave it. No wonder Max was so reverential.

'Come on, Mia, you're losing!' he yelled. He thwacked the blue hippo's lever again and again, gobbling up plastic balls. There was nothing for it: I hit the green hippo's lever, snaffling a few balls of my own. It felt like my brain was shaking inside my cranium – I forced myself not to think about the shameful reasons why. Max was manic now, only sated once his hippo had gorged himself. He sat back on his haunches. 'You are very, very shit at Hungry Hippos,' he said, eyeing my reaction. 'You are fuck at it.'

'You definitely won,' I agreed, tracking the trepidation

that was rising in his face. 'I bet you're not allowed to swear like that at home. Or at school.' We eyed each other. 'But I'm not angry if you use those words in here with me. We just have to agree they stay inside our session.'

'OK,' he said solemnly.

'As long as you don't hurt yourself, hurt anyone else or take something away with you when you leave, you can use our sessions however you like.'

Max took that in. 'Fuck,' he pronounced, clear and confident. 'Poo,' he added, voice rising an octave. 'Wee. Fart.'

His face had lit up now.

'How does it make you feel when you say those words?' I asked him. I could see him struggle to find an answer and I jumped to my feet. 'Poo!' I shouted, jumping in the air, all instinct. Max followed suit, springing up.

'Wee!' he shouted. His swearing dictionary had reassuring limitations. 'Shit! Fart!'

He was grinning now, anger moving through his body and out into the ether. We jumped and shouted until we collapsed back down into a heap on the green beanbag, me trying not to think too hard about the dubious brown stains that peppered it. He brought his body close to mine, almost touching, the beans shifting and sliding beneath our weight.

'Was that fun?' I asked him, looking down into his owlish face. He nodded, glasses wobbling on his nose. 'I could talk to your daddy, and tell him we swore in a way that wasn't naughty. Sometimes when we're angry or sad it can be good to find a way to turn it into a noise or a movement. Perhaps you and Daddy can come up with some different ways to do that together?'

Max looked up at me, his face a picture of heartbreak. My own heart seized for a second, both for him and also not. I couldn't allow Patrick's stricken face to seep into my consciousness as I looked into his.

'I want my mummy to do that with me . . .'

'I know, Max. I can see you're very sad she's not here. It *is* very sad.'

His lip began to quiver, his face crumbling. Then he suddenly stood, the movement sudden, almost violent. 'Mummy. Not you! You're just a stinky lady who smells like a poo.'

For a paranoid moment I wondered if my fetid pores were leaking alcohol, but looking at him, I could see that the insult wasn't about me. Quite the opposite: it was about who I wasn't. Who wasn't ever going to come back and plant a Marilyn kiss on his warm bedtime skin ever again. I took a pause to consider my next move. I stood up too. I pulled at the fabric of the white shirt I'd hastily thrown on, gave it a theatrical sniff as I smiled at him. I'd told him it was his session: I was going to let him lead the way and see where he took us. Hopefully not head first down a toilet.

'Hmm, I don't *think* I smell like a poo.'

Max was emphatic. 'You do. You do smell like one.'

Anyone who'd walked in on our session right at that second would have been perfectly entitled to believe that therapy was the most pointless pile of magic beans known to man. I kept going, feeling my way.

'So why do you think I smell like a poo?'

'Because . . .' He was red in the face now, almost bursting out of his body with emotion. 'Because you're naughty. You ask too many things. When you're naughty you don't get treats.'

'And when do you get treats?'

'When you're good, stupid.'

'And what's being good? When are you good?'

It was the quick fire round. Max's eyes gleamed with determination behind his glasses.

'When you do exactly what your mummy tells you.' Now she was gone – his compass, his everything – he had no way to navigate the world. And here I was, giving him a whole new bunch of rules which came with a hefty price tag: that unbearable absence. 'When you zip up.' Again, that motion, his fingers slashing an imaginary zip across his face. What was locked up behind there?

'And what about when you're not good? Then what happens?'

His legs buckled. He sat back down on the beanbag, energy draining away.

His answer, when it came, had the bleak finality of a prisoner walking the corridors towards the electric chair. 'Then you get in bad trouble.'

'OK,' I said, dropping to the floor, and kneeling on the scratchy carpet a foot or so away from him. 'Max, what happens when you get in bad trouble?'

'I never did,' he said, voice small, head low. 'Not before. I was quiet as a grey mouse.'

Something was pulsing in the energy between us, something I couldn't yet identify. I went with the one piece I was sure of.

'Max,' I said, pausing until his eyes rolled upwards towards me. 'I want you to know that what happened to your mummy has got nothing to do with you. It's a very, very sad thing. You couldn't have done anything to stop it. Sometimes very unfair things happen in life which make us sad and angry, and we have to have lots of people to love us and talk to us. And lots of people do love you. Shall we make a list?'

Max nodded. 'Daddy,' he said. 'And Jessica?'

'She's your sister?' I asked.

'Half-sister,' he said firmly. 'My mummy is not her mummy.'

Had she taught him to be emphatic about that?

'Who else?'

'Jack. He's my half-brother. And Lisa. She's their mummy, not my stepmother.' This family tree was like his own complex mathematical equation. 'And Mr Grieve. When he came to see me and Mummy she said I could call him Peter.'

The hairs on my arms started to bristle.

'So did he come and visit?'

He nodded. 'The other children didn't know. They wouldn't have played with me.'

'So it was a secret? Did you keep it zipped up?' I asked, aping his zipping motion.

'Yes. He came to see me when I was in the hospital too.'

He emitted a manic laugh, the cry of an insincere hyena. 'Not really!'

Hospital again. I thought of that grim image from last night, Lysette defiantly snorting up her line, fronds of ivy lacing the picture-perfect building behind her. Had Sarah overdosed in Kimberley's show home? Was that what her garbled confession was straining towards? But surely if she'd been hospitalised it would have come out by now?

'You talked about hospital last time too, didn't you?'

His eyes slid away, back to Hungry Hippos. He idly flicked at the blue lever.

'When I was four we lived in Texas. I had a horse.'

It was patently Woody-related nonsense. I glanced up at the clock, angry with myself: time had run away with me, and I really wanted a moment to close this properly. Luckily there was no sign as yet of Joshua's pinched face peering through the classroom window.

'You're good at telling the time, aren't you?' I said, pointing at the classroom clock, with its thick black hands. Max nodded.

'Once I said Peter, not Mr Grieve, but only the mummy who was helping with my reading heard me.'

Perhaps Sarah wasn't the only cataclysmic loss he'd experienced. Joshua had simply told him that Mr Grieve wouldn't be there next term, keen to protect him from any more horrors, but if his teacher meant more to him than anyone knew, he might be stuck trying to make sense of another trauma – a secret one this time. I looked down at his bent head, his wisps of hair. I wanted so much to help him, but there was no time to excavate what it was he was saying. And if I left it half cooked, it would make my own disappearance even more brutal.

'Max, do you remember I told you that I don't live here? That we were only going to see each other two times?' He nodded solemnly. 'So we have to say a forever goodbye today.'

'OK,' he said, eyes drifting out of the window.

'I've really enjoyed spending time with you. Thank you for talking to me. There are other people who do what I do – people you can play with and talk about your mummy who aren't your family – if you liked it.'

'OK,' he said again, the word snapping out as hard and abrupt as the jaws of the plastic hippos. I hoped I hadn't already done more harm than good, started something I couldn't finish. At least I could tell Joshua that he'd responded, that he seemed to have extracted some comfort and there would be merit in finding someone who could be an ongoing presence for him. I looked to the door: still no sign of his dad.

'Shall we find your stuff?' I said. He'd brought in a backpack, Woody popping out of the top along with a matching Woody water bottle, loved into scuffed oblivion. He went to find it, then crossed to the bookshelf. He pulled out *The Gruffalo*, slipping it into the bag.

'Max?' I said. 'That's not yours, is it? Do you remember what we said about not taking things away? If you leave it here, you'll be able to see it when you come back to school.'

He turned towards me, expression mutinous.

'It is mine.'

When children do this, it's not naughtiness – it's about wanting to take away a piece of the work into a chaotic outside world. But keeping the boundaries, saying no, is part of what keeps them feeling safe. I smiled at him, let him know I wasn't angry.

'Do you have your own, special copy of *The Gruffalo* at home you can read?'

'I want this one.'

The one we'd read from together.

'I understand that, Max, but you can't take it home. It's for all the children to enjoy. You, as well. And I bet you have your own copy that you get to decide if people can read.'

He clutched his backpack to his torso like I was about to rugby tackle him, his face lit up by his fury.

'It's my book,' he yelled. 'I'm taking it. You can't stop me.'

I kept my voice deliberately calm. 'Max, I know you want it . . .'

'Fuck and poo,' he shouted, just as the door swung open. There was Lisa, a look of horror on her face, rooted to the spot – it was probably my own embarrassment looking for a target, but I couldn't help thinking her exaggerated expression had a whiff of bad am-dram about it. 'Wee and fart!' added Max for good measure, too consumed by rage to even notice her. Unlike me, Lisa was immaculate, even if her tailored navy trousers lacked London chic. Her severe bob barely moved as her head swivelled between us. I hated how apologetic the smile I flung at her was. How much of last night's shameful display had reached her gold-studded ears?

'Max, Lisa's here to get you now. Let's put the book back on the shelf, and say goodbye to each other.'

Max stilled, his body rigid. He turned to look at her, little warmth in his face.

'Max!' said Lisa, her face full of righteous purpose. 'Don't be such a rude little boy. You know better than that.'

'It's OK,' I said, trying to communicate with my eyes that she didn't need to shame him. 'We've been blowing off some steam today – we said it was OK to swear inside the session. I'll give Dad a call and tell him all about it.'

I smiled at Max again, and he robotically headed for the bookshelf, putting *The Gruffalo* back where he'd found it. He seemed to pack away all his rage with it, his face blank. I knelt down to his level, made sure I communicated I wasn't angry in my goodbye, but my words barely seemed to register. Where had he gone? I knew in that moment how hard it would be to stop worrying about him.

I was right too. And every shred of that worry would turn out to be justified.

CHAPTER TWENTY-FIVE

Once Max and Lisa had left, I sank back into the rocky embrace of the beanbag, and took a deep pull from my bottle of water. Therapy clients don't work like break-ups: there's no formula for length of relationship versus length of time you feel their loss. I looked over to my handbag, discreetly stowed under a squat table. Now I could retrieve it, I didn't much want to. At least for now I could imagine that Patrick had left a message full of forgiveness and understanding. Called me 'darling' with that particular gentle lilt that growing up on the mean streets of Holloway with Irish parents had injected into his speech. I crossed to it slowly, bargaining with each tread. I stared disbelievingly at the blank screen, willing it to be different, tears rolling down my cheeks unbidden. I wanted to blame Jim – try him for ruining my life for a second time – but I knew that I was my own worst enemy.

There was no warning knock. As the creaky door swung wide, I wiped frantically at my eyes, regretting my decision to try and make my hungover self pass for human with an excess of eye make-up.

Lisa's face was all curiosity. 'Oh, I'm sorry. Is this a bad time?'

'No, no,' I said. I'd stopped my tears, but I knew there was nothing to be done about my giveaway panda eyes. 'I'm fine. Where's Max?'

She stood in the doorway, ramrod straight, her car key swinging from her middle finger.

'Oh, he's all strapped in just outside, eyes glued to his iPad. I'm sure you've got all sorts of thoughts about modern children and screen time!' I gave her a smile that definitely didn't reach my smudgy eyes: I could really do without this. 'I should get back, but – I couldn't help but be concerned . . .'

She paused significantly. Modern children weren't the problem here: it was modern parents. She wasn't Max's mum – not even his stepmum, as he'd made very clear – but she was in a kind of loco parentis role. How much should I share? I stood up, took a deep breath.

'Max is having a lot of feelings right now . . . being able to discharge his justified rage is really important. And discharging on me is a pretty safe place to do it. It's possible he also had some feelings about the fact I was leaving him too.'

Lisa gave a dry titter. 'With respect, he barely knows you.'

'It's not about me, it's about what I represent. I don't want to blind you with science,' I so did, 'but it's something we call transference. He's gone through a major loss. Other losses, however small, will echo off that. I'm a woman, not so different in age from his mum, which might make it more acute.'

Lisa's gaze was cold and steady.

'Which brings me to my – well, our – other worry. Could this really have been a good idea? If anything, he's seemed more distressed since he's had these appointments, even the impromptu one in Lysette's garden. Lots of tears, lots of disobedience and back chat. Joshua . . .' She paused, her face shifting, less mask-like now. 'You must understand, he's experiencing the most excruciating pressure. It will get better – I know him well enough to know he'll come out the other side – but right now, dealing with this rage is almost more than he can cope with.'

I was struggling to keep the exasperation out of my face. Why do people expect children to soak up trauma like obedient little sponges? When we'd met at The Crumpet, Joshua had been taciturn and distant, but he had seemed to have a handle on all of this.

'I do appreciate that's hard, but in my experience it's much better in the long run if children *do* act up. Buried trauma is deeply destructive, not just for them, but for the whole family. I can talk in more depth to Joshua if he'd find that helpful.'

I thought the patent truth of it might pacify her, but I saw her dark brown eyes flash, her chin rise imperceptibly.

'Well, thank you, Mia,' she said, imperious. She gripped hold of her key more tightly, the metal tip pointing towards me. It was as if I was a serf, requiring swift dismissal. 'And I'm sorry to ambush you at what's obviously a very difficult time for you too.' She let her gaze linger on my smudgy, ravaged face and I unconsciously raised a hand to wipe at it. 'We'll be on our way. And of course, this is goodbye – I'm sure after all of this you'll be itching to get back to the big city!'

It was the thing I wanted most, and the thing I wanted least, all at the same time. They're the most disturbing moments of all: those snatches of time where none of the threads inside of you knit into a whole.

*

The sun had lost that sporadic intensity it had in early summer, replaced with that deceptive incarnation which heralds the arrival of autumn. It still looked like summer, but there was an underlying coldness that pinched you with its sly, chilly fingers when you least expected it.

The streets of Little Copping were coursing with people. I slipped my way through, sunglasses clamped on, hoping I wouldn't run into anyone I knew. Lysette had left a couple of angry messages, demanding to know what was going on. I hadn't been able to face calling her back quite yet. I understood why she was angry about Jim and me – particularly once the scene had been moulded and shaped by Kimberley's retelling – but I also suspected there was a strange kind of relief in being able to move the spotlight. Her pinched face, her wild eyes – the half-confession she'd blurted out was haunting me. I knew now how bad her situation really was, and I needed to have my wits about me before I spoke to her.

I rang Patrick, yet again, without much hope of success. I'd given up leaving messages about ten calls ago, but by now I was desperate, gut-wrenchingly aware of how horrible it was to not know he was there – quietly, if distractedly, adoring me. His love was a steady heartbeat, not a racing pulse, which had made it all too easy to take for granted. Not now – there's no way that you can ignore a cardiac arrest. I listened to his voicemail, the sound of his voice making the lump in my throat so big I didn't know if a message was even possible.

'Patrick, it's me. All I can think about is you. I'm dealing with all of this – this life and death stuff – and all I can think about is how lucky I am to have you. Or to have had you. Please don't let it be that.' I paused, choked by a sob, then ran on, aware that soon his voicemail would cut me off: multiple messages was bordering on bunny boiler behaviour. 'Last night looked so much worse than it was. I know I should've told you that Jim had – that I'd seen him again – but I didn't want to hurt you. I know that's a lame excuse. I'm so, so . . .' but before I could lay on another pathetic sorry, the smug-sounding automated message trilled that I was out of time.

There was already so much I longed to tell him, and it had been less than twenty-four hours since we'd had that back and forth whilst he hunted down a baguette in Pret A Manger. It had seemed scrappy to that unlovely princess part of me, but the way he had effortlessly integrated me into the fabric of his life now felt like the ultimate compliment. I wanted to pour out my fears for Lysette, my paralysis about what was best to do. I wanted to ask him how, with that in mind, I should dance around Snake Hips Krall, particularly when Roger would be eagerly spectating. And most of all I wanted to make him slow down and tell me what he was thinking and feeling – to pay him proper attention. I stopped a moment outside the hardware shop, winded by his absence, and swivelled the small diamond on my ring finger as if it had magical powers and could transmit a message to him across time and space.

Then I forced myself onwards, past the newsagent, grateful to see that a premier league footballer's quickie divorce had knocked the deaths off the front pages. But there was the local paper, a beaming picture of Little Copping's golden couple splashed across the front, all white teeth and perfect hair. *Charity Triumph!* it said. Triumph was absolutely the last word I associated with last night's events. I crossed the cobbled square and traversed the village green, the station now in sight. At that moment, I finally heard the beep of my phone. I scrabbled in my bag, pulled it out. My heart was pounding, which made the disappointment even more crushing: Jim.

Hey Mia, you OK? Let's just forget about last night. Nothing happened anyway – I told Lysette that – and she's gonna make sure Kimberley keeps quiet. Delete after reading! C u in another 20 years x

I growled with fury, stabbing at my phone to wipe his message off the screen. Kimberley wasn't some obedient minion, eager to do his bidding: there was every chance this would get back to his wife, coloured in and embellished for good measure. Perhaps it didn't matter to them – perhaps Little Copping was a hotbed of swinging parties – but from the way that Rowena had gripped his wandering hands, I didn't believe it. It was hurtful too, although the fact it hurt made me even more infuriated with myself. What we'd talked about was real and important, something that had been left unsaid twenty years. How had I still not learnt my lesson? Of course he couldn't be relied on to acknowledge what mattered in life.

My phone beeped again. This time I raised it without a sense of hope, but finally it was Patrick.

> Got yr message. I need some time to think – I think you do too. Let's talk next week. Please don't contact me again till then. Good luck with Krall today, Patrick.

Even now, even in the aftermath of my deception, he was still tracking the detail of my life – it was almost too much to bear. The train was pulling into the station: I knew I couldn't let myself collapse. I slowly paced the remaining distance, pulling ragged breaths into my centre. How much had this tragedy ultimately cost us? It took all my strength to respect his wishes, to not call and call until he was forced to pick up, just to get rid of me. I'm not sure I would've succeeded if I hadn't been able to see the train doors slamming, known that Roger was right there waiting for me.

*

Roger was standing in the booking office, tall and suave, taking in his surroundings. When he saw me, he shot out a hand for a firm shake, as if we were two world leaders posing for the cameras before we retired to discuss the fastest route to world peace.

'Mia,' he said. His keen gaze rested on me, searching for the right sentence. Saying I looked well would've been inappropriately dishonest, undermining our professional code of honour. 'You've obviously been giving this situation your all.'

I cast a quick, darting glance around myself in the way that I'd grown prone to. The silver-haired man behind the glass was pretending to be busy with his gigantic ticket machine, the chubby young couple on the island of benches had ceased crunching their grab bag of crisps. I could no longer tell what was paranoia and what was self-preservation.

'Shall we head into the village?' I said, forcing an empty smile.

'Lead on,' agreed Roger, immediately pulling open the door for me.

*

We were tucked into a musty booth, right at the back of the pub, a few feet away from the well-worn, pocked dartboard. It wasn't the perfect environment for a supervision session, but it was all we had. Roger was returning from the bar, a friendly smile plastered on his smooth face, unaware of Rita's sharp gaze burning a laser between his shoulder blades. 'It'll be lunchtime soon,' she'd snapped, when I'd told her we needed a quiet spot for a meeting. 'I know you like your pow-wows, but I can't guarantee you peace and quiet once we fill up.'

'One orange juice and soda for you, and a Diet Coke for me!' said Roger, landing them on the table. 'When I used to work in conflict zones, there was nothing quite like an ice cold Coke in the burning heat.'

Textbook technique – share a moment of personal vulnerability to build intimacy and trust.

'I can't imagine how you did it. I'd last about seven minutes in a war zone.'

'Would you?' asked Roger. 'The way you were talking when we Skyped was almost like you were in a war zone of your very own down here. How have things been progressing? It would be good to get an overview before we meet with Lawrence.'

Lawrence. His best buddy Lawrence. I couldn't think *Snake Hips*: it would make that golf-ball-sized lump rise back up in my throat and choke me. I took a swig of my drink, the ice cubes rising up and rattling painfully against my front teeth.

'Well, it's all but over!' I said, my smile bright and bland. 'I did what I came to do, which was provide support. I'm particularly glad to have worked with Max, Sarah's little boy, and from my conversation with her widower I think he might seriously contemplate finding ongoing support for him.'

'Mmm,' said Roger, giving the sound a meaningful burr. 'But you did mention that some of the statements he was making were' – he dropped his voice – 'concerning to you.'

I was tired, my zeal all but gone. I worried desperately for Lysette, for Max, but it felt like anything I did was liable to cause more harm than good. It was as if we were watching a drama on an old TV, the arial at a dodgy angle, the picture too blurry and static-filled to be identifiable. Making guesses was a dangerous game.

'I certainly think it's a complicated community.' Max's face flashed up for me – that zipping motion that felt like a vow. 'It sounds like Peter and Sarah most probably were involved. And obviously you know about the accusations Kimberley Farthing made and then withdrew against him.' Her name tasted bitter in my mouth. So too did the accusation.

'What about the drugs?' asked Roger, quick as a flash. 'Are the Farthings aware of that?'

'I think it's possible there was drug taking, and it's possible Kimberley was aware of that.' She was cunning, the way she didn't even acknowledge the flakes of powder on the wrought-iron table. Plausible deniability. 'But – lots of people take recreational drugs. There's no reason to think it's connected.'

'But could it be? If Sarah was taking drugs?'

I shrugged, sipped from my icy drink.

'It's possible. Anything's possible.' Lysette reared up for me now; the desperation in her grief-ravaged face when she'd asked for that loan, the eerily contrasting wads of cash that Jim described, the determination with which she'd pulled out the wrap. But none of that had been when I was on official business. I had no obligation to share it with Roger. 'All the evidence suggests it was a love affair gone wrong.'

'Is that what you believe, Mia? From everything Judith told me, from the feedback I've had, my understanding is that you're deeply intuitive. That it was your intuition that got the police all the way to Christopher Vine.'

I felt an answering flicker of it, a crackle. *He didn't do it* – the conviction whispered through me, but then I reminded myself that I wasn't some kind of tribal elder with a medicine ball. All I needed to do right now was get home and attend to my real life. Nothing I did or said would bring Sarah back, and I couldn't take the risk of causing Lysette – the person who had brought me here, my friend of the ages – more trauma.

'I don't know anything definitive to the contrary, and I certainly don't want to confuse things with half-truths and suggestions.'

Roger looked around the pub, buying himself a moment's thinking time.

'I get that – I admire your loyalty, your integrity – but I'm also here to help you steer a steady path through any legal responsibilities you might have around disclosure.'

'Thank you. I appreciate that.'

When Roger turned his ice blue gaze on me it was like a searchlight on dark water. I didn't flinch.

'OK – well let's talk in more depth about your recent sessions. We'll also need to cover the layer of complication offered by the fact that your oldest friend is right at the hub.'

Fun times. Cake-munching Krall – with his growing certainty that this was an open and shut case – would be a breeze after this. I knew as I thought it that my logic was dangerous – supervision was meant to be a support to me, a support to my clients, not an exercise in evasion. The last time I'd treated it that way, I'd nearly got myself killed.

Why was I so stubborn, so determined not to learn from my own mistakes?

CHAPTER TWENTY-SIX

'Are we meeting him in The Crumpet?' Roger gave me a look of bemusement. 'It's a restaurant – well, more of a tea shop. It's where I met him last time.'

We were standing in the lane outside The Black Bull now: it was almost as though the scenery had pulled out all the stops to seduce Roger. The fields were splayed out in front of us, greeny-gold in the afternoon light, whilst the rushing stream bubbled its way past, the ducks providing a symphony of quacks.

'No, we're meeting him at the police station,' he said, seemingly unmoved. 'I asked Ruth behind the bar to call a cab when I settled the bill.'

'Rita,' I said, unnecessarily. I should've seen in his expression what I was failing to notice – I had gone dangerously native.

'Aah, here it is,' said Roger, as a bashed-up white saloon car pulled up next to us.

*

The police station loomed up in front of us, that forbidding grey slab of concrete. I gave a little internal shudder at the memory of Jim meeting me on the steps, the guilty comfort it had shot through me.

I could chalk that up as yet another thing to avoid sharing with Roger. I'd described this morning's session with Max, but as with our Gruffalo encounter, the pieces that unsettled me were hard to grasp hold of, found as much in the spaces between the words as they were in the words themselves. To be fair to Roger, he'd done what he was supposed to do: helped me identify those pieces and jigsaw them together into a clearer shape.

'It sounds like you are picking up on something beyond simple grief,' he'd said. 'If he was aware her relationship with his teacher was transgressive – just the fact he couldn't tell his classmates he saw him in his home – he'll be left with an extra complication. Something he might feel he can't talk to the surviving parent about out of loyalty to his mum.'

'No, I get that,' I'd said, mind racing with all the add-ons I didn't want to bring to the party. Of course he'd gone back to the drugs, asked me if anything else had emerged, and I'd shaken my head, not quite trusting myself to speak. Last night was still a noisy, painful blur, scrambled footage that I needed to rewind and play back frame by frame.

The cab swung into the car park, the heavy metal pole swinging upwards like an execution in reverse.

'Here we are,' said Roger, who was clearly a master at stating the obvious.

He palmed the driver some cash, then led the way towards the looming grey building. I felt a furious stab of resentment as I looked up at it: I should've listened to that whisper of instinct, not the shout of my ego. I knew that getting drawn into this case could only cause trouble – what I hadn't known was quite how much.

Lawrence Krall was standing in the tatty reception area, as if he couldn't wait a second longer to see us. He lacked the twinkle he'd had at The Crumpet, his face solemn and closed. He held open the heavy steel door that led into the bowels of the station, and took us up in the lift to the meeting room where this had all begun. Once we were sitting around the Formica table, he turned serious eyes on us.

'First of all, thank you both for taking the time to come and see me here,' he said. He looked at Roger. 'Mia should probably cover her ears, but I was frankly intimidated by how perceptive she was about the various players when we last met. It certainly helped us excavate things.'

My skin prickled with unease. The last thing I wanted was to take centre stage.

'And of course you found that CCTV footage,' I said. 'You were struggling with a lack of hard evidence.'

Lawrence gave a sage nod. 'And – as you so wisely pointed out – the limits of supposition, rather than proof.'

'I think we're all agreed on Mia's talent,' said Roger, giving me the kind of patronising smile you might give your star pupil as they step up to receive the fifth form science trophy. 'Which is why we both felt it would be useful for us to have a debrief before you return to London. Make sure you're not leaving with any information that doesn't seem important, but is actually more relevant than you know.'

'Absolutely,' agreed Krall.

At that moment, I realised – with crushing, hungover certainty – that I should have wasted less of our time together evading Roger's questions, and more time perfecting the duet we were duty bound to sing here. 'I feel fairly confident I've got nothing that's relevant to share . . .'

Roger smoothly interrupted. 'As I mentioned, my specialism is around trauma, so I've been helping Mia work through what might just be garbled shock – particularly with her friend . . .'

'Ah yes, Lysette Allen,' said Lawrence. There was something about the way he said it – the steely precision with which he enunciated the syllables – that made me almost leap out of my chair and run from the room to warn her that she needed to watch her back.

I'd tuned Roger out but he was still giving forth. 'And what could potentially be worthy of discussion.'

'Well, let me get you up to speed with where we are,' said Lawrence, 'confidentially of course. And see where any information you have might slot into the current story we're telling. See if you approve.'

'Fine,' I said, trying to force the tiny word to sound cooperative and open.

Lawrence smiled, his eyes not leaving my face. 'The CCTV was obviously a game changer. We now have proof that Sarah was with Peter Grieve, in the vicinity of the car park, within two hours of her death. We've tracked down more footage of Peter, solo, in the immediate area within half an hour of her fall. We've also had some eye witnesses come forward, who remember them sitting in a coffee shop close by that day, engrossed in each other's company. And it seems it was a regular meeting point for them, safely out of the way of Little Copping's prying eyes.'

I had more than a little sympathy with that desire.

'Is there more?' I asked.

'There is, yes,' said Lawrence, his face serious. 'I'm not sure you're going to like it, though.'

'Oh?' I said. Roger was positively wriggling in his seat, poised for the next revelation. *A woman's dead*, I wanted to yell at him, *her son's heart is breaking. This isn't juicy material for your next lecture.*

'We've uncovered what we think is a drug ring, connected to Sarah.' He paused, let his words sink in. My heart thumped in my chest. Don't say it. 'And also your friend Lysette Allen.'

'Exactly as you suspected!' said Roger, triumphant. Lawrence watched us closely: bingo, said his eyes. 'Well done, Mia.'

'Well no, not exactly,' I snapped, turning deliberately towards Lawrence, forgetting in my frustration that, for better or worse, Roger was my boss. 'Can you elaborate?'

'Sarah didn't come from Little Copping, or anywhere remotely like it,' said Lawrence. I remembered her parents, the desperation on their faces, the way they'd felt just a little bit out of place, even when they were disguised in the dark uniform of funeral clothes. There was something about them that refused to blend with the tasteful oatmeal hues of the Bryants' well-appointed home. 'She was from a run-down little town outside King's Lynn. Not many opportunities. She hung around with a rough crowd, got a caution for being drunk and disorderly when she was a teenager.'

'Right,' I said. Words of more than one syllable seemed to be beyond my reach.

'Judging by phone records and email accounts we've managed to uncover, she kept in touch with some of those people more closely than her husband ever knew. I'd go so far as to say she had a secret life.'

Why does the past pull on us so insistently, its cold fingers refusing to loosen their grip even when all they offer is the strangulation of our present? The truth seemed so self-evident in that moment. I should have known – my work meant I should have known enough to keep its allure at bay.

'And you think that's what got her killed?' said Roger.

'No, not directly,' said Lawrence. 'But in going through those records, adding in bank statements and tallying up the timelines, we started to see a pattern emerging. Large cash withdrawals, calls to a known drug dealer, petrol receipts from the garage on the outskirts of King's Lynn. The kind of sums we're talking about are not personal use. And unfortunately there are cash withdrawals from Lysette's accounts that tie in too closely to be coincidental. Apparently her behaviour – and her spending habits – had become erratic months before Sarah's death.'

Lawrence watched for my reaction. I couldn't hear this. Couldn't bear where it might go. Couldn't bear my own egotistical conviction that I could have changed the course of it if only I'd spent less of the last year listening to my clients, and more time listening to my best friend.

'So how does this relate to Sarah's death?' I demanded, aware how shrill my voice sounded.

'We think that Peter Grieve knew what was going on, was even complicit. We've found footage of his car number plate in the vicinity of the known drug dealer on one of the dates in question. We've found a burner phone, with texts on it we can only assume were between him and Sarah.'

'What kind of texts?' I asked.

'Loving is the best word I can use,' said Lawrence.

'So not sexual?'

He paused, looked askance.

'No, not as such.'

Roger cut in. 'So are you saying that your working hypothesis remains that Peter killed Sarah? An intense affair gone wrong, with other complications thrown in?'

'Exactly,' said Lawrence, sitting back. 'And if Lysette – the person closest to Sarah – was involved in some petty drug dealing, she'd have every reason not to reveal their affair.'

The words burst out of me. 'But it's all still a narrative! And if there was drug dealing – which is something I can't ever imagine Lysette doing – well, whoever it was would have had to be passing drugs on to someone.' Those two pairs of heels clacking across the stone floor – Kimberley was part of this. She certainly hadn't flinched when I'd called her out on the coke outside. 'What about their friends?'

I tried to push away the image of her and Sarah, cash overflowing from their purses, bags bulging with treats. Dealing was too big a word, surely?

Lawrence had drawn back in his chair, his warmth all but drained away. There was something else going on here.

'Do you have anything specific you want to share here, Mia?' said Roger.

'No.' No one spoke. 'I just don't know why you're assuming that – if any of this is true – Lysette was the only person involved.' I was spooling through all of it – every moment of these last, fraught weeks – summoning up my defence. 'But also, Lysette's my oldest friend. She's not an angel, but she's also no way a drug dealer. The idea is just ridiculous.'

'I hear what you're saying,' said Lawrence, bringing my blood to boiling point, 'but it's marked how much more cooperation we've had from the other players. And if we could win her cooperation, we might be looking at a major drug trial. The person in question has been of interest for some time.'

I spat out her name. 'Kimberley. She's been helping you.'

'Yes, the Farthings have been extremely helpful,' said Lawrence mildly. 'Obviously Nigel Farthing's ministerial position gives him a special insight into the challenges we face with the war on drugs.'

And some – he was facing the challenge closer to home than they could ever imagine. Both men looked at my flushed face with the expression of a couple of Victorian doctors in proximity to a hysterical female in need of sedation.

'You're quite happy with your hypothesis about Sarah and Peter,' I said. 'You've moved on to a whole new agenda, haven't you?'

I'd riled Lawrence now. His dark eyes flashed a warning. 'If you're asking if I'm happy about the tragic death of a young mother, I can assure you that I'm not. If you're asking if I'm pleased to have the chance to prevent more devastation, then yes, I am. I think you'll find it's part of my job description.'

We sat there, eyeing each other. I took a slow, deliberate breath to buy myself some calm. I needed to keep my status in the room. The stakes were higher than I'd ever imagined.

'So how can I help you?' I asked, forcing myself to smile. Roger gave me a look of quiet approval.

'Firstly with information,' said Lawrence. 'What led you to believe that Sarah was taking drugs before she died?'

'I can't even remember,' I said, my stomach lurching with the knowledge that my statement was more lie than truth. 'It was maybe implied more than it was spoken.'

Roger leapt in. 'Didn't you mention a conversation with your ex-partner, Lysette's brother?'

Lawrence gave a slow smile.

'Possibly, but it was more than that. There was general chatter. Nothing specific.'

The last thing I wanted was them questioning Jim on my behest. Lawrence eyeballed me, unimpressed.

'Let me level with you. We're not looking to pursue charges against Lysette. What we do want is as much clarity on Sarah's death as we can get prior to the inquest, and also a way into a major drug operation that extends across the whole south-east and beyond.'

Lysette's face last night – stray specks of powder around her nose, her eyes crazed – had been a picture of desperation. Whatever secrets she was carrying around were destroying her. But being locked in an interview room, being forced to reveal what it was that she'd been party to, the darkness of which I suspected ran far deeper than Lawrence even knew – could be the ultimate destruction.

'If there is a whole drug gang that Sarah was mixed up with, surely that means there could be other suspects for her murder?'

Lawrence's tone was icy. 'Possibly.'

My brain was whirring, thinking back to what Patrick said when he heard Krall was on the case.

'Did you always know? Did you always think there was something bigger going on? Is that why you were assigned to this?'

He shrugged, cagey. 'We had our suspicions. I didn't know that Lysette's brother was your ex-partner?'

I tried to match his evasiveness. 'More like childhood sweetheart. We went out for a summer when we were teen-agers.' Lawrence didn't speak. 'Water under the bridge. He's married and I'm ...' I willed my voice not to crack. 'I'm engaged.'

He'd sensed my breaking. I was fatally weakened now, more prey than equal.

'So you don't think that Lysette Allen has taken drugs in recent months?'

The room closed in on me, airless and stifling. The lie I'd have to tell was too stark, too damning. Roger's eyes were trained on me. I drew myself up in my seat, almost haughty.

'I do really want to help you, Lawrence, but I don't feel able to answer that question.'

'But you're her friend.'

My throat felt tight, my skin blazing with heat. 'You never know everything about another person though, do you?'

I felt sick to my stomach. In my refusal to answer, I'd given him the answer he wanted. Roger looked distinctly unimpressed, but Lawrence leant back in his chair, struggling to keep the satisfaction out of the smile he gave me.

'Mia, the last thing I want to do is compromise you. You've been enormously helpful, and the work you've done in the community has been a huge support to us. Let's leave it there for today, and if we need to interview you more formally, I'll be in touch.'

He had what he needed: the winning hand of cards which would ensure that Lysette had to fold. What had I done? Words started to tumble out of me.

'Lysette isn't – if she got herself mixed up in something, it will have started with the best intentions. She loved Sarah.

Sarah loved her. She's – she's someone who goes all in. It's what I've always loved about her too.' Both of them looked utterly unmoved by me. I blundered on, frustration and desperation a dangerous cocktail. 'If you're pressurising Lysette with what you think she's hiding, you should keep an open mind. I'd guarantee she's not the only one with secrets. I'd look hard at why Kimberley's so keen to keep control of the story. It seems to me that she's the one with the most to lose.'

'Again, is there anything specific?' asked Lawrence.

It suddenly seemed so clear to me what was happening. The Farthings' power and influence being used to devastating effect. If Kimberley lost her sheen, things might look very different.

'Ask her about Susan,' I said. 'Do you remember, the ex-nanny I told you about? I'm sure there's something connected to her – something that happened – which she's determined to keep quiet.'

Lawrence didn't even deign to note down the name, simply stood up.

'Thank you again. I'd ask that you don't share any of what we've discussed with Lysette – or indeed with anyone – at this stage. We're at a particularly critical point in the investigation.'

Roger shot out a firm hand.

'You can rely on our professional discretion,' he said.

We were well and truly dismissed.

CHAPTER TWENTY-SEVEN

This wasn't the final night I'd pictured. I'd imagined Lysette and me coming full circle: me reading an adoring Saffron a bedtime story, then sharing a bottle of wine on the tatty, comfy green sofa where we'd huddled up when I first arrived. We'd acknowledge the hard edges we'd hit these last few weeks, but know instinctively it was already healing. Instead I was perched on the lip of Rita's wafer-thin mattress, fiddling obsessively with the tassels on the scratchy beige bedspread. Dusk was gathering through the porthole of a window, the crescent moon a curved slash of light. My time here was so nearly over – I wanted to snatch it back, force it to afford me a second chance.

'She really can't speak?'

It was Ged I was calling now. I'd given up leaving messages for Lysette, my calls cutting out in that hurtfully abrupt way after a tell-tale couple of rings. It was her who'd been trying to call me only a few hours ago – what had happened in the interim?

'She's . . .' Ged paused, the silence full to bursting. 'She's not herself, you know that. She's having a down day.' Otherwise known as a comedown – I didn't say it. How much did Ged actually know? 'I'm sure she'll be in touch tomorrow.'

'But I'm leaving tomorrow,' I said, my voice full of wheedling desperation.

His voice was infused with the warmth that came so easily to him, instantly soothing the sting. 'Course you are!' he said. 'Come round on your way to the station. Saffron'll never forgive me if she misses the chance to show you her new shoes.'

'Bows?' I asked.

'Obviously.'

Another pregnant pause, both of us craving the chance to confide, both of us holding ourselves back. I broke first.

'Ged, is there anything I can do? Anything at all? I know I haven't exactly been friend of the year while I've been here . . .'

He sounded so weary. 'You tried.'

'I did, and I fucked up, but I wouldn't forgive myself if . . .' The *if* seemed to splinter and multiply, each version more frightening than the last. Lawrence Krall's face, filled with grim purpose. Lysette's broken terror. What destination was all of this hurtling towards?

Ged's voice cracked. 'I know, Mia. I know.'

Was he crying?

'Ged?'

'I'm not sure we're gonna make it.' This sob was audible. He turned it into a throat-clear, shook it off. 'I shouldn't be saying anything.'

'You two are great,' I said, uselessly. '*You're* great.' He was – even though he was yet another man I'd underesti-mated. I'd wished for someone for her who was more of a provider, unable to see, for many years, that what he did provide was solid gold.

'It's hard though, isn't it?'

It was difficult to argue with that.

'Ged, this isn't just me and Lysette winding each other up. I need . . .' I stopped abruptly: my promise to Lawrence of confidentiality was legally binding. 'She needs to be very careful. Please tell her that from me.'

*

Sleep was a long time coming. When it finally descended it was more like a coma. My phone cut through it, shrieking like a shrill banshee, my hand wheeling around in the half-light in search of it. Lysette. I missed it by a nanosecond, but as soon as it had stopped, it started its relentless pealing all over again.

'Lys?'

Her voice was shaking. 'You've gone too far now, Mia. You've gone too fucking far.'

Had Lawrence Krall already pulled her in? Nausea rose up in me like a sick wave.

'Lys, hang on. They said I couldn't speak to you. I did try to call . . .'

'What, you care more what a fucking tabloid feels than what I feel? Did you get paid for it, then?'

'What are you talking about?'

'Oh, come on. Are you on a roll? Are you lying to every-one now, not just Patrick?'

I hadn't yet been awake long enough to remember the painful state of affairs between Patrick and me. My voice was like ice when I replied. 'Like I said, I don't know what you're talking about.'

'Have a look at your friend April's front page exclusive. Everyone else will be once they wake up.'

'She's not my friend . . .'

But before I'd got the chance to ask any more, I'd been abandoned to an angry dial tone.

*

The cobbled streets were half empty, Little Copping still rubbing sleep from its eyes. I half walked, half ran to the newsagent, my heart thumping harder and harder in my chest. I slowed as I approached, the urgency draining out of me. Now my feet were like lead weights.

There it was. Thick black capitals that looked a mile high. *Sarah Death: Sex Shame In Paradise*. There below in smaller letters: *Exclusive from April Greening*. There was a close-up of a laughing Sarah, a shot of Peter just below it. The other half of the cover was given over to a picture of the school. At that moment I longed acutely for the grimy anonymity of the Holloway Road. Gareth, the newsagent, was standing sentry behind the counter, arms folded over the top of his mountainous belly, barely encased in his tight brown polo shirt. I'd bought a fair few bottles of water and less lurid

papers from him and his wife by now, had never got away
with less than five minutes of chat.

'Hi. Can I grab . . .' The words tailed off. Gareth's slack,
grey face was like stone. He gave a curt nod, thrust the paper
at me like he was parrying a blow. Of course I only had a
note. He snatched it from my hand, loudly rootling in the
till for change.

'There you go,' he said, dropping it into my hand.

I often encourage my clients to check out their more dis-
tressing interpretations of the world, not stay locked up in
the torture chamber of internal paranoia.

'I'm heading back to London today,' I said, deliberately
cheerful.

He had the grace to mutter, but he made sure it was loud
enough for me to hear.

'Good riddance.'

I stumbled past the rack of sweets, the bags of crisps, back
out into the quaint beauty of the village. Right then it felt
as ugly as sin.

*

I managed to slip upstairs without encountering either Rita
or any of my fellow guests. At least I could be fairly confident
that April would've scuttled back to London like a sewer rat,
a far safer place to bask in her mucky triumph. I spread the
newspaper out on my unmade bed, hands shaking. As I did
so, I caught a glimpse of a grainy photo inside. It couldn't
be. It was from the function – a snatched picture of me,

over-made up, my mouth open – with Lysette visibly dodging the camera. 'Best friends,' it said underneath. Next to it was a picture of Kimberley and Nigel, freshly out of the car, loving smiles plastered on.

I could barely focus: the black print swirled in front of my eyes like a busy tribe of worker ants. I forced myself to track it.

The case of murdered young mum Sarah Bryant – close pal of Cabinet minister Nigel Farthing's wife Kimberley – took a dramatic turn yesterday as a source close to the investigation poured scorn on the case against the prime suspect, pervy teacher Peter Grieve. Grieve, who had a history of stalking women, killed himself on the day of the tragic beauty's funeral, leaving behind a desperate suicide note, a chilling reply to the mystery message found unsent on Sarah's phone. Footage released last week showed the pair laughing and joking next to the car park where she plunged to her death an hour later. But police shrink Mia Cosgrove – who is giving therapy to the grieving family – spoke out angrily against their methods. 'Peter's not here to defend himself,' she said. 'He was hysterical at the funeral. They shouldn't make assumptions.'

I was hot with rage. She'd stitched my words together like a patchwork quilt, made it sound like a formal interview. How could I have been stupid enough to utter a single syllable? I turned the page, praying it wouldn't get worse. Of course it did.

We can also exclusively reveal a nest of scandals and secrets which have rocked the picture-perfect village before and after Sarah's death plunge.

The school quiz night that descended into mayhem after it was revealed that Peter Grieve had been STALKING glam political wife Kimberley Farthing. A source said she was 'shaken and distressed' by the shocking confrontation.

Hubby Joshua Bryant is leaning heavily on ex-wife Lisa, the mother of his first two children, who he abandoned for waitress Sarah – almost twenty years his junior – after their sex-fuelled affair. 'It's the bravest thing he can do,' was Cosgrove's bizarre claim.

Partying mum of three Lysette Allen – close friend of the Cracker style expert as well as the victim – fired off a drunken rant at Sarah's devastated parents after the funeral. 'She knows way more than she's telling the police,' speculated a source. The shrink was forced to move out of her best friend's home after a devastating row. She was later seen having an intimate meal in the village pub with her pal's married brother, desperately seeking clues for what's triggering Allen's out of control behaviour.

This week the tight-knit community turned out in force for a lavish charity ball hosted by Nigel Farthing, who refused to comment on recent developments. Police are expected to announce within days that they are no longer looking for any further suspects in connection to the murder, with an inquest pencilled for the New Year.

It was horrific. I collapsed backwards onto the unyielding mattress, the room spinning like I was drunk. I wished I could cry – purge the distress from my body – but my anger was too rigid and hard to juice out any tears. I sat up, trying Patrick first. I was growing to hate the breezy professionalism of his voicemail.

'Patrick it's me. Obviously it's me. I don't know if you've seen the awful story that April's written, but please ignore it. I did have lunch with him . . .' I paused, aware how awful this could sound. 'But it was just lunch. I wanted to find out about Lysette. That bit's true, even if the rest of it is total bollocks. Nothing I can say sounds good, and I know it's about to cut out, but I love you. Please know that. I love you. Marrying you is the thing I want most in the world.'

The truth of that statement stopped me in my tracks; none of this, not Sarah, not Lysette, not even whether or not we had children mattered in the face of it. As I tried to formulate the next sentence the beep bossily informed it was too late. I fell backwards again, tears streaming down my face. After what felt like a snotty, damp age I gathered myself to call Lysette. I think part of me hoped she wouldn't pick up, but she answered after a single ring.

'Are you proud of yourself, Miss Cracker style expert?'

I could almost see her angry quotation marks.

'I barely spoke to her. She's taken a couple of innocuous remarks I made about not jumping to conclusions and puffed them up into a story. Don't fall for it, Lys, please! We need to be on the same side right now.'

My phone gave a beep, as I was talking and I ripped it from my ear, hoping it was Patrick. No – it was a text from Joshua.

You disgust me.

The hard simplicity of it smashed into me like a body blow. Max was right there for me in that moment, his face a living haunting. I hoped this wouldn't spell the end of him getting the help he needed.

'No!' shouted Lysette. 'I'm not falling for this, any more. It's not just those awful quotes. You told her about the funeral . . .'

'Of course I didn't . . .'

'You went and bitched to her about . . . about you moving out and then you went running off to cosy up to Jim. Who is married by the way – at least that's something she got right.'

You sanctimonious bitch. I had the self-preservation not to say it.

'We were both worried about you,' I said. 'And she only knew you'd thrown me out because of something she heard me say to Joshua.'

Lysette kept getting angrier. 'I didn't throw you out. And I can't believe you went round broadcasting that I did.'

'It wasn't like that.'

'You must've told her about the quiz night . . .'

'Hang on, why *must* I have told her about the quiz night? Of course I didn't. Plenty of people know far more about that than me. April's been here for days, making nice with everyone she can find.'

'Yeah, and people who are actually from here have had the good sense to ignore her.' She had a point. 'Kimberley's furious about it. That bit about her being shaken and distressed — it's so humiliating for her.'

I heard it then, the puppeteer accidentally clearing his throat from behind the scenes. *Shaken and distressed* — that phrase was pure Kimberley. A perfect snapshot of her version of events, all of which added weight to the case against Peter.

The words spewed before I had the calm to yank them back in. 'What if Kimberley talked to her?'

Lysette gave an angry snort. 'You're fucking unbelievable. Why have you got this weird vendetta against her? That's completely ridiculous.'

It wasn't, it really wasn't. Suddenly it was starting to come together in my mind: her endless sly remarks about Sarah, the rage she couldn't quite suppress. Could she even have killed her? No — murder was a step too far, surely?

'You said yourself you didn't believe what she'd said about Peter after the quiz night. When Sarah died, you were adamant he hadn't done it.' She paused a second, caught by what I'd said, but she'd gone too far to turn back. I thought about how it must have felt reading that damning clutch of words — *partying mum of three*. 'Lys, this is us. You know I'd never do anything to hurt you.'

The calm that she affected made me crumble to dust. 'I don't know how you can say that on a day like today. I wish you'd never come here. Stop talking to people, go back to

London and leave me alone. I mean it, Mia, I don't want to hear from you again.'

'Lysette, please!' It was more a sob than a coherent utterance. 'I promise you I barely spoke to her. You're my best friend, you know that.' I couldn't help but look at her: the laughing picture of Sarah plastered across the front of the paper. I said it again. 'You're my best friend.' My phone had been consistently beeping with competing calls, and now, as I waited in hope for her response, I could see how many there were from Lawrence Krall. 'We need to keep looking out for each other.'

She didn't hear it, the coded whisper I was trying to convey underneath the foghorn reminder of how much we had always meant to each other.

'It's too late.'

'Lysette, don't hang up. You mustn't trust Kimberley. I know you think I'm being paranoid, but I'm not. She's caused all of this.'

Lysette gave an exasperated sigh.

'Goodbye, Mia,' she said, cutting the call.

This time when I lay down I wondered if I'd ever find the strength to get back up again.

*

It was an hour or so later, when I heard that tentative knocking on the door. By then I'd spoken to Krall, spoken to Roger, proclaimed my innocence. Roger had warned me about the danger of breathing a word to the press, but I also sensed a certain satisfaction at seeing his new protégée placed firmly at the centre of a front-page case. Krall was more brusque, my usefulness all but gone now. As he'd hung up, he'd made sure to tell me that my tip about Susan was a complete dead-end. I ignored the knocking at first, wondering if it was Rita with a curt reminder of check-out time. When it came a third time, more loudly now, I reluctantly crossed the tiny room and opened up.

Her hair was bluntly cut, a spiky blonde frame around her square face, the highlights having a whiff of a supermarket DIY job. Her skin was grey, showing signs of the emotional strain that radiated out of her dark eyes. There was something familiar about her, but I couldn't place her. It would make sense that she worked here, but there was something about her pulsing energy that told me that she was more than one of Rita's minions, sent to tell me it was time to pack up.

'Hi,' I said, keeping the door at an unwelcoming angle that was neither closed nor properly open.

'Are you Mia Cosgrove?'

My heart thumped hard in my chest.

'Why?'

'You are, aren't you? I need to speak to you. I'm Jennifer. Peter's sister. You're the only one talking any sense.'

CHAPTER TWENTY-EIGHT

'So how did you find me?'

I'd swept last night's clothes off the uncomfortable chair in the corner, offered her a cup of tea. The room had a tiny travel kettle, along with a handful of UHT milk pods and some greying bags. She'd accepted, a fact I was excessively grateful for: it gave me something to do, a way to give this bizarre scenario a recognisable ritual. The room was full of steam by now. I concentrated on pouring boiling water into the tannin-stained mugs, flicking open the milk with my fingernails. The lumpy home-made manicure I'd given them for the ball was already starting to peel and chip.

'Just took a chance,' she said. 'I looked at that story, and I thought – if I was you, I wouldn't be showing my face round here.' I could hear the hostility in her tone – I hoped it was more for the 'here' than it was for me. 'There's nowhere else to stay, and it said you'd been eating in the pub. Snuck up the back stairs and tried every room till you answered.'

I handed her the mug, noticing how much her hand shook as she took it. I knew then how much of her spikiness was bravado: it had taken a lot for her to get this far. I sat down on the bed, discreetly smoothing the rumpled counterpane. I wanted her to go. I wanted her to calm down, realise I was an irrelevance, and let me get back to trying to salvage my car crash of a life.

'You must have really wanted to track me down.' We made eye contact for a second before she looked downwards into her steaming mug. 'I'm so sorry about Peter.'

'Yeah . . . well.' She ground to a halt. 'Thanks.' She looked up again, gathering strength. Her eyes were ringed with inky liner, lashes so thick and stiff with mascara that they were like tiny spears. A column of gold rings ran up each of her ear lobes, a skull punctuating the left. It all looked so painful. 'He wasn't some fucking pervert. You know that, don't you? He would never have killed anyone, let alone her.'

I had nothing to give, and yet there she was in front of me, vibrating with grief. I couldn't harden myself against her.

'I can't imagine how horrible it is, reading all those head-lines about your own brother. I didn't give that journalist an interview, just so you know.' Jennifer's shoulders slumped low, and I realised instantaneously that she was the only person who'd hoped that I had. In her mind, I'd been her brother's staunch defender, a beacon of hope in a hostile universe. 'She cobbled together a few things I said in passing. But I do think anyone has the right to be innocent till proven guilty.'

I saw it then – that same look of rabid emotional hunger that had burned from Sarah's mother's eyes. 'Did you know him?' she demanded.

'I didn't meet him properly – I only saw him at the funeral. And once outside the school.' I paused, not wanting to cross an invisible line, masquerade as what she hoped I was. 'He was very sweet with my god-daughter.'

Could you stop being a godmother, or was it only God who had the power to take that away? My gaze flicked unconsciously downwards to my left hand: to that tiny, twinkling diamond that I also refused to stop believing in. Then I thought about what had been taken away from her at a stroke. And now what was left: her memory of who her brother had been was being taken by stealth, brick by brick.

'You must've known, just from that,' she said firmly. 'Must've been totally obvious to a shrink that he'd never do something like that.'

'I . . .'

Jennifer saved me, running on before I could come up with the kind of fudged reply I was duty bound to give her.

'He loved kids, he was amazing with them. Well, apart from when he was one himself. He hated school, got bullied. He was too soft.'

'Maybe it was the softness that made him such a brilliant teacher?' I said. 'Lots of people have said that about him, you know.'

I wanted her to hear it, to know there was more than one narrative going around about who he was. What I didn't tell her was how strange the energy felt when people acknowledged that brilliance, the postscript left unspoken.

'He always wanted to be a teacher. He's the only one of us

who got to university.' She rolled her eyes, her fingers worrying at the hem of her denim jacket. 'Had debts up to his eyeballs.'

The cramped bedroom felt soupy and airless, but I didn't want to break her flow by crossing the room and opening the tiny window. It only let in a little sunlight, the room dingy and claustrophobic.

'Do you have more siblings?' I asked her.

'No, I meant our mum and dad. It's just me and Peter.' His name caught in her throat, and my heart clenched in silent reply. 'I was gutted when they came back with a little brother for me.' She gave a quick, pained smile. 'Wasn't what I ordered. I used to put him in my old dresses when he was little. Probably didn't help with the softness.'

'Were you always close?' She gave a half-shrug, her face shadowed by complicated memories. I could sense survivor guilt: that inevitable bargaining – the belief that if you'd only played your part differently, the world would have moulded itself into an entirely different shape. 'I think it can be hard when someone dies, not to feel like you're duty bound to only remember the good bits.'

A sooty tear fell from Jennifer's eye. I scooted into the tiny en suite, handed her a wad of thin, scratchy loo paper.

'Sorry,' I said, 'I'm afraid it's the best I've got.'

She fought hard against her tears, but they traced black lines down the contours of her face. I knelt on the scratchy carpet at her feet, wishing there was a second chair I could pull up.

'I'm sorry,' she said, hiccuping through the sobs. 'I didn't come here to cry on you. I don't want a free appointment or anything.'

'Please don't apologise, I imagine it's completely over-whelming. You're going through hell – losing a sibling is tragic enough. But with everything else that's happened, it must feel unbearable.'

Jennifer gave me a look of damp gratitude, words start-ing to tumble out of her. 'I loved him, no question, but he could bug the shit out of me too.' Her dark eyes pleaded for absolution. 'He was so worried about every little thing, what everyone thought of him. I think he was a bit OCD, if I'm honest. It was me that persuaded him to go to the doctor and now . . . now they're using that to make out he was some kind of fucking psycho.'

I looked up at her from my vantage point on the floor.

'The stigma around mental health is kind of medieval. I have so many people – particularly men – who come to me feeling ashamed of asking for help, when it's the bravest thing they can do. You did really well to get him through the door.'

Jennifer's hands balled up into tight fists, the chunky silver rings she wore glinting like knuckledusters. 'It didn't do any fucking good though, did it?'

Her anger was so palpable that it felt like the third person in the room. Or maybe the fourth. Sometimes acknowledg-ing the obvious is all you can do.

'It must feel so unfair.'

'It's not what was meant to happen, you know?' Her voice swung upwards with emotion. 'We were driving up to the church in that big black car – I remember him being chris-tened there, he screamed his head off – and I was thinking, this was meant to be your wedding. I'm not meant to stand up there and talk about you being dead. No one else wanted to do it, but it wasn't what I signed up for either. And there were all these photographers ... fucking vampires.'

She clamped her hand across her heart, shrank backwards in the chair, as if she could somehow ward off what had already happened. She was pale, visibly shaking, the memory too visceral to allow tears. I stood up, put a tentative arm around her denim-clad shoulders. She softened to my touch, a shuddering sob suddenly erupting from her body. She wiped her nose on the sleeve of her jeans jacket.

'Sorry, that was disgusting!' she said, laughing for the first time.

'No, I'm a terrible host. You needed some more bog roll from the cash and carry and I didn't get it for you.' Now we were both laughing. 'Do you want another cup of tea?' I asked her gently.

Jennifer nodded, sweeping the tears from her face and finding her poise. She was brave, I could tell. 'I didn't come for this, I really didn't. I came because I know he didn't do it. My mum and dad have given up, they're just broken by it. I couldn't save him. I've got to get this bit right.'

I nodded, trying not to convey to her the hopelessness of her fight. I see it again and again, the bargaining that goes on with death. The desperate fight for control that the bereaved wage against an unseen tormentor.

'What do you think happened?' I said, still fussing with the kettle.

Jennifer was sharp again. 'I think he got fucked over, that's what happened. I told him to leave, but because of that other school he said he'd never get another job. Our parents used all their savings to get him through uni—'

I cut across her, wanting to make sure the lines were clear. 'Listen, Jennifer, I'm not working on this case. I'm happy to talk, but you need to know that. I can't help in a practical way.'

She gave a sharp nod, the words barely registering. I handed her the mug, and she took a swift sip from it.

'They're making out he was some kind of sex pest, but he just got involved with a woman who was getting divorced at the other school, and the headmistress made a song and dance about it. So when she started pestering him, with who her husband was . . .'

I sat back down on the bed. 'What, Sarah?'

'No, the other one.' She spat the words out. 'Madam. You know, Kimberley Farthing.'

'What, Kimberley was harassing *him*?'

She positively vibrated with conviction.

'Yes! I know everyone thinks it was the other way round, but it's bullshit. Did you not know? From your mate? I thought that might be why you were standing up for him.'

My mind was spinning. 'Harassing him how?'

'Whole thing – sending him all these WhatsApp messages about what she wanted him to do to her. Calling at night. Touching him. You know, just a little bit too long at drop-off.'

I saw a flash of that manicured hand, the vice it formed around Jake's bicep in The Crumpet. The cow eyes at the ball. He couldn't afford to throw her off either.

Jennifer carried on. 'He started thinking it was something he'd done. He was good-looking, but he didn't ever feel like it. Think he still felt like the little shrimpy kid no one wanted to pair up with in PE.'

Her eyes were far away, back there with the little brother she hadn't been able to protect – had probably shaken and cajoled, shaming him without ever meaning to. One thing I know from my work is that tough love is overrated.

'So what about that whole quiz night thing?' I asked.

'He said she followed him out to the toilets, tried to kiss him. He pushed her off, and she went storming back in and told her husband he'd grabbed her.' Jennifer's face twisted with anger. 'Poor her, she hadn't wanted to tell him, Peter had been harassing her for months.'

'But didn't he have the messages?'

'He was scared. He'd already deleted them, hoped it'd go away. I think he blamed himself a bit too – he got himself all screwed up about whether he'd led her on.'

I felt a stab of anger – it was the same way Kimberley had made me feel, like I was the one who'd committed a crime when she'd tried to stick her tongue in my mouth.

'Jesus. Poor Peter.'

'The headmaster was fuck all help, too scared of offending

his celebrity parents.' I thought back to Ian; the half-sentences that tailed off, his lack of enthusiasm about going deep with the work, despite his obvious trauma. It made sense. 'The one person who believed him was Sarah.'

'Were they already friends?'

'Friends is one word for it. I could just tell for a while that he was hung up on someone. He was such a soppy thing, he'd just get this look in his eyes, you know? But he wouldn't talk about it – not till after the quiz night. Then he needed a big sister.'

I watched as a wave of pain crashed over her, too big to contain – it felt as though it soaked both of us to the skin.

'And you did your best to help him,' I said, looking into her eyes. 'What happened to him – it's not your fault.'

She gave a frustrated shrug. 'He always wanted someone to love, but the thing was, it was always the wrong person.'

I checked myself. The man she described was troubled: could it be that he sold his sister a version of events that made him whiter than white? I didn't want to be blinded by a heady feeling of vindication.

'I wonder why, if Sarah knew he was telling the truth, she didn't talk to Ian for him? I didn't know her well, but she certainly wasn't mousy.'

Jennifer's eyes flashed: she was the one person who hated Kimberley more than I did. 'She might've tried. Trust me, it wouldn't have helped him. Have you seen their new climbing frame? The Japanese garden? That Farthing bitch knows how to buy her way through life.'

A chill ran through me. Maybe Sarah did. Maybe that's what got her killed. *I'm sorry too* could mean all kinds of things.

'Jennifer – do you think they were having an affair?'

Jennifer dropped her eyes, as if she was carrying Peter's private shames.

'He wanted it, no question, but she wouldn't go there. Happy to hang out with him, and call him all hours. But she wasn't putting out.'

'Really?'

She was boiling with injustice. 'They all used him, Mia. He'd have done anything for Sarah. He got really depressed about her. Felt like the one person he'd ever loved, he couldn't have.' She tried and failed to raise a smile. 'Happiness was never my brother's speciality.'

Not sexual, that was what Krall had said, *more loving*.

'Have you told the police all of this? The guy in charge is Lawrence Kr—'

'Of course I fucking have,' snapped Jennifer. 'They don't care. They've got this letter where he begged Sarah to leave her husband: you'd think it was the Bible, the way they're behaving. There's his DNA on her clothes' – she made angry quotation marks in the air – 'a history of inappropriate behaviour. Oh and you can't call back WhatsApp messages apparently, only texts. I bet she knew that.'

'I'm so sorry.'

'And he's dead!' She was almost shouting now, tears threatening again. 'No one cares that much about a dead man's reputation. We care – we've had our lives destroyed – but once the headlines stop, everyone else gets to move on.' She looked at me, face naked and vulnerable. 'We don't. I can't move on if it means leaving my brother behind.'

Jennifer started to sob, head dropped over her forearms, her broad shoulders heaving.

'I could talk to Lawrence Krall ...' I said, aware as the words left my mouth how useless they were. Even if he still cared what I thought, he was already enthralled by the next chapter, had no desire to turn the pages backwards. Jennifer's head, still bowed, shook a vigorous no.

'People like her get to decide about people like me,' she said, her voice muffled.

'What, Kimberley?'

'Yeah,' she said, jerking her head up, eyes blazing amidst the watery remains of her make-up. 'I had this stupid fairy tale that you knew what had happened. That you knew who really did it, so they wouldn't pin it on Peter. Cos trust me, no one wants to listen to his sister. Let alone his sister who works in Tesco.'

Something stirred in me then, something primal and dangerous. The problem was, at that moment it felt like I had nothing left to lose. I did believe her – I'd always believed, with an illogical conviction, in Peter's innocence. And if he hadn't done it, then someone else had.

CHAPTER TWENTY-NINE

'Just here is fine. Perfect, in fact.'

The cab driver stared into his rear-view mirror, his lined and baggy eyes alight with suspicion.

'D'you want me to ring the buzzer? Normally do when people get dropped here.'

We both looked towards the fortress that was the Farthing residence. In my feverish state, the gates seemed higher and spikier than ever. I knew this whole mission was insane, and yet somehow I couldn't stop.

'No, I'm all good.'

He peered at me a second longer before he finally caved. 'I'll get your bags out.'

Then I was stranded on the verge outside Kimberley's house, the wheels of my suitcase sinking into the muddy grass. I pulled its dead weight towards the intercom, gave the cab driver a determined wave. Hopefully he couldn't see my hand shaking as I pretended to push the buzzer.

I needed a minute more. I took some deep breaths, composed myself, but before I could buzz, the screen of the intercom lit up. Kimberley was framed in the square, hair swept up into a high ponytail that accentuated the sharp triangle of her cheekbones, skin bare and luminous.

'Mia? Is that you? What a treat!'

She was already taking control of the situation: this time, I wasn't going to let it happen.

'I thought I'd drop by before I went back.'

'Come in, come in,' she said, a jarring buzz coming out of the shiny intercom.

I couldn't dawdle, couldn't give myself any more time to think, I strode up the sweeping drive, yanking my heavy suitcase behind me. I squared my shoulders as I languished outside the closed front door: she'd obviously decided to reverse her strategy and make me wait. Finally it swung open, her face also opening up into a broad and empty smile. She leaned in, gave me a staccato kiss on each cheek. She was dressed in expensive-looking yoga gear, the teal fabric so tight against her skinny body I could almost count her ribs.

'What a surprise!' she said. 'You really are in transit. Just dump the luggage here.'

'Thanks.'

'So, Mia, you've been a naughty girl!' she said, heading towards the kitchen, the words flung over a bony shoulder.

The cavernous kitchen was spotless.

'What, the press story? No — no I actually haven't. She cobbled together a few throwaway remarks and made it sound like an interview.'

She grabbed two tall glasses, stuck them under the noisy ice-maker.

'You live and learn. Obviously with Nigel's job, I've had to become a professional at dealing with the gutter press. You won't be doing that again in a hurry!'

She thrust a glass towards me, a look of amused pity on her face.

'Yes,' I said, reaching for it, 'I've noticed how skilled you are at controlling your public image. It's quite a talent.'

'I wish they hadn't used those photos from the other night . . .' she said, blue eyes trained on me, waiting for a reaction. 'Have you recovered yet?'

'From which part of it, Kimberley? Seeing that my best friend has a serious drug habit? From my continued knowledge that there are secrets being guarded which are torturing her and making her problems even worse?'

Kimberley paused a second, keeping her face deliberately blank. Cut-price injectables were certainly an advantage in this scenario.

'I was wondering more about that little incident in Priory Quad. Jake said it was a quite a scene in the end. I'm sure you'll be glad to get back to London and start patching things up with, with – Pat? I think we're all just concerned to protect poor Rowena.'

The shame still tasted bitter and metallic. 'Nothing happened, Kimberley.' I felt myself flush, hated it. 'It was actually nothing.'

Kimberley took a mouthful of ice cold water, gazed at me.

'We're all used to a country pace of life, I'm afraid. Our "nothings" don't involve front-page exclusives and adultery.'

'I'd hardly call a two-second kiss adultery!' Kimberley's sense of triumph was tangible. 'And as for your country pace of life – as far as I know, you're not all that opposed to a spot of adultery yourself when the mood takes you.'

I'd finally got to her: two high spots of scarlet splashed those angular cheekbones. She gripped the granite counter. 'I'm sorry?'

I didn't care now: I was going to lay it all out, and see how she handled it.

'You weren't scared of Peter; Peter was scared of you! You were stalking him – not the other way round. And he didn't have a chance against someone like you.'

'Where have you got this rubbish from?' said Kimberley, with a snort of derision. 'The fact Peter was stalking me is well documented. Me not pressing charges – it was an act of kindness.'

I ignored her.

'And as for the drugs – I bet you've manipulated that with the police. Pushed the blame onto Sarah and Lysette when they were buying them for the whole lot of you.'

Kimberley gave an affected shudder. 'Those two, unfortunately, didn't know where to stop. Where the line was, if you'll pardon the pun.'

She was clever: the 'pun' was designed to convey the idea she was still entirely in control. I was going to have to go to the one place no one was comfortable going to break her down.

'Oh yes, and I don't know the full story with Susan ...'
I saw something flash in her ice blue eyes, something that
was fearful and dangerous all at once, 'but I know whatever
happened with her is something you don't want getting out.
There's a reason she was rushed back to Romania before
anyone could ask her any awkward questions.'

Kimberley was silent for a few seconds – then she smiled
and reached deliberately for my tall, slippery glass.

'More water?'

'No.'

She crossed to the fridge, shot a noisy torrent into her own
glass. When she spoke, her voice was a sing-song.

'People tell you stories all day, don't they, Mia? Ask for
your pearls of wisdom. It's no wonder you've been telling
your stories to Lawrence Krall, assuming he'll think you're
this wise oracle. Unfortunately, even if anyone did care
what you thought – and they really don't – you're way off
the mark. I suggest you trot back to London with your little
wheelie case and put all of this behind you.'

'Really? I'm completely wrong, am I? You've got too
much at stake. Too much to lose. Whatever you said to
Lysette – whatever lies you told her about me – I know that
it was you who talked to April. That unnamed source saying
you were shaken and distressed – consider it named. I know
you're pulling the strings.' My whole body was shaking, and
not just with anger. I felt frightened too. I was trapped inside
her remote, gated house, taking her apart.

'The sad fact that you seem unable to comprehend is that

you've destroyed your relationship with your supposed best friend all by yourself.' She gave me one of her maddening smiles, but I could see a vein throbbing in her neck. She was feeling the pressure now. 'It was all about Sarah for Lysette. It had been for a long time. You're just someone to lend her cash and listen to her whining. Sarah was the star.'

The first thing that hit me was the poison intended for me, but it didn't stop there. The venom directed towards Sarah was deadly. It was another chink.

'I think you hated Sarah. You worship youth, don't you? You stuff your face full of chemicals, you chase boys half your age. She had all of that for real.'

Kimberley's beautiful face twisted into something ugly in front of my eyes. When she spoke her voice had lost its careful elocution.

'Listen to me, you little bitch, this is over. Get out of my house. Don't come back here. If you do . . .' Her face was pinched and white. 'Trust me, Mia, I can make things very difficult for you. I'm sure they look pretty bleak right now, but know this, they could get a lot worse. What's the phrase? Friends in high places.'

We stood on either side of her granite counter, our eyes locked.

'Did you do it, Kimberley? Did you push her off?'

Her eyes flicked away, flicked back.

'Don't be so ridiculous. I can't believe anyone pays good money to listen to your ludicrous fantasies.'

I said it again, more softly this time.

'Did you?'

Something was pulsing, straining to come out. But before it exploded, we were ambushed. Lysette stormed into the kitchen, every bit as wild and desperate as she'd been at the ball.

'Just stop it! Stop it, OK?'

Kimberley took a step towards her.

'I told you to stay upstairs and rest. I'm handling this.' Her voice was soothing now, almost soporific. That was why she'd taken so long to come to the door – it was more than a simple power play. 'You don't need to worry.'

Lysette thrust her phone at us.

'The police are looking for me.' It was only now that I noticed the way her words were slurring. 'They've been to the house. My kids have seen the police on the doorstep asking for their mum. I'm all over the papers . . .'

'Lysette . . .' I said, stepping towards her, but Kimberley had got there first. She snaked a skinny arm around Lysette's shaking body.

'Let's get you back upstairs. I'll call Lawrence, tell him you're safe here and we'll go and talk to him later.'

Lysette flung her arms wide, shook Kimberley off.

'No! I can't do this any more. I can't . . .'

'She's right,' I said. 'She can't dodge questioning.' A nauseous wave of guilt washed over me as I remembered Lawrence's satisfaction at my refusal to answer his questions. Kimberley was ignoring me, face full of faux concern for Lysette. 'None of you can.'

'I can't do it,' Lysette repeated, bleak and hopeless.

'Do what, Lys?' I said, forcing eye contact from where I stood. 'What happened?'

Her face broke apart in front of my eyes.

'All of it!' she wailed. She turned to Kimberley, eyes pleading. 'All of it.'

Kimberley turned on me, furious.

'I clearly remember asking you to leave my home.'

'There's no way I'm leaving her in this state. Especially not with you.'

Lysette half staggered, gripping the counter. This time I moved to her side.

'Lys, look at me . . .' She focused on me, but then her gaze slid away. 'Have you taken something?' This didn't seem like coke, it was more like she was drunk. But no, that wasn't right either.

'I'm just so tired!' she said, pleading. 'I can't keep holding on to it.'

'What do you mean?' I said. 'What really happened to Sarah?'

'No!'

She was so frustrating, so child-like. I shot a look at a glowering Kimberley. What would she do if I kept refusing to leave? Patrick's warning echoed through my head: how much did she have to lose? I shivered, my desperation to speak to him reaching a fever pitch.

'I think we should call Ged,' I said.

'No!' said the two of them, in unison. The union gave

402

Kimberley confidence. She handcuffed Lysette's upper arm with a pinching grip.

'Come on, let's go back upstairs. This will all feel better once you've got some sleep. You're still in shock from' – she cast me a look of pure disgust – 'from her betrayal.'

'I didn't say those things,' I said, pleading myself now. 'You've got to believe that. If anyone knows how to manipulate this situation it's her! Don't trust her.'

Lysette slammed her hands down hard on the granite counter. When she spoke, her words suddenly sounded clear, definitive.

'Stop it, OK? Both of you.' She looked at me. 'I need – I need to show you something. I can't keep hold of it any more. You're the only one who might understand it.'

*

Lysette's battered Fiat Punto was stowed in Kimberley's garage. Kimberley was still loudly complaining as Lysette aimed her key at the boot with a shaking hand.

'I don't know what you think you're doing,' she said, her shrill voice like a blade. 'Don't encourage her to hang around here. She's on her way back to London. Have you forgotten what you woke up to this morning?'

Lysette ignored her. I should've been triumphant at this fact, but there was something almost robotic – trance-like – about her movements. The boot sprang open: she crossed to it and slowly peeled back the rubber floor. There, underneath, was a red leather book. She handed it to me, solemn.

'What is that?' demanded Kimberley, ponytail flying through the air like a weapon as she looked between us. 'What on earth are you doing?'

Lysette's words had that sticky quality again, like they couldn't quite separate from each other. 'Sarah's diary,' she said. She gave a half-sob. 'I want you to read it.'

It felt heavy in my hands. 'How did you get it?'

'Just read it, OK? I can't . . .'

She gave way to a proper, juddering sob. I put my arm around her.

'Let's go inside.'

'Absolutely not!' said Kimberley. 'You don't set foot in my house.'

I wanted to whisk her away, but Kimberley was too dangerous to leave to her own devices. Besides, Lysette was in no fit state to travel. She'd crumpled to the floor by now, the back of her head leaning against the car's bumper. I felt that deep unease again, that sense that something was badly wrong with her.

'Seriously?' I said to Kimberley. 'Look at her, there's something not right.' She'd folded her arms across her chest, was staring at both of us like we were a pair of guttersnipes.

'I'm fine, Mia, stop fussing,' said Lysette, waving a hand at me. It looped unsteadily through the air, then gripped the diary. She opened it. 'Please!'

I sat down on the grimy garage floor. 'Fine.'

Our bodies were pushed up together on the ground. Lysette pushing the book towards me, opening it at a specific page. There was an odd, unexpected comfort in the midst of this darkness. I could feel her bodily warmth, that familiar closeness that I now knew had been in hiding, not extinguished.

Kimberley was still hovering above us, refusing to back away. I looked down at the slanting writing, my body prickling with vulnerability.

I spy, with my little eye – YOU. I watched her today, I watched her come out of her house and climb into her car, and I felt sick.

I settled myself on the hard ground as best I could, and began to read.

CHAPTER THIRTY

I'd nearly finished now. Lysette had only directed me to a few of the entries, and I'd barely spoken as I'd read them. I'd been trying to tune out Kimberley, who was jabbing at the pages, providing her own commentary. We were at the last one, written less than a month before her death.

June 30th 2015

I can't believe it happened. The one thing I knew for certain about myself was that I was a good mum. Now I don't even have that to keep me sane.

I can't believe I let it happen. Lysette kept saying it wasn't my fault, they all did, but I knew it was. Kimberley was making out she was being kind, but she just wanted it to go away, for me to shut up and forget about it. She'd thrown money at the problem and I was supposed to be grateful. So was Susan.

406

I'll never forget. I promise you that, Max, I'll never forget. I'll be a new mummy.

He let me cry and cry outside the hospital. He held me tight, those muscly arms wrapped around me, and my tears soaked through his T-shirt. It's different now. It HAS started now. I wanted to tell him that, but it would have hurt him too much. Or maybe it was me I was protecting – maybe I was scared of what it would mean if he took it right inside his big heart.

At least it's made me stop obsessing about her. I didn't think about her at all the rest of the week. When I'm not thinking about Max, all I can think about is him.

Feels good to write that. All I can think about is him.

Later I lay in his arms, and we both cried. I was in my bra and pants, like I was fourteen years old. 'It's OK,' he said, making my hair wet with his tears, 'I love you no matter what.' The way he talks – like a book of poems. But it wasn't. It wasn't really. 'I'm sorry,' I whispered, but I don't know if he even heard.

I had to go then, but I couldn't tell him where. I wanted to, I really did. I haven't got all the money, and it's not like another fucking late credit card payment. Thing is, I know he'd insist on helping. He'd sell his stuff, he'd find a night job. And I can't take any more from him.

I'm Sorry. Next time I tell him, I'm going to have to make sure he hears me.

Tears streamed down Lysette's ravaged face. 'She couldn't talk to me,' she said. 'Maybe if she'd talked to me we could've sorted it out.' She looked at me, pleading. 'Do you think she was shagging him all the time?'

My eyes rolled upwards towards Kimberley, my heart beating a swift tattoo in my chest. When I'd accused her in the kitchen I'd only half meant it, but now I'd read Sarah's words, the sense we were trapped here, behind her high iron gates, was becoming increasingly frightening. Surely Lori would reappear with the children soon?

'No, of course she wasn't!' snapped Kimberley. 'She was pining after him, and stalking me. She says it there – she was parked outside my home. She was a very disturbed young woman.' She gave a theatrical shudder. 'I've told people again and again how unsafe I felt.'

I jumped to my feet, whipped around to face her. I needed to stay strong. 'Can you – just for five minutes – stop talking about yourself?' I turned my attention back to Lysette. 'How did you get the diary? Did she give it to you?'

If she had done – if she'd been preparing to leave this earth – then it would change everything. I almost wanted her to say yes – for there to be a possibility it was a tragedy instead of an act of evil – but she was shaking her head in shame.

'I picked up Max the day it happened. I knew where she kept it, right at the back of her wardrobe.'

'How come?' I asked.

'She told me, she said she was frightened of Joshua reading it. She said he had a temper, but no one else ever saw it.'

It was an odd, teenage hiding place if she really didn't want him to see it. Were the words she'd written between the pages a desperate bid for his attention as much as anything?

'You *took* it?' said Kimberley, her voice flipping upwards.

'Wow.' I knew she was deliberately making Lysette feel worse, but the fact was that she had removed and concealed key evidence – her prospects with the police were looking increasingly grim. I felt sick at the memory of Krall's ferocious determination to use her culpability to get what he wanted.

Lysette crumpled further towards the floor, her words slipping and slurring again. 'She said . . . she said to me once that she was terrified of him when he got really angry. And . . .' She turned an intense gaze upwards towards Kimberley. 'We didn't know what was in there, did we?'

A twisting darkness crossed Kimberley's face, like one of those incoming tornadoes that are so severe and specific that they get their very own name. In that moment I couldn't remember why I'd ever found her beautiful.

'So she was terrified of him?' I asked. It kind of tallied now I'd read her description of their relationship. There was something incredibly bleak, incredibly distant about Joshua. His smiles – rare and fleeting – were like winter.

'She only said it a couple of times,' said Lysette. 'Other times she'd talk about him like he was completely amazing. Like they were dating, or something.'

My brain was whirring. 'Did you read it as soon as you had it? Can you fill in the blanks in what she's writing?'

Lysette gave a sob. 'No. I only read it today, I didn't want to be another person who betrayed her.' I saw that sense of shame creep back through her. 'And if I didn't know what it said, then I didn't have to worry about it.'

'All it does is confirm the truth . . .' Self-doubt was

409

creeping into Kimberley's haughty tone, the fear that she'd no longer be able to control the narrative. 'That Peter was obsessed with me, and that he was also a terrifying predator. That ...'

She saw something in my face that silenced her.

'No, it doesn't!' I shouted. 'She was frightened of Joshua finding it – we know that. So she says "him" the whole time, keeps it deniable. Well, what if "him" is two people?' It had been percolating all the time I'd been reading, but now the truth was fully emerging. 'Peter is one "him", but the "him" she's really craving and can't have, that's Joshua.'

Kimberley rolled her eyes. 'Joshua was her husband, Mia.'

'You of all people should know marriage isn't perfect,' I said. I was spooling back through what Jennifer said, how Peter had been pining for Sarah, never getting what he wanted. 'I bet she was in her bra and pants with *Peter*, not with Joshua,' I said. 'She couldn't go through with having sex. Betraying her husband.'

Marriage isn't perfect – I was actually parroting a phrase I'd heard from Joshua, his eyes cold and dark as he'd uttered it. I thought too about the text he'd sent me that morning – 'You disgust me' – it was so stark, so brutal. Poor Sarah. I've seen it so many times, the kind of abuse that leaves no visible scars but does devastating damage. Had that loud, bubbly persona been a way to hide the low self-esteem that was keeping her trapped?

I kept going. 'What if *he* was the one having an affair ...'

'Is this another chance for you to air your ridiculous suggestion that I killed her?'

I ignored Kimberley, dropped to my knees on the grimy, uncomfortable floor so that I was at eye level with Lysette.

'Lys, do you think it's possible Joshua was cheating on her? Is that what she's writing about?'

Lysette looked shamefaced.

'I told her she was being paranoid. But she wasn't, was she?' Lysette looked up towards Kimberley, who was determinedly refusing to make eye contact. 'Lisa. She thought he was still in love with her.'

'Lisa?' I gasped.

Suddenly it was all starting to click into place. The motherly frustration she displayed with Max, like he was her wayward third. Even the way she said Joshua's name, the three syllables like a melody. It was frustrated love that she was singing about.

'Oh my God,' said Lysette, 'she was right! And then, what happened with Max . . .' Lysette started to sob. 'She had such a terrible time, and then she died!'

'You don't know they were having an affair,' snapped Kimberley. 'There's no proof.'

I needed to keep Lysette focused. I put an arm around her heaving shoulders.

'What did happen with Max?' I asked, urgent. 'You can tell me, Lys.'

Kimberley was riled now. 'Don't answer her!'

Lysette leant backwards, twisted her head so she could look at me. There was a strange kind of serenity about her, the relief of knowing it was time to unburden herself.

Her voice was a whisper. 'He swallowed a pill. We thought he was asleep upstairs.' She pointed a shaky hand towards the house. 'But he came down, and took it out of her handbag. Susan pretended he was her son at A and E, and we got him out before social services could get involved. Peter helped us.'

I felt a wave of sickness wash over me: little Max. My God, how must Sarah have felt? How could you live with that knowledge?

'So he took an E, or something, from her purse? Lys, the police think she was dealing drugs, and that you were involved.'

Kimberley grabbed my shoulder so hard that it felt like a punch.

'I know how you do this, the way you wheedle information out of people. This isn't your business. She needs a lawyer if she's going to talk, and she certainly doesn't need to talk to you.'

I flung my arms back violently, still focused on Lysette. 'Get off me. Why don't you do something useful and get her some water?'

Lysette's voice shook with fear. 'It wasn't dealing! It was just – something fun on a Friday night. You know – well, you don't, but – a few lines, a few drinks. It was meant to be harmless.'

Now Kimberley wanted out – deniability had always been her saving grace. As she set off towards the house, Lysette continued, vomiting up words in her desperation to get them out.

'And yeah, we were the ones who picked it up, and we did make a few quid here and there. Like nothing real, just a bit of money for clothes.' Her face had that pleading quality that broke my heart, like she was hoping I could take it all away. 'I know it sounds awful, but I never have any cash. And, look at this . . .'

She gestured towards the massive house that loomed over us. How naive I was, the first time I came here, to think that the disparity didn't sting. I didn't care about my professional responsibilities, my legal responsibilities – any of it. I just wanted to protect my friend. She'd made a monumental fuck-up, but she'd never wanted to hurt anyone.

'Is that why she was in the car park?'

Lysette gave a weary nod. 'She used to meet the dealer there.'

'The police know about the dealing, Lys. They want to use you to get into the supply chain. Find the gang who are smuggling drugs in.'

Lysette gave a strangled sob. 'I could go to prison!'

I tried to control my own terror, keep my voice soothing. 'I don't think it'll come to that. They just want to scare you into giving them information. I think you just need to cooperate.'

What if it wasn't as simple as that? What if cooperating brought all kinds of dangers that Lawrence Krall had no interest in protecting her from?

Lysette's fists were balled up in her lap. 'It was Kimberley – fucking Kimberley – who made it bigger, buying stuff for their posh friends who wanted to get high without having to get their hands dirty. I knew we should've said no, but Sarah liked it. She used to joke they'd be doing it in Number 10 cos of us.'

Kimberley was sailing back towards us now, a single tall glass held aloft in her right hand like a gleaming spear.

'And I owe them money!' she continued. 'Sarah died with debts . . . drugs we hadn't paid them for. I gave them what I could the night before the funeral, but . . .'

At least we were finally on the same side. I squeezed her shaking body. 'It's going to be all right, Lys. We'll find a way through it.'

Kimberley was getting closer. Lysette stood up, a little unsteady.

'I can't talk to her now. She'll never tell the truth. I'm going to the bathroom.'

'Lys . . .'

I knew instinctively we shouldn't separate, but she was already pushing past Kimberley and heading for the house. I stood up, walked out of the garage.

'Well, I hope you're pleased with yourself,' said Kimberley, who'd rediscovered her self-righteous poise during her absence. 'Before you tipped up uninvited, I'd calmed her down. Now she looks . . .' An expression of disgust blew across her face. 'Well, she's in a terrible state.'

'You're just as responsible as she is,' I spat. 'You're an ena-bler – you're just clever enough to keep it all under wraps. You and your entitled friends. Your sleazy husband.'

It was midday, the sun burning down on us. I felt sticky and uncomfortable, stranded there in the sweeping driveway scalded by heat.

Kimberley's nostrils flared, her hand tightly gripping the glass. 'Just go, will you? You've caused nothing but pain and distress since you arrived here.'

I shook my head. 'No. I want to know how long you knew that Joshua and Lisa were having an affair?'

I saw something cross her face – a tiny tell. 'I don't know what you're talking about.'

'I think you do,' I said, emboldened. 'That's not a civilised divorce, it's the absolute opposite. It's a man who wanted to believe he was something he wasn't, and then got cold feet. She's your friend and you know everyone's business.'

'Another lovely fairy tale . . .'

'You're up to your neck in it, Kimberley, whether you like it or not. Your friends in high places – I'm not sure how much use they'll be.'

I could see the rigid set of her jaw. I was gaining the upper hand.

'Lisa had every right to be angry with Sarah.' Kimberley spat the words out. 'And you need to get out of my house. Stop spreading lies about me. You know nothing about it . . .'

'I know enough to know that you covered up a child's drug overdose in your own home . . .' I looked straight at her, challenge in my eyes. 'Today's papers have got nothing on tomorrow's.'

I'd pushed her too far now. She looked like she was on

the verge of lunging at me, but before she could, Lysette reappeared from the back door. As she walked towards us, I could sense there was something deeply wrong. She was more floating than walking, almost as if she wasn't tethered to the ground. I hurried to her. Her pupils were too big, her pallor deathly white.

'Hi, Mia,' she said, a strange, almost ethereal smile wreathing her face.

'What's wrong? Have you taken something, Lys? We need to get you inside.'

Kimberley regarded us coldly, making no move to help.

'Come on!' I said, insistent. 'She's really not in a good way.' I cupped Lysette's pale face in my hands. 'What have you taken?'

Lysette gestured towards Kimberley.

'Just, you know, what she gave me earlier. And then I took a couple more. I'm so tired. We should never have let it happen.' She started to cry. 'Max needed his mummy.' She turned on Kimberley. 'You shouldn't . . . you shouldn't have told her.' Her words were slurring and accusatory, all at once. 'You told Lisa, didn't you?'

Panic swept Kimberley's face, but in the moment I was too distracted by Lysette to demand to know why. She was growing paler and paler, her body swaying with the effort of staying upright. I started half walking, half dragging her towards the house.

'Kimberley, what's she taken?'

Kimberley waved an airy hand.

'I just gave her an Amblin, they're completely harmless.'

'But I found the ones you like at the back of the cupboard too,' added Lysette. She turned to me. 'It makes you feel really light inside, Mia. It's nice.'

A wave of dread washed through me at the memory of Kimberley's overflowing medicine cabinet. Of course I didn't know the names on the tiny labels – any pharmacist would be proud of that professional haul. In her desperate state, Lysette could've taken a cocktail of just about anything.

'Great, so you've basically encouraged her to swallow a pick and mix of prescription drugs.' We were in the doorway by then. Lysette slumped downwards at the foot of the stairs.

'She's fine,' said Kimberley, reaching down and pulling at the skin around her eyes like she was an animal. Her own hands were shaking now. Even she knew this had all gone too far – that no amount of blacked-out windows and posed photo opps could hide how corrupted she'd become.

I was shouting now. 'She's not! You know she's not. I'm calling 999.'

I reached for the landline on the elegant occasional table, but as I did, Kimberley made that familiar bony handcuff around my wrist.

'Stop. I'll call a private doctor. It'll be quicker. Much nicer for her too.'

I shook her off. Lysette was even paler now, her head slumping sideways. I fought to stay calm.

'You're the worst kind of Tory, aren't you?' I hissed, running to the kitchen for my phone. I jabbed the numbers in with a shaking hand. Kimberley was just a minute behind.

'Stop! I've called a doctor already.'

'No, you haven't.' I went to speak to the operator.

'Ambulance. I need an ambulance at—' Shit – I had absolutely no idea what the address was here. We were in the middle of nowhere. 'At Nigel Farthing's home . . .' Kimberley knocked the phone clean out of my hand, the two of us left scrabbling on the Tuscan tiles in pursuit of it. I was almost crying with fear and frustration. We shouldn't be leaving Lysette – barely conscious – on her own, and yet in order to look after her I had to find a way to ring for help.

I ignored the sirens at first, imagined they were a part of my fevered and desperate imagination. But then the intercom started buzzing incessantly, loud and determined, like a mutant insect in a horror film. They must have been using a loud hailer.

'Police. Open up.'

Kimberley stood up, somehow finding her Teflon poise between the ground and the sky. She fixed a smile on her face, ready to charm whomever was on the other side of her expensive security system. She was actually reassured by their arrival, so confident was she in her authority.

'It's over,' I told her, 'you know that, don't you?'

She looked at me through narrowed eyes as I scrabbled to my feet, her index finger hovering over the buzzer. 'Lysette just needs us to be strong for her now, Mia.'

I had to crack her open. I see it too much: how far self-belief can take someone, particularly when it's fused with a polished exterior. The authorities wouldn't want to destroy the illusion unless they absolutely had to, particularly if it required a humiliating climb down on their part.

'You think no one's going to believe her because of the state she's in, but there's the diary. All those drugs that weren't prescribed to you that you've got stashed upstairs.' It wasn't enough. I was throwing out bait now, hoping something would get a bite. What had Lysette said, before she'd slid into incoherence? *You shouldn't have told Lisa.* Suddenly the pieces started to coalesce in my mind. The naked panic I'd seen in Kimberley's eyes was making perfect sense.

'You told Lisa about Max's accident, didn't you? You made sure you had someone who'd say Max overdosing in your house was all down to Sarah if it came out. But what it did – what it made her do – was decide to take what she thought was rightfully hers.'

Tiny things – even Lisa's body language when she'd come to collect Max from the school. There was something so proprietary about it – a brooding, dangerous anger at my interference. If I made her feel that way, how much anger did Sarah elicit? Kimberley's finger wavered, not quite depressing the button.

'I don't know what you're talking about . . .' There was no conviction in her voice now. There was too much stacking up.

'And if it was Lisa who killed her, I don't believe for a second you didn't know about it. I bet you've been colluding with her to keep Peter as the prime suspect. That would've suited you perfectly – the ultimate revenge for him telling you he didn't want you. He didn't, did he? He only wanted Sarah. You couldn't stand it.'

Her denial was almost childlike, her power draining away before my eyes. 'He did want me! He was obsessed with me.'

'That's what happened, isn't it?' Kimberley's stare was unwavering, but she didn't deny it. I softened my tone. 'You can still keep yourself relatively squeaky clean, give Nigel's career a chance to survive. You just need to give them enough. If they think you've only just realised she did it, that you're still the one who's cooperating . . .'

She gave an almost imperceptible nod. I pushed my way past her, slammed my palm against the buzzer. Now her face twisted into an expression of pure hatred.

'Sarah was a bitch, and so are you.'

'Yeah, and you might not have killed her but you've got blood on your hands.'

'I wish you'd never come here,' she spat.

I looked her straight in the eye.

'Do you know what, so do I.'

*

The two paramedics were low on the ground, huddled around Lysette. I watched them anxiously, my heartbeat refusing to slow. They looked too young to trust with this. Eventually the boyish-looking male, his dark hair gelled flat against his head (the view I'd had for the last fifteen minutes) looked up at me.

'She's gonna be OK. We'll take her in, but the fact she's still conscious is a really good sign. Means we don't need to pump her stomach. We'll take those drugs with us to the hospital.'

Lysette was mumbling, words starting to come a little more clearly. Kimberley looked down, wide-eyed, at the little brown bottles she'd been forced to bring down from the bathroom.

'I'm so sorry, I had no idea. You know – a friend in LA just gave them to me to help me sleep on the flight. I mean . . .'

She turned towards Lawrence Krall, who was standing a few feet away, taking in the whole scene. I could see that something had shifted for him: there was a shrewdness in the way that he looked at her. She sensed it too, her stream of justifications dying away.

The diary lay there on the hall carpet. I handed it to Krall.

'This is Sarah's diary. I think it will change your thinking quite a bit, don't you agree, Kimberley?'

Her eyes flashed, but she gave a meek nod.

'Yes. We put quite a few pieces of the puzzle together before . . .' She clutched at herself. 'Before all of this happened.'

'Mia.' It was Lysette, reaching out a shaking hand from the stretcher. 'Mia, will you come with me?'

I felt my eyes fill with hot tears.

'Of course I will!'

'I need you with me.'

'Don't worry, I'm there.'

421

CHAPTER THIRTY-ONE

It was dark by the time the train pulled in, but King's Cross was still teeming with humans. I struggled to get my suitcase – my faithful, four-wheeled friend – down from the luggage rack as passengers pushed past me without a backward glance. Once I was on the platform, I was carried along in the slipstream of rushing, harried people, headphones clamped on, eyes trained straight ahead. Now it was London that felt like a foreign country. The truth was, I was no more Zen than any of them. I was out of practice, and – even though I'd lived my whole life here – I was as lost as a teenage exchange student with no guidebook and three halting words of English.

I'd spent the rest of the day in the police station going over what had unfolded at Kimberley's house. I'd kept my tone calm and measured, my exhaustion making it easier to mask my emotions. Krall was discreet, but I divined from the little he'd shared that even Kimberley had decided it was time to open up and provide her carefully curated version of the truth. He was too clever, too smooth, to resist implying that all of this was where he'd always been heading, but we both knew it was a lie.

Lysette was staying in hospital overnight: the fact they considered her a suicide risk meant that Lawrence had promised they'd go gently when they questioned her. I didn't believe she was – I knew her well enough to know she'd never do that to her family – but if it meant she'd be treated with more kindness, I had no intention of disabusing them of the notion. Lisa had already been brought in for questioning by the time I'd left.

I pushed my ticket through the barrier, and then came to a juddering stop halfway to the exit. There I was, between Starbucks and WHSmith, people tutting as they swerved past me and my luggage. I averted my eyes from the headlines, longing for them to be nothing more than tomorrow's fish and chip wrapping. What had it all been for? In that moment I felt utterly alone. Sarah jolted her way into my consciousness, her scribbled, desperate words still chasing circles in my mind. How alone had she felt, up there in the car park, awaiting her death without even knowing it? We never know what's coming next. I felt my lips move, the thought becoming a whisper. And me – becoming a mad person, who muttered to herself in train stations.

This couldn't go on. The fact that the words were true – the fact that we really do never know – was why it couldn't go on.

*

I stood there in the taxi queue, my stomach doing somersaults. Not good somersaults – not the fizzy, excitable kind that herald positive things. This was more doomed, internal churning – ancient machinery that creaked and shook. I tried not to think about Patrick dropping me off here, kissing me goodbye as I promised it would only be a short few days. Or the very first time – the night we first kissed, him begging me to take him seriously, to not assume he was using me for information, rain drizzling and spitting on us and neither of us caring. Was it supreme arrogance to be doing what I was doing? My feet kept carrying me forward: I didn't seem to have a choice.

The cab journey was interminable. Of course I had a chatty driver, the kind I'd have bonded with on a different day, but who immediately took against me after I rejected two of his cheery opening gambits. We sat there in stony silence on the Euston Road, the traffic rock solid, the meter ticking ever upwards like a hungry gremlin. Eventually we arrived in Kennington, pulling up outside my second police station of the day. I overthanked and overtipped, even though by now the fare was about half my month's salary, refusing any help with the dead weight of my suitcase.

'You OK, love?' he said, looking up at the building and suddenly seeing my surly behaviour in a different light.

I was about to throw out a platitude, but then I stopped myself.

'No, not really,' I said, smiling, grateful for the small kindness. 'But I might be soon.'

'Take care, OK?'

That was exactly what I hadn't done. It was what had brought me here, to this very moment, alone on a South London street corner.

'Thanks,' I said, too heartfelt, then wrapped a blistered palm around the suitcase's handle and lugged it towards the glowing mouth of the door.

*

It was a deliberate move. I knew if I texted him, or called his mobile, he'd firmly and politely tell me to respect his time-line and burrow his way back under his mountain of papers. I told the receptionist that we had an appointment, gave her the blandest name I could come up with, then perched myself on an uncomfortable orange plastic chair and prayed that he'd fall for it.

A few interminable minutes passed. Then he appeared, coming through the swing doors, every detail of him so familiar and so precious. I drank all of it up, greedy and pro-prietary, before he even saw me. The way his crumpled shirt refused to stay confined inside the trousers of his unstylish suit. The way his red hair insisted on sticking up at unruly angles however much product he lashed through it. The gentleness of his brown eyes, even when he wasn't focusing on something that moved him.

Then he did see me. I do this in my room, look for the expression a client has before they've arranged their features into an acceptable huddle. It tells me what they're really feeling, rather than the press release that's liable to come out of their mouth. The last look he'd given me – as he revved his engine and sped away from Cambridge – was one of deep hurt, a hurt which had translated into my own body and made me ache with it. I hadn't been able to imagine anything worse than the pain of hurting him so deeply, but this – this look of cold disdain – turned out to be infinitely more agonising.

He stood over me, his voice a hiss. 'I can't do this, Mia. *You* can't do this.'

I got to my feet, looked up at him.

'But I just did.'

His jaw pulsed, his face white with anger. I'd misplayed it. It was too us, that teasing intimacy, and I'd lost the right to an us.

'I'm not your chew toy, OK? I'm not here to be tossed around and thrown away depending on how you happen to be feeling.'

The receptionist was eyeing us, straining to hear. She wasn't the only one. It wasn't the most savoury place I'd ever been, and I didn't relish asking any of the other people nearby to give us some privacy.

I spoke in an undertone. 'Patrick, can we just go outside?'

'No!' The word reverberated in the air. 'No, we can't.' He directed a scowl towards my suitcase. 'You can go and stay in the flat. I'll sleep here if I have to. Just go somewhere else tomorrow.'

'Is that why you think I'm here? Because I'm too tight to

pay for a hotel?' Tears of frustration sprung to my eyes. 'I love you, Patrick.'

He paused, considered me.

'Do you, Mia, or do you just think you do?'

The question – the fact that he felt he had to ask it – made me curl up inside with shame.

'How can you even need to ask that?' I tipped my left hand forwards, subtly reminding him of that symbol of commitment. 'We're getting married, we're trying for a baby.' I was clinging desperately to the present tense, losing purchase as his face remained impassive. 'I've been stupid and thoughtless, but I never stopped loving you.'

'You've got some slick little therapist phrase, haven't you? Something about love being a verb, not an adjective?' His gaze burned into me now. 'In fact, you've got a lot of slick little phrases, Mia. They're kind of your stock in trade.'

That almost hurt the most, the idea that I was a seller of snake oil, trading a version of myself which was nothing but a pile of empty theories.

'Please ...' My eyes were brimming with tears by now. 'Please just come outside. Five minutes.'

Patrick leant his face downwards until our noses almost bumped. For one insane, happy second I thought he was going to kiss me.

'You don't get to call the shots any more.'

'Stop it!' I said. 'Stop talking like it's over.'

I regretted the words as soon as I'd uttered them. A look of genuine sadness breathed across Patrick's face.

'I don't know how we'd ever come back from here.'

I sat down heavily, my body suddenly leaden. The legs of the chair gave an earsplitting metallic squeal as they scraped the ground in protest. I could still hear the ringing phones and ranged voices, but they'd receded into a kind of white noise. I saw a moment of calculation in Patrick's eyes, the chance of escape. Then he sat down next to me, his body kept deliberately rigid and distant.

'I didn't shag him. I kissed him, and there's no excuse for that and I know I wasn't completely honest with you – but to end things over it ... unless,' the unless was almost too painful, too scorching, to express, 'unless you'd just stopped wanting it anyway.'

A look of pure rage mangled Patrick's face. How was it that everything I said to this man – the person I thought I knew best in the world – was so utterly misjudged? I longed to touch him, to abandon the clumsiness of words and instead simply connect our two bodies, and yet to have reached across the thin strip of air that lay between us would have been nothing short of an assault.

'Don't you dare try and turn this round on me. That is so fucking ...' He shook with anger. 'Insulting.' He paused, his dark eyes narrow and dangerous. Patrick is essentially kind: watching him weigh up his next words – his reluctance to let them loose on me – made my skin prickle with dread. 'When I met you, you were all wounded from your relationship with your dad. How he'd abandoned you, abandoned your mum, never even made an honest woman of her. Made you pick the worst kind of men. But . . .' He cocked his head, considered me as if he barely knew me. As if he was deciding whether it was worth striking up a conversation. 'I think now I worry that you're a little bit like him. You don't seem all that bothered about getting married. You've been seeing that arsehole behind my back, and to be honest, I don't really care if you shagged him – you certainly made him feel like you'd welcome him kissing you. And nothing I do is enough for you. You still think, after all of this – after the last thing I did was dodge about a hundred speed cameras on the M25 to surprise you after a twelve-hour work day – that it's me who couldn't be arsed.'

Time seemed to judder to a halt. I felt mortally wounded, like his words had sliced into the tenderest parts of my flesh. In that moment it felt like the quickest remedy was to launch my own coruscating attack. To flush out those hidden vul-nerabilities of his that he'd gradually exposed to me – those things we can choose to either love or despise another person for – and turn them into weapons of war. I took a breath, time starting to tick forward again. I clutched a tiny corner of his jacket sleeve between my two fingers, the fabric rough and scratchy to my touch. I looked straight at him.

'Please, will you just come outside?'

I think he sensed that something important had shifted, that we could no longer afford to have this conversation in angry whispers, surrounded by prying eyes. He nodded solemnly, then followed me out. I stopped underneath the sodium glow of a tall street lamp, ignoring the discarded remains of a box of chicken wings, the bits of rubbish that were casually blowing around our feet. It was chilly, the cold in my bones adding to the sense that I'd been away for years, not weeks. Patrick looked down at me, that familiar face still so unnervingly unreadable.

'Mia . . .'

We were standing on the outskirts of a housing estate, the windows of a nearby block lit up at random, like the open doors of an advent calendar halfway through December. What was going on in all those homes – in all those lives – as my own life hung in the balance?

'Let me talk now, OK?' I took a breath – I couldn't hide between theories, or counter arguments. All I had now was my most vulnerable self, even though part of me didn't want to risk bringing her here. 'You know me well enough to know how much that would hurt me. My dad was abusive, he was cruel, and I don't think I am those things. But he was the way he was because he was blind, and I think I *have* been that. I haven't noticed that I'm not making you feel like I'm excited about us getting married. I got too caught up in what was going on in Little Copping. And I have to ask myself why.' Patrick was watching me, his face still. I stumbled on. 'I think I've been scared. I want this so much . . . I want this so much that it scares me.' I wanted to reach up and touch him, but his face was too immovable to risk it. 'What if I lose you? What if we bore each other, or our differences . . .'

It came from left field. 'You never bore me.'

'You never bore me!' I looked up at him, sensing a chink.

'Jim bores me. He's so fucking boring. He's exactly the same as he was twenty years ago. I just needed to know that. That it wasn't me . . .'

'Wasn't you?'

'That I didn't make all of it happen. That if it was my only chance to have a baby, that the fact I didn't . . .' I had to just let the sob come, I couldn't hold it in. 'Wasn't my fault.' I risked looking at him properly. 'You can have a baby till you're a hundred.'

Patrick smiled. It was unexpected, precious. 'I am modelling myself on Hugh Hefner, it's true.'

'You would look good in a jacuzzi. In your Speedos. With the Bunnies.'

It was Patrick's turn to look vulnerable. 'The problem is, there's only one Bunny I want.'

'Then . . .'

He cut across me. 'We'd need to go slow, OK? Just build up the trust again. I don't want to feel like I'm having to chase you. Like you're this elusive, mysterious creature and I'm some lumbering peasant trying to drag you down the Holloway Road to church in my wagon.'

'I'm sorry if I've ever made you feel like that. Sometimes I feel like I'm this ancient blue stocking, and you're this hotshot lawyer who doesn't ever want to come home from work.' I paused. 'You do work all the time.'

'So do you,' he countered, but then it was his turn to pause. 'It was all I had before you. Truth is, it'd be all I'd have without you.'

'No, it wouldn't. There'd be some perky blonde from Tinder . . .'

He silenced me with a wave of his hand. 'Well done, by the way. Well done for what you did there.'

'You knew?'

'Snake Hips called me himself. Think he was worried the story would get told wrong if he didn't assert his take.'

'Of course.'

Patrick was right to warn me not to trust him.

He moved a wisp of my hair away from my face. My whole body tingled to his touch. 'I was frustrated with you, but you were right to keep pushing.'

I risked taking his hand in mine.

'But I learnt it from you.' He smiled. 'You know the things we find most annoying in other people tend to be the things we find most annoying about ourselves.'

'Yeah, thanks, Dr Freud,' he said, taking our intertwined hands and wrapping us up together. 'Shall we go home?'

'Are you sure? Do you need to get your stuff?'

'I've got all my stuff with me. I knew it'd be you. No one in the world is called Jane Brown.' He looked down at me. 'You're not as clever as you think you are, just FYI.'

I felt myself begin to breathe, let him lead me towards the headlights and exhaust fumes of the main road. Behind us, a mangy fox scuttled out from the undergrowth in pursuit of the chicken bones.

'Trust me, I know that now.'

CHAPTER THIRTY-TWO

Three Months Later

I spotted her before she saw me. Lysette's hair hung loose, falling in soft waves around her shoulders. She was wearing a pair of jeans, snug in the right way, with a red-and-white Breton top slung on over them. I felt a lump in my throat and couldn't immediately identify why it was there. Then I suddenly knew – it was that she finally looked like herself again. She was neither a sparkly confection nor an exhausted mess: she was simply Lysette.

Then she saw me, pushing and wriggling through the crush of tables towards me as I stood up. We hugged so hard that I could hear her heartbeat.

'Shall I go up to the counter?' she said, casting a trepidatious look at the queue. I probably shouldn't have picked somewhere right in the middle of Covent Garden. Backpacks and buggies abounded. 'I need a fix.' She saw my face. 'Jesus, Mia, I'm teasing you. Caffeine. I need caffeine.'

'Let's go together,' I said. 'No, we'll lose the table. I'll go.'

It was ridiculous how flustered I was. It had been a full three months since we'd seen each other. The truth was, I hadn't been able to face going back to Little Copping – I couldn't help feeling that it had cast a dangerous spell over me, taken too much – and she'd been consumed by the fall-out from everything that had gone down there.

I inched slowly forward in the queue, treating us to some kind of complicated gluten-free blondie from the bountiful cake selection when I finally got to the front. I wasn't even opposed to gluten: it was more the satisfying sense that I'd never have been able to get it in The Crumpet. I dumped our coffees and cake on the table and sat back down.

'It's so good to see you,' I said. 'I'm sorry I didn't . . . I just couldn't. You understand, don't you?'

Lysette waved a dismissive hand. 'Jesus, Mia, after everything I put you through? I tell you, by the time the moving van was packed up, I couldn't wait to see the back of Little Copping either.'

'How is it where you are?' I asked. We'd barely spoken on the phone – most of our contact had been texts or emails. It meant I'd had headlines more than anything. 'Can you imagine it feeling like home?'

'Well, obviously we didn't have a choice,' she said. Her face began to crumple. 'I just feel so bad for what I've put them all through. It's a miracle . . .' Her voice was shaking now. 'Ged's a saint.'

'Um,' I stuck up my hand, trying to lighten the mood, 'so's Patrick.'

The fact she smiled, knew I wasn't trivialising what she'd been through, made warmth spread right through my body. We were still us. We wouldn't have to start again.

'Saint Patrick O'Leary,' she said, 'sounds good.' She paused, eyes full of sadness. 'I put them through all of that, and now they've had to move halfway across the country.'

'You need to be safe.'

'They might never have come after me, and it's not like we've got witness protection anyway, but even if the police hadn't pushed for it, I couldn't have stayed there. I couldn't be running into Kimberley in The Crumpet.' Lysette feigned a twee wave. 'Oh, how are you? No thanks!'

'She's a . . .' I restrained myself. Just. 'She's a total C word.'

'You called it, Mia.' She put her hand over mine. 'I'm sorry I didn't listen to you.' She paused. 'Maybe I didn't want to hear it.'

'What do you mean?'

Her face was full of emotion. 'I felt like you'd hate me if you knew about it all.'

'I could never hate you!'

She put a hand up to silence me.

'It's just – I felt like I'd done so much shit you'd NEVER do. And you're the person who knows me better than anyone. You knew me when I had spots, and those suede cowboy boots with the nasty gold studs up the side. You're like – my conscience.'

My words were lumpy and choked. 'I don't want to be your conscience. I'm not – I'm so not qualified for that. I only

435

ever want to be your . . .' I paused again, ashamed of my own childishness. I had to say it. 'Your best friend.'

'You're not really that,' she said, and my heart plummeted downwards. 'You're more than that. You're in my bones. You're my sister, really.' She smiled a smile that told me she understood how it had felt. 'It was different with Sarah. It was more like an affair.'

'What do you mean?'

'I did love her . . .'

Lysette's eyes filled with tears, her jaw clenching tightly to keep them at bay. She took a darting look round the crowded café, not wanting to make a fool of herself. 'You know, the thing is, I'm convinced she never did shag Peter. She didn't want Joshua to be right about her, or any of the other people who were judging her. I watched that footage again, from the day it . . .' She took a breath in. 'She's cuddling into him, it's not like – "I need to rip your clothes off". I bet she was still putting him off. He made her feel safe. She really struggled to feel safe.'

'And Joshua looked safe from the outside, but the way he treated her meant he was the absolute opposite.'

Lysette's eyes narrowed at the thought of him. 'I think she did mad things to stay on top. That gave her a funny kind of safety. But I wish she'd told me what she was covering up by acting that way. I should never have got involved with the . . .' Her eyes darted around again. 'You know.'

'You made a mistake.' I covered her hand with my own. 'You really can forgive yourself for it now.'

I could see in her face it was a big ask. It would've been for me, too.

'I knew she didn't like Lisa, but I had no idea it was such an obsession.' Her eyes were full of sadness again. 'I didn't want you to judge me, and I guess she didn't want me to judge her. So stupid.'

'I wish you had told me.'

'Me too.'

'Lys, have you . . .' I was trying to be delicate. 'Have you properly stopped?'

She wrinkled up her pretty face.

'I really have. You were right to tell me to go and talk to someone, and because of taking the pills, they were falling over themselves to find me a counsellor. Me and Ged have been going to someone together too.'

'That's brilliant. It's a really brave thing to do.'

She gave a half-shrug. 'We needed to do something. I hadn't been in a good place for a long time, and I was stupid to think it wasn't damaging us.'

'I'm sorry that I didn't *notice*! You say I'm your conscience but maybe . . . maybe I wanted you to be my picture-perfect family. Didn't want to see the cracks. Maybe I made it hard for you to tell me? I want you to be able to be honest.'

'Same same,' said Lysette, sounding so young suddenly. 'Saffron's beside herself I'm seeing you without her.'

The thought of her chubby face, her bee-faced wellies – I missed her every bit as fiercely as she missed me. 'How's it been for her, moving schools? Saying goodbye to Max?'

The thought of him was still deeply upsetting to me. I didn't want to say it out loud: I knew how much Lysette would also be worrying about him.

'They Skype a bit.' She could see it in my face. 'He's doing pretty well, Mia. The shock of it – I think it's changed Joshua quite a lot. He did find him a therapist, and the school are looking out for him too.'

'Do you really think Joshua didn't know Lisa had done it?' Lysette shrugged.

'Didn't, or didn't want to. They're kind of the same thing after a point.' She smiled. 'Look at me, all psychologically astute. Might start doing your job.'

'You knew something wasn't right though, didn't you?' I paused. 'Well, you knew that Peter didn't do it.'

'I got so confused in the end.' A wave of grief swept across her face, her eyes going somewhere far away. 'I was scared – I wanted the truth, but I also wanted it to all go away.'

'It's understandable,' I said.

'I always knew she wouldn't have done that to Max – killed herself, I mean. I wish she'd told me how paranoid she was about Lisa. No – that's the point. She wasn't paranoid. Joshua made her feel like she was.'

'No one listened to you. Not even me.' I held her gaze. 'You are astute. You don't give yourself enough credit for all the things you're amazing at.'

'You're pretty amazing, the way you got to the bottom of it all.'

I laughed, squeezed her hand.

'Or I'm a nosy bitch.'

'Or you're a nosy bitch AND you're amazing. Your friend April will be crawling all over the courtroom, I bet.'

I shuddered. I still experienced a strange kind of PTSD when I thought about all of that — trapped in that hamster cage of a room, bickering with Patrick down a tinny phone line, April lurking on the landing, scavenging for information.

'It's still a few months away, isn't it?'

'Yeah,' said Lysette, 'March or so. She's confessed, so it's only going to be a question of how long she goes down for.'

'I bet Kimberley hasn't been to see her once,' I said.

'She was *shocked*,' said Lysette, her impression pitch perfect. 'She only knew once she'd read the diary and put two and two together. If only I'd have shared it sooner. Blah blah.' She looked ashamed. 'I should've done. In fact, I should never have taken it.'

I shook my head.

'You know, I bet Joshua would've found it and got rid of it. Or the police would've read it all wrong.' I paused. 'You were trying to protect her too.'

She took my hand again.

'Thanks, conscience.'

'No, I'm resigning from that job. Don't even try and recruit me.' I took a slug of my cold decaf, a bite of the gluten-free monstrosity. 'It pisses me off, the way Kimberley's body swerved all of it when she was right in the middle all along.'

Lysette waved a dismissive hand, then swooped in for the remaining lump of cake.

'Disgusting! The cake – well, all of it. I can't think like that, Mia. It'd drive me mad. Thing about Kimberley is, she's naturally bitter and twisted. She's her very own, one-woman prison cell. Helena and Alex have dropped her; I've gone. She'll be scrabbling around for a new coven. Nigel's never there, and I bet he's got a little black book bigger than Bill Clinton's. Let's just forget about her.'

I sighed, breath squeezing out of me like a pair of enthusiastically handled bellows. I was expelling all of it, the residue finally leaving my body. Lysette has that simplicity to her nature, that ability to let go and be in the moment. I'm more of a brooder.

'You're right. I don't want to be your conscience, but can you be my guru?'

Lysette giggled. 'I do rock an orange robe.'

'Orange is so in this year.' I suddenly saw the time. 'Shit. Patrick's leaving at six. We're going somewhere with starchy tablecloths and loads of courses which could only seat us at toddlers' suppertime.'

'Is it his birthday?'

'No.' I smiled, relief spreading through me, as it still did every time I thought how close I'd come to destroying things between us. I realised in tandem that neither Lysette nor I had so much as mentioned Jim. That was an even bigger relief – I didn't need to devote any more energy to that man. It was only by seeing him again that I'd known how much he was draining me: a background app with some pointless function you'll never need, that robs your battery of all the power you need for the real things. 'We're just trying to do a date night every week. They always seem to be a bit random.'

Lysette smiled, pleased for me. 'Random's good.'

We hadn't talked about babies either. That suited me too. Patrick and I had decided not to think too hard about it for the next few months. There was still a certain fragility between us, a new way of relating that was taking shape.

'Yeah, it is.'

We weaved our way towards the exit, grabbing our thick winter coats from the hooks by the door. Now it was time to say goodbye, it inevitably felt too soon.

'Never again,' said Lysette, giving me a short, fierce hug.

'Never again,' I repeated, matching her for fierceness. Then, more quietly, 'Always.'

'Always,' she echoed, the word spoken directly into my ear.

I stepped out of the muggy warmth of the café into a sharp winter's evening. It was December, and the streets were thronged with desperate shoppers, their eyes alight with present panic. I took it slowly, felt each footfall hit the pavement, not caring about the jostling or the irritating Christmas songs that blared out of shops or the filthy pigeons that pecked at overflowing bins.

I was here. Here was home, and I was here.

Acknowledgements

With thanks to Jo Dickinson for putting up with me for yet another book! It's been a joy working with you, as always. Thanks too to the rest of the Simon & Schuster team, particularly Sara-Jade Virtue, Carla Josephson and Emma Capron. Huge thanks also to Sheila Crowley at Curtis Brown and the wider team there. Thanks too to the fabulous Lucinda Prain at Casarotto.

Thanks also due to Sophia Parsons for a therapist's perspective (and all-round friendship excellence) and Anne Mensah for being the world's most overqualified script editor. Thanks to the Brann/Sutherlands for letting me type all through Christmas on a tiny Canadian island as my deadline loomed. Thanks to Carol Biss for so many things. Thanks to all my lovely colleagues at 42 for being – well – lovely, and for Dan Walker for some excellent notes.

Thanks due too to my lovely family. This is the first book that my beloved grandmother wasn't the first to read. I miss you every day.

Thanks lastly due to Eugenie Furniss and the Furniss Lawton team.